SALEM'S CHILDREN

By Mary Leader

TRIAD

SALEM'S CHILDREN

SALEM'S CHILDREN

Mary Leader

Coward, McCann & Geoghegan, Inc.
New York

Library of Congress Cataloging in Publication Data

Leader, Mary.
    Salem's children.

    I. Title.
PZ4.L4344Sal   1979 [PS3562.E18]   813'.5'4   78-24115
ISBN 0-698-10724-1

To Leslie Cross, my friend and mentor, who was
"Wes" in TRIAD and who, before his death in 1977,
gave me criticism and encouragement which helped shape
Salem's Children,

and to

Robert and Beryl Graves

and to

my mother, whose dearest dream
was for me to become an author, and through whom
I am descended from the Stoughtons.

Acknowledgments

I would like to express my heartfelt gratitude to the many people who have helped me research *Salem's Children*, with especial thanks to:

Richard Trask, archivist, Danvers Archival Center, Danvers (formerly Salem Village), Mass., and direct descendant of Mary Esty; David Little, former director, Essex Institute, Salem, Mass.; Dr. Hans Naegli, M.D., doctor of medicine and psychiatry (and student of Carl Gustave Jung), Zurich, Switzerland, after whom I modeled Dr. Brun; Dr. Alan Reed, M.D., assistant clinical professor of psychiatry at the Medical College of Wisconsin, founder of Underground Switchboard, Milwaukee, and author of treatises on cocaine and other drugs; Dr. John Hurley, M.D., oncologist and surgical director, Deaconess Hospital, Milwaukee; Dr. Kuang Shim Kim, M.D., Milwaukee; Dr. Michael T. Jaekels, M.D., Milwaukee; Mrs. Delia Decorah Maisell, a full-blooded Winnebago and descendant of the great Chief Decorah; Dr. Nancy Lurie, anthropologist and authority on American Indians, Milwaukee Museum; Lady Cybele, a family tradition witch in Madison, Wis.; Stewart Farrar, author of *What Witches Do*, and high priest of his coven in London, England; Eric Maple, author of *The Dark World of Witches*, who took me "witch-hunting" (in a pleasant sense) in Essex County, England; Mrs. Joy Ertel and her staff at the Weyenberg Library, Mequon, Wis.; Lieutenant Richard Burgard and Detective Robert Silverwood of the Mequon Police Department; Mrs. Lynn Sewall Honeck, direct descendant of Samuel Sewall, author of *Sewall's Diary* and associate justice of the Massachusetts appellate court of oyer and terminer, 1692; James Brindley, former mayor of Richland Center, Wis.; and above all, to my editor, Patricia B. Soliman, whose faith in *Salem's Children* and her discerning criticism have been my lodestar in the writing of this book.

SALEM'S CHILDREN

Chapter One

An insistent ringing shattered my slumber. Wildly, unable to orient myself, I groped in the dark until my fingers closed over the smooth plastic.

"Submit—Submit, do you hear me?" came the whisper. "I know you're there, Submit. We hate you—we hate you . . ."

The words trailed off into faint breathing at the other end of the line, then a click and the line went dead.

"Kid stuff!" I muttered, trying to resettle my weary body into the sagging, alien mattress—but the last dregs of slumber had drained away and reality crowded in on me. This was Aunt Bo's great bed, arced between twin walls of intricately carved walnut. It may have conformed to her more ample contours, but to me it was a torture rack. Only exhaustion—on this, my first night in the house Aunt Bo had unexpectedly willed me—had granted me any sleep at all, and I found myself devoutly praying for an early arrival of the van from New York with my own furnishings. I'd had misgivings about occupying Aunt Bo's room—at least so soon—but Dana, the half-Indian woman who had been Aunt Bo's companion during the last few years of her life, had already installed my things, and I'd been too tired to protest.

Folding myself into the fetal position proved no answer; I immediately slid down into the center of the bed, my knees pressing against my chin. In desperation, I piled the pillows high against the ornate headboard, sat up, and switched on the light. Laid across the cedar chest was a down comforter. I folded it tightly and slid it under my legs. This helped, but still I didn't sleep. Somewhere out there in the dark was someone who knew me and didn't want me there—someone who knew the name I seldom used, who was perhaps voicing Peacehaven's real feelings about me.

But that was being morbid. I rose and tiptoed into the room where my two daughters lay sleeping; Cariad in her crib and Rowan in the big bed, relaxed and rosy in the soft glow of the nightlight. Dana had bundled them into bed as soon as she'd given us a light supper, and they'd fallen asleep with hardly a murmur, tired out from the long drive from New York.

It was a quiet, unheralded entry we'd made that afternoon into Peacehaven, here in the southwest corner of Wisconsin. The town had seemed empty as we drove along the main street, but that was natural since it was the dinner hour. I tried to point out old landmarks to Rowan, but many no longer existed.

"There—over there!" I exclaimed, pointing to a red brick building with large plate glass windows. "That's where your great-grandfather's general store used to be. Looks like it's a teen shop now."

How had I once thought it so large and imposing?

"I didn't know little towns had parking meters," Rowan said.

"Where? I don't see any."

"There!" she pointed.

"That?" I began to laugh. "That's the old hitching post your great-grandfather had in front of his store. All the merchants used to have them, but I see the others have been taken down."

Rowan sat quietly, holding the baby in her lap as I chattered on, trying to re-create the Peacehaven that had once charmed me.

"I'll just drive around the corner and show you the Congregational Church where your grandparents were married. Your great-grandmother donated the pipe organ in memory of— It's gone!" I exclaimed, staring down a street that dead-ended at a broad expanse of water. "I never thought the river would get this far!"

I drove slowly past the wrought iron gate and a length of the iron fence that had once surrounded the graveyard. These, and a buckled section of cement walk on a collapsing bank gave a brief amen to what had once been Peacehaven's leading church. Someone had planted pretty blue morning glories along the fence, as though to give the cemetery one final, everblooming bouquet. Farther down the riverbank a small boy fished from a toppled tombstone.

I tried to explain that the river had been shifting its channel for over a century, gradually inundating the town, but my daughter was unaffected by the loss. "What are those funny little islands out in the river?"

"Sandbars. They appear and disappear. We used to go out there in canoes and have picnics." *Until that was spoiled for me,* I remembered, gripping the wheel tightly.

"Weren't you afraid they'd sink while you were on them?"

"It doesn't happen that quickly. People sometimes camp there all night." I turned back toward the main street.

"What's that?" Rowan pointed to a stone monument in the square. "It looks like an upside down 'L.' "

"It's supposed to look like a gallows."

She was puzzled. "I thought they burned the witches."

"They didn't burn them, they hanged them."

"Here?"

"Oh, not here," I said hurriedly, "in Salem in—uh—1692," reading the date off the base of the monument. "About a century and a half later, Joshua Martin, Aunt Bo's great-grandfather, led a group of descendants of so-called witches out here to Peacehaven. Joshua's ancestress, Susanna Martin, was one of those hanged. He founded Peacehaven as a memorial to the victims of the witchcraft trials. They used to make a big thing of it, but it's more a town legend now—and a badge of distinction, I suppose."

"If Aunt Bo was descended from a witch, then we must be, too," she reflected, a note of pride in her voice.

"Sorry, Rowan. We can't claim it; we aren't related on that side."

"Oh." Obvious disappointment.

The sun was already descending in the west and I knew we should be getting on, but I was enjoying just sitting here and chatting with my daughter—a rare occurrence these days.

"Do you think there are any witches here now?"

"No, of course not! There's no such thing," I laughed. "They even sell broomsticks here without anyone getting nervous."

"There are witchcraft shops in New York," she said skeptically.

"That's different. That's business."

"What did the Salem witches do that was so bad?" she asked after a pause.

"Oh," I hesitated, trying to remember. "People imagined they did everything from souring milk to murdering babies."

Rowan studied the monument. The stone noose was attached to the granite gallows by a massive wrought-iron ring.

"I'll bet that noose would swing," she speculated. "Let's try it."

"We'll do it another day— Dana's expecting us for supper." I sighed. "It's not going to be the same without Aunt Bo. I wish you could have known her, Rowan."

But my daughter had lapsed into one of her too-frequent silences. She shifted Cariad in her arms and nuzzled her gently. I turned the car up a street leading to the bluff road, feeling pangs of guilt as we flashed by the homes of Peacehaven. I hadn't visited Aunt Bo since before my marriage, and yet she had willed most of her property to me, a half-niece, instead of her full niece and nephew. I could see her now: tall, heavily built, her dark gray-streaked hair swept into a French twist, color high and eyes alight whenever the conversation got around to politics or social conditions, her acousticon—she never could get the hang of a hearing aid—pushed forward to catch her listener's replies.

We proceeded along the elm-arched street, once completely vaulted by dense foliage, but now showing the ravages of dutch elm disease. I slowed as we came to a large, pale yellow clapboard house with black shutters and white trim.

"That's where Aunt Bee and Uncle George Proctor used to live." I said, but Rowan gave no sign she heard me. "Your cousin Ward and his wife live there now." I tried to think of something that would interest her. "They have a daughter who's only about a year older than you—and a son in medical school."

I thought I detected a flicker of interest in the blue eyes half-turned away from me, but her mouth remained set. I stepped on the accelerator again and soon the canopy of elms slid away to reveal a lofty bluff ahead of us, the top momentarily obscured by a towering chimney rock that rose from the slope at the base of the escarpment.

"That's old Earthmaker's Tomahawk pointing to the sky," I explained. "The Indians believe the chimney rock is sacred and—" I paused as the rough outline of a house perched above a limestone outcropping—its great windows flaming in the sunset—hove into view. "There it is! The Phoenix!" I cried.

"It's funny-looking," Rowan said. "It sticks out in all directions."

"It's a beautiful house!" I protested. "Frank Lloyd Wright designed it to make it look like part of the bluff."

"Who was he?"

Well, at least my daughter didn't know everything. "A famous architect who used to live near here. Some people didn't like him, but Aunt Bo championed him, so when her house burned down he insisted on designing a new one for her. You see, his own home burned several times, so he understood. The two of them had a glorious time planning and arguing, because Aunt Bo could be just as stubborn as he. For instance, she wanted a tower. He told her she'd soon be too old for climbing stairs, which made her all the more determined.

" 'I need a tower,' she declared, 'so I can watch over Peacehaven by day and the heavens by night. As for the stairs, I'll climb them until the day I die.' And that's just what she did."

The Phoenix slid from sight as the road followed a chicken wing pattern up the side of the bluff. I pulled into the driveway of a small white house burrowed into the hillside where a tiny, spare figure with a shock of crew-cut white hair was working away at the woodpile.

"Hi, Darcy!" I called. She dropped her axe and came toward us, wiping her hands on her faded jeans. She was just as I remembered her—the same wrinkled, weather-beaten face, her hair only a little whiter.

"Well, for land's sakes, if it isn't the crown princess herself!"

Her grip ground the bones of my hand together. "Good to see you, Darcy," I said, flexing my hand. "Is Hannah in the house?"

Her mouth drooped. "Hannah died eight years ago. I live here with my husband. He's inside restoring a melodeon."

Darcy with a *husband*? Her relationship with Hannah had been whispered about in town for years. What were the gossips saying now?

"Cariad? What kind of a name is that?" she boomed after I'd introduced my daughters.

"It's Welsh for 'love,'" I explained. Naming her Cariad had been my requiem for Owen, her father.

"You wouldn't be wanting a kitten, would you?"

"How many do you have now?" Darcy and her cats! She hadn't changed.

"Twenty-nine. I could spare two or three."

"We'll have to think about it, Darcy. We'd better get on up to the house now. Dana's expecting us."

"I'm not sure a kitten would be good for Cari," Rowan interjected primly. "They take the breath away from babies."

Darcy squinted. "You been tellin' her old wives' tales, Mitti?"

"No. Where'd you hear that, Rowan?"

Her cobalt eyes widened. "But, Mother, I was sure you—well, maybe it was one of the kids at school. Cats are witch animals, aren't they?"

"Only on Hallowe'en, dear."

"What about Midsummer Eve? Don't witches and cats come out then?"

"I wouldn't know. I don't even know when Midsummer Eve is," I confessed.

"It's tomorrow night," she said with thirteen-year-old superiority.

I was duly impressed. "How did you know that, darling?"

"Oh, I belonged to a coven at school. We had seances and worked the ouija board and everything—creepy!"

Child's play, I told myself—but more than ever I felt my decision to move out here had been right. "If you're talking about that high-powered club that was always asking for assessments, I'm not sorry you're out of it. You never mentioned witchcraft."

18

"It was a secret. We signed in blood and they put a curse on you if you told. But now I don't belong anymore, it doesn't matter."

"Rowan, I don't think I like the idea of you fooling around with such things," I reproved her.

"I thought you didn't believe in 'such things.' "

"I don't, but—"

"Anyway, we weren't *real* witches," she assured me. "They're bad. The only people we ever cursed were our teachers."

"That was bad, too," I said sternly. "Besides, you shouldn't keep secrets from me."

"I keep secrets from you all the time, Mother." She averted her eyes as she shifted the baby in her arms.

Darcy intervened. "I used to belong to a secret spy organization when I was her age," she said. "And if cats are witches' familiars, then I know what that makes me— twenty-nine times over!" She chuckled. "I s'pose it's the witch blood in me."

Rowan leaned forward, almost crushing Cariad, who whimpered in her sleep. "You have witch blood?"

"Yep! Like most people here. 'Ceptin' you, Mitti."

"I hope you won't hold that against me," I laughed.

"Never have, have I?" she snorted. "Though there's some as does, I expect—especially lately. Too bad you're related only by marriage. You don't have any Salem blood at all."

"Witch blood, you mean," I teased.

"Martyr's blood," she corrected me stiffly.

"I was only using your term, Darcy."

"It's all right for me to joke about it—I've got witch blood from both sides. But it wouldn't be smart for you to. Understand what I mean?"

I nodded, a ripple of apprehension at the back of my mind.

"You make me wonder if I'll ever be accepted."

"Sure you will—if you respect the rules. And I'll help you, Mitti, all I can. But don't ask me to come to the party."

"Party!"

"Well, not really—more of a welcoming by relatives and friends. They're all coming up to the Phoenix tomorrow night." She ran her lean, brown-patched hand over the white hairs on her chin. "You know me—never did like to dress up, and I refuse to be part of a snooping bee. There's a lot I'd like to say, but I guess I'd better not. Come back and meet Marion when you have time."

"Marion?" Then I remembered. "Your husband? What's your last name now, Darcy?"

"Zagrodnik." Her eyes twinkled. "Try to wrap these Anglo-Saxon tongues here around that one! But at least Marion is spelled with an 'o.' "

"She's gross!" Rowan observed as we continued up the side of the bluff. "I thought she was a man."

"Sometimes I think she thinks so, too. But don't be so critical of the natives, young lady. That won't make you popular."

After a moment she asked in a small, stifled voice, "Do we have to live here, Mother?"

"You'll grow to love it!" I tried to sound convincing. "We'll go canoeing and we'll—"

A loud barking broke into my sentence. Heralding our approach was a majestic golden retriever, which stood at the entrance to the vast turn-around that separated the two houses on the top of the bluff. One was the Phoenix—so newly mine—and the other, a smaller building, was the oldest house in Peacehaven, once Joshua Martin's home. This, the lawyer had written, Aunt Bo had willed to Dana. Two more dissimilar structures could hardly be found, I reflected, glancing from the free-form, contemporary lines of the Phoenix to the austere brown gables.

"Freya! Quiet!" A tall, statuesque woman with gray braids hanging almost to her waist came limping across the gravel to greet us. *This must be Dana*, I thought, noting how the sinking sun gilded her high cheekbones and made dark hollows of her eyes.

"Down, Freya!" the woman commanded.

"She's all right," I replied, letting the dog sniff my hands. "She's beautiful! She's going to have pups, isn't she?" I straightened up and extended my hand. "You're Dana! Aunt Bo wrote so much about you."

"She always wanted us to meet, Mrs. Llewellyn," she replied formally.

"Please, I want you to call me Mitti," I said, taking the baby from Rowan so she could climb out. "This is Rowan and the baby is Cariad—Cari for short." My voice quivered. "I'm not sure I want to go in. I can't imagine the Phoenix without Aunt Bo."

"Your aunt will always be here," she said quietly. "Such a woman never dies. Now, you must come in; I have made supper for you. Let me take the little one."

I expected Cariad to start screaming, but to my surprise she snuggled up to the woman, and a soft light crept into the blue eyes that were so strange to behold in an Indian face. It seemed a good sign—again, I felt glad of my decision to move here.

*   *   *

Now, I tucked Cari's plump little arm back under her coverlet and turned to Rowan. Her long silken lashes followed the curve of her cheeks, a shade darker than the gold-red curls sprawled on the pillow. In this moment she was mine—all mine. Impulsively I reached out and stroked the soft contour of her cheek, then quickly drew my hand away as even in her sleep she seemed to shrink from my touch. She turned over on her side, her back to me.

"Daddy . . ." she breathed.

Chapter Two

Back in my room as I sat down before the marble-topped dressing table, the fragrance of Aunt Bo assailed me—a heavy, woodsy scent of bath powder and cologne. Her toilet articles were still set out: the ornate silver-backed hairbrush, hand mirror and comb, a small cloisonné tray full of hairpins, and a handpainted china hair receiver. Through the hole in the top I could see a wad of fuzzy gray hair combings—the last tangible evidence of Aunt Bo. A board creaked behind me and I stared into the mirror, half expecting to see her there, holding out her acousticon, but there was nothing—only my own tired face superimposed on the room behind me. Still, I couldn't rid myself of the impression that she was there watching.

I hoped she wouldn't regret the plan I already had for redecorating this house. In spite of the contemporary architecture, Aunt Bo—Bo for Boadicea—had perversely filled it with Victorian antiques. Those articles that hadn't been saved when the original house burned, she had faithfully sought to reproduce from antique shops as far away as Milwaukee and Chicago. I heard something rustle on the wallpaper, like silk skirts brushing against it. But if Aunt Bo was there, I welcomed her presence. After that phone call, I was going to need all the support I could get—even from the astral plane. My counterpart in the mirror smiled at my little joke.

Submit! Whoever had called had known my Christian name. My father had been a clergyman, which meant we moved every few years. How I used to dread those first days at a new school while the kids got their mileage out of the new girl with the weird name! How to explain that my mother was fanatic about family genealogy? And that she couldn't carry her babies full term? The ninth attempt, I was supposed to be the ninth disaster. Mother went into post-partum psychosis and for days walked with her ancestors.

"Submit!" she repeated over and over. "Name her Submit! 'Submit unto the Lord!' "

I know now that she found the name in one of our family genealogies. My father, thinking to please her, had me christened 'Submit' and recorded it before he or anyone else realized I wasn't going to follow my brothers and sisters into limbo. Mother snapped back to reality the day I was taken out of the incubator and placed in her arms.

"Submit!" she puzzled. "What a peculiar name! Who did that to her?" Then, seeing my father's face, she realized that he'd done it out of love. She said no more, but did her best to make it up to me by nicknaming me

Mitti—and anyone who wants to be my friend had better call me that.

Owen didn't care though. He had loved to ruffle my feathers by calling me Submit. A Welshman with the Welsh talent for singing, he could also tease so charmingly that one didn't mind. *But no,* I told myself as I climbed back into bed. I wouldn't let the memories invade me—Owen's meteoric rise as a musical comedy star on Broadway, the inevitable stresses, his resultant addiction to cocaine—psychological, if not physical, but that's just as bad—the deterioration of our marriage, then death . . .

I rolled over, trying to find a comfortable spot, but another thought brought me up short: Rowan. She blamed *me* for Owen's accident, as if I held the power to project destruction, nor would she let me forget it. Rowan, who was thus named because it rhymed with Owen, and because her hair was the color of the rowan berries that flamed over the hillsides in her father's native Wales—Rowan was a living reminder of that cold day in Switzerland, when we were told by the police that Owen's car had been crushed by a van, his body mangled beyond recognition. Rowan had been hysterical. She'd shrieked at the young Swiss officer, who tried to calm her. "You don't understand! My Daddy's dead! And Mommy *wanted* him dead!" Then she broke off into great, wrenching sobs and went limp, dragging his hand with her as she slumped to the ground.

"Rowan, darling!" I knelt beside her and tried to take her in my arms. The Swiss had relinquished his hold and now she flailed at me with her fists.

"Don't touch me! Don't touch me!"

"Call a doctor, *bitte!*" I pleaded. "Rowan—sweetheart!

25

Mommy *loved* Daddy," I cried, the tears streaming down my face. "You just don't understand—oh my God, Rowan, how can I make you understand?"

She'd gone suddenly still and cold and white, her eyes glittering. "I *don't* believe you," she breathed. "I hate you, Mother! I hate you!"

The phone jangled again, bringing me back to the present. I stared at it, knowing that if the ringing kept up sheer curiosity would force me to answer . . .

"Submit—Submit—move away—move away—" the caller chanted in her syrupy voice. "We don't want you here . . ."

Silence now, but she was still there, listening.

"Whoever you are, why don't you tell it to my face?" I exclaimed angrily, then bit my lip. That was exactly what she wanted—to know she had reached me. I slammed down the receiver, then picked it up again, intending to dial the operator to see what could be done about such calls—but the line was still engaged, only her breathing echoing along the wires. I spun the dial, glorying in the painful static I must be making, but whoever it was hung on until I set the phone back down on the hook.

The ensuing quiet was almost suffocating. Years in New York had made me more attuned to noise than to this stillness. Now, my ears began to pick up little sounds I wouldn't have noticed otherwise—soft scratchings on the wallpaper, the death rattle of the refrigerator as it concluded its cycle, the warble of an owl abruptly suspended, a soft bleating and the dull clink of a bell rapped on wood—was there a goat in the neighborhood?—and, threading through it all, a low humming sound—almost like a soft chanting.

26

I settled down into the hostile bed again and sat propped up against the pillows. There had been something familiar about that voice, but my acquaintanceship was limited, as I'd only spent my summers here. I didn't really belong—not in the sense the others did. My grandfather had moved to Peacehaven when he bought the town's general store, and he'd made things right by marrying the granddaughter of Joshua Martin. Aunt Bo and Aunt Bee had been the offspring of that marriage, but my mother came from his second wife, who was not from Peacehaven. Nor was my father, so I was totally an outsider. Aunt Bo, who never married, inherited the bulk of her father's property, including the Martin holdings—and now in turn had willed most of it to me. The windfall had been welcome, for Owen had left very little. But resentment was natural. Darcy had tagged it right when she had called me the crown princess.

Could it have been Charity Carrier on the phone? Aunt Bee's oldest child and first in line to inherit, she'd always seemed formidable to me, tiny and doll-like though she was. Tattletale and voice of conscience she'd been to her young brothers, Ward and Gareth. But anonymous phone calls in the middle of the night? Not Charity!

As for Alison, Ward's wife—out of the question!

There was Darcy, who was distantly related, but she couldn't whisper if she tried. Besides, Aunt Bo had left her some money and clear title to the house in which she'd formerly been a tenant.

Another face came to mind—Iris. But she'd left town years ago. Iris Faulkner—I could still see her. Peacehaven's *femme fatale*. She and her father, the judge, had lived in the big house that straddled a rock islet and the tip of a tiny peninsula jutting out from the town. Some said Iris' mother drowned in the miniature strait that ran through the basement and that her body floated on down to the Mississippi. Others maintained she'd eloped with a traveling salesman. There was no grave for her in the Peacehaven cemetery.

Since Judge Faulkner always retired early, there was much speculation about a light often seen burning in the turreted room overlooking the river. Perhaps the servants put it there for a beacon, but gossips said it was Iris signaling her lovers. How many egos had she bruised? Ward had escaped because he was devoted to Alison. Gareth only toyed with her at first, but I had reason to believe that he, too, finally succumbed—if only I could forget! Gareth—sweet Gareth . . .

At my age I was beneath Iris' notice. How I had longed for her sophistication! I considered dyeing my hair red, but no dye would have produced her subtle shade of amber. Nor could I assume her air of mystery. Try as hard as I did to copy her indolent casualness, it never came across. So I'd been inordinately excited when she invited me to go canoeing with her that hazy summer day.

We dropped anchor near a sandbar and let the canoe rock gently in the current as we ate the sandwiches she'd brought. Iris dabbled her hand in the little eddies that swirled around us, her amber hair rippling over the pale skin of her breasts.

"We're anchored over the original Peacehaven," she mused.

I gazed across the expanse of water toward the present town sprawled along the shore. "This far out?"

"Farther. It extended over to the opposite shore line. Imagine the people down there in their houses or sitting in their church pews—or in their privies."

"But I heard it wasn't that way at all," I protested. "No

one got drowned when the city sank—it was gradual."

"So they say," she sighed. "It would have been so much grander my way. I can just see the land collapsing and the water rushing in, like it did when a section of bank was washed out from under our house. Of course, I didn't really see it happen at all. I was sleeping and I dreamed that the river was my lover—that it could take on the shape of a man and come to me. And the next morning when I awoke, there was that big gap under the house, so maybe I wasn't dreaming after all. He was exciting as no boy has ever been. Father had the house reinforced and we just let the river flow beneath it. The way he took out that chunk of land—all in one night! Nothing can hold him back. I could never understand why he was so gentle with Peacehaven. I'd have drowned them all. Listen! Hear the church bells down there?"

"That's a cowbell across the river," I scoffed.

"No, no, it isn't!" she insisted. "It's church bells—the First Church of Satan!"

Her voice was hypnotic.

"The city in the sea!" I burst out.

"The what?"

"It's a legend my mother told me about the city of Ys off the coast of Brittany. Their princess, Ahès, was very wicked. When she tired of her lovers she had them killed—for her one true love was the sea itself. One day she stole her father's key to the sea gates and when the waters came boiling in, the people were drowned and she became a mermaid luring sailors to their death. They say that when the tide is low, you can see her beckoning in the waves and hear the cathedral bells."

I paused, afraid of boring her, but her eyes were glowing.

"Fabulous!" she exclaimed. "I'd like to have been that

29

princess. The name 'Ahès' even sounds like 'Iris!' Think of the power she had over people—over men! Only the sea was worthy to be her bridegroom."

She stopped. Someone was calling to us from the bank. My cousin Gareth stood there in swimming trunks, the sun gilding his bronzed body. He looked sturdy but I knew—and so did she—that he was still recovering from an appendectomy.

"Gareth!" she called through cupped hands. "I bet him five dollars he couldn't swim out to us."

"You didn't!" I cried, dismayed. "He's not well enough yet!"

She merely smiled as he poised for a dive. I tried to wave him back—too late. He slid into the water and swam toward us with powerful strokes.

"Let's go get him," I pleaded, trying to reach around her to pull up anchor, but she pushed me away.

"Leave him alone!" she hissed. "He'd hate for us to make a sissy out of him."

Helplessly I watched as the cramp seized him. He struggled to keep afloat, clawed at the eddy that caught him, whirled him around, then sucked him under. Still Iris guarded the anchor. In desperation I tried to throw myself out of the canoe, and swim to him, but she caught hold of my arm and forced me back down. Then she balanced herself delicately, her gold-green eyes glittering, and flashed into the water. I hoisted anchor and paddled toward the spot where I'd seen him go down, but we never found him. *She'd* come out the heroine, denying the bet and saying she'd held me back to save me from drowning myself.

But I must push away such memories—I must remember the good times in Peacehaven; the golden summers, rambles through the woods, muddy excursions in the caves, and riding ponies at a nearby farm. Idyllic—that was Peacehaven in contrast to the clamor and crowding of New York. In Peacehaven, even tragedy was tinged with romance.

My own recent tragedy was not similarly tinged. After Rowan's hysterics over Owen's death, she had withdrawn into herself until Cariad's posthumous birth gave her a new interest. She forgot her dolls and lavished her affection on the baby to the point of excluding me. Was this revenge? No—I could have fought that—but I felt she was trying to *protect* Cariad from me.

Her schoolwork suffered. Was it because I couldn't afford to give her the things she'd been used to? Cocaine and gambling debts had eaten up much of Owen's estate. Aunt Bo's bequest had seemed heaven-sent . . .

Yet here I was, staring at the phone, almost a live thing now, waiting to pounce. Well, I'd stop that. I unplugged it and lay back. Just in time. It began to ring downstairs. So let it ring—and ring—and ring—

My tired body slumped into the bottomless pit in the center of the bed, slipped through—and I was out of it. I cast a swift backward glance at a form lying there quietly and then I was out into the night—

"There th'art! Where'st tha been, miss? Mun I do thy chores so my daughter can walk out with her fine young gentleman? Be thankful I hanna told thy father about it. His heart be set on thee marryin' the cooper fellow, if'n he bespeaks thee."

"Daughter?" Why was she calling me that? And what quaint speech! This wasn't my mother—this bent, wizened woman

31

with a swollen stomach, lugging a milk pail into a kitchen I'd never seen before. A huge fireplace dominated the room. Suspended by chains from its blackened inner walls were a great cauldron of steaming water and a smaller stewpot. Down on the hearth a haunch of venison was turning slowly, propelled by a counterweighted rope that took all day to unwind. But how did I know that?

She set the milk down on the table, swatted the flies away and covered it with a cloth, then shuffled over to the stewpot to give it a stir. "Thy sister Becky warn't as choosy," she complained, her cheeks reddened and bright from the savory steam. "She be content to be a Goodwife, and mind thee, that man o' hers'll be a big landowner someday. But e'en that wouldna satisfy thee. The title o' Goodwife is nae good enow. Tha'd have a fine house in Dorchester wi' silver plate and linen and the right to be called Mistress Sto . . ."

"Mother, be you silent!" Did I say that? It was as if someone else within me, long asleep, had just awakened. This woman bore no resemblance to my mother, and yet there was something in her voice that was familiar—as were these surroundings—like an old garment hung in a closet and forgotten, then rediscovered and tried on once more. Words came tumbling out of me.

" 'Tisn't so!" I protested. "I would he weren't a gentleman. Then might you believe I love him for himself. And he swears he loves me, too."

Who was I? And where? I touched my dress—coarse woolen stuff of a dark red. I owned nothing like this and yet it seemed to belong to me. Nor did it seem strange that the long braids falling across my breasts were tawny yellow, not my own mahogany color.

" 'S'blood!" she was swearing under her breath. "What has love to do with a good marriage? Like as not he'll have thy maidenhead and be off with him."

"I' faith, he could have had that a long time ago if 'tweren't that he's for the ministry and all so pure." The shock in her face made me relent. "Nay, Mother, I wouldna allow that. I'll be no gentleman's jade."

She tasted the stew, sloshing it around in her mouth critically, then reached for more salt. " 'Twere an evil day when he first came to this house," she complained. "Ye gained a lover and lost a friend."

"Dorcas?" I snorted. "She was ne'er a friend and he'd only a passing fancy for her."

"I still say it was an evil day," she reiterated.

" 'Twere a rainy one, I'll allow." I luxuriated in the memory of it. His horse had thrown a shoe in the rain and he hadn't been able to journey on that night. I remembered casting shy glances at the tall, slender, young man seated on the inglenook. He was still in mourning for his father, so he said, though he had died five years past fighting the king back in England. I suspected the son wore his somber habit not so much out of deference for the old man, but because it suited his taste. Yet, firelight did elfin things to his deep-set eyes and his long, narrow face. This was the first time we'd met, but I'd heard about him from Dorcas, who said he'd been coming to our village to oversee some of the properties he and his older brother Thomas had inherited.

"I didna mean the rain, though to be sure, it might've held off a day or two, so he wouldna ha' spent the night under our roof," the woman grumbled. "Faith, I know not why any maid would take to such a moody chap. He'll be a strict un, I'll warrant. As if our lives weren't gloomy enow with all this piety. Many's the time I wish for the old days when we could dance around the Maypole and celebrate Christmas with the Yule log and the Lord o' Misrule and—"

"Mother, you talk like a Papist!" I cried, peering out the

window to make sure no one had been listening. "If people were to hear you, 'twould go ill with you."

She stood with her arms akimbo, the spoon dripping a thick, brown liquid on the floor. A long gray cat dropped down from the windowsill and began to lap it up.

"The time will come," she said distantly, "when one belief will understand another, and the sooner the better, but we'll ne'er know it. And the time will come, too, when no woman will be a Goodwife, and there'll not be the gulf 'twixt yeoman and gentleman—but that's a long time a comin'. Mary, m'lass, I see nought but black around thy young gentleman. I know not what it means, but I fear for thee."

"His grandfather was no more than a country parson."

"*But* a younger son of a baronet! He'd ha' done better in Papist days. Then he might ha' been bishop."

" 'Tis better to be a poor parson with a wife and children than a bishop in a lonely palace," I said pompously.

" 'S'nails!" she exclaimed irreverently. "Think ye the bishops and cardinals didn't have their doxies?"

Anything was to be expected of Papists, even to horns sprouting out of their heads! Oh, I'd gotten her to bristling for sure!

I felt a pang of remorse as I watched her bend down painfully to pet the cat. This baby was sure to be a boy, it taxed her so.

" 'Twas only teasing you I was, Mother. My young gentleman's in Cambridge and won't be here for a fortnight. I went out to return those eggs we borrowed from Goody Tompkins, and 'twas a fair thing I did, for now I know she's no friend."

She looked up at me through black slits. "Aye, I believe it. My Grimalkin's been a spittin' at her. There's my little love— thou didst try to warn me," she crooned to the gray shadow

34

rubbing against her leg. "Now tell me, what has that busybody got up her sleeve?"

"She and her gossip, Goody Stebbins, will be here this afternoon with a squash pie they baked."

She wiped her hands carefully on her apron. "I'faith, that might be called Christian charity, but methinks I like it not. Do thee tell me what tha knowst—and how is it ye spy on our neighbors?"

"Not spy!" I protested. "As I came along the fence to her backyard, I heard voices on the other side. She and Goody Stebbins were chucklin' like a couple o' magpies about how they put an old broken scissors in the pie. When they give it to you, if you drop the pie or show fear o't, they'll cry out on you."

She snorted. "So they'd have me for a witch, would they? 'Iron,' they say, 'no witch can abide by iron.' Thankful Tompkins is a fool. Thinketh she I can stand o'er my iron kettles day after day and then be afeard o' her silly scissors? Albeit, I like not iron—'tis not a seemly metal. 'Tis hard and ugly and full o' death. Only today my paring knife turned on me." She showed me a long, jagged cut on her thumb. "I thankee, m'girl, for warning me. Oh, 'twill be like needles going through me, but I'll not be frighted, for I be ready for it." She wiped her hands on her apron. "Ah, Mary, I've been a burden to ye, but th'art a good lass."

" 'Tisn't you this time, Mother," I said slowly. "Dorcas is Goody Tompkins' niece and methinks she put her up to this to spite me."

"Aye, it may be, yet there are many who fear me—e'en though they've ne'er proved nought."

"Nor shall. I know you to be a Gospel woman, Mother."

"Ah, but I can do things they can't," she sighed, lowering herself down on the inglenook. Grimalkin sprang to her shoulder, and one worn hand caressed him gently. "Things they say come from the Devil—but I'll swear, Mary, ye'll not find the name o' Goody Towne in the Black Man's book."

"Goody Stebbins says you turned yourself into a black cat and pounced on her bed, Wednesday night last."

She spat into the fire. "Like as not she'd been at the ale again, and I don't need the Sight to know that. But 'tis too free I've been with my remedies. Is't wrong to cure where the leech has failed? Yet folks be 'feared of my powers. My willow and dandelion tea healed Ezra Herrick's rheumatism. Since Mistress Conant's been taking my foxglove tea, her ankles no longer swell and her sinking spells be gone—and that after Dr. Endicott could do nought to help her. But 'twas foolish o' me to warn Matt Hubbard, where others could hear, that he'd be killed by Indians if he went hunting afore Michaelmas. I see'd it so plain, him lyin' there with the arrow through him. And when it happened the tongues started waggin'. But when they need me, they still come. When her man got took wi' back pain, Goody Tompkins came for my birchbark remedy, but then his urine turned to blood and she vowed I'd poisoned him. These things do not work in a day."

Grimalkin glared at me with narrowed eyes as I took the hand that had been stroking him, and yet I cannot think he had much pleasure in that hand, so gnarled and rough.

"Do not fear," I said softly, "those two gossips willna dare cry you out. Your birch bark will work—he's been takin' it on the sly. When Goody Tompkins returns home, she'll find her Goodman's passed the stone."

Her eyes gentled and she cupped her hand under my chin. "Mary, m'lass, th'art the one o' my children who has the Sight." Her face compressed into a thousand wrinkles. "Aye, but keep it close. It can cause thee nought but harm. Those who have it not think it be from the Devil."

"Think you it might?"

She shook her head. "Nay, 'tis from the Old Ones. And if tha'st read the Scriptures, tha'll see Our Lord had it, too. Now get on wi' thy chores. Isaac is coming to call on thee tonight."

I drew my breath in sharply. "How do you know?"

She touched her hand to her head. "That is how I know. Right now he hurries his work so he'll be through in time." She winced. "Och! I knew it! There be a blackened nail for me to treat tonight. Nay, I'll let thee do the treatin'. Tha hast a better balm for him."

"I prithee, Mother, do not make me. Belike he'll take it for a sign o' love, and if he bespeaks me, I know Father'll give consent. But I shan't marry him. I do not love Isaac. He is good and kind, but that is nae enow to make me want to bear his children."

There was sorrow in her eyes. "Mary, ye've e'er been the headstrong one, though I might say little Sarah is some'at like 'ee. Ye look too high. Do not try to wed out o' thy class."

I flung back my head. "I ken my William loves me and that's all that matters!" I took her hand again. "Tell me what you see! Nought? Know you not your own daughter's future?"

But I was talking to nothing. There was no woman, no hearth. I was dissolving back into the quiet form on the bed and sinking into a deep, deep sleep.

Chapter Three

Much as I had longed for my own bed, I was dismayed when my furniture was delivered ahead of schedule the next morning. I had just stumbled back to bed after giving Cari her morning feeding when the van arrived, squealing its way into the drive. With the party scheduled for tonight, this was all I needed! I hadn't brought a lot of furniture with me, but I could imagine the whispers about any changes I'd make in the house. One relative, it seemed, couldn't wait for the party. Charity appeared just as the movers were carrying Aunt Bo's dresser over to Dana's house.

"Careful of those marble tops!" I panted, hurrying after them, and coming face to face with my cousin.

"So you're tearing it apart already!" Charity motioned to the men to set it down. Slight as she was, there was command in her presence. She ran her hand over the smooth marble. "I see you don't appreciate things like this. My house is all Victorian. Aunt Bo said she wanted me to have this, but I take it she forgot."

"Well, be my guest, Charity," I told her. "It really doesn't suit the early American style of Dana's house either."

"No, I wouldn't think of it," she said tersely. "I don't beg for things that belong to others. Let it be on your conscience what's done with it."

"Oh, really, Charity—Dana was taking this only to accommodate me. It's too fine a piece of furniture to store. Would you like the big bed, too?" I asked out of pure malice.

"Well—if you're sure—" Her pride and acquisitiveness met head on. "I can call Ward to send over a truck."

I led her into the kitchen. "Coffee?"

"No, thank you," she said, twisting her gloved hands.

I remembered—Charity was never without gloves, even on hot days. But where was the old poise? She kept blinking and her lips quivered slightly as she spoke.

"I was going to ask you to run over to Richland Center with me," she said, "but I see you're busy. Do you suppose Rowan would like to come? I could show her around a bit."

I felt guilty for my hard thoughts. "That's nice of you, Charity. I'll go and ask her."

"And tell the men not to scratch any of *my* furniture!"

Rowan was not ecstatic. "Do I have to? Run around with a pokey old aunt, I mean?"

"She's not your aunt, she's your cousin—but I suppose it *would* be best for you to address her as 'aunt.' Go on, sweetheart. Then you won't have to help with the unpacking," I bribed her.

"Oh, all right," she assented grudgingly, "but I'm sure I'll hate it." She aimed a kick at the headboard of Aunt Bo's bed, which the movers had propped up against the wall.

Ward's wife Alison arrived with an aspic just after the movers left.

"Thought you wouldn't want to bother with lunch," she explained.

I thanked her. "I just hope I can get things in shape for tonight."

"Frankly, I think the whole thing's an imposition, even if we are bringing the food. I tried to get them to wait a few days, but no go. So I came over to offer my help."

The day was a scorcher. Sticky beads of perspiration darkened my halter between my breasts. Alison accepted a glass of lemonade. She'd aged more than I had anticipated. Her brown eyes were still as luminous as they were the day she married my cousin Ward, but now the fine skin was sallow parchment stretched taut over her bones, and her hair, though swept ingeniously into a figure eight at the nape of her neck, was the color of spun aluminum. I noticed with concern how emaciated were the long legs below her white shorts.

"Where are the children?" she asked.

"Charity took Rowan out for the day and Cari's fallen asleep in her playpen."

"Well, don't disturb her. What can I do? Unpack china?"

"No, that'll have to wait until I can clear some space in the cupboards. You can show me where everything's kept. Dana's settling her things at her house."

Alison began opening and closing cabinet doors. "Have you seen Dr. Brun yet?"

40

"No, he and Dana should be here in a little while. I'm looking forward to meeting him again."

"People here don't know what to make of him. They can't understand why he wants to go poking around in caves—a man of his age. I confess, he has even me confused. Did you ever hear of a Prince Madog?"

The strange name reminded me of my first meeting with Dr. Brun in New York, just after Owen had begun work on *Lucifer*, a rock musical based on *Paradise Lost*. A famous Swiss archaeologist, psychiatrist and controversial theologian, Dr. Brun had acted as a consultant on the play. He and Owen had spent hours discussing religion in our Village apartment. My father had been impressed by his writings, and I found this rather gnomelike gentleman, with his Van Dyke beard, white hair, and a patch over one eye to be not only remarkable, but compassionate. He'd noticed the amulet that Aunt Bo had given me as a child, and become very excited, asking me all sorts of questions and then recounting the legend of the Welsh prince Madog who'd supposedly come to America before Columbus and, with his party, intermarried into an Indian tribe. It was Dr. Brun's theory that the tribe had migrated to the area which was now Peacehaven and that the cave in which my amulet had been found might be an old Indian burial ground. He'd vowed to come to Peacehaven some day to explore . . .

I suddenly realized that Alison was awaiting my reply. "Yes," I said quickly. "Dr. Brun told me the legend, and of his theory—but I never thought he'd actually come here to prove it." I fingered my amulet. "Strange that this bit of metal would cause such excitement. I hope for Dr. Brun's sake the cave really exists. Too bad old Two Knives isn't still alive."

"But his daughter lives here."

"She does?"

"Yes—Dana. Didn't you know?"

"No, I didn't. She should know about a cave."

"She says not, but you can never tell with her. Dana's like the river—she's quiet on the surface, but her secrets are like submerged sandbars. Looking for something?"

"The paring knife. I thought I'd cut up some celery sticks."

She took one with a long, curving blade out of a drawer.

"Was there something wrong about Charity's taking Rowan out?" I demanded suddenly.

"N-no. Why do you ask?"

"The look on your face when I told you."

"Well, just between us, Charity has some odd quirks," she said, taking plates out of the cupboard. "Not that I blame her. As a doctor's wife she's supposed to show a brave face to the world, but she's had a rough time of it. First there was Mark's death—"

"Mark dead!" I was aghast. "I thought he was in medical school. Aunt Bo didn't write about that."

"No, she wouldn't. It affected her too deeply, as it did all of us. Our Bruce, especially. He's studying medicine now. He always wanted to do everything Mark did."

"What happened to Mark?"

"No one really knows. His body was washed up on the river bank just a little downstream from the Faulkner house. He must have gone for a midnight swim—kids do crazy things. There were no marks of violence."

Near the Faulkner house! "Was Iris here then?" I asked.

"Yes, but she claimed she didn't hear or see anything.

Charity was devastated. I think that's what really made her lose the baby."

"Baby? At her age?"

"Yes, after all those years she'd gotten pregnant again. Some women would have wanted to shoot themselves, but both Charity and Damon were delighted. Anyway, right after Mark's death the baby was stillborn and she got it in her head that Dana had killed the child by overlooking her."

"By what?"

"Overlooking her—it's an old Salem term for the Evil Eye. It happened here. She tripped on the circular stairs leading to the tower. Dana kept her from falling, but when the baby was born dead several weeks later, she swore Dana had killed the baby with her glance."

"How absurd! What did Damon say?"

"That the child—a girl—died of natural causes; but Charity couldn't be persuaded. There *is* a rumor that Dana's own people thought she was a witch. Charity went so far as to hint that Dana had something to do with Mark's death, too."

"I should think Damon would have sent her to a psychiatrist."

"Oh, he did, but I don't think the analyst ever rid her of her obsession—beyond helping her gain a measure of self-control. She seldom talks about it now and we don't dare speak of it to her. But you know Charity. When she gets an idea in her head, it's impossible to get it out. I just hope she doesn't monopolize Rowan."

"Why should she do that?"

"Ever since she lost the baby she gets—well, crushes on adolescent girls in town. My Linda was first. Charity took her places, showered gifts on her, even had a bedroom decorated in pink, with a pink ruffled canopy bed, so Linda could sleep over. I believe she envisions her Elaine as a girl about Rowan's age. Anyway, the situation with Linda got so thick it became an embarrassment, and I was about to protest when she dropped her like a hot potato and turned her attentions to Cissie Osburn instead."

"Melvin's daughter?"

"Yes. He married Elspeth Bishop and they operate his father's funeral home now. Then after Cissie it was Jessica Willard and after that Lucy Leroi, the minister's daughter—and so on. I suppose it'll be Rowan's turn now. Just don't let Charity take your daughter away from you."

I thanked her. "I need you, Alison, to fill in the blanks. Darcy's marriage, for instance. I'd always thought—"

"So had everyone else. Marion came to Peacehaven with a partner who had emphysema and moved out here for his health. Their antique shop was a failure. The town had them tagged as gay right off the bat."

"But homosexuality isn't new to Peacehaven. After all, Darcy and Hannah . . ."

Alison shook her head. "Homegrown lesbians can be swept under the rug much more easily than outsiders. When his partner died, Marion was utterly lost. Then the town rowdies began to harass him. I think they might eventually have done him physical harm, but Darcy spirited him out of town, and when they returned a week later—Darcy and Marion were man and wife."

"In that order?"

"That was a slip, but it raises a good question. Which is which? Darcy does all the heavy work around the place. Marion cooks and cleans and polishes antiques.

44

Darcy lowered her status a little, but Marion is now under the protective wing of local kinship and—what the devil is that?" she exclaimed as a commotion outside brought us both to the window. "What has Mother's Little Darling done now?"

Dana was chasing a teen-aged boy down the drive. A plaintive bleating sounded in the background.

"That's Junior Osburn," Alison said, turning to me. "Dirty little bully! I'll bet he was teasing Dana's goat."

"So that's the bleating I heard last night. I didn't know Dana had a goat."

The boy ducked just as Dana aimed a blow, danced out of reach, then turned and made an obscene gesture.

"Rotten little punk!" Alison sputtered. "Trouble is, he'll pay Dana back in some underhanded way and then he'll go down to the Patch and brag about it."

"The Patch?"

"Iris Faulkner's store. She's back in town, you know."

The knife slipped in my hand and gashed my thumb. *Iron is not a seemly metal!* Where had I heard that? I held my hand under cold water, more to suppress a sudden rush of nausea than to stem the blood.

"I—I thought she'd married and moved away long ago," I said.

"She did, but after two husbands she's back—and so's her maiden name. She operates the Patch where your grandfather's general store used to be. Sells levis, leather purses, macramé, records—teen stuff. Her store is a hangout for the kids from all over the county—Peacehaven's equivalent of a discothèque. Rowan will be down there before you know it."

Heaven forbid! "Who owns the building now?"

"She does. Judge Faulkner bought it from Ward's

mother years ago. He left his fortune in trust to Iris, provided she lives in Peacehaven. Being fresh out of husbands and money, she had little choice."

"She was divorced twice?"

"Not divorced—widowed."

"Natural causes?"

She gave me a sharp look. "You still think she was to blame for Gareth's death, don't you?"

"No one else does, so—forget it."

"Some do," Alison said, snapping off a stalk of celery. "At first your story seemed incredible, and of course the Faulkners had influence, but afterwards . . . Well, nothing much was said—Peacehaven likes to bury its dirty linen—but folks began to shun her, even the boys."

"And now?"

"Oh, she's back in the fold—reconstituted by our present minister, who's a real hell-raiser."

I had had enough of Iris for the moment. "Tell me about Dana," I said. "She—she's strange. I heard an odd noise last night—like someone chanting or something. It must have been her."

"Dana's—Dana," she shrugged. "Some think she's a witch. One of her Indian ancestors was a medicine man and her English mother and grandmother were supposed to have had powers."

"What do you mean—powers?"

"Oh, second sight, controlling the weather, that sort of thing. Dana knows a lot about herbs."

"Do you believe that?"

She showed me a tiny scar on her right middle finger. "I had a wart there. Damon excised it, but it grew back. So Dana mixed sesame oil with the juice of impatiens, then plunged a red hot poker into the mixture. She told me to apply this 'medicine' three times a day for three days. It was a blend of two remedies, she said. If one didn't work the other would. And it did."

The scar showed white against the sallow, purple-veined hand.

"Are you well, Alison?" I asked.

She withdrew her hand quickly. "I—I'm fine."

"You look as if you'd been on a hunger strike."

"Me? I eat like a horse."

"Maybe Dana could give you a tonic."

"I did ask Damon about it," she admitted. "He said it was hypertension and gave me tranquilizers."

I was about to tell her it wasn't her nature to be nervous when Dana and Dr. Brun entered.

"Always I have trouble with that one," she was fuming. "Once he stuck Darcy's cat's tail in wet cement and left the poor thing out in the woods to starve. I found Jupiter trying to drag a hunk of concrete. The tail was so infected I had to cut it off. Now he's tried to burn my Caper. Singed his beard off with a propane torch."

"Only the hair is burned," Dr. Brun soothed her. He turned to me and held out his hand. "So nice to see you after all this time."

I greeted him warmly. "Sit down, you two. Alison brought this aspic."

"Am I invited, too?"

"Damon!"

The object of my first girlhood crush stood in the door—handsomer than ever now, his dark hair silvered. I had adored him secretly and iniquitously even after he married Charity. Perhaps it had been his unattainability.

But now, as he kissed me, I was conscious only of the wetness of his mouth. So much for schoolgirl romance!

47

"Do join us," I said.

"No thanks, I'm making house calls. I just thought I'd see if you needed anything from the farmers' market."

I opened the refrigerator, favoring my bandaged thumb. "I could use some eggs."

"What did you do to yourself?"

"My knife slipped."

"Better let me check it."

"No, really, it's nothing."

"Okay, but keep it clean. A dozen enough?"

"Plenty. Thanks, Damon."

As his Mark IV glided out of the drive, another car rounded the crest of the hill. "Well, if it isn't the pope himself!" Alison exclaimed irreverently. Dana and Dr. Brun exchanged amused glances. "It's the pastor of the Community church," she went on. "Couldn't wait for the party. Remember Gladys?"

"The church organist? Sure! Did she ever marry?"

"Gladys Pudeator, the preacher-eater! No, but she's still trying. I think our previous minister resigned because he was tired of dodging her. She was in her wig phase then. People used to lay bets on which one she'd wear next. After that it was yoga. I think she's into pyramids now."

"Is the new pastor single?" I asked.

"He's a widower, and before he gets here, I'd better warn you that people are already pairing you off with him—or Gregory Towne, the newspaper editor. But beware Iris. Her tentacles are out, too."

"Ach, you disappoint me, Mrs. Proctor," Dr. Brun sighed with mock seriousness. "Am I not also eligible? A little old, perhaps, but not *too* old, I hope."

He did seem young and robust for his rather advanced

age. Maybe it was his tan or what he was wearing—an open-necked white shirt, and brown shorts.

"You'll always be eligible, doctor," I assured him.

"You're coming to the party tonight, I hope."

"*Nein, danke.* Such an event is for family and I must work on my book. Another time, *meine liebe Freundin.* Ah, *guten Morgen,*" he addressed the man who entered now. "Mrs. Llewellyn, may I present Lucian Leroi."

The newcomer had already had lunch, but he accepted the glass of lemonade I offered. As he sipped it, I watched him covertly, wondering why anyone would cast him as a suitor. He was of medium height, and his dark hair—shot with silver—swept back from a sunken, sallow face. Then I looked into his eyes—compelling, smoky eyes set deep in the hollows beneath peaked eyebrows. I felt myself shiver, whether from like or dislike I couldn't tell. I was about to ask him to say grace when Alison anticipated me.

"Dr. Brun was just about to say the blessing," she lied smoothly, nudging me under the table. Dana looked at her gratefully.

"I came to extend the right hand of fellowship," he said after the amen.

What would ministers do without that cliché?

"I would like to welcome you to Community church," he continued. "As you may know, the Congregational church no longer exists. Except for a few Catholics, who go to mass elsewhere, most of the people here attend Community or," he looked straight at my guests, "just don't go at all."

Alison flushed. "Sorry, Lucian," she said. "You know Ward and I have never been much for formal religion. We're like Aunt Bo."

"And a pity," he mourned. "You and Ward are basically such good people. I pray that I may bring you to Jesus while there's still time. It was a day of rejoicing when I brought Brother and Sister Carrier into the fold," he added.

"Damon and Charity?" I'd never thought of them as religious.

"Yes, they've been born again, Submit."

I stiffened. "Where did you hear that name? Everyone here calls me Mitti, as do all my—friends." Had he gotten the name from my anonymous phone caller?

His brow puckered. "I don't remember, but I think it's a lovely name. 'Submit unto the Lord!' *Have* you given yourself unto the Lord?" He spread his hands on the table—narrow palms sprouting thin, crooked fingers with tufts of black hair between the knuckles. "Have you truly, Submit?"

"My father was a clergyman," I replied. This man had no right to conduct an inquisition.

"You evade me," he said. "Being a minister's daughter doesn't exempt you from making your own decision. I sincerely hope you have." There was a distinct threat in his tone.

"My father preached a loving God," I declared. "He said if there is a hell, it'll be one of mental anguish."

Something flickered in those haunted eyes, as though a door had opened and shut. "And that would be the worst hell of all," he said.

"Agreed. But surely a God of Love would give the soul a chance to redeem itself."

"You can't mean you believe in reincarnation!"

Dana, who had been sitting there, remote and withdrawn, suddenly leaned forward, listening intently.

50

"I don't know," I confessed. "It's a tempting theory, although when I try to believe in it, it evades me, and when I try not to, there it is—luring me with its utter logic."

"Your father would be shocked to hear you say that."

"No," I replied, squaring off. "I don't think he would. I can't see anything unChristian about a concept in which the individual soul can work toward perfection during the course of various lives—whether on this planet or others, or on different planes of existence. One lifetime is too short to work out our karma."

"Karma? I hope you haven't been influenced by this recent interest in the occult and witchcraft, Sub—uh—Mitti," he said, staring at Dana. "That's satanic."

"I must see to Caper," Dana excused herself abruptly.

"The thing that always perturbs me," said Dr. Brun after she'd gone, "is the potency ascribed to Satan. He is not a creator God, he's a negative quantity. Without us to do his works he is nothing. You just said that anything in the supernatural realm is satanic. Let me remind you that the most supernatural force of all is God. May I suggest, sir, that you reread the twelfth chapter of First Corinthians?"

Lucian rose. "It is also written, 'Thou shalt not suffer a witch to live,' " he quoted, putting down his empty glass.

"More lemonade?" Alison asked sweetly.

"No, thank you," he said. "I have other calls to make."

As his car scraped on the gravel outside, she muttered, "He has a burr under his saddle because Aunt Bo had Dr. Brun preach the funeral sermon. And besides," she laughed, "I don't think he likes to linger with publicans and sinners."

51

Dr. Brun sighed. "And this is *Peace*haven!"

"Salem means peace," I observed unnecessarily.

"My grandfather," Alison said, "told me Salem was originally named 'Naumkeag' after the Indians who lived there. The Puritans, who thought the natives were the lost tribes of Israel, believed 'Naumkeag' was Hebrew for 'comfort haven.' Hence, 'Peacehaven.' "

The phone rang. I took it off its hook, my throat tightening.

"Hello? Submit?" came the taunting, sing-song whisper. "Submit, why did you return? We hate you. Move away, Submit . . ."

"Someone has a poor idea of a joke," I mumbled.

"Submit—move away. We warn you. Take your daughters and go. We are many. Did you cut yourself today? We willed it—and that is only the beginning—"

I slammed the receiver down and sat staring at the cut on my thumb.

Chapter Four

With the help of Dana and Alison I was able to get things into fair shape before the invasion began. Unpacked boxes were either shoved into the back hall or stashed in unoccupied bedrooms. One of the first things I did was to strip the heavy plush velvet drapes from the huge picture windows to bring the lush panorama of the countryside indoors.

Rowan came in carrying a large dress box, her eyes shining. Charity had taken her to the Patch and bought her a long denim skirt with fringed hem and a gauze blouse, which she insisted on wearing to the party. In spite of the ninety-degree weather, I shuddered when my daughter said, "It's a *really* neat store! Iris says she knows you. She read my palm this afternoon."

"Oh?" I tried to keep my voice calm. "And what did she say?"

"She said I'm going to be a movie star and marry a rich man, but that a woman with dark brown hair is my enemy." Rowan stood in front of the pier glass in my bedroom, holding up the new skirt to her slight figure. Without turning her head she said, "You have dark brown hair, Mother."

They came, bearing casseroles and salads and cakes and cookies, Ward and Alison first.

"I'll be right behind you to cue you on names," she had promised before she went home to change. Time had been kind to Ward. Only a slight sprinkling of gray dusted his dark hair, and the squint at the corners of his hazel eyes was more a gift of the sun than aging. He held me at arm's length, scanning me with the same quizzical, fond look he'd always had for me. Did he remember the adventures that he and Gareth and I used to have?

Aunt Jenny Pudeator arrived next, with her daughters—Gladys and her sister Muriel, and Muriel's husband, Caleb Toothaker. "Mitti, child, it's a treat to see you. My, how you've grown!" Aunt Jenny squeezed my hands between her two plump ones. Everyone kissed me warmly except Caleb, who stood glumly to one side—long, gaunt hands thrust into his pockets. Muriel had once been almost a beauty, but now her hair hung in yellow strings and her skin was drawn into fine pleats around her mouth and chin. Life with Caleb couldn't have been easy. He was a ruthless man, who, with his half-brother Tyler Bishop, the bank president, was known for making some very sharp deals.

Damon Carrier's greeting was to reach for my lips. His wife's lids narrowed, and I offered him my cheek instead.

"We don't often see such beauty in Peacehaven," he said, scanning my gold crêpe pants and low-cut top. "But you always were a heartbreaker."

I pushed him away. "You never had eyes for anyone but your wife, Damon."

She shot me a grateful look, then turned to greet Rowan, who was pirouetting in front of her.

"See? I wore them, Aunt Charity. They're cool!"

My cousin's face flushed with pleasure as Rowan wound her arm around her waist. Doll-like Charity, already shorter than my daughter. I might have envied her Rowan's warmth if I hadn't remembered about Mark and the baby. Still, a warning bell sounded in my mind. There may be enemies among your guests tonight, Dana had told me before the party.

"And here are Elspeth and Melvin Osburn," Alison broke in. "You remember them—she was Elspeth Bishop." I did—just barely. The town's mortician, he now looked like one of his own customers. Elspeth, Caleb's half-sister, was as colorless as her husband, but her high-gabled nose, sunken cheeks and close-set eyes gave her face more character.

"It's a pleasure to see you two again," I murmured.

"You *must* come over soon!" Elspeth gushed. "I want Junior and Cissie to get acquainted with Rowan."

Junior, the torturer!

"Excuse me," I said as the doorbell rang again.

Ward returned with a tall, blond, studious-looking man who had to stoop slightly as he entered.

"Mitti, I want you to meet Gregory Towne, editor of our newspaper."

His fingers gripping my hand were long and well-shaped. Brown eyes smiled through heavy-rimmed

55

glasses, sending the blood pounding in my ears. I had never seen this man before, but there was something about him—I pushed the thought away, hardly aware my hand had lingered in his. For the first time since Owen's death, I was seeing a man as a man, yet no two could have been more dissimilar. There was a slight movement at the other end of the room—Rowan was staring at our joined hands. I quickly withdrew mine.

"Owner of the paper now as well," Damon broke in. "That's one thing Aunt Bo didn't leave you, Mitti."

"I'm sure Aunt Bo knew the better thing to do with *The Puritan*," I said quickly, trying to cover the newcomer's embarrassment.

"Your aunt was very generous," he said. "I want to do a series of features about her—how she campaigned for suffrage, helped unwed mothers, worked among the mentally retarded—I hope you'll be willing to help me, Mitti."

"I'll be glad to."

"Now don't get Mitti involved in any crusades," Charity cautioned sharply. "Aunt Bo caused enough trouble—almost got herself arrested more than once."

I felt a twinge of annoyance at her disloyalty.

"Suffrage!" Caleb sniffed. "We can thank meddling women like Bo Severance for laying the foundation for this goddam women's lib."

"We *have* been wondering, Mitti—" Damon said, helping himself to a handful of nuts, "you were always so fond of Aunt Bo—you're not going to go around stirring things up, are you?"

"Don't worry, Damon." There was a dangerous quiver in my voice. "I'm not for women's lib—I'm for man's enslavement."

Ward and Alison's laughter died as the others sat there uncomfortably. Gregory Towne came to my rescue.

"In that case we men are doomed. I, for one, surrender."

Smooth, I thought, wondering how a man of his caliber could make an adequate living out of so small a newspaper as the Peacehaven *Puritan*.

Ward answered my unspoken question. "Greg has a fellowship from Harvard for a study of the descendants of Salem victims—he happens to be descended from one himself, and," with the old familiar, teasing smile, "since we are just about the most concentrated and isolated group of witch progeny in existence, he chose us as a test case."

Greg frowned. "I liked your term 'victim' better," he said. "The real witches were their accusers." How intense he was!

"You honestly think they were practicing witchcraft?" I asked in amazement, settling onto the sofa.

"It depends on what you mean by witchcraft," he replied. He seated himself on the inglenook. "It varies from age to age. To the Puritans, witchcraft was a contractual affair. To curry the Devil's favor, you signed his black book and performed his evil works. In that sense I think there was witchcraft—I don't mean anyone actually signed such a book, but I believe certain people did dedicate themselves to mischief. The indigent, undesirables, incapacitated and elderly posed a financial burden on society. It would have been to the advantage of the ruling class—magistrates, government officials, clergy, and large property holders—to sift out those elements in the population. The crime of witchcraft, which carried the death penalty, provided the means."

Ward pulled his pipe from his pocket. "Not all the victims were poor or burdensome."

"As heretics they were considered burdensome," Greg argued. "And anyone with enemies ran the risk of being accused of heresy."

"But why only Salem?" Ward countered.

"Historians have never come up with a satisfactory answer to that," Greg replied. "They cite ill will between neighbors, fear of the Crown, fear of the Indians, of disease, of Satan, mass hysteria, and antipathy between various church congregations—but these were common to every community. There had to be another factor—a catalyst—but what that was we may never know. I'm hoping to find a clue here."

"Were any of the accused really guilty?" I asked.

"Yes. Dorcas Hoar probably was," Greg said. "She saved her life with an eleventh hour confession, incriminating others. She had a previous reputation for sorcery. Today we'd call her an extortionist—a Massachusetts Fagin, you might say. She read palms and told fortunes, mostly among servants and children, predicting dire fates for them if they didn't bring her stolen goods. She *should* have been hanged. But most, I believe, were innocent."

"Oh, come on, Greg!" This from Alison, who entered with a steaming percolator, followed by Dana trundling a teacart. "It's intriguing to think one has witch ancestors. I just wish I could use some witchcraft on my housework!"

Only Ward and I laughed, although Greg smiled. The others were clearly shocked.

"Really, Alison!" her sister-in-law scolded. "How can you be so flippant? If you'd felt the Evil Eye like I—"

"Careful, Char," Damon warned her.

"—like *they* said they did," she corrected herself. "Damn it, Alison, you've got me arguing on the wrong side." Her hand shook as she brought the lighter to her cigarette.

"But why were the founders of Peacehaven, who were separated from the Salem tragedy by at least a century and a half, still so bitter?" I asked, trying to cover Charity's confusion.

"You say that because you're really not one of us, Mitti," she reminded me ungratefully.

"Legal murder isn't easily forgotten," Greg explained. "Did you know that the bill of attainder stands to this day against seven of the twenty who were executed? The Massachusetts legislature passed a resolution in 1957 condemning the legal proceedings at the trials, but that did nothing to reverse the convictions."

"But why harbor old resentments?" I persisted. "You can't unhang those unfortunates."

"We can clear their names," he pointed out.

"Who believes them guilty now?"

"The world does," Damon blurted out. "The name of Salem is still synonymous with witchcraft and satanism."

"And Salem profits handsomely from its reputation," Ward commented sardonically. "Why're you so vehement, Damon? I never heard you talk that way before."

"I admit I never thought much about it until lately, but Lucian's made me see things differently. Witchcraft— that is, satanism—is coming to the surface again after lying low for centuries."

"Oh, come on, Damon," Ward snorted, "you certainly don't believe there's anything to that hocus-pocus."

59

His brother-in-law forked into his food impatiently. "The thing that concerns me is that criminals can operate in the guise of witches or satanists—and we may've had a taste of that right here in Peacehaven."

Behind me, Muriel gasped.

"I agree with Mitti," Alison said hastily. "It's about time this town got over its hang-ups."

"Forget our heritage? Never!" Damon said. "I suppose this is as good a time as any to make an announcement. Lucian has suggested we put on a pageant about Salem. Greg's writing the script. We'll all wear period costumes—like they do in Williamsburg—and those of us in the pageant will rehearse until we're so professional people will come from all over to see it. It'll be Peacehaven's passion play!"

"The young girls will have the best parts," Charity volunteered. "If Rowan's like her father, she'll play the lead among the girls."

"Oh, that would be great!" Rowan embraced her.

I observed them wistfully and turned away, accidentally knocking the spoon off my plate. Greg and I bent over simultaneously, our hands closing over it. I straightened to see Rowan looking at me strangely.

"Just a minute, Aunt Charity!" she blurted out. "I've got something upstairs I want to bring down for you to hear."

Greg brought us back to the pageant. "I hear you were a commercial artist in New York, Mitti. Would you do the scenery?"

How could I resist those clear brown eyes? "I'd love to. It would take study, of course."

"Oh, I'll help you." His tone was intimate now, as though we were the only ones in the room. "I'll drop off material for you and we can go over it together."

"That would be fi—"

I checked myself as the strains of "Frenzy" intruded. Rowan came in carrying her tape recorder, a strange smile on her face, as Owen's voice filled the room, bringing back unendurable memories of our violent arguments over his last role—the one that drove him to his cocaine addiction—and that one, awful night . . .

"Rowan, dear," I said between clenched teeth, "please turn that off. This is not the proper time."

She turned up the volume.

"Turn it off!" I was on my feet now.

She switched off the cassette. "That was my Daddy," she said. "Mother doesn't like me to play it. She wants to forget him, but I won't—and I don't want anyone else to. My daddy was a superstar."

"Rowan!" I cried out, swaying slightly. Greg's hand at my elbow steadied me.

"You're very young, my dear," Alison told her gently. "Someday you will understand that—after a great loss— certain songs make us very sad."

"But it's natural for Rowan to be proud of her father," Charity defended her.

"Sweetheart," I began, trying to recover my composure, "you're obviously very tired, and tired little girls must go to bed."

Rowan's eyes glittered defiantly as Owen's voice blared forth again. I held out my hand.

"Let me have the cassette, dear."

She held her ground.

"Let me have it!"

Eye to eye—I mustn't yield, mustn't waver or blink— how long could she keep this up? I swallowed hard to

61

hold back the tears—then she broke and ran out of the room.

I crumpled inside. "I'm sorry," I apologized, switching off the recorder. *Somebody say something,* I pleaded silently. *Don't just sit around and think!*

Gladys came to my rescue. "Where's Lucian?" she asked in the little girl's voice so out of keeping with her massive body.

"Oh, then you've met him!" she exclaimed when I told her he'd be late. "We're so fortunate to have a man of his caliber in Peacehaven. He's brought us salvation. He's made remarkable changes, like his 'stones into bread' drive for the missions. He heaps up a pile of stones in front of the church. One stone is removed for each offering until the pile is gone."

"Didn't Satan try to make Christ turn stones into bread?" Ward, the iconoclast, offered.

"Did he?" Gladys was distressed. "Oh, but Lucian's no devil—he's a saint and his sermons are utterly—what's the matter, Muriel?"

She was holding her head and moaning.

"It's another of her spells coming on, looks like," Caleb said disgustedly. "I guess we'd better get going. C'mon, Mur!" He jerked her to her feet.

"Oh, no!" Gladys pouted. "We've hardly gotten here."

And Lucian hadn't.

"Please," her sister begged, between white lips. "Do you mind, Glad? Besides, mother shouldn't stay out late."

"Oh, fiddlesticks, Muriel," Aunt Jenny huffed, "it's not nearly my bedtime. Where's Dana? I want to talk to her."

"She's busy in the kitchen," Alison said. "I'll get her."

"No, never mind," Caleb checked her. "We really must

leave. I know what happens when Muriel gets one of these attacks."

"Muriel's never been the same since her little girl was killed," Charity said as we heard the Toothakers's car grind down the hill.

"Let's not go into that. That was six months ago." Her husband cut her off as forks were suspended in midair. Greg, over on the inglenook, turned his eyes away. Something was wrong.

"Really," I said, "you might as well tell me. I'll find out soon enough in this town."

They looked from one to another, hesitant to begin. Greg spoke finally. "Susie Toothaker was found in a farmer's field not far from here—murdered. She was only seven."

The shadows on the cathedral ceiling, formed by the beams arching overhead, pressed in on us. "Who did it?" I asked.

"Nobody knows."

"Probably some transient," Ward said.

"Nothing like this ever happened before we became integrated here in Peacehaven," Charity observed, fidgeting with her rings.

Ward turned to her in annoyance. "Will you knock it off? Darrell Jackson's a fine man and the best manager I've ever had at the lumberyard."

"It's a pity the school board never saw fit to employ his wife," Alison added. "Rhoda Jackson has a doctorate in education."

"I was secretary of the school board then and I resent that," Elspeth snapped. "How many parents here would like to have their children taught by a colored woman? I, for one, wouldn't. Look at that black activist son of hers!"

63

"Why shouldn't Quentin want to help his people?" Ward growled. "He's done nothing criminal. He's a top law student and I'll lay you odds he'll be a legislator or congressman someday."

"Not from this district he won't!" Charity declared. "Not while I live here. How do you know *he* didn't kill that little girl? He was in town at the time."

Damon shook his head. "More likely it was one of those weirdos who bought Aunt Bo's farm."

"A couple who own a witchcraft supply store in Madison have made a country home of the farm," Greg explained. "They appear to take it pretty seriously—at least they hold regular meetings, and—"

"Damn insult—bringing witchcraft here," Damon stormed.

"I thought it was taboo to persecute witchcraft in Peacehaven," Ward observed drily.

"Not at all," Damon retorted. "It's only forbidden to accuse falsely. If we harbor characters like that, we're liable to have Salem all over again."

"They're really fixing up the old farm," Ward said. "They've been buying lumber for repairs."

"So that's why you defend them! Good business for you."

"Oh, come off it, Damon!"

Elspeth waved a bite of cake in the air. "Harold Toothaker's gone to their meetings. Maybe *he* killed Susie. Everyone knows he was terribly jealous of his baby sister. And now that he's a witch—"

"Now honey, that's getting a bit farfetched," Melvin objected.

"Not at all," she retorted. "You saw those queer signs carved on her body when we laid her out—like a ritual murder. It took plenty of make-up to fix her up—and a wig, too."

"Sweetheart!" Melvin's cup slammed down on its saucer. "Those are professional secrets!"

Upstairs Alice Cooper yowled. My head throbbed. Rowan must be asleep by now. I went to the kitchen and asked Dana to go up and turn off the recorder.

"Actually, there were two types of wounds," Damon said. "Some looked as if she'd been attacked by a wild beast—maybe a wolf—but others could have been made by a knife—crosses, swastikas, crescents, stars—you name it."

"Like the Manson murders," Elspeth said.

I shivered as the music stopped abruptly and Dana ran into the room.

"They're gone—their beds are empty!"

My throat contracted. The walls swam around me and the beams overhead rotated like the blades of a ceiling fan.

"You're sure you looked everywhere?" Ward's voice.

"Everywhere but outside."

"Everybody start searching!" Damon said.

As I struggled for control I saw Dana sink to a crouch on the floor intoning unintelligible words. "I—see—them," she reverted to English. "Come, I will take you to them."

She led us across the parking lot and into the woods. Dark had thoroughly descended and I floundered over rocks and undergrowth. My flaring pants caught on the brambles, but I paid no heed. I fought off a vine that wound around my arm as if it were something live. Somewhere in the distance what sounded like tom-toms were beating.

"Do you hear that?" I gasped, catching someone's arm. Greg's hand closed over mine.

"Probably those witches," I heard Damon mutter.

"It's Midsummer Eve," Charity's weary voice fluttered through the dark. "They're having a sabbat—maybe a sacrifice."

"Shut up!" Damon snapped.

Midsummer's Eve—Rowan had said something about that. Oh God! Rituals in the night and a little girl murdered. I clung to Greg's hand, flinching as a spruce branch slapped me smartly in the face. An owl hooted. What was the old belief? When an owl hoots someone dies?

Again the sound of tom-toms in counterpoint with chanting.

"That's where they held their meetings in Salem," Charity said. "Out in the parson's pasture."

"At least our minister doesn't own a pasture," Greg reminded her. All the while I felt his hand pressing mine. Even in my distress I was conscious of an inner strength in him buoying me up. If it had been Owen, I would have had to be the stronger one. But I was being unfair—Rowan wasn't Greg's daughter.

Dana loomed ahead of us, the wind filling out her skirt. I touched her arm. "Where are you taking us?"

"Where I saw them. Do not worry. The little girls are safe."

A thin ray of light caught up with us and passed us, then came Ward, at the other end, holding a flashlight. The beam swept past Dana to pick up something white against the blackness.

"There! Did I not tell you we'd find them?"

She seemed a miniature madonna, enveloped in the

66

halo of the flashlight, her back to a great burled oak, the baby in her arms. The slender beam caught the red-gold hair cascading down her shoulders and glinted on the star sapphires of her eyes. How beautiful she is! I marvelled, then chilled. She was a statue holding a live baby, which whimpered and squirmed in her rigid grip. Alison took Cariad from her with some difficulty.

Damon took hold of her wrist. "Appears to be some sort of catalepsy," he muttered as he released her. "Her pulse is about half the normal rate and her respiration's slow, too." He waved his hand in front of her unblinking eyes.

"What could cause that?" I asked tremulously.

"A number of things—hysteria for one, or—"

Or schizophrenia, I supplied mentally, grateful he hadn't added that for the others to hear.

"Or demonic possession," Charity said.

"Now, whatever made you say a thing like that?" Damon said impatiently as he lifted Rowan's lids and peered into her pupils with Ward's flashlight.

"You read too many novels," Ward reproved his sister.

"She's overtired, poor child," Alison said. "Maybe she overheard us talking about Susie and—"

The bushes rustled and a dark figure stepped into the narrow beam of the flash—Lucian!

"I found her that way," he told us. "As I was parking my car in your drive, Mitti, I saw her disappearing into the woods. I went after her, but it was hard to follow in the dark, and when I got here, there wasn't a thing I could do."

"Were they alone? Did you see anyone else?" Ward asked.

"No, no one."

67

"I'll have to examine her at the house," Damon said, trying to lift her. Suddenly the statue came to life and struck out at him furiously, kicking and screaming and tearing at his face until he let go. Immediately she began to prance around in a circle, chucking her tongue as though riding a horse.

"Git along with ye, Robin, or I'll fetch a clout to thy 'ead, I will." One small foot thrashed in the air kicking her invisible mount in the belly. In the dim light her feet seemed more to dangle than to be making contact with the ground.

"Good Lord!" someone exclaimed.

"In the name of Jesus—" Lucian began.

She somersaulted forward, thrown by her phantom steed, and lay on the ground—her limbs jerking convulsively, eyes rolling backward until only the whites showed.

"Do ye be silent!" she cried, sticking her fingers in her ears. " 'Tis a name that sickens me!"

She flopped over on her stomach, arching her back grotesquely so that her neck and heels were touching. I could hear her vertebrae grinding together, and her tongue lolled out of one corner of her mouth. I knelt down to try to straighten her limbs, but she jerked away.

"You burned me!" she cried out. "Let me go! Let me go!"

I drew back in horror, the stench of burning flesh in my nostrils. Was I hallucinating, too? Greg lifted me gently from my knees, but he, too, was shuddering, shaken by an emotion he couldn't control. Charity advanced on Dana, who was standing to one side, her face a mass of shadows in the dim light.

"Is this your doing? Will she die like my baby did?"

"Charity! We don't talk like that, do we?" Damon warned her. She shrank back and covered her face with her hands.

A twig snapped and Dr. Brun appeared, holding a lantern.

"Something has happened?" he asked, his accent heavy in his excitement. *"Ach! Was ist los?"* as the ray of his lantern fell across Rowan's tortured form. "It is the little one. Perhaps I can be of help—I have had experience with this—"

"We'll attend to her," Damon brushed him aside. Bracing, he strained to tear her hands from her ankles, but her grip remained fixed.

"My God, this is straight out of Cotton Mather!" Greg exclaimed.

"All right, Melvin, let's get her up," Damon ordered, but her hands closed about her throat. "Stop them! Oh, stop them!" she shrieked. "They're nailing me down!" she tugged at an invisible spike.

"What she needs is a good spanking," I heard Elspeth murmur to her husband.

"Come here, Ward—you, too, Greg—give us a hand, will you?" The doctor grunted as he and Melvin and Lucian struggled to lift the child. The five of them interlocked their arms beneath her and heaved, but Rowan remained welded to the soil. She was screaming and I with her. Alison gripped my hand.

The men drew back, wiping the sweat from their foreheads.

"There must be an explanation." This from Ward, the realist.

Damon shook his head. "Damnedest thing I ever saw."

This time Dr. Brun didn't ask. He waved them back

imperiously as he crouched beside Rowan and murmured softly. Her face contorted and her body writhed helplessly, still held by the invisible spike. One hand clawed at his face. Suddenly her own contorted and a voice cried out in anguish, "No, no, don't use that name—don't, don't!" Agony turned to cunning, "Why call on *him* when *we* are here to serve you?"

"How can I call on you if I don't know your name?" the doctor asked slyly.

"We are *not* one—we are Seven . . ." A deep, coarse chuckle issued from her throat. "Did you think we'd tell you? Let you gain power over us?"

The veins stood out in Dr. Brun's temples and every muscle was quivering.

"I'll not play guessing games with you," he replied. "I know you, Old Adversary, and for all your selves you are but one. I adjure you in the name of God the Father, Son and Holy Spirit—"

Talons raked his face, leaving long red stripes against the pale skin. He reeled momentarily, but his hands remained poised above Rowan's body, which thrashed from one side to the other, shuddering as unseen blows rained on her.

There was sudden silence. She lay as though dead— then slowly sat up, twisting her head around until I could hear her vertebrae grind.

"Dana," came a mocking voice, "why do you hide there in the shadows? You have served us in the past. Did you think you could escape us now?"

Dana's face was chiseled adamantine, but I saw her waver slightly and her hand gripped her skirt.

"Come, we can use you. It's the saints who serve us best."

"Be quiet!" The rocks reverberated with Dr. Brun's voice. "I command you in the name of the Father and the Son and the Holy Spirit—be gone from this child!"

Snarls and hisses and then macabre laughter floated off into the night. Rowan's head jerked back and her mouth opened wide, taking in great gulps of air.

"Rowan," Dr. Brun said gently, "listen to me, child. You—Rowan—have the power to cast out evil from yourself—*if you so will!* If you do not, it will return again and again. I know—I have dealt with this before."

She gagged and her eyes bulged as a ball swelled in her windpipe, crept slowly up the line of her throat, and into her mouth. Then, with a loud hiss, it was gone. She lay there, limp and spent, her cheeks wet with tears.

He lifted her easily. Her head fell against his chest as the half-light plowed deep furrows in his haggard face.

"She will sleep now," he told us. "Let us return to the house."

Chapter Five

Now, even my own bed couldn't induce sleep. The events of the day and their terrifying climax had strained every nerve to its limit. The phone was silent—but that, too, was unnerving. I could see a hand hovering over a dial somewhere out there. Had news of tonight's episode traveled already? Would Rowan be marked as "odd"?

My cousins had stayed for awhile after the others left. Rowan wanted Dr. Brun to remain with her until she went to sleep, so the Proctors and the Carriers and I sat downstairs, sipping coffee and groping for explanations.

"The child was overwrought," Alison tried to reassure me. "Moving to a strange place—meeting relatives she's never known."

"She was obviously mimicking *The Exorcist*," Charity said, her own qualms forgotten. "Did you *let* her see that, Mitti?"

"No, but it's possible she and some of her classmates played hookey and went."

"I think we're all forgetting something," Alison said. "We were just as spooked as she was. Something unnatural was going on out there."

"I think we spooked ourselves," Ward remarked. "All that talk about Susie and—who knows? As you suggested earlier, Alison, maybe Rowan overheard and got upset." He fell silent. Ward had a great belief in disbelief.

"As you say, we were in a suggestible state," Damon agreed. "Catalepsy is a frightening phenomenon."

"*Mass* catalepsy, I'd say," Alison remarked.

Damon gave an embarrassed laugh. "Lucky thing you didn't serve liquor tonight, Mitti. I'd be heading for AA in the morning. If you'll let me, I want to do some tests on Rowan—routine blood tests—and she should have a Rorschach."

"You mean you want her to see a psychiatrist," I bridled.

"Just as a precaution," he soothed me. "We may not find anything. Alison's probably right—just nervous strain."

"Maybe that Indian woman put a spell on her," Charity proposed. Ward and Damon exchanged despairing glances. "Or that Swiss doctor. He could have hypnotized the lot of us. You saw how *he* had no trouble lifting her after five of you failed."

Damon knocked the ashes from his pipe. "You know, she may have something there. Mass hypnosis. That's fairly well documented."

"So is the phenomenon of possession," Dr. Brun said, entering. "Call it what you will—hysteria or actual demonic manifestation, it does exist. She fell asleep

73

almost immediately," he added, answering my unspoken question.

"Oesterreich has written about possession," Damon conceded. "And there are many Catholic treatises on the subject, but I consider those highly unreliable. Catholics love their myths."

Dr. Brun smiled slightly. "Would you accept the word of Cotton Mather, that most dedicated of Protestant Puritans? He wrote in his *Memorable Providences* about four children in Boston who were bewitched by an Irish washerwoman. He and his wife took the oldest child, Martha, into their home to pray for her deliverance."

"Strange thing," he continued, "Rowan's symptoms tonight were nearly identical—the imaginary horse, the contortions, her hands and feet fastened together, the impalement to the ground, the voices, the swelling in her throat—Cotton Mather records all those manifestations."

"Superstitious hogwash," Damon said. "That old buzzard Mather was a witch hunter; naturally he'd lie to make himself look good."

"Mather was hardly an *old* buzzard—he was in his twenties at the time, and I don't believe he was lying," Dr. Brun said mildly. "I've treated similar cases. One in Zurich involved a young man who suffered seizures in which he became violent and would babble in Arabic, a language of which he had no knowledge—"

Damon rose and took his wife by the arm. "Let's go," he rasped. "I'd forgotten we have a writer here who will apparently go to any length for sensationalism—even if he has to re-create *The Exorcist*."

Dr. Brun gave him a puzzled look. "Exorcist? What is that? A book?"

Now, as I lay in my bed, I wondered what *had* made

Rowan take Cariad and run away? Maybe Ward had the right idea. I certainly hoped she wasn't taking revenge on me. *Had* something frightened her? *Had* someone lured her out? Dr. Brun? Lucian?

Upset by my suspicions, I climbed out of bed and grabbed my robe, intending to get some fresh air, and determined to shake the anxiety that gripped me.

Two figures stood in the country mist between the Phoenix and Dana's house, and as I approached, I heard Dana's distinct tones.

"Anyway," she was saying, "it's not respectable to be possessed in Peacehaven. The people here have been trying too long to prove their ancestors *weren't* witches . . . Mitti! Is anything wrong?"

"No," I replied, joining them, "I just couldn't sleep."

Dr. Brun led us over to the steps to sit down, and I felt a rush of despair.

"What is the town going to think about Rowan—about what happened tonight?"

"They were too much a part of it, this time," he tried to reassure me. "You saw five men unable to lift her."

"Yet you did," I observed. "Take care they don't label you a wizard, Dr. Brun."

"Oh, I'm quite certain they have long ago."

"Did Rowan say anything about why she ran away like that?"

He shook his head. "She was so sleepy I didn't want to question her. Does she ever sleepwalk?"

"I've never known her to. Damon wants to do some tests and send her to a psychiatrist. Do you think it's necessary?"

"I do think it would be wise for her to take a Rorschach test."

My fingernails were stabbing my palms. "Would it have to be done right away? With moving and all, everything is so upset—"

"But, of course! Take your time! We'll watch her closely, and if other things occur . . . But this may be stress-induced—just an isolated incident."

"As for blood tests," I hurried on, "Rowan had a complete physical just before we left New York. I wanted her own pediatrician to do it. Everything was normal."

"There are more sophisticated tests—" he began.

"No!" I was adamant. "I won't have it! I can still see the blood spurting from that little girl's neck in *The Exorcist*. I *won't* have Rowan subjected to gruesome tests like that. By themselves they'd be enough to push a sensitive child over the edge." My nails were inflicting genuine pain now, but my hands refused to unclasp.

Dr. Brun laid his hand over my clenched fists. Warmth stole into them and slowly they relaxed. "I agree, Mitti. The best course is to wait and see, and try as much as possible to make her forget the whole incident. Not that she'll remember what happened out there—she won't, but others will undoubtedly talk to her about it."

My tension was easing. "You don't really believe in demons, do you?" I asked.

He touched his eye-patch lightly. "I owe that to a demon in the Amazon. The kindest, gentlest man you could imagine began to show classic symptoms of possession. Like you, I didn't believe in such things, and I tried to treat him as a psychiatrist and medical man would. I lost an eye and gained wisdom. So I tried exorcism and the man was cured."

"Oh well, in primitive cultures people are easily suggestible," I observed. "They only have to know that someone's sticking pins in their image or has put a curse on them and they curl up and die of fright."

"And those telephone calls you get don't affect you?" he asked.

"Not enough to cause me to be possessed."

"Yet if it were to be carried to an extreme, you might not only become fear-ridden, but vulnerable to psychic attack."

"Couldn't this possession thing be a handy excuse for certain kinds of behavior?"

"In some cases, yes. But to all my patients I stress that we must be responsible for the actions of the entities we choose to harbor, be they angels or demons."

"In other words—we still have free will. Do you think Rowan has deliberately opened herself up to demonic possession? I can't believe that."

"She's done it unthinkingly. However, she wasn't alone in it tonight. Rowan was a sounding board for the imperfections in all of us. She's a sensitive child and I suspect she's still suffering from the trauma of her father's death."

More than you know, I thought, as a thousand questions in my mind clamored to be heard. "I have such a strange feeling about Peacehaven," I said. "It's as if this tiny town has been suspended in a particular spot in time, with all sorts of coincidences, that aren't coincidences at all, rushing in upon it—as if all the forces of the universe were converging here for some terrible event just as they did in Salem nearly three hundred years ago. You, Dr. Brun, why are you here? To explore our caves? That may be your reason, but maybe God has another. The same for Greg and Lucian. And perhaps it was all part of the same plan for Aunt Bo to reverse her will, bringing me and my daughters here at this moment. All of us fulfilling one divine—or infernal—purpose. It's like sitting on the San Andreas fault, waiting for California to drop into the ocean."

"Or Peacehaven to fall into the river," he said.

Dana and I sat without talking for some time after Dr. Brun left us. I longed for bed, but was too tired to make the effort to get there.

Dana spoke first. "Look, the mist is lifting!"

It was indeed. The old house with its faceted windows was emerging to the rear and west of the parking lot. I became aware of a dull, metallic clank against the fenced-in enclosure behind the house.

"Come, I'll introduce you to Caper," Dana said, reaching out her hand.

"Oh—the goat," I remembered. "How is he, by the way?"

"Fine, except for a wounded ego now his beard is gone."

The little goat came trotting out of his pen toward me, reaching out his black head for me to pet. I gingerly held out my hand, and he immediately caught hold of the sleeve of my robe.

"Caper, behave!" Dana commanded. He obeyed, relinquishing my sleeve intact.

"He's a gentleman," she said, stroking him. "A gentleman 'it,' that is, which keeps him smelling sweet. He earns his room and board by grazing the dandelions and burdock and other weeds, although I've kept him penned up since he wandered into town and ate one of Elspeth's plum trees."

As I put out my hand again, Caper spooked, sidling away toward the back door of the Phoenix.

"He'd like to be let in for a few minutes, but it's too late now," she explained.

"You let Caper in the house?" I asked, taken aback.

"Just into the kitchen for a bowl of cereal now and then." Then, seeing the dismay in my face, she added, "He's housebroken."

About this time Caper wheeled about and started back toward me. I retreated, envisioning a well-aimed butt, but just as he got to me he put on the brakes, lowered his head and rubbed his face against my robe. He *was* a gentleman!

"You intrigue me, Dana," I said as we turned back to the house. "Tell me about yourself. I know you took wonderful care of Aunt Bo. And you well deserved that," I said, pointing to the old house which was now hers. In the mercury light it looked black, but it was really a dark brown.

"Some people resent her bequest," Dana said. "They think it should have stayed in the family."

I took her hand. "You are family now, Dana. Try to remember that. Please tell me more about yourself."

"There isn't much to tell. My mother was resented by my father's people, partly because she was a white woman, but more because she was known to have the Sight. Winnebagoes fear witches. So we left the reservation and came here to live. Father said this land once belonged to his people—they'd held councils here on this bluff."

"All the more reason for you to have the house," I said.

"Father took odd jobs, but never did prosper. Then, after my mother died, your Aunt Bo took us in. She gave

79

my father a steady job and let him build a little cabin back in the woods. When he died, she sent me to college to study teaching and nursing, after which I returned to the reservation to help my people. I married a Winnebago man, but he died young and we had no children. I continued to teach for many years until one of my students died suddenly. Then the gray-haired women of the tribe remembered my mother—and they accused me of being a witch and stealing the child's unused years so I might live longer. I didn't blame them. I knew this had happened so that I could go to your aunt and say, 'Aunt Bo'—for that is what I called her, too—'I am no longer of any use to my people, so let me stay with you!' You see, I couldn't tell her she wasn't able to take care of herself anymore. She had to feel she was taking care of me."

"No wonder Aunt Bo loved you so much, Dana," I said softly.

"Thank you for that, Mitti. Now, at last, I feel the house is really mine."

She spoke with pride and I followed her gaze over to the house Joshua Martin had built. It loomed tall and forbidding with its high, narrow gables, dark brown clapboarding and mullioned windows. It was said that Martin had deliberately copied the House of Seven Gables in Salem—although it wasn't known as that then, since it was before Hawthorne had immortalized it. Martin even slanted the doors in the way the old sea captain had in the original house so they would always swing closed unless someone propped them open. And he, too, had a hidden staircase beside the chimney that led to a secret room upstairs. Little did he know it would come in handy before the Civil War for hiding fugitive slaves.

"There is a problem though," Dana went on. "In a

town like Peacehaven, if Dr. Brun and I stay there alone—even at our age—there's bound to be talk, and that might be hard for you."

"It would be no one's business," I scoffed.

"No," she said firmly. "You have Rowan and Cari to think of. I have a plan in mind which I hope you'll approve—I know Aunt Bo would."

Sly fox!

"There's an old woman in town, who is crippled with arthritis and needs care. Her house on the river is threatened with collapse. Her son wants to send her to a nursing home, but since there are none in Peacehaven, she'd be sent away where she'd have no friends. I have a large room where she could stay and keep her treasures, and her friends could visit her."

"Oh, Dana, after all those years of taking care of Aunt Bo!" The enormity of her generosity stunned me. "I should think you'd want some freedom."

Her chin lifted. "I've always been free and this is something I wish to do."

"Mightn't you be accused of operating a nursing home without a license?"

"I checked into that. She will 'rent' a room from me. She has Social Security and Medicare. But her son might object."

"Why? Nursing homes are expensive."

"Not in his case. He deals constantly with nursing homes and social agencies."

Who was this insensitive son? I wondered angrily.

"I do not understand this," she continued. "Among my people it is an honor to be old, for with age comes wisdom. Agh, I talk too much." She turned toward her house.

"Wait, Dana," I stopped her. "You haven't told me—

who is this old lady? Do I know her?" A suspicion rose in my mind. "Not Damon's mother!"

"But she worked so hard to put him through medical school!" I exclaimed when she admitted it was. Damon's grandfather had once owned nearly half the town, most of which was now under the river. What was left of his fortune Damon's father had squandered. Mrs. Carrier, a slight, frail woman, had taken in laundry, baked and sewed and cleaned—anything to scrape together the money for Damon to complete his education. "There's plenty of room in his home."

"He says she and Charity would never get on. To tell the truth, I think he's ashamed of his mother. He seldom visits her. And because she's lonely and in pain she's taken to drinking in secret and has been seen drunk in public several times."

"Mightn't an alcoholic be too much to handle?"

"She's not an alcoholic!" The reprimand was implicit. "Just lonely. She won't need to drink here because she'll be among friends—I hope."

I winced at her scorn. "I didn't mean it that way, Dana. Have her here, by all means." Damon would be furious, but that rather enhanced the idea.

"You say that easily, but when it happens you may regret it."

"Why should I? It's very Christian of you."

"People here do not think of me as a Christian, Mitti."

"I'd call it Christian charity," I floundered.

"You think Christians have a monopoly on charity?" she asked.

"Well, no," I stammered. "However, when I spoke of Christian charity I used the wrong term. I meant a deed of love, such as Christ might have performed." Who was this woman who was alternately Indian and inscrutable, warm and impulsive as the Celtic blood in her, and as coolly intellectual as her Anglo-Saxon heritage?

"Christ is another matter," she said simply, then shrugged. "It is not the hour for religious discussion."

No, it wasn't. I wrapped my robe tighter around me as I became aware of the night chill. Somewhere down in the town a dog barked. We should both get to bed, yet I lingered. "Has Dr. Brun explored our cave at the back of the bluff, Dana?"

I felt a withdrawal in her. "Yes. He found nothing."

"I remember a deep drop-off right at the entrance. My cousins and I had to put planks across to get into the cave. But I—well I thought I saw footholds in the steep wall. There could be a lower level. I wanted to try climbing down with a rope, but Ward said it was too dangerous."

"And right he was," she said severely. "Dr. Brun has had several narrow escapes in other caves. I hope he won't take any risks in ours."

There was no use pursuing the subject. I turned back toward the Phoenix. A cow lowed somewhere in the distance. Suddenly I felt desolate—frightened. This was so different from the Peacehaven I'd known.

"Oh, Dana," I burst out, "nothing here is the way I expected it to be!"

"Nothing ever is," she replied. "Time doesn't give us reruns."

"No, but—" I stopped. The phone was ringing in my house. I instinctively clutched her arm. "I—I don't want to answer that."

"I'll get it," she said.

"Hello?"

Click!

She hung up, giving me a long look. "Leave it off the hook tonight," she suggested. "You need your sleep."

"Who could it be, Dana?" I whispered.

But her eyes were fixed on something far away.

"I can't see it yet," she came back to me at last. "I tried, but I can't get through." Then she brightened. "But neither can the other person now, so go to bed."

Chapter Six

Two weeks passed before I finally climbed the circular staircase to Aunt Bo's tower. To be truthful, deep at the back of my mind was the thought of Aunt Bo dying there. It wasn't the physical death that frightened me, but so many disturbing things had happened in this first week in Peacehaven that I had begun to doubt my own powers of perception. I don't know what I expected to find. Perhaps I feared seeing her shade appearing and disappearing? Whatever it was, I was unable to shake my unease.

Now, as I gazed out over the panorama of river valley and crag-crested bluffs ranged around the horizon, and luxuriated in the cool breeze sweeping through the circuit of windows, I laughed at myself. Aunt Bo's great black leather chair was there, but no ghostly apparition— only a natural sagging from use, and on her vast mahogany desk the papers and newspaper clippings were neatly stacked, probably by Dana, as Aunt Bo never straightened anything.

Orderliness was the only imprint Death had laid upon the place. I should have known. Death and Aunt Bo had nothing in common. Instead, my spirit lifted, and my fingers tingled with longing to paint the jumbled bluffs crowded one upon another until they lay blue upon the horizon.

The phone on the desk jingled, startling me, but it was only Darcy. Would Rowan and I come to dinner soon? And why hadn't we been down to pick out a kitten?

As I hung up, I realized I was trembling. Would I ever get over my dread of those threatening calls? So many *different* voices! How efficiently they'd cancelled out the first syllable of Peacehaven!

Now Cariad posed a problem. Even though she had yet to take her first step, she was lightning on all fours and an incorrigible streaker. I had to make a rule that all screen doors be latched, because she had learned to push them out. I mentally checked now. Yes, they were secure. Besides, Rowan had come in and would watch over her sister.

In the sparkling clear day I could see the faint outlines of the Blue Mounds to the southeast and the Platteville Mounds to the southwest. Looking straight down, I saw Mrs. Carrier seated on a lawn chair in front of Dana's house, her white head bent over a rag doll she was making for Cari.

Freya lay at her feet enjoying the morning sun—then she was up, running swiftly across the lawn in spite of the pups swelling her belly, barking frantically. I froze. A little pink form was scooting over the grass toward the edge of the bluff. Freya circled her, trying to force her back, but Cariad apparently thought the big dog was playing a game and kept right on. I plummeted down the stairs, two steps at a time, praying.

By the time I reached her, Cari was lying on her back, shrieking, with Freya crouched by her side, one big paw over her chest. Cariad reached out to me, only to experience a second betrayal as I scooped her up and proceeded to polish her firm little bottom with as much vigor as my shaking hand could muster.

Rowan came running. "Why did you leave the side door unlatched?" she demanded angrily.

"I?" I was thunderstruck. "You came in last."

"I came in the back door," she retorted. "Maybe I shouldn't have left her alone with you."

I was too stunned to reply. No use trying to convince her that I had had to unhook the screen to get out just now. I went back in, the tears stinging my lids. Cari, bless her, vindicated me at once. As soon as I put her down inside the house, she darted on all fours for the side door again, pulled herself up by the knob and deftly slid open the bolt.

Clearly, new measures had to be taken. After I'd secured the wailing infant in the nursery, I called Ward and requested fencing to make a safe play yard and door chains that would be too high for Cari to reach. Later I confronted Rowan.

"I think you owe me an apology," I told her.

"I'm going to wash my hair," she said coldly, heading toward the bathroom.

"Rowan, I want an apology."

She whipped around. "They say if a woman doesn't like her husband, she may resent his children."

Cold steel sliced through me. "Where did you hear such a thing?"

"I-Iris," she faltered.

I fought for self control. "You go there?"

"All the kids do. It's a neat place."

"And she said that about me?" My voice shook.

"Oh no!" Her blue eyes opened wide. "She was just talking in general. I—I didn't tell her a thing, Mother—honest!"

But Iris had guessed something and was using it. "I don't like you going down there, Rowan. I don't trust her—for reasons I'd rather not discuss. Just don't judge me by what Iris says. I love both you and Cari deeply."

"Oh?" The cynicism in that one word twisted the shaft, but my frustration was covered by the arrival of a delivery truck driven by a tall young man with an Afro and pointed beard. He barely acknowledged my greeting as he unloaded the lumber and set about erecting the fence in the spot I indicated. He was naked to the waist and the muscles under his skin rippled in the sunlight as he swung his sledgehammer.

"May I get you some coffee or a cold drink?" I asked.

"No, thank you." His reply was curt.

"You must be Quentin Jackson," I ventured.

If he was surprised, he didn't show it. "Uncle Tom's terrorist son, right?"

The bitterness in his tone caught me off balance. "I believe 'black activist' was the term," I said, remembering Elspeth's remark. "And that is quite something else."

"Not to these people here. It's a dirty word."

"So is the term 'Uncle Tom'—particularly when you apply it to your own father."

He set the sledgehammer against the post he'd just driven in, squinting at me in the bright sun.

"Well—" he began, puzzled. "I thought you'd deny it—what people say, I mean. I shouldn't have called my father an Uncle Tom." His hands clenched about the invisible thing that was hurting him. "It's just that—well, he's so gentle. Does his work. No trouble, no complaints. 'Good old Darrell,' folks here say, 'he's an okay nigger. Stays in his place.' "

"It's not a bad place—manager."

"Oh, the job's good enough. Mr. Proctor's fair, I'll admit that. It's my mother I'm thinking about."

"The only woman in town with a doctorate," I said.

"You knew about that?" he said in surprise.

"Alison Proctor told me."

"She would—she's not like the others," he conceded.

"For what it's worth, I don't understand the school board—unless they felt they couldn't afford her."

"No way. She offered to teach for less than her degree warranted."

"That must have been before the Equal Opportunities Law was passed. Why doesn't she apply now?"

"Not a chance. She has pride." He paused. "Dr. Carrier was chairman at that time. I think he and his wife would have kept me from going to school here if they could have. They didn't like me chumming around with their son."

"You knew Mark then!"

"He was my best friend," he said quietly.

"I didn't know he'd drowned until I came back here."

"It's something nobody talks about." He picked up a post and jammed it viciously into the hole he'd dug.

"What do you know of—of his death?" I asked.

"Only the official story." He swung his mallet at the post.

89

And you don't believe it! "Did he know Mrs. Faulkner?"

He straightened up and I knew I'd touched a chord. "He was fascinated by her."

"But she was so much older. Surely they weren't—"

"I wouldn't know about that." He was on the defensive now. "I was at the University when it happened. Lucky for me."

"Why do you say that?"

"Wouldn't they have just loved to hang something like that on me! You can never trust a ho . . ." He stopped.

"A honky?" Again the look of surprise. "You trusted Mark," I reminded him.

He leaned on his sledgehammer. "Mark was different—I think. If he'd lived longer, he might have disappointed me, too, like most whites."

Freya sidled up to Quentin, her tail wagging vigorously. He ran his sinewy fingers over her wavy coat. "Howya, ol' girl?"

"That's my heroine of the moment," I said, grateful the subject had been changed. "If it hadn't been for her . . ." I couldn't bring myself to finish.

He lifted her muzzle. "If you want to feel like a god, just look into a dog's eyes," he said, ruffling her fur. "Somebody stole my big shepherd. I know who did it, but I can't prove it."

"If you knew who it was, why didn't you confront him and demand your dog back?"

"It wasn't that simple. He didn't have Duke anymore. Laboratories pay good prices for dogs. Or maybe someone wanted to make a fighter out of him. Dogfighters like German shepherds."

"Dogfighters around here?"

"They go all over to collect dogs. Do you know these

90

days a good fighting dog brings as much as three or four grand? Only Duke wouldn't have made out. He was too gentle."

Quentin didn't trust anyone, I thought. It was possible the dog had run off or been killed on the highway.

"Unless they abused him into being mean," he added. "I hope I'm wrong. I'd like to think whoever got him treated him decently." His voice trailed off. Damon was coming across the lawn and Quentin was glaring at him with pure hatred in his eyes.

"Excuse me, please," I said hastily.

Damon's face was livid. He pointed to his mother. "H-how long has she been here?" he stammered in his fury. "Why wasn't I told of this? I had arrangements made at the county nursing home."

"Your mother preferred to come here. She's over eighteen and under senility. I really don't know what you can do about it."

He drew his hand back, as if to strike me, then dropped it. "She needs constant care, competent nursing care."

"Was she getting it where she was—alone?"

The telltale vein bulged in his forehead. "I can have that woman prosecuted for operating a nursing home without a license."

"Nursing home, Damon? Your mother's paying room and board."

"With what?"

"None of your money, to be sure," I answered tartly. "But she does have social security and if Dana considers that sufficient, I think that's her business, don't you?"

"The whole town will talk," he protested.

"The whole town is talking," I answered, "but they'll stop if you let on that it was your idea."

He knew he was defeated. "Well, if this is what she

wants, I suppose I'll have to go along with it. But if anything happens to her—I'll see that Indian woman answer for it." Then he managed a limp smile. "I'm sorry I blew up, Mitti, but I *am* concerned about my mother."

"Then why didn't you take her into your home?"

He shook his head. "You must have noticed. Charity has—problems. Can you see her and my mother getting along?"

No, I couldn't. I held my breath as Dana came toward us, but to my surprise, Damon greeted her amiably and made an about-face. "My mother appears to be happy here. Perhaps I can add something to the stipend she pays you."

She took his measure. "She's paying me adequately."

"No, I insist," he persisted. "But we'll talk about that later. Right now I must get over to the Redds'."

"Esther having difficulty with her pregnancy?" Dana asked. "Her tubes should be tied."

"I know, I know," he sighed. "You think I haven't told Homer? He wants a son, and if this is another girl, he'll try again—even if it kills Esther." He glanced at his wristwatch. "I'd better be going. I've a golf date later." He went over to his mother, spoke to her briefly, gave her white hair a hurried pat, then climbed into his auto.

As the Lincoln headed down the hill, a smaller car came careening into the drive. Brakes and tires screeched on the loose gravel as the vehicle, its rear end obscenely elevated, spun around and headed back down the bluff road, too fast for me to see who was driving. Freya was standing on the grass just off the drive. Suddenly the car swerved toward her without braking. There was a sickening crunch and the dog's body was catapulted through the air. The driver leaned out of the window, gave a whoop and vanished down the drive.

Freya was struggling unsuccessfully to stand on shattered legs when we reached her. Several ribs were white against her golden coat and blood was pouring from her flanks and mouth. A red haze enveloped me. "He should burn!" I heard myself scream. "Burn! God damn you—burn!"

As the mists began to clear, I saw Rowan running past me and Dana kneeling by the suffering animal, which looked up through her agony with trusting, loving eyes. Her mistress ran her hand tenderly over the dog's eyes and mouth, crooning unintelligibly, drawing the hurt out of the heaving body. One paw reached out and touched Dana on the knee. Then a blade flashed and Freya lay still but for slight movements in her distended belly. Swiftly Dana slit it open, reached in and pulled a mass of pups from the cavity. With deft strokes she opened one amniotic sac after another. Eight tiny sparks of life, but only one kindled. It squirmed almost imperceptibly at first, then more vigorously as the woman massaged it and breathed into its mouth. The knife lay in the grass at her side, its long, wide blade and strangely carved black handle glistening with blood. The pup gave a faint squeal. Dana turned to me with tear-blinded eyes.

"It is a little male," she said. "If he lives, I will give him to you, Mitti."

She rose with difficulty, cradling the wet little thing in her arms. Rowan had disappeared, but Quentin was gently stuffing the dead puppies back into the dog's body. A flash of unspoken understanding traveled between him and Dana. He picked Freya up and carried her around to the back of the old house, where he began to dig a grave under a lilac bush.

Moving like an automaton, I was hosing away the blood when Rowan came running back up the road. She

93

rushed at me headlong, then stopped short, a sudden scrim of fear clouding her eyes. Slowly, carefully, she began to edge around me, as though I represented some unspeakable horror.

"What's wrong, sweetheart?" I half-whispered.

She shook her head, still backing away.

"Rowan, answer me! What's wrong?" I took hold of her arms.

"Don't you touch me!" Her scream broke into a sob as she struggled to break my grasp, red blotches mottling her white face and neck.

"Tell me, Rowan," I pleaded. "I'm your mother."

"That's just it," she responded through chattering teeth. "You're my mother! Did you have to be? You *wished* him dead—I heard you—and he hit a tree and the car exploded and he burned down there at the bottom of the bluff."

"What are you talking about? Who burned?"

"Junior Osburn. Didn't you hear the crash? He didn't make the turn. Mr. Osburn came with the hearse and he didn't even know it was his own son until they told him."

"I—I didn't hear," I breathed, releasing her. "Rowan, I couldn't make that happen. I don't have any such power."

Her hands went to her face. "Daddy?" she whispered through her fingers. "Daddy, too?"

"Oh, my darling, you must never believe such—"

I was protesting to thin air. She had run into the house.

I stood there shocked into immobility until Dana took my arm to lead me inside. "My God, Mitti!" she said in a low voice as we walked, "you are one of us. You have the power. You don't know it, but you have the power. God help you—it could destroy you, too."

*   *   *

Rowan was just hanging up the telephone when I returned to the house.

"I'm going over to Aunt Charity's," she announced.

"I'll take you," I said.

"You don't need to." She seemed calmer now. "You might not get through. The road was blocked when I was down there. It's not far and I'd like the walk—I really would." Dark red-brown lashes opened wide with apparent candor, but I felt she was holding something back.

"Rowan—" I started, undecided whether to reopen the subject.

She made my decision for me. "I know. I was upset, that's all. You couldn't have that kind of power."

I breathed more easily. "And the same with your daddy, Rowan. You know I had nothing to do with that."

Her eyes averted. "Just forget it, Mother—I won't tell Aunt Charity anything."

That's my girl, I thought gratefully. Rowan had always been very close about family matters—too close, I thought. Even I was excluded. But in the relief of the moment I let her go, even though something warned me not to.

Afterwards, I dressed Cari and went with her over to Dana's, where she at once went into squeals of delight over the puppy. "You look exhausted. Leave the baby with me and go somewhere alone," Dana said, scanning my face.

"You surely don't believe I had anything to do with—with Junior's death," I protested.

She bent over the pup, which was lapping warm milk from the tip of her finger. "I felt the force of it," she said in a low tone. "It was a normal reaction, Mitti, but some people have powers that could blow this world apart if they're not controlled, especially the Old Souls."

None of this made sense to me—nor did I care to unravel it just then. "You're sure Cari won't be too much trouble?" I asked.

"Not in the least. She might as well get to know her new playmate."

"You should keep him, Dana. You just lost Freya."

She shook her head. "He'll be safer with you."

That didn't make any better sense, but I obeyed orders and plunged into the woods behind the house, guided subconsciously by an old memory. Prickly ash and hawthorn lashed out at my bare legs as I went, but they were more than compensated for by the lush fronds of ferns, wild geranium, spikenard and countless other plants I couldn't name. Wild grapes, five-leaf ivy, columbine and nightshade made liaison with the lower vegetation and the trees. Here—whether in the tough, gnarled tree trunks or the slenderest flower stem—surged the lifeblood of the earth mother.

This had been my secret sanctuary when I was a child. A wind fugue echoed through the grove and somewhere a cardinal burst forth in glorious antiphony. I moved along a narrow aisle slick with pine needles until I came to a circular Lady chapel carpeted with a fine, soft, supple grass and bordered by the darker green moss at the base of the trees. A tall, stalwart ash and graceful, frilly maple, their limbs intertwined, were sacristans here—Philemon and Baucis I used to call them, but now they were father and mother to me, and I embraced them in turn, pressing my cheek to their cool, rough trunks, striving to draw their strength into my body. Did I detect a beating within? No, only my own heart pounding against the bark. I sank down into the grass and lay with my head pillowed on the moss.

"The truth—the truth—" the branches murmured above me, "you must—face—it—" How often had my parents said that!

And yet, what was the truth . . . reality? Surely not what Rowan believed. That she had retracted her accusation was little comfort. Had she done so merely to avoid conflict? Or worse, because she *was* afraid of me? Even Dana believed I held a secret power within me.

I opened my eyes to erase the horror projected on the interior of my lids, but still I saw it—the hurtling car, the great, trusting, unsuspecting dog by the road, the deliberate cruelty that had made me want to destroy. To me, in that moment, it hadn't been a boy—not even a human being—and my mind had expunged it, like an obscenity erased from a blackboard. What was worse, aware as I was now that *It* had been a boy and human, I couldn't honestly feel regret. I wouldn't wish him dead *now*, but neither could I wish him back again. Yet how horrible for Melvin to come with the hearse and find his own son! And Elspeth—what was she doing now? Did they know about my outburst?

If they did, surely they didn't believe in such medieval things as curses! Hadn't their own ancestors been accused of laying curses, and didn't Peacehaven repudiate such ideas? No matter what I might have cried out in the horror of the moment, it could not possibly have caused their son's death.

But what disturbed me most was that Rowan had linked Junior's death with her father's. I'd thought the wound nearly healed, but it had only closed over, an abscess poisoning her young, misunderstanding mind—and for me, recalling the memory of that night in Switzerland, that hideous night . . .

I'd been lying in our bedroom, content, enjoying the child moving within me, when Owen had entered. He was drunk—or high—and I'd recoiled from the stench of sweat that pasted his red curls to his brow and dampened his shirt. His hand dug cruelly into my breast as he turned me to him, the other hand forcing itself between my legs.

"Not tonight, Owen," I pleaded, trying to remove his eager hands. In this state, what might he do to the baby?

But my protest only succeeded in inflaming him. He flung himself across me, sinking his teeth into my breast. I threw my knee into his groin and caught him off balance, but he lunged at me again. In desperation, I rolled out of the bed and reached behind me, groping for something on my dressing table. My fingers closed over a tall, cut-glass perfume vial.

"Touch me and I'll use this!"

My words penetrated his fogged brain. For a moment I thought he would attack again and I held the bottle ready, but something had gone out of him and he hunched out of the room. I slammed the door and slumped against the frame, listening to him prowl the living room, kicking furniture, throwing books off the shelves. A vase crashed to the floor. Then the score of *Lucifer* blared from the tape deck.

I became aware of my fingers still cramped around the perfume bottle and set it down, then sank back onto the bed, clutching my gown, feeling defiled, contaminated. By my own husband! By Owen, to whom I would have given anything—no, not anything, not my self respect. I had been handled like a beast by a beast—and all because of the silvery white powder that had hollowed out Owen's mind and body until he was no more than a shell wherein the demon could flourish. This was what had assaulted me—not Owen— and it would wear off in a few hours. Tomorrow, if he took no more cocaine, he would be himself. This time perhaps he would listen to me, would realize this couldn't go on.

I had sat up—new fears gripping me. Rowan mustn't see him like this, and he was in no state to be left alone. He might run out on the mountainside and stumble over the cliff or fall into the frigid Alpine stream that boiled down the nearby slope. Snatching up my robe, I ran into the living room, where the tape had just reeled into "Frenzy." How I hated that melody! Its furious staccato, the throat-raking emotion and wild intensity—using the drug to perfect these had made him into the creature that had invaded my bedroom. I snapped off the recorder and was heading for the front door when sounds from Rowan's bedroom halted me. I pushed open her door.

"Will it hurt, Daddy?"

Owen was crouching over Rowan, who lay with her baby doll clasped to her breast. It had belonged to my mother, a shell-tinted bisque head on a stuffed fabric body.

"No, darling," his voice grated. "You are my beautiful little queen—so soft and white!" His hand moved down—"Don't push it away. Let me—let me, please! It would feel so good—throw that damn doll away!" He yanked it out of her arms and flung it on the floor. The head exploded.

"Why did you do that, Daddy?"

"I'll get you another. I'll get you all the dolls in the world—only let me . . ."

"Daddy, you're heavy—"

I caught Owen by the hair tumbling over the nape of

his neck and yanked him back, bringing his face within inches of mine. "May God strike you dead!" I screamed, thrusting him away from me so that he hit the floor. Slowly he turned over and began to crawl out of the room. Rowan was crying softly behind me. At the door, Owen grabbed the knob, pulled himself up and stood there rocking back and forth like an unstrung marionette, the fires dying out of his eyes and his jaw gone slack. I tried to push him out of the room, but he leaned back on my hands, digging in with his long legs. Summoning all my strength, I finally managed to steer him into the guest suite, where I undressed him and put him to bed.

When I returned, Rowan was trying to fit bits of bisque together and crooning to her headless child.

"We'll get you another," I consoled her.

"I know. Daddy said so," she replied listlessly.

"Oh, darling, I'm so sorry," I exclaimed, putting my arms around her, but she pushed me away.

"Why did you knock Daddy down?"

"Because he was sick." That didn't make any sense. I could read it on her face: you don't hit sick people.

"He was delirious," I lied. "He didn't know what he was doing." That, at least, was true. "He might have hurt you."

"He only wanted to love me—he said so. It was an accident."

I was dumbfounded—what could I say? "Of course, he loves you, sweetheart. But your Daddy is sick in a different way and sometimes you have to be rough with that kind of sickness. You know how the doctor takes a little hammer and hits you on the knee sometimes."

"And tickles my foot," she giggled. I hoped I'd made her forget, but the scared, white look returned as she continued to toy with the jagged shards. "They don't fit together," she mourned. "My dolly's broken and so is Daddy."

"Come on, sweetheart, I'll tuck you in," I had said, but she shrugged me off, turning an old, old face to me.

"I don't need you anymore," was all she replied.

Here was the beginning of her hostility. In the stress of the moment, my mind had blanked out those fatal words, "May God strike you dead!" But she had remembered, and now, as I lay here in the woods, so did I. "May God strike you dead!" And He had done so.

But surely God hadn't rolled that truck over Owen's Mercedes at my bidding. God commands. He doesn't obey. Curses are only words and they are nothing. But wrong! Prayers, too, are words.

So this was why Rowan shunned me, why she hovered over Cariad. If I could destroy their father, mightn't I destroy them, too?

But now that she was older, didn't she understand what Owen had been trying to do? Apparently she had repressed his actions just as thoroughly as I had my terrible words until this moment. Well, I'd wanted her to forget, hadn't I? Hadn't I fostered the notion that her Daddy could do no wrong? Shielded her from the effects of his cocaine addiction?

I had kept Rowan's memory of her father untarnished, no matter what it cost me. I suppose I'd hoped that as she matured she'd gradually come to understand, although to explain to her what Owen had been trying to do to her that night was unthinkable. But after today, what hope had I?

I longed to confide in Dr. Brun, but he'd admired Owen's work and I wanted everyone to remember my husband for the good in him, for the pleasure he'd given them. He'd taken cocaine, not to indulge himself, but to perfect his art—like the scientist whose experiments lead him to create the monster that destroys him.

Oh yes, these I had done: kept Owen's image intact in Rowan's eyes, shielded him from the world, given Cariad her name in his memory, and sought to find excuse and counterbalance for his misdeeds—but now I was faced with the truth. I had done these things more out of duty and pride than forgiveness. For Owen lay on my heart like a stone and I would never, never truly forgive him!

Sunlight seeped through the fan vaulting of the branches overhead. Natural incenses overpowered me. I drifted back to the happy times before those terrible years—*back, back—before we'd ever heard of a show named Lucifer—before there was a Rowan toddling around our sunny, plant-filled Village apartment—back to the first days of our marriage when Owen and I would take the ferry over to Staten Island and walk along the beach, stooping now and then to empty sand from our shoes—and we'd lie on the sand, listening to the wild, sweet song of the sea—and I'd reach up to touch Owen's face as he bent over me . . . this was not Staten Island!— and this was not Owen! . . . this was the one who always came to me in this twilight world, his face a shadow beneath his broad-brimmed, high, buckled hat, his great cape wrapped around me as I nestled against his heart . . . then the harsh cry of a gull slashing past—oh, what did I do?—was it something I said?—why did he leave me? . . . come back, oh, come back! . . . must this dream always turn out this way—oh, dream it again and make it turn out right . . .*

*And he was there again . . . I'd not let him get away
this time . . . my hand traced the fine, firm features . . .*

"Mitti," a voice said gently.

Mitti? Who was that? My name was Mary . . . Mitti was
on the other side of my lids . . .

My lashes fluttered open. He was still there, but the hat
was gone and the eyes were those of Gregory Towne.

Chapter Seven

"Oh, I beg your pardon— I guess I was dreaming," I stammered, withdrawing my hand.

"I knew it was too good to be true," he sighed, seating himself with his back to the ash. The sun filtering through the leaves glinted on his blond hair and highlighted the rugged planes of his face. He had stuck his glasses into his shirt pocket and this was the first time I'd seen him without them. Who did he remind me of— Gareth? But Gareth had known how to laugh.

"I was dreaming that Owen—my husband—had come back," I explained, "and then it was someone else— someone I've known for a long time, but only in dreams. Haven't you ever had a recurring dream?"

He broke off a dried fern and drew it gently across my nose. "Strange you should mention that. For a moment, when I saw you lying there, it was as if my favorite dream had come to life."

Boy, what a line! And I had let myself in for it!

"She's always blonde, though, and your hair is dark."

"I'll bet she bleaches her hair," I teased. Was it possible he was serious?

"Not *her* hair. She doesn't belong to this century. She's a natural wheaten blonde—not that I prefer blondes," he amended hastily. "You know what your hair reminds me of?"

He didn't belong to this century either—a swain, not a swinger, I decided.

"Brown satin," he answered himself. "Like an evening gown my mother had. She was beautiful in it. Your hair has that sheen and," he lifted one of my long locks with his fern, "where the sunlight strikes it, it has all the colors of the rainbow." He paused and I waited, both expectant and wary, but he only said, "Forgive me—I hope you don't think I was being too personal."

"This is the only nice thing that's happened all day."

"I could have guessed," he replied. "Dana told me you'd had a severe shock."

"No worse than she. Oh, Greg, did she tell you about Freya? And—and the accident?" I was close to losing control again. His hands took firm hold of my shoulders.

"I covered the story," he said. "Junior asked for what he got. I'm sorry for his parents, but in a way it was their fault, too."

"They may think it was mine."

"Yours!"

"I—I cursed him when I saw him intentionally run the dog down," I confessed, feeling both relieved and foolish in the telling of it.

"I heard. I would have done the same."

I stared at him. "Who told you?"

"I overheard Mrs. Carrier tell Irv Good—the sheriff—when he came up to question witnesses."

"Then it'll be all over town," I groaned.

"Unfortunately, yes. But you still had nothing to do with Junior's missing that turn."

"I hope Elspeth and Melvin realize that."

"That may be a problem," he frowned. "Elspeth's naturally morbid. Melvin was a fool to let her see the body." He stopped at the sight of my stricken face.

Leaf shadows pressed in on me and I shuddered. "I wish I could do something to help them."

"Lucian was with them when I left. He'll comfort them."

I dug in the moss absently, heedless of the dirt collecting under my fingernails. "Are you sure? There's something about him that—that disturbs me. I haven't been to church yet for that reason . . ."

Cowbells in the distance tolled an angelus. We sat there in silence until a wren somewhere in the wood put an end to our reverie.

"How's the puppy doing?" I asked.

"Dana thinks he's going to make it. She's rigged up an incubator out of a box and a light bulb. What'll you name him?"

I hadn't thought about that, but it was nice to feel life could resume with a certain amount of normalcy.

"Any ideas?"

"How about 'Caesar'?"

"No, sounds too much like a Great Dane, but if you mean the manner of his birth, why not 'Macduff'?"

"Who 'was from his mother's womb untimely ripped'? Not bad! He looks like a shaggy Scot."

A wave of guilt washed over me again. I leaned against

the tree, fighting for equilibrium in the dizzy whirl of images around me—the boy's cruelty, the cruelty within me responding, Freya lying there, suffering, Rowan's accusation and the fear underlying it—and that last night with Owen. I bit my lip to hold back the tears.

"I came to talk to you about the pageant." Greg's change of subject was deliberate, commanding, steadying. "—to remind you that you promised to help with the art work."

"I haven't forgotten," I said, brushing some teardrops from my cheeks. "But I'll need material on Salem's history."

"There's an excellent Salem collection up in your tower and I'll help you." He rolled over on his stomach and looked up at me quizzically. "You can start with my script. I just *happen* to have a copy here." He pulled a bulky manuscript out of a small briefcase he had with him. Our hands touched as I took it, sending a chain reaction through every cell in my body. Yet it was not a purely physical sensation. It was more a feeling of recognition, of having known the touch of this hand before. There was both pleasure and distaste in it.

"You know so much more about the theater than I," he was saying. "I'm almost embarrassed to show this to you. I'd appreciate any suggestions you might have."

A footnote on the first page caught my eye. "What does this mean—*The War of the Covens?*"

"That's the title of my doctoral dissertation. It's my theory that New England, in colonial times, was divided into any number of covens practicing witchcraft under a distinct caste system. In other words, not only were there covens among artisans and farmers, but among the upper class, who employed popular superstition to their own advantage. It wouldn't have been new. According to Margaret Murray, the Plantagenets were practicing witches."

"But strict Puritans? Brought up to abhor witchcraft?"

"Only when the other guy did it. The Puritans didn't hesitate to use fire to fight fire. They relied on 'wise women' or 'white witches' like a certain Mrs. Carver, whose 'shining spirits' convinced Cotton Mather that another storm of witchcraft was about to descend on Massachusetts. And Mather himself practiced exorcism. According to his *Memorable Providences*, he drove demons out of the Goodwin children in Boston, especially the girl Martha."

"Yes, Dr. Brun mentioned that after—after Rowan had that strange seizure. I was surprised to find he knew so much about our New England history."

"Dr. Brun is an amazing man."

"He seemed to think Rowan's symptoms were much like Martha Goodwin's. Were they really?"

"So much so I didn't know if I should mention it. Your little girl never had access to Mather's book, did she?"

I shook my head, my face flaming. "Are you intimating that Rowan was faking?"

"Not at all. I was thinking of the power of suggestion. I'll bring you Mather's book sometime. We descendants of the Britons are still susceptible to such things— druidism and pagan beliefs are ingrained in us. What do you do when you say everything is going fine, your car runs, your family is healthy—"

"I knock on wood, of course. And if I get a stye in my eye, I spit on a gold ring and rub my lid and the stye goes away."

"You're kidding."

108

"No, I'm not. It really works. My mother taught me."

"There—you're superstitious, too."

I leaned back against my tree. "It's not superstition if it works and I know it does, although I don't know why."

"You're proving my point. All its invasions made England a melting pot of religions. When Christianity arrived, it spread its mantle over the old beliefs, but they're still there and when the mantle slips they show through. To hate witchcraft is to believe in it, and if you believe in it, you naturally resort to countermagic and violence to eradicate it. And that's what's dangerous. Hysteria breaks out and then nobody is safe. For instance, among those hanged in Salem were two women whose younger brother was my direct ancestor . . ."

I groaned inwardly—another genealogy buff like my mother!

". . . so I have a natural interest in them. Even the judges hesitated to find such staunch church members guilty, but they didn't dare go against the panic they themselves had fostered. The older sister, Rebecca Nurse, is perhaps the most cited case of wronged innocence, but the younger—Mary Esty—was, of all the victims, the most intelligent and literate. Her famous petition, written in her own hand to the appellate judges, pleaded, not for her own life, but for more caution in future trials, and for a reexamination of confessing witches, lest they belie themselves to save their lives and thus be damned. Imagine a condemned woman having the compassion to worry about the weak!" His brown eyes glowed. "Mary Esty haunts me, Mitti. She was a restless spirit. According to the record, her ghost stopped the whole miserable affair."

"You don't really believe that, do you?"

"The recorders did. So did my ancestor, Bered Towne. He was sixteen years younger than Mary, who was fifty-eight at the time of her death. His mother had died bearing him, so Mary was more like a mother to him than a sister."

Mary—Towne—Esty! Those were names right out of my dream—where the worn little woman with a swollen belly sat by the fire, stroking her cat!

"He became a stonecutter by trade—" he went on, "gravestones mostly, I imagine, as Death was always with them in those days. During the first part of his life he was probably content to make the crude little slabs you see so often in New England, with incised skulls and other symbols, but after Mary's death, he spent nearly eight years in England perfecting his craft. When one of the Salem judges, Lieutenant Governor William Stoughton, died in 1701, Towne was commissioned to carve the marble for his tombstone in Dorchester. He produced a masterpiece, for he had become a sculptor—and an avenging angel as well. He carved with a double-edged blade."

"How do you mean?"

"At one end of the tomb he reproduced the Stoughton family arms. At the other, he carved a pair of skulls with stylized ribs which, gruesome as they are, are the work of a master. In addition, hovering above the two skeletons, is a winged figure with an hourglass in the center, which probably means 'Tempus fugit.' Yet, if you look at the wings and hourglass in a certain light, they take on the appearance of a vampire. The story handed down in our family is that old Towne deliberately avenged his sisters. There is no reference to that in the fragments of his diary that have survived, but he did mention his hatred of Stoughton."

I absently picked at the green part of a leaf, denuding its skeletal structure. "Why Stoughton and not the other judges?"

"Because he was chief justice at the trials, I imagine, and he never recanted as his associate, Samuel Sewall, did after his favorite daughter died. Sewall thought his Sarah's death was God's punishment and he made public penance—but not Stoughton, who was furious when Governor Phips called off the trials."

Greg pursed up his lips in an imitation of an austere despot and thundered, " 'We were in a way to have cleared the land of witches . . . Who it is that obstructs the course of justice I know not.' "

I applauded. "You should play Stoughton in the pageant!" To my surprise, he said he'd enjoy portraying the old curmudgeon. "Be careful," I warned. "To make him believable, you must try to understand his viewpoint and—portray the humanity in the man."

"If he had any," he growled. "If Sewall could admit his error, why couldn't Stoughton?"

"But Sewall had lost a child."

"Stoughton didn't have any to lose. He never married."

"So he couldn't feel God's retribution like Sewall did."

Greg frowned. "I hardly expected you to defend an arrogant bigot—"

"And upper class witch, if your theory is correct," I reminded him. "American history is more fascinating than I realized. Maybe that's how we're being governed now—by bell, book and tape recorder."

Now he laughed. "We are a witchy country at that," he

conceded. *"Thirteen* colonies—a coven, if you will— represented by *thirteen pentacles* in a magic circle on our original flag."

"And don't forget the *thirteen* stripes!" I supplied.

"What's worse, we keep adding pentacles," he continued the game. "Two more states and we'll have four covens."

"Or a deck of cards."

He reached in his pocket and pulled out a dollar. "Ever notice this pyramid with the shining eye at the top?"

I shook my head. "Just goes to show you can look at a thing all your life and never see it."

"That's straight out of the Cabala."

"Or Masonry."

"That's about the same thing. Ever read the history of the Templars?"

I confessed I hadn't. *"The Occult Background of Red-Blooded, God-fearing America!* What a great title for a book!" I exclaimed. "Do you suppose we still have covens in the government?"

"In Washington, anything can happen." He drew himself up to a sitting position, his face level with mine—so close his features blurred. I struggled against a desire to brush my lips against his—yet the impulse seemed not to belong to Mitti Llewellyn, but to another woman totally removed from me.

Leaves rustled and we drew apart as a shadow fell across us. She was little changed—the same translucent eyes and pale skin, her lips curved in their salamander smile.

Greg was the first to recover. "Taking the day off, Iris?"

"I closed the shop in deference to the Osburns." *What*

112

are you doing? her eyes asked me. "And I brought your daughter home."

I sprang to my feet. "Rowan? She was at the Carriers'!"

She shrugged. "No, she was at my house. She knew Charity and Muriel were going to La Crosse today." She turned eloquent eyes to Greg. "It's so important to give children a chance to communicate."

The bitch! Trying to make me look like a delinquent mother! My anger fused into pain. Had Rowan lied to me? What had she told Iris?

"It's been a long time, Mitti," she continued.

Not long enough! "Excuse me," I said aloud. "I must get back to Rowan. I don't think she should be left alone."

The counter rebuke failed to penetrate. "Of course," she replied in a soothing tone, laying a proprietary hand on Greg's arm. "Walk me home, darling." He shifted uncomfortably. "Greg and I love to go for long walks," she added.

"I thought swimming was your sport!" I blurted out before I could stop myself.

Her pupils were almost nonexistent in the yellow-green irises. "We enjoy that, too, don't we, Greg?" She tugged at his arm. "Come on, darling, Rowan needs her mother. Let's go."

"By all means—don't let me keep you." I turned away. If Greg was going to let her tow him around, I wanted no more of him.

"Wait a minute, Mitti!" he checked me. "Sorry, Iris, Mitti and I are working on the pageant. Some other time."

Greg stayed only long enough to explain some notations in his script, but the length of his stay wasn't important. She had forced a confrontation and it had backfired. As for Rowan, that was another matter. After Greg dropped me off at the Phoenix I knocked at her door.

Our eyes met in the mirror where she sat combing her curls, and she looked away. "You said you were going to your aunt's, Rowan."

"I was, but she wasn't home."

"You *knew* she'd gone to La Crosse. Iris told me. We may have our differences, Rowan, but I never thought you'd lie to me."

"I didn't. I never said I called Aunt Charity."

"But you went to Iris' house knowing I thought you were at your aunt's."

"Yes," she flung at me defiantly. Again the warning bell in my mind—don't make too much of this. Don't turn Iris into forbidden fruit. "And she was nice enough to walk home with you." I tried to sound convincing and perhaps succeeded, for she shot me a startled look.

"I—uh—I didn't talk about us," she volunteered.

"I didn't think you would."

I hurried out. The phone was ringing in my room.

"Sub—mi—t!" A male voice this time. "We warned you—we hate you—witch! Move away—move away!"

I dropped the phone, stared at it through several more rings, then jerked it off the hook.

"Listen you! Oh, it's you, Charity, I'm sorry! I thought it was—someone else. When did you get back? Then you haven't heard—oh, you have? Yes, it was a terrible thing. I'm so sorry for Elspeth and Melvin. Rowan? Yes, she's here. I'll get her—"

I stumbled over something as I went to call Rowan. After she'd taken the phone I bent to pick it up. It was a tiny model racing car, battered and crushed. Inside was a lump of charcoal.

Chapter Eight

The sanctuary of the Community Church throbbed with Gounod's "Sanctus" as Alison and I took our places in one of the pews. I glanced up toward the organ in surprise. Surely Gladys Pudeator couldn't have improved to this extent! My memory hadn't played me false. A slender, dark woman was at the console.

"Is that Quentin's mother? I didn't know she was an organist," I whispered to Alison.

"Yes—and a very good one. Gladys is on vacation."

Ambers and yellows predominated in the stained glass windows, casting a saffron light over the sanctuary. Names of Peacehaven families filled the "In Memoriams" beneath the windows—Nurses, Cloyces, Carriers, Toothakers and others, dividing them from those who had joined since the collapse of the Congregational Church.

Charity and Damon came down the aisle and slid into

a pew farther forward. We half-rose as a powerfully built man of medium height, followed by a diminutive woman and a great, shuffling hulk of a boy, bulldozed over us to get to the other end of our pew.

"Irving and Mavis Good," Alison whispered. "He's the sheriff—and that's their son Jonah," she added as the young man slouched down next to his mother.

I sensed the apology in Alison's tone. Jonah was watching us with a vacant stare. His child's face was set in a small head on top of his massive man's body. I tried not to notice him, looking beyond him to his father. Irv Good, once the town bully, now the sheriff! Deep lines creased his features and his huge fists were covered with scars, some still raw. His wife sat with shoulders bowed, nervously fidgeting with loose strands of graying hair.

"Her father owned Scott's bakery."

Not Mavis Scott! Surely this bent, shriveled woman with knob-knuckled hands couldn't be the beautiful Mavis I remembered!

Alison answered my look. "You'd look like that, too, if you were married to Captain Bligh. Oh, and here comes another arm of the law—Peacehaven's police chief, sheriff's deputy and patrolman."

All these titles belonged to one man, whom I recognized as Gareth's friend, Jim Willard. Preceding him were his wife, a girl about Rowan's age, and a small boy. The mother and daughter were both petite and dark, but the boy, small as he was, was already rawboned and lanky like his father.

A door creaked open and the choir filed into the chancel. I was relieved to see the Osburns weren't there. Then a worse possibility set my skin to prickling. They might be somewhere behind me, watching. *Come on now, you're being paranoid*, I scolded myself.

Lucian, clad in a black robe with scarlet stole, mounted the pulpit. Rhoda Jackson's back tensed as she modulated into the firm, resounding strains of the doxology. Latecomers hurried to take their places—Muriel and Caleb Toothaker just ahead of the Goods, while to our right a woman bulging with child tried to wedge herself into our pew. Her ruddy-faced, sturdily-built husband waited behind her, making no effort to assist or to conceal his boredom. Two girls stood quietly behind their father.

"The Redds," Alison breathed.

Where had I heard that name? Oh yes, Damon had been on his way to their house the morning Freya was killed. Why did everything have to remind me of that? I turned around to see if I could locate my daughter. Lucian and his daughter Lucy had come by early to pick up Rowan for Sunday school. The girls were several pews behind us on the other side of the sanctuary. Lucy, a frail child with cascading ash-blonde hair that framed her pale, thin face, sat rigid and quiet, staring up at her father. Rowan leaned away from her, whispering to—I bit my lip—Iris Faulkner, who turned and looked at me triumphantly.

The collection plate floated past. Just in time I checked myself from dropping in a crumpled Kleenex instead of the bill I'd taken from my purse. Alison glanced at me in amusement.

"Here come Mr. and Mrs. Big," she mouthed under cover of the next hymn. "Tyler and Rosalind Bishop. Too late for the collection, as usual. He's the bank president. Stuffed shirts," she added, "but you'd like their daughter. She's with the Peace Corps in Africa."

She hushed as Lucian rose and laid his hand on the

large pulpit Bible. He put on his glasses, then removed them again—for dramatic effect, I thought at first, but then I saw he was distracted by something at the rear. Greg was making his way slowly down the aisle, his eyes scanning the congregation in search of someone. I saw Iris motion to the girls to slide over, but he ignored them and continued on until he reached our pew. With an apologetic nod he squeezed past the Redds and sat down next to me. Only then did he seem to become aware of an awkward pause in the service and a deep flush spread over his face.

Lucian cleared his throat. "Brothers and Sisters," he began in that peculiarly compelling voice. "Instead of my usual text, I'd like to read a speech that was delivered to an undercover group by a man wanted by the authorities . . ." His eyebrows formed two circumflexes as he ran his finger along the page. "This man told his agents the following: 'Do not think that I have come to bring peace, but a sword. For I have come to set a man against his father, and a daughter against her mother, and a daughter-in-law against her mother-in-law.' Harsh words, you say? Then listen to this: 'If anyone comes to me and does not hate his own father and mother and wife and children and brothers and sisters, yes, and even his own life, he cannot be my disciple.'

"Who was this wild-eyed subversive and where was he? In Berkeley? Belfast? Beirut? What would you have done had you been there? Called in the FBI or the CIA? Well, my friends, you were born too late. By nearly two thousand years. This rabble rouser, this instigator of familial disobedience, was Our Lord and Savior, Jesus Christ. He was talking about priorities. Not even our family obligations can supercede our loyalty to Him."

119

What was he doing? Setting the children up in judgment over their elders? My father would have decried such an interpretation.

"This may seem severe indeed," he went on in a gentler tone, "yet He said the same thing in a different way—'I am the Way, the Truth and the Life: no man cometh unto the Father but by me.' Jew and Gentile were asked to depart from the beliefs of their parents to follow Him, and He asks it of us today. Beware, all ye who are not born again in Christ lest your children learn to hate you. Jesus demands loyalty and there can be no backsliding.

"My friends," his robe fell bat-like from his upraised arms, "everywhere true Christians are ringed around with the synagogue of Satan described by the Apostle John in Revelations—those who claim to be Christians but are not because they have never truly given their hearts to Jesus. They know not the baptism of the Spirit. Let me tell you about this 'synagogue' . . ."

It was a vivid picture he painted—a wilderness of unsaved Christians, atheists, pagans, blasphemers, and backsliders. There was no denying the power of Lucian's delivery. But then he switched to the other side of the picture, a "synagogue of Christ." Why do preachers generally make the good side sound so dull? Feet began to shuffle, noses were blown and coughs became endemic. The sheriff, who had been cooling himself with a fan labeled, "Jesus Saves! Courtesy of the Osburn Funeral Home," checked his watch and began to kick the pew ahead. Muriel Toothaker turned around and gave him a dirty look. Homer Redd and Tyler Bishop were unabashedly asleep.

"And can we be saved by our works alone?" Lucian's

fist came down on the pulpit. Heads snapped back, only to droop again as the minister settled into calmer tones. I tried futilely to concentrate, but the distant hum of a motorboat pulled me out the window. How long before the river would begin to wash at the foundations of this building? Another five years—or three or two—and this part of Peacehaven would be submerged with canoers gliding over head, unaware of the buildings slumbering in the mud below . . .

Wake up! Listen to the sermon! Again I tried to concentrate. Christ this—Christ that—who *was* this Christ he was talking about? Not the one my father had preached. But Lucian didn't really preach—he delivered commercials: Christ, the All-in-One, buffered, anti-histamine, antacid, multivitamin tablet to be taken before meals and at bedtime . . .

Greg's arm pressed against mine, doing little to keep my attention on the sermon. My blood pounded and my hand clamored to be held.

"Now if anyone today should desire to give his heart to Christ," Lucian's voice was husky with emotion, "if he or she will come forward . . ."

He waited. No one moved. "Don't put it off," he urged. "We had a warning this week. A fine young member of this congregation was taken from us suddenly and tragically. He had been saved, praise the Lord! We have that blessed assurance that he is now with Jesus, hallelujah! But had he not—"

There was a muffled sob somewhere at the back of the church. Elspeth! My nails dug into my hands. Did he think he could console the Osburns this way? I could forgive him for that, if that was his intent. But he'd known the truth about Junior—he'd admitted that to me himself. How could he be so hypocritical about a boy who tortured helpless animals, whose last act had been one of unadulterated cruelty? It was false witness!

"Jesus stands at the door and waits," Lucian was saying, "holding his arms out to you, sorrowing because you hesitate . . ." His eyes rested on me, trying to draw me forward, his will battling mine. I fought against this sinister, hypnotic power that had nothing to do with his words. Our eyes locked in a mortal struggle as we hung suspended in an atmosphere charged with something almost unendurable, something that almost, but not quite, unlocked a memory . . .

"Do you worry that choosing Jesus might cause consternation in your family? That they might object to your allegiance to someone above and beyond them? Christ gave you no alternative. If you would come into His fold, you must be willing to hate your mother and your father—"

He hadn't been talking to me at all! I heard footsteps behind me—saw heads turning and nodding approval. Rowan came down the aisle and knelt at his feet.

Chapter Nine

Although I wasn't entirely convinced Rowan's "rebirth" was genuine, I had to acknowledge there were fringe benefits. She seemed less afraid of me, as though going forward had put her beyond my reach. But better than that, she was thoroughly accepted now in Peacehaven. Whatever demons had seized her in the woods that night were considered exorcised. The story had been told and retold, but if any stigma had been attached to her it was gone now. The most accepted theory was Charity's suggestion that the men's failure to lift Rowan had been the result of mass hypnosis—induced, possibly, by Dana and/or Dr. Brun.

But a saint around the house is a cross for anyone to bear. Matters came to a head one day while I was pinning a hem for her in front of the full-length mirror in the dining room, and a sudden move on her part ran a pin into my thumb.

"Damn!" I exclaimed without thinking.

My daughter responded with cloying sweetness. "If only I could bring you to Christ!"

"Your grandparents did that when I was a little girl."

She was dubious. "Did you go forward?"

"Turn around!" I said, rapping the yardstick on the floor.

"Well, did you?"

"I did when I joined the church."

"Pooh! Everybody does that! That doesn't mean you've made a commitment."

"Doesn't it? It meant that to me."

"But did you see a blinding light? Did Jesus hold out His hand to you?"

"Is that what happened to you?" I asked.

"Yes! I said, 'Dear Lord Jesus, take me!' And the roof of the church opened up and there He was, smiling at me, while underneath me Satan cursed and sank into his fiery pit. He had dark hair and He—well, He looked kind of like Lucian, except he had a beard and a white robe."

"Satan?"

She stamped her foot. "No, Mother! Jesus!"

So Lucian had become a Christ figure in her mind in a sort of spiritual kidnapping: "If you would be my disciple, you must hate your mother!" I was surprised she hadn't identified Christ with her father, but then Lucian had worked hard at his own image.

"So your whole life will be changed from now on?"

"Naturally," she replied, then, suspiciously, "What do you mean?"

"Well, you'll have to do your tasks cheerfully and—oh yes—you'll read a whole chapter in your Bible every day."

"Well . . ."

"And you must be very courteous to people—Dana, for instance. You haven't been very nice to her."

"Did she say that?"

"No, she wouldn't, but I've seen how you avoid her and sometimes you're almost rude."

"I don't trust her. She's a witch."

"Who said that?"

"Everybody does."

"I thought witchhunts were forbidden in Peacehaven."

"Not against real witches. Iris read the tarot for me and said I must beware of a woman of foreign blood who is a witch."

"American Indian is hardly foreign," I scoffed.

"She's English and Welsh, too," she parried.

"So are we."

That stopped her for a moment. "Well, anyway, everyone is positive it was Dana who bewitched me."

"You weren't bewitched. You had a nightmare."

"Nightmares don't glue you to the ground. People say she put a hex on me."

So the rumor had progressed from hypnotic suggestion to downright sorcery! My mind reeled. Was this the twentieth century?

"Did you see *The Exorcist*, Rowan?" I asked abruptly.

"You wouldn't let me."

"But you did anyway?"

"No, I wanted to until I heard how people were throwing up."

I repressed a desire to laugh. "But the kids talked about it?"

"Yeah. The bed went up and down and her head went

round and round and—" her eyes widened. "Did I do that?"

"No, of course not," I assured her. "It was nothing like that. Those were only special effects."

"Aunt Charity says I did."

"Aunt Charity says a lot of things. So Iris reads the tarot as well as palms."

"Oh yes, and she's promised to make an astrological chart for me and she goes into trances and talks in a funny language."

"And you call Dana a witch!"

"That's different. Iris is divinely inspired—Lucian says so."

"I thought he didn't approve of such things."

"Mostly he doesn't. But he says Iris uses them to the glory of God, especially when she talks in tongues, like in the Bible. And he's the one who got me to go forward. Ouch! You stuck me!"

"Sorry about that." I reached for the yardstick with a shaking hand. "Stand still!"

"I don't have to obey you—you haven't been born again."

Damn Lucian! *No, God, I don't mean that!*

"What do you have against Iris?" Rowan asked abruptly.

I longed to tell her, but I knew she wouldn't believe me. "I don't know her very well," I began.

"Yes, you do," she interrupted. "You're afraid of her, aren't you? She might tell the truth about Uncle Gareth."

I grabbed her shoulders and spun her around. "What are you talking about?"

The blue eyes faltered. "I—I don't know what she meant. She wouldn't say, except that—that—"

"Except what?"

"That Uncle Gareth drowned when he was trying to swim out to your boat."

I was deathly cold. "And what else, Rowan?"

"That's all. She said you wouldn't want her to talk about it." She drew a quivery breath. "Did you curse him, too?"

"Of course not!" So that was what Iris was hinting! "I tried to save him." Something in my face touched Rowan ever so slightly. Her hand brushed my arm.

"Everyone knows about Junior," she said. "but I didn't tell. And I would never say anything about Daddy."

My eyes misted and I reached for her hand, but she moved away. "I don't talk about family matters," she said flatly, and ran out the door, nearly crashing into Dr. Brun.

"You're just in time for a cool drink," I told him. "Why don't you go out and sit in one of the lawn chairs on the eastern side where it's shady? What will you have?"

"A shandy, bitte. I'm just back from Gays Mills and I'm thirsty."

"Gays Mills is pretty far away," I observed as I carried out a couple of shandies, Macduff padding after me with an enormous milkbone in his mouth. "I thought the cave was supposed to be near our river, not the Kickapoo."

"Ja, but I've been through all the caves around here."

"What about Bogus Bluff?"

"That also. What a place. Like the Minoan labyrinth. I had to use Ariadne's trick or I would have been lost."

"Counterfeiters hid in Bogus Bluff during the Civil War—that's how it got its name. The Feds had a hard time chasing them out."

"All the more reason for that not to be the cave. They

127

would have found what I'm looking for."

"Just what *are* you seeking?" I sipped at my shandy. "I never have heard the whole story. All I know is that it has to do with my amulet and a Welsh prince named Madog."

"I'm on the trail of a myth my Welsh mother used to tell me. I thought it was nothing more until I learned that in legend lies the truth of our past. Heinrich Schliemann, using the landmarks Homer described in the *Iliad*, dug down and found Troy. Archaeologists using the Bible as a guide have discovered places like Ur and Jericho. To be a good archaeologist one *must* believe in the myths."

His attention was distracted by a honeybee crawling out of the coral orifice of one of the blossoms on the trumpet vine that wound up the stone wall of the house. The bee, frowzy with pollen, hovered a moment, then took off.

"There, you see? It is as I said," Dr. Brun exclaimed. "She is going home to her hive to tell the others a myth about all the beautiful flowers here, full of nectar. Now, if they were humans they'd say, 'Ja? Trumpet-shaped goblets? How far? Ten miles? Very funny! Tell us another.' But all this little bee has to do is to tell her myth in a little dance like this—"

To my astonishment he hopped up and began to slap his knees and spin this way and that, for all the world like a gnome in *Lederhosen*. I couldn't keep from laughing.

"Ah, now! The smiles come out!" he cried as he resumed his seat. "When I came, something was wrong, I think? So, as I was telling you, the bee dances her myth and the others come for honey. I, too. I saw your amulet and I believed."

"It's incredible. This little scrap of silver was enough evidence to bring you back here again—halfway around the world."

He shook his head. "*Nein!* I am crazy, but not that crazy. I did other research. Many archaeologists like myself believe that Columbus was not the first European to come here."

"Then you think Leif Ericsson reached mainland America."

"*Natürlich!* And many others much earlier. I have found carvings in South America that lead me to believe the Phoenicians were engaged in a lively commerce between the two hemispheres as early as 2000 B.C. Then there's the myth about St. Brendan who sailed west from Ireland in the sixth century and discovered a wonderful island. Perhaps he did, perhaps he didn't, but there are standing stones in your state of Maine with some strange inscriptions on them. Once thought to be runes, they've recently been identified as old Gaelic, and some scholars claim there are many Celtic words in the Algonquin language."

"That fits in with something Dana said," I told him. "The Winnebagoes don't believe they come from Asia. 'We originated here!' they insist."

The blue eyes twinkled. "They're not the only Indians who believe that, and they may be right. Maybe the Orientals are descendants of Indians who followed the sun. Who's to say *this* wasn't the Garden of Eden? But we'll leave that for another time. Let's get back to 1170 A.D., when, according to the story, Prince Madog sailed west and landed at Mobile Bay. Leaving part of his men in the company of friendly Indians, he returned to Wales to get more colonists. A record exists that a 'Madawc' sailed from the Isle of Lundy in Bristol Bay in 1171. Ironically, the Spanish made Prince Madog historically important by their very efforts to prove the story a fabrication. At the same time, Henry VII of England, a Tudor and a Welshman, strove to prove the truth of the tale to give England a prior claim over the Spanish to the Americas."

"Did anyone ever find any proof either way?"

"There are ruins of forts in Georgia, Alabama, and Tennessee that were constructed with a kind of concrete peculiar to the early Welsh. The Daughters of the American Revolution even erected a monument to Madog at Fort Morgan on Mobile Bay."

"But I can't see what any of this would have to do with a cave in Peacehaven."

"It's thought that the Welshmen were absorbed into the friendly Indian tribe, which migrated westward over several centuries. You see, when Englishmen began to explore this country, they kept coming back with tales of Welsh-speaking Indians. Finally, in the last century, a painter by the name of Catlin—"

"George Catlin? The one who painted Indians?"

"*Ja.* He became convinced that the Mandan Indians in North Dakota could be descendants of Madog's men. He compiled a list of similar words in Mandan and Welsh and pointed out that the Mandan 'bullboats,' which were made of wicker frames covered with hides, were much like the Welsh and Irish coracles. Their pottery resembled Celtic pottery and they had blue glass beads similar to those found on Lundy Island, from which, you will remember, Madog embarked on his second voyage. The Mandans had a Noah story in their mythology which they could have derived from the Christian Welsh, and they honored a 'big canoe,' sort of an ark, in their ceremonies, in which they believed their ancestors had arrived from the east after a great deluge. Catlin also noted that Mandan Indians were lighter in complexion and often had blue eyes."

He reached over and took my amulet into his broad hand. "Now we come to Peacehaven and this. It is very old."

"Could it be carbon tested?"

He shook his head. "Alas, the carbon 14 test works only on organic materials. But the runic characters, if that is what they are, of an 'M' and a 'D' intrigued me. Might that not stand for 'Madog?' I asked myself. Indians treasure their relics. But how could it be found in a Wisconsin cave when the Mandans live in the Dakotas? Then I asked—did they *all* go up the Missouri? Might not a band of them have continued up the Mississippi until they reached the mouth of this river, then followed it until they came to what is now Peacehaven? And since this is Winnebago territory, is it not likely there was commerce—or warfare—between the two tribes? This might explain another mystery—why there are similarities between Mandan and Winnebago that are not found in other Siouan tongues.

"As for the cave—was it a burial place? Not likely. The Mandans never used to bury their dead. They placed them on scaffolds. No, I think this was a scene of disaster—pestilence, starvation, tribal wars—who knows? It's all conjecture, I realize, but I am at the time of life when I believe in catering to my whims. Besides, I have the quiet here that enables me to write my book."

Macduff had fallen asleep in my lap. Stroking the puppy wool thoughtfully, I said, "I assume you've explored our cave."

"*Aber natürlich!* First of all. It is a beautiful cave, but I found nothing, even though I trained lights into the drop-off at the entrance. There was only sheer wall and rubble. As for the chambers, they are empty of everything but rock formations and that is disappointing, because I felt—" he hesitated.

"You felt what?"

He shifted uncomfortably. "You'll think me foolish."

"You? Never!"

"Then I tell you. It's hard to describe, but there is a feeling about that cave—a tragic chill. Most caves are cold, but this wasn't a matter of temperature. Still, I found nothing."

"Maybe Dana's father removed everything."

"Dana's father!"

"Yes. He gave Aunt Bo the amulet."

"I didn't know that. Dana doesn't talk about herself. No, an Indian would not have disturbed such a place."

Macduff stirred and yawned. Sharp puppy teeth nibbled at my arm. I tapped him on the nose and pushed him off my lap.

"I wonder if you've noticed . . ." I began, then stopped. I'd been about to ask him if he'd noticed the indentations in the walls of the crevice, then I remembered Dana's warning. If he should fall and be hurt or killed, I'd never forgive myself. And it could happen, I was convinced of that. Superimposed upon the incessant humming and industry on a late summer afternoon was the sensation of something else, something that brooded

132

and bided its time. Had it only just come? Or had it always been there?

"You were about to say?" Dr. Brun was looking at me strangely.

"Never mind. I—I forgot."

The question was still on his face, but we were distracted by a car door slamming. Rowan came running out of the house.

"Hi, Lucian! Hi, Lucy!"

It was a timely interruption.

Chapter Ten

"Y ou have company," the doctor said, rising. "I'll go."

But Lucian barred his way. "Ah, the *Herr Doktor Brun*," he said with a tinge of mockery. "Don't let us disturb you. I was just dropping Lucy off. I'll be on my way."

"Stay awhile, Lucian," I invited, hoping he wouldn't, but he promptly sank down in a lawn chair and tilted it back comfortably.

"Please don't leave, Dr. Brun," I begged. "I'll bring more lemonade for everyone. Rowan dear, would you go see if Cari is awake, and if she is, bring her down?"

Rowan had returned with the baby by the time I came outside with lemonade and cookies. She seated herself cross-legged at Lucy's feet. Lucy sat prim and nervous on the edge of her chair, her short skirt tucked in neatly under her bare thighs, thin hands clasped about her knees. Dark blue veins showed through the transparent white skin of her face, and the great round spectacles framed her myopic eyes, giving her an owlish look. Certainly she didn't resemble her father. Perhaps she took after her mother. When had she died? What a lonely life the child must have had, brought up mostly in the care of housekeepers!

"Mother and her lemonade!" Rowan was protesting. "Wouldn't you rather have soda, Lucy?"

"N-no, this will be fine," the girl murmured uncertainly, as if she were afraid of offending me. I went back to the house to get glasses. When I returned, Rowan was speaking to Lucian.

"Mother thinks Iris is a witch! I wish you'd tell her that's not so."

"I never said that!" I protested, passing the tray to Lucian. "I did wonder how you countenance her dabbling in the occult."

He cleared his throat. "It's hard to explain, I know. I myself had doubts about her at first. But she has convinced me she uses her—er—talents for God's purpose. She doesn't do it for money and it's what she knows best. Sometimes one must fight fire with fire. Through her qualified use of astrology and palmistry, she manages to get close to her young friends and steer them into—into right thinking. She's really quite remarkable."

"Then it doesn't bother you for Lucy to hang around her shop?"

"On the contrary. I'm grateful that Iris is kind enough to provide Peacehaven with an unofficial youth center."

"I was afraid of Iris at first. Sometimes she talks in a funny language, but Daddy said the Disciples did that, too, so I wasn't afraid anymore," Lucy blurted out. A

135

bright pink suffused her fair skin and her pale eyes blinked behind the thick lenses, making her look more owl-like than ever.

Her father was obviously annoyed. "She means Iris talks in tongues," he explained.

"Yes, Rowan mentioned something about that to me," I said.

"Do you pray in tongues?" Dr. Brun asked suddenly.

"No," Lucian admitted. "The good Lord has never given me the gift."

Dr. Brun leaned forward. "What does talking in tongues mean to you, Lucian?"

A wary look came into the minister's eyes. "Since I've never done it, I'll have to describe it the way Iris does. She says she suddenly finds herself praying—or praising—in words whose meaning she doesn't know. She just knows it's God's language and He prefers to hear that rather than any other."

"If she doesn't know what she's praying about, how does she know she's praying for something good or, for that matter, that she's even praying to God?" I asked.

"By the exaltation she feels," Lucian answered. "It's certainly a Christian phenomenon. Paul lists the gift of tongues in that same chapter in Corinthians you once cited to me, Martin."

Dr. Brun absentmindedly tore off a tendril of trumpet vine and began toying with it. "It is a problem to which I've given much thought," he said. "I know there are many sincerely religious people who think they have the gift of tongues, and perhaps they do. Yet, according to the Book of Acts, Pentecost was the coming together of people of many nations, cultures and languages to be of one spirit, one religious mind, and through this miracle, all languages became one. It seemed to each man that everyone else spoke in his own language. They *knew* what they were talking about; the Bible says so explicitly. 'And how hear we every man in our own tongue, wherein we were born?' It is my prayer that someday we will attain Pentecost again—the power of universal understanding. But when we do, I think we, as well as God, will know what we are praying about. Unintelligible gibberish could be the utterings of demons, you know."

The lines at the corners of Lucian's mouth were drawn down. "Are you trying to say Mrs. Faulkner's gift isn't genuine? That it comes from Satan?"

Dr. Brun set his drink aside and stood up, silhouetted against the western sky so that tongues of flame seemed to emanate from the tousled white hair. "I do not speak of individual cases," he said. "Nor do I make accusations. I merely gave you my interpretation. Now I must go. An old man gets long-winded and tiresome at times."

After he'd left, Rowan took Lucy up to her room to listen to records. Soon the decibels were flying out the window and I suggested to Lucian that we take a walk and give our ears a break. As we came around the house to the west side I saw Dana stooping over something below one of the windows. When she straightened, I saw she was holding a tiny blue bird in the hollow of her hand.

"Did it hit the window?" I never could shake a sense of personal guilt when my house brought death to one of these creatures.

Dana nodded, manipulating its miniscule breast. Lightly she breathed into the parted beak. After a long moment, the eyes opened half way. She continued to stroke it, murmuring words in what I supposed was Winnebago. The eyes became two round black beads in a violet-hued head. The azure wings fluttered. Dana looked up with a smile.

"The heart is beating again. Now I will warm my little brother with my hands so he does not die of shock. See, he struggles. That is good. The wings aren't broken because he doesn't drag them." She set the indigo bunting on a sunny ledge, where he teetered back and forth groggily on the warm stone. In the sunlight his feathers shaded from sapphire to peacock blue, with elegant black tips on his wings—a living jewel.

"Isn't he beautiful?" I exclaimed, gently touching his throat. His tiny black and white beak investigated my finger and for one moment I imagined he recognized me as a friend, but he spread his wings, tested them a second, then flipped himself into the air. Dana laughed at my disappointment.

"Never expect gratitude from a wild bird," she said. "Think how you'd feel if you woke up to find a giant stroking your throat."

"We run a wildlife rescue squad here," I explained to Lucian, who was scowling at Dana's retreating figure.

We had reached a mound of shelf rock that formed a natural bench at the edge of the bluff. Just a few feet away the weathered column of Tomahawk Rock reared from the base of the cliff. Below, beneath a canopy of elms and maples, the townspeople were going about their business. Farther out, the river lay like a gilded serpent in the late afternoon sun. Closing my eyes, I let myself go limp against the stone, yet my nerves remained alert—sensually aware of the man beside me. I was conscious of his hand lying next to mine, not quite touching. Why did I have such ambivalent feelings toward both him and Greg? Yet it was not quite the same. I was undeniably drawn to Greg, as I had once thought I never would be to any man but Owen, but I couldn't banish the sensation of some force—or forces—outside us both keeping us apart. With Lucian it was the opposite. Lucian-the-man repelled me and Lucian-the-minister irritated me. It was only that other personality of which I caught occasional glimpses that held an almost sinister attraction. Which one was sitting beside me now? His little finger crossed mine. Such a slight, innocent gesture! And yet somehow I felt violated—partly because of the response deep inside my own body.

"I'm glad you brought Lucy today," I said, withdrawing my hand.

"It's been lonely for her without a mother," he said. "There're just the two of us. Mrs. Soames, our housekeeper, isn't very congenial. She's a stubborn old soul. For some odd reason she has a hang-up about Iris. Lucy invited her to dinner and Mrs. Soames refused to cook it."

Well, chalk one up for Mrs. Soames! I thought.

"She reminds me of Dana," he went on. "She eavesdrops."

"Dana *never* does that!" I was indignant.

"Why was she hanging around just now? You can't tell me it was that bird."

"If anyone has a right here she has! She probably came over to look in on Cari and Macduff. She's awfully good about that."

"You like her, don't you?"

"Yes, very much."

"Well, if I were you I'd go slow with her. There's a lot we don't know."

I turned on him angrily. "There's a lot you don't know about me, Lucian, so you'd better go slow with me, too. I

139

hope you're not one of those foolish people who think she's a witch!"

"Did I say that?"

"No, but you've heard others say it and you believed them, didn't you?"

"Let's just say I don't trust her. She's not a Christian—"

"She believes in Christ—she said so."

"I doubt it. Although I hope, for her sake—and yours, that it's so." He smiled. "Let's not quarrel, Mitti. Even though you're very beautiful when your eyes flash like that."

He caught me off guard. I wanted no flattery from him and quickly changed the subject. "Has anyone ever told you the legend of Tomahawk Rock?" I gave him no chance to answer. "The Indians say it was put there by Earthmaker, to be a protection from tornadoes and other natural disasters."

"It hasn't managed to keep the river away," he observed.

"Maybe its protection begins up here. Do you realize that rock's only a few feet from us, but the drop in between makes it miles away? Sometimes I'm tempted to build a bridge out to it."

"Why don't you?"

"That would be cheating."

"Why?"

"Because it's good to have a solid example of the unattainable. God should have some places where He alone can stand."

Unwittingly, I had flung down the gauntlet. A curious light came into his eyes and I thought how very unlike a clergyman he looked at that moment.

"You know," he said slowly, "I think I could ju—ust make it."

"Lucian, you're not serious!" He crouched low. "Don't! You'll fall!"

But he was already running and now he sprang—over the void between the face of the bluff and the flat top of the rock. The jump was a good one—if he could check his momentum, if he didn't slip. Visions of his body toppling over the other side and hurtling down onto the sharp rocks below flashed before me, but he landed lightly and surely, swayed dizzily a moment, then regained his balance. He turned around slowly and faced me triumphantly.

"Now it's mine as well as God's!" he cried. "I'm standing on the pinnacle of the temple just as Christ did."

"Yes, and the Devil put him there!" I shouted back. Now what could he do? The rock had no running room for a return leap. He seemed oblivious to danger, standing with arms uplifted as the setting sun enveloped him in flaming robes. His eyes sought me out, but this wasn't Lucian. *Simon Magus preparing to fly* came to my mind. But that was an apocryphal tale—remote and unreal, while the scene before me had roused a sensation of having been personally involved in some ancient drama, of having known this man eons ago.

"I'm in God's place!" he shouted. "Now do you know me? I *am* God! Why do you not fall down and worship me?"

I was too shocked to answer. A sudden rage shook him and a spate of unintelligible words spewed from his mouth. Though I couldn't understand their meaning, there was no mistaking the venom in them. Then a cloud drifted over the lowering sun, divesting him of his robes, turning him back into Lucian again—a slight man in red sport shirt and pants. His mouth had gone slack, his face ashen, and sweat was beginning to break out on his brow as for the first time he seemed to realize where he was. He hunched down to make the return jump, lost his nerve and lowered himself cautiously to all fours on the tiny island in the sky.

"I—I can't do it," he gasped, gripping the stone.

"Don't try! I'll go for help." I started for the shed to get the extension ladder, but Dana was already coming with it, and Dr. Brun was sprinting toward us with a coil of rope. He tossed one end to Lucian and called to him to tie it around his waist. The other end Dr. Brun fastened to an oak tree nearby. Then the three of us hoisted the ladder across the void and held it fast.

Lucian crawled out on it, but the ladder sagged with his weight and he scrambled back.

"Don't worry, it will hold," Dr. Brun assured him. "If not, the rope will keep you from falling."

Again he tried and again he pulled back.

"You must trust us," Dr. Brun persisted.

Lucian's eyes darted from face to face. I don't suppose that in all of Peacehaven he could have found three people he trusted less. He shook his head and clung to his pinnacle. Dr. Brun lost patience. "Very well, if you won't let us help you, get off the way you came." He walked to the tree and began to work with the knot in the rope.

"No, no," Lucian shouted, "I'll do it! Don't leave me!"

Slowly he inched his way across while the ladder creaked and swayed and we kept the rope taut.

"Don't know what could have made me do that," the

minister muttered shamefacedly when he was safely back on the bluff.

"I told you—the Devil," I teased, then felt sorry. It was really indecent to unman him any further. In his chagrin Lucian was more likable, if not lovable, than he'd ever been. "At least you may have established a record," I consoled him. "You're probably the first person ever to stand on Tomahawk Rock."

"You won't say anything about this, will you?" he asked anxiously.

"Why should we?" Dana flung back at him as she and Dr. Brun started away. "Winnebago boys do it all the time at the Dells."

"What language were you using?" I asked after they'd gone. "I couldn't understand a word."

"Language?" he puzzled, then his eyes lighted. "Do you suppose I was talking in tongues? That must be it— the Holy Spirit's come down upon me!"

"It really didn't sound like the Holy Spirit talking— you were too angry. Right at first, though, you spoke in English—said you were God and wondered why I didn't worship you."

He caught my wrist. "I said I was God? Oh, my dear Mitti, I *must* have given you a terrible shock for you to imagine any such thing. That would be blasphemy!" He stroked my hand. "I did give you a turn, didn't I?"

Chapter Eleven

Ladybug, Ladybug!
At last you are home!
But where are your children
While with witches you roam?

So now I had a bad poet on the line, I thought, more amused than frightened. The phone had been ringing as I came in the house after a long day of driving in the country with Dana. We had gone out to Aunt Bo's old farm so that Dana could deliver her herbs to Dylan, the new owner, for his witchcraft shop in Madison. Then we'd stopped by the Hobbs farm to drop off some groceries for old Ruby Hobbs, who couldn't drive and who'd lived alone since her brother'd died two years before. Half-deaf, unkempt, and suspicious of strangers,

Ruby was the embodiment of the stereotype witch. In Salem she would have swung without the hysteria. Her farmhouse was typical, too—no plumbing, no electricity, rooms filled with junk and festooned with cobwebs. Her one luxury was a telephone. I asked if I might call Rowan to tell her to put the meatloaf in the oven.

"If you pay me twenty cents," she answered tartly. Then a slow red crept in under the grime on her cheeks as she caught the reproach in Dana's eye. "Sorry—guess I shouldn't have said that—you bringin' my things like you did. It's the sheriff that makes me mad. Now he's renting my barn, he thinks he can use my phone all he pleases, and I have limited service."

After leaving Ruby, Dana and I had dropped in at the Redd farm—what a contrast!—to see Esther and the new baby, and then came home. Now this sinister phone call—the first in weeks. Who could know about our visit to Dylan's "witch" farm? I'd said nothing about it to either Rowan or Esther.

My fingers tensed on the instrument. Someone at the other end of the line was listening. So was I, a smell of fear in my nostrils. By now Cari and Macduff should have come tumbling to greet me. And I didn't hear Rowan's cassette playing upstairs.

As I started to hang up the phone, the listener spoke again:

> Ladybug! Ladybug!
> Have you no care?
> Look the house over—
> They're not anywhere!

145

Macduff was howling in the play yard outside, but the interior of the house was a black hole in space. "Rowan! Cariad! Don't play games! Where are you?"

My search finally led me to the tower, where I picked up the phone and started to dial Jim Willard, then checked myself. This wasn't—I *wouldn't* have it be a police matter! I mustn't think about Susie Toothaker. I dialed Darcy's number. Marion answered. No, they hadn't seen the girls. Alison next—no, neither had she. Nor had any of Rowan's friends. I tried Greg, but there was no answer either at his apartment or at the newspaper. I felt an unreasoning anger at his not being available when I needed him most. Lucian was home, but could give me no information. Nor could Elspeth. Did I detect gloating in her voice? Muriel Toothaker sounded genuinely worried and begged me to call the moment I found them. *My anxiety must be showing,* I thought. Finally, reluctantly, I called the Patch. Edna Bradbury, Iris' assistant, answered.

"No, I haven't seen them. Why don't you call Iris at home? It's her day off."

I flipped to the F's in the Peacehaven section of the county telephone book . . . *Faulkner, Iris.* The letters blurred and I leaned dizzily against Aunt Bo's desk as the tower spun, catapulting me into another room and another time, when I stood before . . .

Dour-faced men in leather doublets gathered around a table at the end of a long hall. One, more formally clad in black, hammered on the rough-hewn oak table with a pine knot gavel, glaring balefully at a woman in a floor-length gown of linsey woolsey who stood a few paces from me. I seemed to know her, but couldn't remember where. This was not my time nor my place and I struggled to free myself of it—to get back to where I belonged as there was something I must do. But Time had turned counterclockwise and I with it. There was no escape.

"Goodwife," the magistrate levelled his gavel at her, "this woman," turning the gavel in my direction, "has made serious allegations against you. How do you plead, Goodwife . . . ?" I nearly laughed out loud. Was it whore he'd called her? 'Struth, that were fitting, for I remembered her now. She still had a stylish cut to her figure and the coarse cloth of her bodice was stretched across still firm breasts. Her sandy hair was gathered into a lace cap—far too fine to be worn by one o' her means.

"How do you plead, Goody Hoar?" the magistrate asked again.

"Not guilty, your honor," with a demure bow of her head.

"Will you repeat the charge, Goody Esty?" he ordered.

No one spoke.

"Goody Esty, I asked ye, will you repeat the charge?" The man was looking at *me!* Was Esty *my* name?

"Aye, your honor," the person I seemed to be stammered, "I charge this woman with corrupting children and servants by intimidation. I know some have accused her of being a witch—"

"And that she be!" a woman called out from among the spectators. "Everyone knows she said she 'ud live poorly as long as her husband William were alive, but after he died she should live better. An' didn't he die the very day she said he would? And hasn't she lived better ever since?"

The gavel pounded. "Silence woman! You were not asked to testify."

But Sarah Bibber o' the prattling tongue was not to be

147

quieted. "Have ye forgotten that ye held an autopsy when poor William died?"

The magistrate made the mistake of replying. "And have ye forgotten that nought came o' that?"

"Humph!" she snorted. "Whoever heard o' the Devil's minions leavin' traces o' their sorcery—less'n they wanted to?"

The gavel made dents in the table. "Constable, remove that woman! Goody Esty, will you continue?"

"I know nought o' her bein' a witch," I testified, "albeit I think it has suited her fancy to pose as one. In sooth, she *has* lived better since her husband died, but I trow 'tis not magic that's done it. She tells fortunes and reads palms to cozen her clients into stealing for her—for they fear they will share William's fate—and she's made her own children her accomplices. I know this to be so because," my voice trembled, "my daughter Sarah was one o' her victims, as was Rebecca, daughter of the Reverend Mr. Hale. That very kerchief she wears about her neck and her bonny lace cap were mine, traded by a ship captain to my husband for barrels he'd made. Sarah confessed she had taken them and some o' my linen and my good piece o' plate and given them to this Dorcas Hoar, who, I doubt not, sold these last, for she told Sarah she would be cursed and die if she didn't obey her."

"She lies, Your Honor," the other shrieked. "This kerchief is me own, given me by an admirer. 'Tis no sin for a widow woman to have an admirer, now is't?"

The magistrate ignored the last remark and turned to me. "Do you accuse this woman of witchcraft?"

"Nay, not witchcraft—thievery! And corrupting children."

"What have you to say for yourself, Goody Hoar?"

"I need say nought for meself," she attested. "The Reverend Mr. Hale will do that. As for her," she smirked at me, "thievery, she claims! She'd not dare accuse me o' witchcraft when everyone knows her own mother was one . . ."

. . . I was riding through a forest glen on my mare. It had
been several months since Dorcas had paid for her crimes—
one morning in the stocks and seizure of what stolen goods
could be found. Most never were. All too light a punishment
in my mind, but the gentle, naïve Reverend Hale, as she
predicted, had interceded for her. Suddenly my horse
whinnied and reared, nearly unseating me. I thought 'twas a
bee stung her, but then a leather thong wrapped around my
neck and jerked me from the saddle. The mare bolted. As I
was getting to my feet, Dorcas strode into the path, reeling in
a great bull whip.

"Are ye daft?" I cried.

"Daft is't you'd call me? When you've been nought but a
thorn in me arse all my life. First you took my William—"

"William!" I exclaimed. "I hardly knew your husband."

She gave a brittle laugh. "Will Hoar? You think I'd've cared
a farthing if you'd taken *him* from me? Don't try to gull me.
'Twas the other William I meant."

"He was never *your* William. He swore it."

"A man's swearing is e'er to be taken lightly—as ye know
well! You wed no better than I, but ships need barrels and
your man throve. Still, you're nought but a cooper's wife wi'
no more right to silks and laces and silverplate than I. Is't my
fault your daughter loved me enow to bring me gifts? An' was't
your right to hold me up to public shame? Me, a poor widow
wi' young 'uns to support?"

"From what I've heard, Dorcas, your day in the stocks has
spread your fame. 'Tisn't only thievery fills your pockets,
Goody Whore!"

She knew what name I'd called her. Her eyes blazed like

marsh fire as she drew back the whip. To run would be useless; I could only stand and stare her down, praying silently. She hesitated, then unleashed the whip, but that one second had been just enough to break the force of the rawhide. I grasped it, feeling the sting of its coils about my arm, but I held on, drawing her to me until our faces were almost touching. Toe to toe, we struggled for control of the whip, although she, having hold of the handle, had the advantage. I know not how it would have ended had not a brown arm encircled her neck and pulled her back.

"No hurt Yawataw's friend!" The point of the squaw's knife was at Dorcas' throat. Yawataw, who'd been my friend from childhood!

Dorcas released the handle, which fell to my side, dangling from the leather still wound around my arm. As Yawataw put away her knife, the marsh fire rekindled. "Someday I'll have my revenge," she snarled, "when there's no filthy, stinking salvage around to help you. If I have to wait all my life—nay, if it be that we meet in another life, I'll get you for this! Your Sarah loves me. Blood does not a daughter make!"

The phone book refocused in my vision, with the name IRIS FAULKNER standing out as though printed in boldface. What tricks had terror been playing on me that I should have had such fancies? Was I becoming psychotic? No, it could be explained easily enough, I thought. My mind had taken similarly shaped pieces from different jigsaw puzzles and put them together, but I could sort them out and put them back in proper order. First of all, there was the unmistakable similarity between Dorcas and Iris. As for the name Mary Esty, I would have gotten that from Greg. Wasn't she the ancestress who'd died at Salem? And with all the talk of a pageant, maybe *I* was acquiring an obsession about Salem. The squaw was easy to explain, too—Dana and her knife had somehow wandered into my dream—if that was what it was. But it hadn't been, had it? A glance at my wristwatch told me that barely any time had elapsed. I put my finger in the dial to call Iris, but instantly thought better of it. How would I know if she lied? Rowan and Cari might be there, held against their wishes, unable to call out—I must get hold of myself! What was the last thing Dorcas had said? *"Blood does not a daughter make!"* It was time to face Iris Faulkner on her own ground.

The north half of the Faulkner house actually bridged the narrow channel between a spur of solid rock and the short peninsula that jutted out from the river bank at that point. One long street bisecting the peninsula led to the driveway and garage. After parking my car I followed a wooden sidewalk along the upriver side of the garage until my footsteps rang hollowly on the span of walk that was supported by pilings over the water. Underneath, the water swirled into sort of a millrace that flowed through portcullis-like gratings on either side of the building. Few people in Peacehaven had ever been inside—with the exception of Iris' lovers. The Faulkners had guarded their privacy well, but it was said the judge had had the channel constructed so he and his daughter could swim there.

Gray wooden steps with white latticework risers led to a wide veranda surrounding the river side of the house like the deck of a sternwheeler. The upper deck was another veranda and both were decorated with white wooden lacework of the river-steamer era. Finding no doorbell, I lifted the brass gargoyle knocker and rapped on the door, which gave unexpectedly to my touch.

The entrance hall was empty. Iris' home was as traditional as her shop was trendy. Farther in was a hall table on which a silver calling card tray—shaped like a cherub holding an artist's palette—was reflected in a tall mirror with lights on either side. Ahead was a broad staircase. A gigantic philodendron in a massive jardinière at the foot of the newel post had climbed to the second floor level.

"Come in!" Iris' voice sounded through the heavy dark gold portières to my left. I pushed them aside and entered a room which at first glance seemed untenanted. I had expected to find a magnificent view of the river, but the stained glass windows above the wainscoting were tightly closed. A tawny Oriental rug on the floor was largely obscured by heavy, ornate furniture upholstered in tufted mauve and amber velvet.

"You're early, lover," the voice said from the depths of a huge wing-back chair. "I hadn't expected you so soon."

My first instinct was to back out hastily, but the urgency of my errand held me. "I'm sorry to intrude, Iris," I began.

She rose, struggling with the last hook on a flowing green silk caftan.

"What are you doing here?" Her wide mouth softened into a smile. "What a nice surprise!" she exclaimed. "I never thought you'd deign to visit me. Sit down and let me get you a drink."

I declined both offers. "I was looking for my daughters."

"Have you lost them? Dear me, how awkward!" She went over to the bar and poured herself a drink. "Sure you won't join me?" She leaned against the bar, letting the caftan fall back from her bare thighs.

I was fuming inwardly. "No, thank you. I'm sorry—I didn't realize you were expecting someone." Confused and embarrassed, I started back through the velvet-hung archway, but her next question spun me around "Did you think you'd find your daughters here?"

"I didn't know. I'd called just about everywhere else." Who was "lover," I wondered—Greg?

She sipped her drink. "Why didn't you just call me?"

I fumbled for an answer. Why did I always feel so defenseless against her? "Perhaps I thought it a good chance to see this fabulous house I've been hearing about all my life."

"Now you're here, let me show you around," she said, replacing her glass on the bar. She didn't believe me, I was certain.

"No—some other time. I must look for Rowan and Cari."

"Oh, come now, how do you know I don't have them chained somewhere?" she asked softly.

"Really, Iris, I'm in no mood for joking. May I use your phone? I want to call Jim Willard."

"The police!" Her pale lashes flicked. "Oh, Mitti, I *am* sorry!" She was all solicitude. "I've been teasing you. Charity came by here on her way to Richland Center to pick up . . . something I'd ordered for her. She had your girls in the car with her."

"But Charity went to Mineral Point with her bridge club today," I said suspiciously.

"It was canceled at the last minute."

I was still unconvinced. "Why didn't Rowan leave a note?"

153

She shrugged. "Oh, you know kids. Besides, you two aren't very close, are you?"

I clenched my teeth, not daring to speak.

"Anyway," she hurried on, "she probably thought she'd get home first. She said you'd called from the Hobbs farm."

Weak with relief, I slumped down in a chair to fight off a wave of dizziness.

"Poor Mitti, you *were* frightened, weren't you? I had no idea," she purred. She was letting me run a few steps before her claws sank into me again. "Here, drink this. You need it."

I drank the brandy gratefully, feeling it unravel knots all the way down to my toes.

"Now you must let me show you something," she said as I handed back the glass. "Something you inspired."

Warmed with brandy and curiosity, I followed her across the hall and through the dining room into a large butler's pantry.

"We're in the 'bridge' part of the house," she said. "Now, watch!" She opened a double trapdoor, revealing a circular metal staircase leading down into the space beneath the house. Light filtered through the crossbars of the gratings and made a checkered pattern on the high concrete walkways on either side of a swift running channel. An aluminum ladder led down into the water.

"Remember the story you once told me about the city in the sea?" she asked after we'd descended.

How could I *ever* forget that day?

She stretched herself full-length on the edge of the channel, letting her hand dabble in the current. "I used to wish I was that princess," she mused, her eyes reflecting the black-green water ribboning through the basement. "I'd dream of drowning Peacehaven just as she did Ys."

"Did you hate Peacehaven so much?"

"Do you have to hate something to want to destroy it? When you see an untrampled field of snow, what do you want to do? Wade through it and destroy its perfection, isn't that so? Besides, I would have made Peacehaven famous. If it hadn't been for Ahès, who would ever have heard of Ys? Salem would be another grubby Massachusetts seaport if it hadn't been for the witch trials." She turned over on her back and pillowed her head in her hands. "At one time the river ran through here unchecked. After you told me about the city of Ys, I suggested to Father that if we dug a deeper channel and installed gratings that could be raised and lowered electrically, we could swim here." Her mouth curved. "I liked to pretend this would be a trysting place for me and the river, and a dumping off place for tiresome lovers. Don't kids get strange notions?"

"Doesn't this ice up in the winter?"

"No, there are hot water pipes and heating elements submerged there. I take a plunge nearly every day except in zero weather."

"Do you let the kids swim here?" I asked apprehensively.

"No, I wouldn't want the responsibility. There's a bad eddy a few yards down from the house. If the grate were raised and someone unaware of the hazard were to try swimming out, he might get sucked into the whirlpool."

Was she really that conscientious or was she veiling a threat?

"When I swim around the rock I always hold onto the pilings until I'm out of the undertow," she continued, giving me a curious look. "I'm really not like your princess after all. If I were, I suppose I'd let the bores drown, but eligible men in Peacehaven are too scarce to be expendable."

Except Mark? flashed through my mind. No, that was unreasonably suspicious of me. Mark would have been much too young for her. But who had been down here? Greg? Lucian?

"Why don't you just swim between the grates?" I wondered.

"In winter I do, but that's tedious. I don't like being trapped behind bars."

"Aren't you afraid a flood might wash your house away?"

"The house is high enough and the rock is solid, unlike the sandstone along the rest of the shore. The only nuisance is the driftwood and loose boats and other things that come floating downriver. I have to hire boys to clear them away. But most things pass by in midstream." She looked pointedly at her wristwatch. "Well, now you've seen it, I won't keep you any longer."

"I might invite Rowan to swim with me sometime," she remarked after we'd returned to the main floor.

Again that hint of menace. "I'd rather you wouldn't, Iris."

"Oh, only between the grates," she assured me.

"I thought you didn't want the responsibility of kids swimming down there," I reminded her.

"But Rowan isn't just another kid," she said, opening the front door. "She and I are very close. Sometimes I think she's more my daughter than yours, Mitti. What's wrong between you two? I hope she'll tell me someday."

"That's hardly your business, is it, Iris?" I snapped.

"I suppose you're right." She placed an icy hand on my shoulder. "I only want to help, Mitti. I think she's afraid of you. Something happened to cause that. I've seen it in her hand."

I thought she was reaching for my hand to bid farewell, but instead she turned it over and began to examine it. "Aha! It's there in yours, too!" she exclaimed. "See that cross? Oh, Mitti, you do have to be careful. I don't have time to do a reading now, but sometime I'll be glad to give you one."

Not if I could help it! I was glad to escape now, even though it was tempting to linger and learn the identity of the expected caller.

"Thank you, but I'm not one to inquire into the future—I have too much trouble with the present," I said, stepping out onto the porch.

"You still distrust me, don't you, Mitti," she sighed. "That's not very wise. Rowan confides in me. I could do a lot for you. *Blood doesn't make a mother-daughter relationship, you know.*"

She might have plucked that sentence right out of my dream! A sense of unreality clung to me as I drove away, so absorbed in my thoughts I almost didn't notice the car headed in the direction from which I'd come, except that it wasn't Greg's Beetle. Then with a slight shock I realized the driver was Quentin Jackson.

Chapter Twelve

Early morning frosts heralded the approach of autumn. Dana and I dragged out all the old sheets, drapes, blankets and bedspreads we could find to cover up our tomatoes and other tender plants at night, hoping desperately to tide them over until Indian summer so we could finish canning. With Darcy in charge, we made forays into the woods after dead trees, which Darcy felled with a chain saw.

Rowan was a freshman in the Richland Center high school. The bus picked her up early and she was seldom home before four. Sometimes, however, she'd get off the bus in town and go to a friend's house or—uneasy thought—Iris' store. So far as I could tell, she always went with a group, but the memory of Iris' swimming pool and the treacherous river beyond haunted me.

Between canning and logging I hadn't had time to read

Greg's script and I realized I needed to study more of Salem's history. I was running out of excuses to give him. I dreaded the task, as though there might be something I didn't want to discover in the dark pages of Salem lore.

A heavy drizzle cancelled the logging one morning and robbed me of my last excuse; so after lunch I snuggled down on the sofa with Greg's script. Rowan, who was home with a cold, was studying in her room. In front of me on the coffee table were reference books I'd brought down from the tower. On a warmer day I would have preferred to study up there, but in this weather I'd opted for a seat near the fire with a woolly pup curled up beside me.

Greg had set his first scene in the kitchen of the Reverend Samuel Parris, where his half-Carib, half-Negro slave, Tituba, was clandestinely tutoring the young girls of Salem Village in the mysteries of *obeah* and witchcraft. For sensitive nine-year-old Betty Parris and neurotic twelve-year-old Anne Putnam, steeped as they were in strict Calvinist teachings against the wiles of Satan and the evil of witchcraft, Tituba's stories of hauntings and spells were all too vivid . . .

I closed my eyes and tried to envision that kitchen. If I was going to design the set I would need more background. I began thumbing through the books I'd spread out on the cocktail table, finally selecting *Witchcraft at Salem* by Chadwick Hansen:

"Early in the year 1692," it said, "several girls of Salem Village . . . began to sicken and display alarming symptoms . . . fits so grotesque and violent that eyewitnesses agreed that the girls could not possibly be acting . . . 'Their motions in their fits,' wrote the Reverend Deodat Lawson, 'are preternatural . . . as a well person could not screw their body into ... being much beyond the ordinary force of the same person when they are in their right mind. ... Their arms, necks and backs ... were turned this way and that way, and returned back again, so as it was impossible for them to do of themselves, and beyond the power of any epileptic fits, or natural disease to effect.'

"There were other symptoms ... temporary loss of hearing, speech and sight; loss of memory, so that some of the girls would not recall what had happened to them in their fits; a choking sensation in the throat; loss of appetite ... they saw specters who tormented them in a variety of ingenious and cruel ways. They felt themselves pinched and bitten, and often there were actual marks upon the skin ...

"For some time the physicians were puzzled, but eventually one of them ... Dr. William Griggs of Salem Village ... produced a diagnosis. 'The evil hand,' he announced, 'is upon them'; the girls were victims of malefic witchcraft ...''

A loud pop issued from a wet log in the fire, answered by a slash of icy rain against the windows. Then a floorboard creaked behind me. I looked up briefly, saw nothing, and started to settle back into my book when I became aware of a shuffling sound behind the sofa. Macduff sat up, low growls in his throat, then dived under the sofa.

A mewing sound set my heart to beating again. Dana's cat? "Phantom?" I called. "How'd you get in here? Here, kitty, kitty, kitty!"

No response. Then a goat bleated. Caper? He *couldn't* have gotten into the house. Whatever it was was creeping around the end of the sofa. Then a touseled red head came into view—Rowan! A laugh died in my throat as she began rolling at my feet, her eyes glazed and staring. My God, it was happening again!

"Stop them, stop them!" she gasped, thrusting out her arms. "They're pinching me. Owww! Don't bite me! Oh, 'tis Goody Nurse and Tituba after me, don't you see them?" She lunged forward and grabbed my knee, then slid back, her hand to her throat, gagging and retching.

I sat transfixed, terrible thoughts racing through my mind. Rowan would have to see a psychiatrist—go into an institution. I fell on my knees and tried to take her into my arms.

"Rowan, Rowan, darling! In the name of God . . ."

Her eyes bulged and her mouth contorted. "Don't say that name!" she shrieked. "My master is Satan! See?" she pointed. "He's coming toward us. Ooooh, he's gross!" The anachronism snapped us both out of it. She began to giggle and I fell back limp on the sofa. Macduff stuck his nose out warily.

"Oh, Rowan, you scared the wits out of me!" I gasped.

"How was I? I really had you going, didn't I?"

"Yes, and if you *ever* do that again, I . . ."

She shook her curls out of her eyes. "That's just it! I *want* to do it again—in the pageant. This was an audition. I've been reading Greg's script and the part of Anne Putnam is the best teen-age role. I know you're on the casting committee—"

"And for that reason I can't give my daughter the best part. What would the other girls say? They've lived here all along and are direct descendants of the witches." For a moment we had seemed so close. I hated to refuse her.

"That doesn't mean they can act," she frowned. "Iris and Greg and Lucian all say I'd be best in the part. You just don't want me to do anything I want to."

There was no doubt about it—she'd inherited her father's talent, but if I was to help with casting and directing, how could I in good conscience give her the lead?

"Listen, sweetheart, you were good just now—frighteningly good, but I can't give you the part. It'll be up to the rest of the committee. You'll have to audition for them and if they think you're right—"

She slammed her fist down on the coffee table. "I am right! You know that. But the committee members wouldn't care about that. Like Mr. and Mrs. Osburn—they'll want Cissie to have the part and Mrs. Willard will fight for Jessica—"

"Rowan, let me finish! You already named three people on your side—"

"Iris isn't on the committee."

"Well, Greg and Lucian are. Leave it to them."

She sat down beside me and laid her hand on my arm. "You'll talk to them, won't you, Mommy?" It had been years since she called me that. "You'll vote for me, won't you?"

I hated to be honest. "No, I'll have to abstain. Let the others choose you. Then nobody will have any complaints. Believe me, that's the best way."

The thunderstorm broke. "Damn you!" Macduff scooted under the sofa again. "You hate me because I'm like Daddy. I wish you weren't my mother. I wish Iris was—or Aunt Charity—or anybody but—" She clapped her hand over her mouth, terror in her eyes, as if I might suddenly turn on her. "I—I didn't mean that exactly."

And yet I knew she had.

"Oh, Rowan, I love you! You know I want you to have

the part as much as you want it." I took her in my arms, but it was an empty shell I was holding. I released her and she turned and ran out of the room.

It was some time before I could focus my attention on the script again. I brushed a tear from the paper. If only I could tell Rowan the truth, maybe she'd understand—no, I was weak even to entertain such an idea. Shatter her father's image? Never! I forced myself to read on. Greg had said he was coming over this afternoon.

"Tituba," Greg had written his stage directions with Shavian verbosity, "had deftly interwoven the lore of her Indian and African backgrounds with the superstitions of her English masters, producing heady fare for maidens whose leisure hours were supposed to be spent learning the catechism and scriptures. Life held little pleasurable recreation for the women of those days. The men and boys had the fun of hunting and fishing, but women's tasks were arduous and dull."

No wonder the girls had rebelled! Imagine Rowan and her friends under such restraint! Not that today's youth didn't have their problems, but those Salem lasses— hadn't their actions been a natural bid for attention? What a foolproof way to tyrannize their austere elders! Or could it be written off that way? Were there super- natural forces at work in Salem? Had the girls been bewitched—or, as we would say now, possessed? And the entire adult community at their mercy—teenagers— like Rowan . . .

My eyes refused to focus. A gray spectre of steam curled out of the damp log. I forced myself to reach for the poker to stir the smoke out of the fire . . .

*　　*　　*

163

. . . and stared at the great wooden spoon in my hand. Steam was issuing from a stewpot hanging in a mammoth fireplace. I tasted the contents critically—a bit more spice, but just a mite. Our supply was dwindling and who knew when a ship would arrive with more?

The knotted ropes suspending the straw-filled mattress on the bed in the room overhead groaned. Joshua must be waking—he'd been raving sick with the fever during the night, but I'd brought that down with a clyster. Now he would need nourishment. I climbed the heavy oak stairs with a bowl of venison broth in my hand. My son was still sleeping, his forehead cool and moist to the touch. The deep sleep would make him mend.

I straightened the covers, putting the arm he'd flung out back underneath. There was dirt under his nails, but he'd been so ill I hadn't had the heart to make him wash. His long form stretched across the bed—only thirteen, this youngest of my children, and already his feet were sticking out at the foot of the bed. Thirteen!

About the age of those girls who were giving so much trouble in Salem Village. Bewitched? A spanking was what they needed. Still, i' faith, 'twere not good for young minds to hear Tituba's tales about sabbaths in the parson's pasture where the Black Man . . . Yet those were not just tales, were they? I myself knew too well . . .

A picture of Tituba rose in my mind—black darting irises in yellow-white eyeballs that never met you square; thick, sullen lips, perpetually frowning eyebrows, high cheekbones and a high-arched nose. She'd readily confessed, seemingly delighted to incriminate others. Was this her revenge against free women? Oh, she'd been clever. Her first accusation had been against Sarah Good, a general outcast. Time and a worthless husband had beggared and embittered Sarah, so when people refused to give her handouts, she retaliated with curses.

Tituba's second victim was higher on the social ladder—Gammer Osburn, a woman of prosperity, but didn't everyone know she'd lived with her hired man before she married him? And seven other names were in the Black Man's book, Tituba alleged, but she couldn't read them. Her description could have been applied to any member of the clergy, who always wore black. A thin, long, pale young face came to mind. Aye, even him! But 'twere not fitting to think o' him—with me married these many years to another and mother of his nine children.

It hadn't been a bad marriage, but neither had it been a good one. The lovesick suitor, once secure in the marriage bond, had become overbearing and insensitive. To him lovemaking was for the fulfillment of his immediate need and the Lord's commandment. A woman's feelings were not provided for in Scriptures. Farmer and town cooper he was. I kept his accounts, though it suited him not that I, a woman, could read and write and cipher better than he. Once, when he caught me jotting down notes in a diary, he'd flung it into the fire.

"Think ye're better'n your station, don't ye, lass?" he'd growled. "Ye forget Woman was created to serve Man."

I stole back down the stairs and emptied the broth into the pot. Waste not, want not! I piled more kindling on top of the backstick and stirred the backlog. It was a chill, late March thaw—would it had been snow instead of the sleet lashing at the leaded windows. Damp seeped through the walls and ran in rivulets down onto the floor. No wonder there was so much sickness! I must make a poultice of camomile and mallows in milk for my daughter-in-law, whose breasts had been sore and swelled since her babe was stillborn. And I'd promised some burdock tea and fresh meat to Goody Redington, who was down with the King's Evil, and some concentrate of foxglove for Goody How's sinking spells.

But, except for my sleeping son upstairs, I was blessedly alone today. Solitude never frightened me. True, Indians lurked in the forest around us—salvages considered to be devil-worshippers. What did these simple people know of our Devil? They knew well they were always welcome at my fire, even though Isaac grumbled that they ate up our stores. For what they received, they always gave in return. Yawataw particularly. But then, we'd almost grown up together. Her father, No-Nose, a Naumkeag Indian, had worked at times for mine. He would bring his little girl with him because her mother was dead. My mother had taken the baby Yawataw into our home when her father caught the smallpox that disfigured him—an act many of our neighbors scorned. When No-Nose recovered, he said to my mother, "Indians know you have strong medicine keep away white man's sickness. Your family not sick. Can you keep papoose well?"

Her reply was strange. "It is up to the Cow Mother."

So came the day I lay a-fevered, with running sores on my hands. My mother rejoiced. "The Cow Mother ha' blessed thee, Mary, for ye milk wi' a gentle hand. When the Queen and fine ladies lie abed wi' the pox, ye'll be well and strong. 'Tis a secret I learned from the Old Ones."

That day, when Yawataw came, my mother took out her knife and made two small crosscuts on her arm. Though her dark eyes were puzzled, the girl didn't flinch until with the tip of her knife, my mother smeared the cuts with pus from my sores.

"Aihee!" the child cried fearfully.

"Nay, I do thee good. Ye'll be a mite sick like Mary here, but I vow ye'll ne'er ha' pocks on thy face."

Yawataw did sicken slightly and No-Nose refused to come to

166

work or bring her because he thought my mother had given her the pox. But both of us soon recovered and not long after, when another epidemic hit the Indians, Yawataw went unscathed.

She was a widow now and lived alone in the forest, but she always believed my mother had saved her from smallpox. So now she brought me the herbs her people used for medicine, always waiting until the men were gone. Then I'd hear an owl hoot and there'd she be with her pouch full of Indian medicine. I traded meat and provisions for her herbs, although I think she would have brought them even if I hadn't. 'Twasn't charity I gave her, though Isaac would have called it such had he known, for she paid me in kind with not only her medicines, but with lessons on how to plant and use some of the strange plants of the New World.

She wouldn't come today in this weather. Nor would Sarah, my older daughter, who had her own home to tend now. Hannah was helping her cousin who lay in childbed—I saw to it that Hannah was kept busy, determined not to let her fall into Dorcas' clutches as Sarah had. Isaac and the boys were making barrels in the barn. My spinning was fair caught up. Dinner was merely a matter of dipping stew onto the plates and thawing out a squash pie. There was mending to do, but that could wait until this evening. I would steal—deliberately *steal* from this day. How I longed for one of those books I'd heard were read in Boston and London, but Isaac allowed nought but the Geneva Bible and the Catechism in our house. Well, the Good Book was surely the better reading o' the two, and if my menfolk came in early, they'd see me at my Scriptures and think me the holy woman I was not.

'Twas an old game I played, opening the Bible at random for a message, and it seldom failed me, although, if I landed in the "Begats," I'd have to try a second time. The heavy cover fell open to the family register, where I'd entered births and deaths and weddings: "Married, Isaac Eastick to Mary Towne, May 12, 1655." Isaac had scribbled "Esty" above "Eastick." He liked the short form, but I preferred the old.

I closed my eyes, slit the Bible open with my hand and ran my finger down the page until it stopped, then opened my eyes: *"Thou shalt not suffre a witche to live!"* (Exod. 22:18) I nearly dropped the book. What augured this that I should turn to that dread passage so oft quoted by our clergy of late? I tried again—this time in the New Testament, which should be safer:

"For to one is given by the Spirit the worde of wisdome; to another the worde of knowledge, by the same Spirit." (1 Cor. 12:18)

The "worde of wisdome," our parson had once said, was given to divines like himself and the "worde of knowledge" to the schoolmasters. *"To another is given faith, by the same Spirit—"* What did that mean? There was a notation in the margin: *"To do onely miracles by—"* If the Apostles could work miracles, why hadn't they handed this power down to us? *"—to another the giftes of healing, by the same Spirit—"* Doctors? Nay, our physicians healed more by leeching than by the Spirit and their patients died as oft as not. Could it be that Paul had provided for spiritual healers within the church? If so, where were they now? *"And to another ye operations of great workes—"* I looked to the margin again: *"To work by miracles against Satan—"* Again miracles! In these hard days? Belike they'd be called sorcery. *"—and to another prophecie—"* Anyone daring to prophesy today would be called a witch and a witch must not be suffered to live.

Did that make me a witch—that at times I had "the Sight"? Had I in some unconscious moment made a pact with the Devil? Then would my immortal soul be surely damned. I shuddered, thinking of the dream I'd had last night. I prayed it was nothing more than an over-rich pudding that caused it. Unlike other dreams, which dissolve with waking, this still preyed on my mind:

I had been wandering through the rain—great, drenching torrents—delighting in the knowledge that he was out there, too, soaked to his mortal bones, while the rain touched me not. Still, I hadn't quite withdrawn as yet, and I was lost here in the dark, not knowing what lay ahead of me—

I'd intercepted him on the causeway to Dorchester only moments ago—if I could still measure Time—and well nigh drowned him. How could he have chosen to believe her instead of me? Oh, I'd gloried in heaping up the waves around him, affrighting his poor horse 'till it nigh stumbled off the road and he could go no further, but was forced to return to Boston. Yet all around the voices whispered, "Forgive him, Mary! Forgive!" How could I in my fury? "Then stay here in the half-world!" they chorused. "We've no room for you in ours."

The blockhouse loomed before me. He'd pass here soon. I longed for the benison of his arms about me—hating and loving all at once. If it hadn't been for Dorcas—nay, I mustn't let her meanness trap me into like behavior. I loved him still, e'en though he'd become old and testy and the skin sagged from his chin, and I must somehow break through the mists—

There! Hooves sloshing on the cobblestones!

"Will! Will! Whither does thou ride?" I unthinkingly fell into the old-fashioned form of address.

His horse shied, neighing its alarm. He reined in sharply, then slid to the ground and stood by the animal's head, holding it in check. "There, Prince," he tried to soothe the beast, " 'twas but a wisp of fog that crossed our path. There's no one here. What has come over you tonight? Nearly tumbled me off the causeway, you did, and for no reason, although for a moment I thought I saw—"

He jerked around, his eyes bulging, his face gleaming sickly pale in the half light. "Mary! Nay, it can't be thee! I must be a-fevered or belike 'tis the Devil come to torment me, making me believe I saw thee upon the causeway, thine eyes glowing like swampfire. Hast thou come to finish what thou left undone?"

"Will, Will, hear me—I come to ask forgiveness and to forgive! Listen to me—I love thee!"

"Ah, 'tis indeed a fever in the brain. Methinks she talks to me and stretches out her arms. No longer do her eyes burn, but are wet with rain and tears. Was she innocent after all? Did I wrong thee, Mary?" He dug his fist into the horse's flank. "Nay, 'tis Satan sends me these doubts. I have not erred. I will not have it that I erred! Be thou Lucifer or the Whore of Babylon—nay, be thou the Mary I once loved, thou canst not turn my judgment into a lie!"

"Beloved—" I tried again, but the wind carried my voice away as lightning flashed and he fell to his knees.

"Oh, Lord, my God, Thou who didst bring us, Thy new chosen people, to this wilderness—this promised land—save me from the Tempter!" he prayed, his hands clasped, his cheekbones livid in the gloaming. "Even in all her cunning I loved her. How I longed to set her free, to taste of her body—oh, the fleshpots of Babylon! Did I condemn her because I knew she belonged to another and even if I judged her innocent, I could never know her sweet body? Oh, God, t'is Satan who speaks, undermining my convictions, chastising me for doing Thy work, oh, Lord! Yes, yes, 'twas surely Satan who tempted me to set her free, but I yielded not. I thank Thee, God, that I am not as other men—"

How unconsciously he mouthed the prayer of the Pharisee! My hand was a wisp of moisture on his brow, which he wiped away as he would the rain.

"Listen to me, Will! Let not thine ears be stopped up with bigotry and self-righteousness! Hark to thy doubts! Art thou so sure

*of the Lord's will? Nay, thou art not and this has made thee ill, my
love!"*

*"She stands before me still. Her lips move, but I cannot hear.
How the Devil works to delude me and I am ill, very ill. I cannot
proceed."* He pulled himself up from his knees by clinging to the
horse's bridle. *"Come, Prince, we'll return to Sewall's house!"* He
hoisted himself into the saddle and started off toward Boston, but I
ran before him, weeping and pleading, knowing that soon I must be
drawn back into the mists. *"Will—Will—"*

*He covered his eyes with his arm. "Satan, get thee behind me! I
bruised thy heel today. Get thee gone, Mary! I know thou dost
belong to Satan!"*

I felt myself slipping away. My chance had gone.

*"Nay, William, I belong not to Satan! I belong only to God—
and to thee!"*

I had awakened with that cry. Isaac beside me had not
stirred, but I lay there in the dark, pondering this dream that
had no meaning, yet left me with such unutterable despair.
Now, as I mused by the fire, I roused, shuddering from the
memory of that dream. Next time I made a pudding I'd cut
down on the suet . . .

There was a pounding on the door. Now who would be out
on a miserable day like this?

"Let me in quick, Mary! I ha' bad tidings!" Bered!

"Come in, little brother," I bade him, although at six-foot-
one and forty-two-year of age he was scarcely little. " 'Tis
nothing ill with Thankful or the children, I hope."

"Nay, they thrive."

"And your trade also?"

"Too well. There be always a need for tombstones."

"Then have yourself a plate o' stew whilst ye tell me."

He waved it away. "Rebecca's been cried out on! She be
goin' afore Justices Hathorne and Corwin the morrow!"

171

Not my Rebecca! My saintly older sister, who knew more of the Scriptures than any other woman in Salem Village!

"How can they? Why, she be nigh two 'n seventy! And she so weak wi' stomach pain! Who has done this? Tituba?"

"Nay, 'twas Mistress Ann Putnam who first brought the charge and set her daughter and the other maids to cryin' out that Rebecca's shape torments them."

Ann Putnam, wife of Thomas. She'd e'er been queer, that one. Thinkin' her dead babes'd been killed by sorcery. And the young Anne, a pale, fidgety, delicate child, was her mother's tool. As for Thomas, he was troublesome, jealous that the fortunes of the Nurses and the Estys had prospered while his own had declined.

"And what did Mistress Putnam charge?"

"She claimed little children've been risin' from the grave in their winding sheets, cryin' 'Rebecca Nurse murdered us!' "

"But that's daft, man! Can't the magistrates see that?"

"What wi' girls seein' visions and bein' bitten and pinched and vomiting pins, the magistrates'll believe anything."

"It'll kill Rebecca," I cried, "her bein' so feeble and deaf. She'll not hear the questions and she'll say the wrong thing and—oh, Bered!" I dropped my head against his great chest. " 'Tis one o' God's own they'll be tryin'!"

He folded his arms around me. "Aye, Mary, e'en without this she'd not be likely to last the year out. But 'tis you I tremble for."

My head jerked back. "Me? Whatever for?"

"Things are bein' said—about how you cure people the doctors can't, how you consort with that salvage woman, and how you saved Granny Peabody's dog from being hanged. There's no trust left among us. We look at our neighbors and wonder—be *they* in league wi' the Devil? If my cow sickens, be it a spell? There were little ado when Tituba accused Sarah

Good. She'd uttered enough curses to do for a hundred witches, but when they arrest as faithful a church member as Martha Corey, no one is safe."

"Aye, 'tis true," I recalled. Hadn't Martha's own husband testified against her, all because she hid his saddle so he couldn't ride into town to gawk at the afflicted girls? "Giles should be cried out on himself—'twould serve him right!" I said angrily.

"Gently, Mary, gently," Bered cautioned me. " 'Tis for hot words like that people are bein' accused. Forsooth, they be diggin' up things long forgotten—like Goody Corey's mulatto son."

"I should think she'd paid for that long since," I said crisply. "She swore she was raped, but who believes a woman? Anyway, she's a covenanting member o' the church now. 'Tis more her sharp tongue and her scorn o' the magistrates tha's brought this on her. Honesty rankles more than scandal." I paused. "I didn't mean that about Giles. I wouldn't wish that on anyone."

He leaned against the door jamb, beads of melted sleet standing out on the wool of his mantle.

"Let me dry your cloak by the fire," I begged. "La! For what reason should I be cried out on? I have harmed no one and my children be all legitimate."

"Aye, but Tom Putnam looks with a green eye at the Esty farm. And he and his brother remember the lawsuit over boundaries they lost to your menfolk. They'll get at the Esty men through you."

"Then they be cowards in Salem Village!" I exclaimed. "And fools, too! Did these 'chosen people of God' come here just to fight among themselves? And attack each other through their womenfolk?" I added contemptuously.

He slumped down on the inglenook and leaned wearily

against the chimney place, his long, knotted hands spread on his knees.

" 'Tisn't only that," he persisted. " 'Tis you, Mary. You're a strong woman—you've strong ideas—and for that they whisper about you. Samuel Smith still grumbles about the scolding you gave him five years gone. Your tongue can wound."

"Indeed! I wish I had wounded him wi' more'n my tongue! The scoundrel flouted me in me own house. 'Twas no more'n he deserved."

"But in Ingersoll's ordinary he tells how you flew after him, all invisible, tapped him on the shoulder and then rattled a whole stone wall at him."

I snorted. "Who pays attention to *that* drunken prattler?"

His reply was quiet and chilling. "Just about anyone in Salem Village at the now. They whisper about your simples."

"Oh, pooh! Most of them I learned from our mother."

"And she accused o' witchcraft in her time!" The firelight played wizard with his peaked eyebrows. "I never knew her. You were my real mother."

"And you my first son," stroking his gray-streaked hair and thinking how caring for this baby brother had eased the pain of my lost love. "Now, I'll not let you ride home in this weather on an empty stomach. Do eat a bit o' this stew. 'Tis fair savory."

He dipped his spoon into the steaming bowl absentmindedly. "Make Isaac take you away while there's time," he pleaded.

"You're as daft as the others, Bered, if you think he'd ever leave his coopering. Besides, I mun stand by our sister."

"Ye might do Rebecca more harm than good wi' the doctors sayin' there's more'n medicine goes into your cures, and people claimin' they've seen you mutter words over your simples."

"And if I instill a bit o' the Holy Scriptures into them, what be the harm in that?"

"They say you mutter charms from the Black Book."

I fished a choice hunk of venison from the pot and added it to his stew. "The Bible's covers be as black as any book's and the parson's clothes as black as the Devil's himself, belike. All this talk of a Black Man a-makin' folks sign in his Black Book—who knows but what that meddling Reverend Noyes o' Salem Town or the Reverend Parris mought be up to some unholy doin's . . ." My voice trailed off and I flushed with anger and humiliation as the memory of last All Hallows' Eve in Parris' meadow came back to me now. I wouldn't tell Bered. He was too rash—he'd get us all in trouble and I had no proof. Nor could I identify the man in the heavy black hood and cape.

"You've no friend in the Reverend Parris, Mary," Bered interrupted my thoughts.

"Indeed! How so?"

"Sarah Bibber says you told folk you wouldn't visit our services because you like not lining moneygrubbers' pockets."

"Aye, though I didna call him a moneygrubber. But ye know well his contract allows him to keep for himself any monies given by non-members. 'Tis my right to attend my own church."

"True, but 'tis unsafe to flout a man o' God."

"Then let him act like one instead of a sniveling, penny-pinching Barbadoan peddler," I retorted.

Bered struck his head in despair. "Mary, Mary, if ye cannot bridle your tongue better than that, heaven help you."

"Nay, 'twas said only between us. Eat hearty, Bered," I said, "and give thanks unto the Lord that I don't live in your cantankerous Salem Village, where the parson can't keep the

175

young maids out o' mischief or his congregation content, and everyone in the place clawing and backbiting like a pack o' wildcats. No wonder they cast jaundiced eyes at Topsfield. Here there be no nonsense o' that sort."

He dipped his bread into the gravy thoughtfully, his eyes troubled.

"It can spread, sister," he warned. "It can spread."

Chapter Thirteen

I started to taste the stew myself, but a poker had replaced my spoon. What was happening to me? Dreaming in bed is one thing, but while standing and awake? I willed the poker to turn into a spoon again, but it remained solidly a poker. Thoroughly disturbed, I hung it back on its rack. What was reality—my dreams or my waking life?

I was still pondering when Greg arrived. He glanced at the pile of books. "Doing some research, I see."

"Yes. What's a witch cake?"

"A witch cake was a concoction of rye meal and urine from the bewitched that was fed to a dog. If the animal got the shakes, the afflicted was surely under the spell of a witch. What's the matter?" he broke off. "Is my face dirty?"

I was staring at his glistening countenance. It reminded

me of something. "No, not dirty, Greg, just wet. Here!" I took a fresh tissue and wiped off the raindrops.

"How far have you read?" he asked.

"Just the first scene," I confessed. "You said it wasn't to be put on until next year."

"No, but rehearsals begin this fall for the girls; so they can get their parts down pat—really live them."

"I'm not sure how good that will be for them," I objected. "Rowan, for instance—she's too impressionable."

"Really, Mitti, children take these things in stride. They'll have a ball sending their elders to the gallows."

But you remember Rowan the night of the party, I was about to say, then thought of this afternoon's performance. *Had she shammed that earlier one, too?*

"I suppose I'm being overprotective," I yielded.

"I brought something to show you." He took an envelope out of his pocket and extracted some color snapshots.

"Recognize this?" he asked.

Why did I have to force myself to look? "That must be the monument your ancestor carved—what was his name?"

"Bered—Bered Towne. What's wrong? You're trembling."

"It's chilly in here. Let's come closer to the fire," I said, trying not to remember the rugged man with the sleet melting off his mantle who'd been sitting on the inglenook just now. *"There be always a need for tombstones,"* he'd said.

"It—it's really impressive," I hurried on. "The coat of arms and the plumed knight especially." I shuddered involuntarily at the next view he handed me. "So these

178

are the skeletons and hourglass: You're right—that winged hourglass *does* look like a vampire!"

His attention had wandered to the books on the table. "These are good references here," he said, riffling through them. "Don't expect any of them to agree, however."

"Do historians ever? The name of the game is to get a new angle or the book won't be published."

He frowned. "Isn't it good to get new interpretations?"

"What happens to the original truth? I'll bet someday some bright-eyed historian's going to canonize Hitler and people will believe him because his book's a best seller. You can't judge people of the past in the light of our thinking today. If you were to tell a colonist not to drain a swamp because it might hurt the ecology, he wouldn't have the slightest idea what you were talking about. Or try to convince him that Indians are people with rights, he'd say they are salvages and—"

He looked up in surprise. "You've really been reading up on this, haven't you?"

I was embarrassed. "Well, I started. Why?"

"Because just now you used the old term for 'savage.' In colonial times they called them 'salvages'—like you just did."

It had come out so naturally; yet how would I have known that? "I read books by ESP," I laughed. "I still say it's unfair to judge our ancestors by our present standards."

"Are you trying to justify the witch trials?"

"Not at all. Yet if we had to live with their superstitions and fears, who knows what we might do?"

His eyebrows knitted above his glasses. "But I do write from conviction, not just to sell a book."

I thought how like a little boy he looked at the moment. I suppressed a desire to run my fingers through his softly waving blond hair.

"You know, this is really fine sculpture," I said by way of apology. "Gruesome as they are, those skulls and stylized ribs are a work of art. But why did he carve two skeletons on the stone? Stoughton never married."

"I don't know—I never thought about it," he replied slowly. "The skull was a common motif on colonial tombstones, but I can't remember any other instance where two were used. Of course, this was more elaborate and expensive than most."

"Look at the way those ribs are intertwined. Was Bered Towne trying to say something? Involve the old boy with a woman?"

He shrugged. "Could be—if the old curmudgeon could have loved a woman—or any woman him."

"What makes you think he was unloved? Do historians say so?" I retorted. "How could they know?"

"That's a good question," he conceded. "He was a bachelor, therefore they conclude he was unloved."

"That's not what I've heard about bachelors," I flung back.

"Then there's hope for me?" he said teasingly, reaching out his hand. The response within me died as the hand continued past me to pick up a book with royal blue and red binding. No *wonder* he'd never married!

"Here's an excellent source," he remarked, "Samuel Sewall's *Diary*."

"Sounds deadly dull."

"Not at all. Sewall was the American Pepys. His courtships of eligible widows and his descriptions of colonial life are delightful."

Greg flipped the pages. "He was associate justice at the Salem trials and his notes are invaluable. For instance, see here: 'August 19th, 1692. This day George Burrough, John Willard, John Proctor, Martha Carrier and George Jacobs were executed at Salem, a very great number of Spectators being present. Mr. Cotton Mather was there, Mr. Sims, Hale, Noyes, Chiever, &c. all of them said they were inocent, Carrier and all. Mr. Mather says they all died by a Righteous Sentence. Mr. Burrough by his Speech, Prayer, protestation of his Innocence, did much move unthinking persons, which occasions their speaking hardly concerning his being executed.'

"George Burroughs," Greg explained, "a former minister of Salem Village, nearly saved himself at the last moment by reciting the Lord's Prayer without a flaw—they believed that no witch could get through it without stumbling."

"I notice Sewall called those who were swayed by Burroughs 'unthinking.' "

"Yet Sewall was the first judge to recant. Oh, here's something interesting: 'About noon, at Salem, Giles Corey was pressed to death for standing mute: much pains was used with him two days, one after another, by the Court and Capt. Gardner of Nantucket who had been of his acquaintance: but all in vain.' "

"So Giles got his comeuppance after all! After the way he testified against his wife, he deserved it."

Greg looked up, surprised. "You read farther than I thought."

"Read? Why, everyone's been talking about it . . ." a voice not mine trailed off. "—uh—what does it mean," I changed the subject quickly, "to press a person to death?"

181

"They placed boards on the victim and loaded rocks onto them. If the poor guy didn't confess, they'd pile on more until he was crushed to death. Giles died a hero at the last. Refused to plead either guilty or innocent so that his heirs' property wouldn't be confiscated. Eighty years old and it took two days to dispatch him!"

"Poor old man!" I felt a wave of guilt. Looking over Greg's shoulder, I read aloud: " 'September 20. Now I hear from Salem that about 18 years agoe he was suspected to have stamped and press'd a man to death, but was cleared. Twas not remembered till Ane Putname was told of it by said Corey's Spectre the Sabbath-day night before the Execution.' Did Sewall really believe such nonsense?"

"Not only did he believe it, but that's the sort of testimony that sent twenty people to their deaths. They called it 'spectral evidence.' In other words, Satan could assume the shape of only the guilty—those with whom he had a pact. If you had a grudge against me, all you'd have to do would be to say you saw my shape sitting on the foot of your bed one dark night—"

"If I saw that, it's not witchcraft I'd accuse you of."

The cleft in his chin deepened, but he continued— "and during witchcraft hysteria, that was the most damning type of evidence."

"If a specter appeared today, they'd call it a mistrial."

My quip was lost on him. He'd gotten up and was watching the rain cascade down the great glass walls. Eerie light from a drowned sun trying in vain to penetrate the clouds filled the room. Suddenly he spun around. "Do you know what day this is?"

"—uh—September twenty-second. So?"

"It's the autumnal equinox," he said. "The witches are supposed to hold a sabbath tonight."

I thought of Dylan and his coven out at Aunt Bo's old farm and wondered if they'd be celebrating—inside, I hoped.

"And," he went on, "nearly three hundred years ago today, the last of the Salem executions were carried out, which may or may not have been a coincidence—that is, if an upper class coven were offering sacrifices to their god."

"Oh, Greg, that's way out in left field."

"I know, but it's an intriguing speculation." He turned towards the window again. "Strange—it rained later that same day—Sewall made a note of that."

"Was *she* among them?"

"Who?"

"Your ancestor's sister—Mary Eastick."

He started. "Where did you get *that* name?"

"Why, from you, Greg, don't you remember? You told me about her the day you gave me the script."

"I'm sure I used the name 'Esty'—not 'Eastick'! None of the reference books you have here use that version. So *where* did you get it?"

From the family Bible, I almost told him. But that had been a dream and he wouldn't understand that. Already he looked at me as if *I* were some sort of spectral evidence.

"You must have used the old form unconsciously."

"Didn't you say it was Mary's ghost who prevented more executions?" I asked. "What did you mean by that?"

"It's in the record," he replied, letting himself be sidetracked. "A Wenham girl reported to the Reverend John Hale on November fourteenth that for nearly two months since Mary's execution she'd been afflicted by her 'shape' crying out for vengeance. Mary, it seems, had

183

first visited the girl in spectral form just hours before her execution. 'I am going upon the ladder to be hanged for a witch, but I am innocent, and before a twelve-month be past you shall believe it.' Mary Esty kept her appointment on November twelfth, bringing along the shape of another woman—Hale's own wife, *who was still alive* and of unimpeachable reputation. At last Hale was convinced that devil could take the shape of an *innocent* person and that 'spectral evidence' was a fallacy. The girl reported that Mary Esty swore she'd been put to death wrongfully and she'd come to vindicate herself, crying 'Vengeance! Vengeance!' "

"That last doesn't sound like Mary Esty, does it?" I observed.

"No, it doesn't, but the purge was stopped. What was begun by discarnate beings was ended by one. Spectral evidence was now suspect, and people lost their taste for witchhunting. The governor put an end to the executions in spite of vigorous protests by Stoughton and his clique. But tragically, it was years before many of the accused were freed. Some died in prison. In those days, prisoners had to pay for their board. If they or their families had no money, they were held as debtors even though innocent." He glanced at his watch. "I'd better go."

"Why don't you stay for dinner?"

"I wish I could, but I have to cover a special council meeting tonight. They're drafting a petition to the governor for state aid to keep the river from chomping away at Peacehaven. How about a raincheck?" He kissed me lightly on the forehead and was out the door. Oh well, who could fight city hall?

I picked up the diary, wondering what besides rain had been worthy of Sewall's note on that fatal autumn equinox when eight persons, including Mary Esty, had been hanged. Surely he would have something to say about that!

No, apparently he hadn't found it important. More urgent matters were afoot: "Thursday, Sept. 22, 1692. William Stoughton, Esqr., Mr. Cotton Mather, and Capt. John Higginson with my brother St., were at our house, speaking about publishing some Trials of the Witches . . ." Oho! So they were sensitive about PR in those days, too! I read on, "Mr. Stoughton went away and left us, it began to rain and was very dark, so that getting some way beyond the fortification was fain to come back again . . ." and farther on: "Lieut. Governour coming over the Causey is, by reason of the high Tide, so wet, that is fain to go to bed till sends for dry cloaths to Dorchester . . ."

The rest of the world had been cut off by a gray curtain of rain pounding at the windows. A voice echoed somewhere deep within me:

"Nay, William, I belong not to Satan! I belong only to God—and to thee!"

Chapter Fourteen

Greg had hardly left when Dr. Brun came into the kitchen, shaking the water off his trenchcoat. He perched on the kitchen stool, his skin ruddy-gold and moist from the weather, the water still dripping from his mustache and beard.

"*Was ist los*, Mitti?" he asked. "You have a faraway look."

I hesitated, then said, "I was thinking about making hot chocolate. Would you like some?"

"*Ach, wunderbar!*" he exclaimed.

"Understand, this is part payment for a psychiatric consultation," I said after I'd set out the cups of steaming chocolate. "I expect your bill to be reduced accordingly."

I said it lightly, but there was concern on his face. "Is it about Rowan?" he asked. "She has had another spell?"

"I thought so at first," I replied, "but it was only an act.

She's trying to convince me she should play the teenage lead in the pageant. No, this time I'm the patient. You once told me you have a recurring dream. Well, I have the same problem, but my dreams are getting out of hand. In fact, it's uncanny. They're changing in character, becoming more intense and—well, they concern things that happened centuries ago. Only later do I find out that what I dreamed about really did happen—at least part of it. I find myself beginning to believe in my dreams."

If my symptoms perturbed him, he didn't show it. "Perhaps you'd better start with your original dream," was all he said.

"There were several, actually, but one in particular stands out. I used to dream I was with a man in a tall, Puritan hat, walking beside the sea. We were in love, but then I did something—I don't know what—that alienated him from me forever. Lately, however, I've been having other dreams, all related to the same general period in the Salem area. In most of these dreams I'm older and married to another man. It's as if all the years between Salem and Peacehaven had been stripped away and events that took place then are trickling through a thin wall of time into my brain. Does that sound crazy?"

My cup shook as I tried to sip my chocolate. What would he think? A low laugh snapped the tension building up in me.

"You are asking a psychiatrist if *that* sounds crazy?" He continued to chuckle. "*Meine liebe* Mitti, you'll have to do better than that to make me think you're crazy."

"But there's more," I said, reassured. "In my dreams I seem to be reliving scenes in the life of a person who actually existed. Her name was Mary Towne Esty and she was executed in Salem on this very day in 1692. What's more, Greg is collaterally descended from her."

"*Ach*, well, that is natural," he said. "You picked that up from him."

"Not exactly. Before I ever met Greg I dreamed I was Mary Towne, and I was in the kitchen of our home in Salem Village talking with my mother. She reproached me for spurning the suit of Isaac *Esty*, the *cooper*, and aspiring to be married above my station to a young gentleman from Boston. How could I know those names or that Isaac Esty really was a cooper?"

He shrugged. "Perhaps you heard it all as a child."

"No, the people here weren't obsessed with their heritage then—not like they are now. Oh, they made jokes about their witch ancestry at times, but only in passing. Furthermore, while most of the family names here are right off the Salem gallows, there were no Townes or Estys here then, so I wouldn't have known those names. Do you think there might be something to reincarnation after all?" I asked abruptly.

He didn't answer immediately, but kept stirring his chocolate. "You and Lucian argued about that when you first came," he recalled. "I feel as you do. It's a tempting theory. It hasn't been proven one way or the other, and I don't think anything in the Christian religion demands we choose either side. We can only conjecture and conjecturing produces many possibilities besides reincarnation."

He placed his broad, powerful hands on mine, but in spite of the intimacy of the gesture, he seemed to be speaking from a great distance. "As a scientist and physician, I should accept only those things I can perceive through my five senses, but I cannot. I am basically a metagnostic, which means I believe that a

188

knowledge of the Absolute is attained not through logical or scientific processes, but through a higher con-sciousness—intuition if you will. Man cannot wait for science to prove the Absolute. He must make great mental and spiritual leaps forward beyond the reach of science." He stopped and shook his head. "I sound as though I am beginning another book. To put it simply, my dear Mitti, I believe in a life after death. If my conviction is correct, those Salem people of whom you speak are somewhere, whether reincarnated or on some other plane of existence, call it heaven if you will."

A warmth had stolen over me. I remembered the discussions I used to have with my father.

"And where are those other planes of existence?" he rumbled on. "Maybe, as you say, we're separated from them by a thin wall and Mary Esty's thoughts are coming through to you. Perhaps she's directing them to you."

"But why?" My father had never gone that far. "That's even further out than reincarnation. Why should Mary Esty be trying to get through to me?"

He withdrew his hands and gestured helplessly. "I cannot answer that. Perhaps she wants to communicate something that's been forgotten in time or ..." he paused.

"Or she's trying to warn me of things to come." I shivered.

"It may not be Mary Esty at all. Possibly you picked up someone else's thoughts—Greg's, for instance."

"Before I ever knew him?"

"Thought transference knows no bounds. On the other hand, your dreams may be merely—dreams."

"Even if they come in broad daylight, when I'm wide awake?"

189

"Waking dreams are not unknown." He patted my hand. "Don't worry, Mitti, I don't think you're hallucinating. But you are very sensitive, possibly mediumistic. So were the saints."

"I never thought I had anything in common with them," I laughed, "but you would have had something in common with Mary Esty—both you and Dana. According to my dream, Mary and her mother were versed in ancient medical lore handed down to them from the Old Wives—maybe witches, for that matter. They cured with herbs and rhymes and some of their treatments were astonishingly ahead of their time. For instance, in one dream Mary's mother inoculated an Indian girl with matter from pustules on my—on Mary's hands. You see, I was down with the cowpox and—" I stopped. Dr. Brun had lost his air of detachment and was staring at me.

"It's not possible!" he breathed.

"Of course not! Vaccination hadn't been invented."

"I don't mean that. You just reminded me of a dream I had last night. Perhaps there is something to your theory of a 'thin wall.' I thought I visited a home where the goodwife told me she and her mother had saved some Indians from contracting smallpox by rubbing pus from cowpox into cuts on their arms. I remember being both intrigued and horrified—horrified because the practice sounded like witchcraft. Yet these Indians had remained immune."

"Who—who was this woman?"

"I don't know, but I was Cotton Mather."

It was my turn to stare. "The one who attended the hangings and wrote about the witch trials? He's mentioned in Sewall's *Diary*."

"The same. However, the dream could easily have

190

arisen from my subconscious. You see, I could not call you crazy without pointing a finger at myself. In the course of my theological studies, I became obsessed with John Calvin and Cotton Mather, two of the most brilliant bigots who ever lived. At times it even seemed they were taking me over. Calvin sent Michael Servetus, a Spanish physician and Catholic theologian who dared question the Trinity, to the stake. Cotton Mather, for his part, wrote pamphlets on witchcraft that inflamed the people of Salem. Worst of all, he prevented the reprieve of his fellow divine, George Burroughs.

"Ironically, Mather, years later, provoked the wrath of his contemporaries while making his finest contribution to mankind. Having studied medicine, he became interested in a London physician's paper on smallpox inoculation. During an epidemic in 1721, Mather persuaded Dr. Zabdiel Boylston of Boston to inoculate 241 people. Of these only six died, a remarkable record, especially since they were using the dangerous method of inoculating their patients with smallpox matter, instead of the safer cowpox vaccine Jenner was to 'discover' years later. To people brought up in fear of witchcraft, inoculation seemed perilously close to sorcery. The tables were turned on Cotton Mather. A bomb that fortunately failed to ignite was tossed into his house at the height of the furor.

"How two lives like Calvin's and Mather's could produce such extremes of good and evil was the subject of my master's thesis. Ever since then I've had dreams of Servetus writhing in the flames or George Burroughs dangling at the end of a rope, and I awaken with an excruciating sense of personal guilt. Does that mean I am the reincarnation of Calvin or Mather? Or both? I've no evidence to support that. All my dreams can be traced to what I've read, even the one about vaccination."

Cold tingles were doing a staccato on my skin. "Yet that dream's almost a continuation of mine," I exclaimed. "It's uncanny—you and I knowing each other now and dreaming of past lives in the same chapter of history. Is that how reincarnation works?"

He set down his cup. "According to theory, people who were part of an especially traumatic karma in one era tend to be reincarnated together to work out that same karma at another time. However, they may switch roles. For instance, your father in one incarnation might be your husband, brother, son, or just an acquaintance in the next."

"It could get rather incestuous, couldn't it?"

"Not at all. Reincarnation has nothing to do with blood lines. One is not necessarily reborn into the same family or even the same race. Only the spiritual part of us reincarnates. Incest is purely physical—as is one's sex. A woman in one life may be a man in the next. Jesus said, 'For when they shall rise from the dead, they neither marry, or are given in marriage, but are as the angels which are in heaven.' I think he meant that the soul is universal and has no sex."

"Do you suppose everybody here in Peacehaven today once played a role in the Salem hysteria?" I wondered, overwhelmed by the awesomeness of the thought.

He didn't answer, but sat there pondering, his hands clasped around his knee, staring off into—another time?

"You make that wall seem *paper* thin, Dr. Brun—as if I could reach out and put my hand right through. If that is true and there's anything to the theory of karma, does Peacehaven really have any control over its own destiny?"

"There's always free will," he reminded me.

"True." And at the moment I willed *not* to speak of how the man in the tall hat—William Stoughton—and Greg had become inextricably interwoven in my mind. That would be revealing much too much.

"If reincarnation could be proved," I said after a moment, "it could turn the world around."

"*Ja*," he chuckled, "instead of looking up their ancestors, people would be charting their past lives."

Chapter Fifteen

Charity and Damon arrived unexpectedly after dinner. Rowan had gone back upstairs, Dr. Brun had fallen asleep over a book, and I was trying to learn Winnebago basketry from Dana. Occasionally my glance would stray to Damon's mother, who sat with Cari in the large wingback chair playing the old game about the church and the steeple. It was an enchanting tableau—the old lady leaning forward, her softly waving white hair shimmering beneath the table lamp, while Cari leaned unsteadily against the thin knees. With her golden ringlets, her fawn eyes, and her delicate pink skin, she might have been my bisque doll—why did I have to think of that?

The back door slammed, shattering the moment, and Damon strode in, carrying a bottle of wine and one of brandy. "We're going to celebrate," he announced.

"Celebrate what?"

"Oh, your being here," he replied vaguely.

"I'll get glasses," I said, rising. "Come on into the kitchen and play bartender."

"No, don't go, Mrs. Decorah," Damon said to Dana, who was gathering up her weaving. "This includes you."

She sat down again. "Mitti, I'd prefer some cranberry juice if you have it," she said, casting a warning glance at Mother Carrier.

"Where's Rowan?" Charity asked.

"Sleeping, I hope," I replied. "She's been home with a cold and I want her well enough to go to school tomorrow."

"Oh." She looked disappointed as she set her knitting bag on the floor and sat down near her mother-in-law.

Out in the kitchen I arranged glasses on the tray, got the cranberry juice out of the refrigerator, poured some into a small glass for Cari, and filled two of the wine glasses.

"Come on, Mitti, don't tell me you're going WCTU on me, too," Damon protested.

"I ought to," I said severely. "One is for Dana and one for your mother."

"She won't enjoy being treated like a child."

"But she's very fond of cranberry juice and—isn't it better for her? I mean—" I paused, embarrassed. "Forgive me, she does have a problem, doesn't she?"

"Did Dana tell you that?" He emptied one of the glasses into the sink and proceeded to fill it with wine. "So Dana's been telling tales, has she? Mother staggers at times because of her arthritis. There's no record of alcoholism in our family. Drinkers, yes, but they could handle it. So can Mother a glass of wine."

195

He picked up the tray and brushed past me, leaving me with tears stinging my eyes. As I stood there wiping them, I realized I'd forgotten to carry out the garbage. I picked it up and started for the back door. Voices drifting in from the living room made me pause.

"What is this, son?" I heard Mother Carrier ask.

"Something the doctor ordered," he replied.

"Wine? Oh no, I don't think I'd better, Damon."

"A glass won't hurt, Mother."

I was seething as I deposited the garbage outside, and I gave the back door a vicious swing. Wood closed on wood over the middle finger of my right hand. I reeled into the kitchen, sick with pain. As the others circled about me, Dr. Brun bandaged my finger and Damon gave me a shot for pain. I refused to lie down.

"I'll be all right," I assured them. "Dana, would you put Cari to bed?"

"I hope it isn't serious, Mitti," Mother Carrier said as Dana lifted Cariad off her lap. There was a slight slur in her speech and wine had dribbled on her blue dress. I kissed Cari and gave her a hug.

"Donwanna go to bed," she began to wail.

"It's past bedtime," I said. "Dana will tell you a story."

I sat down giddily on the sofa. The pain-killer was beginning to take effect. Damon brought me a snifter of brandy.

"Here, take this, Mitti," he told me. "It'll be better for you than wine."

I sipped it slowly, feeling the warmth steal through my limbs. He seated himself beside me. "We came up here on business tonight, Mitti," he said, "but if you don't feel up to it, we could postpone it until tomorrow."

Charity looked up from her knitting. "It can't wait too long."

"She's right," he said. "We need to know your answer soon."

A warning bell pinged. What was Damon trying to do? He knew liquor and pain-killers didn't mix. I swirled the brandy in the glass, sniffing it, but left the rest untasted.

"Damon, h-have you s-seen our old home l-lately," his mother remarked irrelevantly, almost hidden in the wingback chair.

"Yes, Mother." His voice was wearily patient. "The front porch is already under water. It won't be standing long."

"I loved that old house. It's l-like me—s-sinking."

I'd never heard her talk like that.

"It was a l-lovely house," she continued. "Wasn't it, son?"

"Yes, Mother," through his teeth. He turned back to us. "She's right. It was one of the fine old places here."

"Remember the clubhouse you built in the maple tree?" she persisted.

"Yes, Mother!" He knocked his pipe impatiently against the ashtray on the end table. "My grandfather was the richest man in town at one time and then the river washed his holdings away. I grew up hating the river, and I mean to prove someday that the Carrier name can't be dragged down by a blind, mindless aberration."

"And I've always loved it," I replied, surprised at his vehemence, "even though it took Gareth. But that wasn't the river's fault."

"You still blame Iris for that, don't you?" Charity's tone was as sharp as her knitting needles.

197

I wasn't going to get into the old argument. "As you say, Damon," I continued, ignoring the interruption, "it's a blind, mindless thing, but human error enters in, too. Forgive me, I must be honest. It seems to me you've done very well. You have the only medical practice in town, a beautiful home; you belong to the country club; you're respected in the community—"

"That's not enough," he retorted, his pipe dangling between his teeth. "The Carriers were leaders in Peacehaven. My grandfather and great-grandfather wanted to build a Utopia here. They were dreamers, but they were practical men, too—honest, hardworking. They chose the low land because it was richer and there was a brisk river traffic. Boats from as far away as New Orleans used to dock at Carrier's landing. Then, bit by bit, it all crumbled away. Was it drink or laziness that wrecked their dreams? No, it was a goddam freak of nature. Yes, I have all those things you mention, Mitti, but I'm still on mortgage hill. My income barely exceeds my expenses. I want latitude to do some really meaningful things, to make the name Carrier a household word again, to develop Peacehaven into the metropolis my grandfather dreamed of." His voice trembled and his eyes flashed with the fire of a zealot. "For years I've struggled to come up with a workable idea and at last I have it. You, Martin," he turned to Dr. Brun, "with your knowledge of archaeology and your worldwide connections, can be of inestimable help when the time comes. But you hold the key to the entire venture, Mitti."

"I? But I'm so new here. I really don't know what I could do."

"Before I go any further, let me say that our committee is prepared to incorporate and issue stock whenever final

198

arrangements are made. In addition to Tyler Bishop, the bank president, and myself, the group includes Caleb Toothaker, Melvin Osburn, Sheriff Good, and others. Naturally, we'll need outside financing and Tyler has arranged for that, too. He's been in touch with a large Chicago syndicate and they're practically committed. I have two alternate proposals to make to you, Mitti—or a possible third. Under any circumstances, you would stand to profit considerably."

"But I have nothing to invest," I said, puzzled. "Aunt Bo left me property, but not a tremendous amount of money. Next year when things are settled, I intend to look for a job."

He laid a sweaty hand on mine. "You don't have to invest a thing, Mitti—not in cash anyway. You'll merely have to sit back and clip coupons."

I laughed uneasily. Where was the catch? Now Damon was on his feet, pacing. "This isn't just a hastily conceived idea. We've been quietly picking up options on a number of properties around here, principally the Hobbs farm.

"We plan to build a combination of resort and residential condominiums on these lands—an entire new city, with homes and schools, a shopping mall and recreation areas, including a country club and a golf course. Where did I put that brandy? Oh, here!" He reached around the wingback chair and picked up the bottle from the lamp table.

"I'll get you a brandy glass," I offered.

"Never mind, this'll do," he said, pouring the liquor into his empty wine glass. Charity's needles, which had stopped, resumed their clicking.

"You know that low part of the Hobbs farm? We'll

199

dredge that out to create an artificial lake. Someday we plan to dig a canal to the river to divert some of that water and reclaim part of the old Peacehaven, but that would be far in the future."

"How are you going to attract people out here?" I wanted to know. "Madison's the closest city of any size and it's beyond convenient commuting distance."

"Are Vail and Aspen dependent on a neighboring metropolis?" he countered. *Condominiums are a fabulous investment."

"But those are ski resorts," I reminded him.

"Granted. We have to have something to attract people out here—something unique—several things in fact. One feature would be the pageant. Some I'm not at liberty to discuss at the moment, but one involves you, Mitti. Therefore, we are offering you the chance to become a major stockholder."

"But I told you, I've no money to invest."

"You have something far more valuable—the cave at the rear of your property. The local legend of a treasure cave is Peacehaven's chief claim to fame at the moment, did you know that? Even more so than our Salem history, although the pageant may change that. Seems some journalist got wind of the cave and included it in a book about lost treasures, like the Lost Dutchman mine and the fabled treasure of Oak Island, so it's not altogether unknown. Now I happen to think it's no more than a myth—what about it, Martin? Aren't you beginning to agree?"

Dr. Brun shook his head wearily. "So far I've found nothing, but I haven't given up. I warn you, however, there's no evidence of Indian burials in Mitti's cave."

"Did you explore it completely?"

"No, but I followed each passage until it narrowed so I could go no farther. Since the rock formations predated the period of Indian occupation in this region, I made no attempt to open them up."

"Frankly, I hope there is no Indian burial cave, because we can capitalize on it when we develop Mitti's cave."

"When you do *what?*" I straightened up. Charity dropped a stitch.

"Depending on what sort of a deal we make with you, of course, Mitti," Damon said, sucking on his pipe. "What we envision is the construction of a gigantic totem pole over the entrance, and a rustic bridge over the crevice that would lead into the two large rooms behind. We'd blast out the stalagmites and stalactites, except a few for atmosphere, and install a lighting system and showcases so we could house a collection of American Indian artifacts. Then, farther back in the cave we could plant skeletons and pottery and Indian jewelry to make it *look* like the treasure cave. If we can ream out the deepest passages, we might let our customers be amateur archaeologists and dig for treasure themselves—for a fee, of course. We'd salt the passages with arrowheads and beads and broken pottery so the lucky ones would get a reward for their labors—good PR, you know. I've read there's a place down south where you can dig for gems at so much an hour. And your Prince Madog story, Martin, would be fabulous publicity—Welsh Indians dug up in Wisconsin!"

"Excuse me," he said, "I am ignorant of such things— would tourist attractions induce people to buy homes here?"

Damon knocked ashes from his pipe into the fireplace. "Not by themselves, no. But the tourist trade would bring in commerce, shops and offices, and the area set aside for light industry would necessitate the construction of homes for workers. In the meantime, the resort area would be developed at one end of the lake with, perhaps, a Playboy-type club. Eventually we'd have the Lake Geneva of western Wisconsin. Then would come the condominiums."

"Now wait a minute, Damon," I objected. "Those are imposing ideas, I'll admit, but they seem terribly 'iffy' to me. Why here? Because of a cave that wouldn't even be authentic?"

"I hardly think a Chicago syndicate would be interested if the project weren't feasible," he said condescendingly.

"But if I were to consent," I ignored the rebuff, "how would you give people access? Would you extend my driveway to the back of the bluff? No, thank you, that's out!"

"That wouldn't be practical," he said. "We'd come in from the other direction where it isn't so precipitous. We've been buying up options on right-of-way acquisitions on properties between the Hobbs farm and the state highway." He stopped pacing and resumed his seat beside me, one hand on my knee. "Now, our plan is to make you one of the principal stockholders or partners in the scheme. You wouldn't have to invest one cent—just your land. Also, we'd like to take an option on Mrs. Decorah's property—that old house is historic and fits in with the pageant. In your case, if you prefer, you could make an outright sale of the land to us and we'd be prepared to take out an option right now. Or you might lease us the land."

"I'd have to give up the Phoenix?"

"Oh no! The land would be divided. If Charity had inherited the property, then we would have devoted the entire parcel to this enterprise, but you can hardly be expected to give up your home. Naturally, Mitti, you needn't make a decision tonight. This is too big a thing to be dealt with lightly." He leaned back and eyed me through the pipe smoke. "Now," dismissing the subject, "how about a game of bridge? Do you play, Dr. Brun?"

"Yes, but wouldn't Monopoly be more appropriate?" he countered quietly.

"I can't play," I said.

"You can't?" Charity's shock was profound. How could anyone get anywhere in Peacehaven if they didn't belong to a bridge club?

"I'm not talking about bridge," I said. "There's no reason to delay my decision. The answer is no—an unqualified no. Go ahead and build your Utopia if you wish, but leave my cave out of it. An ancient Indian burial ground with a fake totem pole over it? That's the sort of thing that makes Indians scalping mad. It's insulting."

My vehemence bewildered him. "Insult! What do you mean? I should think it would flatter the Indians and give them employment, too. We could hire some squaws and braves to stand at the door in costume and sell souvenir totem poles and they could stage their dances."

"Don't you know that totems are sacred to the Indians?"

His contempt was clear. "But those are heathen symbols—the primitive concepts of a savage people. Besides, there are too few Indians to hurt us financially."

"I'm sorry, Damon, but I intend to keep the bluff as it is—a natural preserve."

"I rather think you owe it to us," Charity observed acidly. "If it hadn't been for that Indian woman, Aunt Bo would have left this property to me."

I stiffened. "I can't imagine Aunt Bo succumbing to undue influence at any age. Certainly I never tried to influence her."

Charity jabbed her needle into a new row, but Damon slapped my knee heartily. "Of course, Mitti, we know that! We don't blame you. Now I'm not going to take your answer tonight as final. Think about it. I can understand that the suddenness of this has confused and dismayed you. Besides, you're in no condition to think clearly after that shot I gave you." *Had he banked on that and lost?* "I agree, it does sound bizarre—a totem pole in the back forty—but remember, the cave entrance is a good mile from the Phoenix. You'd hardly know it was there. Think what you'd be doing for Peacehaven! It would revitalize the town, create jobs, give people here a chance at a better life. You could make a real contribution—one Aunt Bo would certainly applaud!"

He was twisting things around so that I would be a first-class heel if I refused.

"Won't you be doing enough, Damon, just to develop a resort area?" I asked.

"We can't do it without the syndicate and they insist on the cave. They say that without that we'd be just another development out in the boondocks. We have to attract people—get our name on the map." A pleading note came into his voice. "There are some of us who think enough of Peacehaven to be willing to go into debt to bring this about. We think you should be willing to do your part."

I swished the brandy around in my glass. "Let's put it this way, Damon," I said. "Right now my answer is negative, but if you can come up with a plan that would have genuine historical and educational value, with minimal disturbance of nature, one that would really benefit people who need it—not the promoters—then and only then would I even consider your proposals. But the totem pole, the fake burial ground, and the amateur archaeology bit—they're all out!"

He spilled some of his brandy in his impatience. "But those things would make the place!" Then he sighed. "You're an incurable romantic, Mitti, but I'm not going to accept a hasty 'no.' After all, how can a woman like you be expected to understand business of this magnitude?"

"And you're an incurable male chauvinist," I shot back. "I wonder why Aunt Bo ever tolerated you. Is Ward in on this?"

He shifted uneasily. "No, he's no visionary—or gambler, either." He consulted his watch. "We'd better be going. I have to be in surgery tomorrow morning and I promised I'd stop by and see Alison on the way."

The old tightening came back into my throat. "She's much too thin. Is she ill, Damon?"

"Oh, just menopausal jitters. Actually, she's strong as a truckhorse. Her ability to heal is fantastic. I excised a mole from her back several years ago. Healed practically overnight."

Dr. Brun cleared his throat and seemed about to say something, but Damon strode past him and reached for the brandy to refill his glass. "One for the road," he was saying, then stopped. "My God, what's happened here?"

The bottle was nearly empty. Mother Carrier's glass thumped down on the carpet.

"Have you disgraced us again, Mother?" he hissed at her.

The old lady lifted her head. "Hello, son," she slurred, flinching as he raised his hand. "I was just following doctor's orders."

Damon slapped her hard on the cheek, leaving three red stripes across the white, crêpe paper skin. She began to cry.

Even Charity winced. "Don't, Damon," she pleaded. "After all, you *did* leave the brandy there."

Dana came swiftly into the room and pushed Damon away. She knelt and put her arms around the old woman, whispering to her and stroking her forehead.

"I think you'd better go, Damon," I said, when I could trust myself to speak. "Unless you apologize to your mother."

"I was merely using shock therapy," he excused himself. "I'm—sorry, Mother." He turned to Dana. "I'm disappointed, Mrs. Decorah. I really thought you were helping her. Now I see she's worse than ever."

A sound like a donkey braying cut short his tirade. The others stood frozen as Rowan crawled into the room, twisting her head this way and that. I had to turn away to hide a smile. She'd improved her act. It was outrageous of her, of course, but it *had* interrupted an awkward moment. Charity fell to her knees beside her.

"Oh, my baby," she moaned. "It's happening again."

Rowan clutched at her aunt's arm. "Stop them! Stop them! They're biting me—pinching me!" She convulsed, gripping her neck and letting her tongue hang out of her mouth. Then she rolled her eyes up at Dana. "Indian woman, why do you torment me?"

Dana went white, her face a tragic mask. I couldn't let this go on any longer. "Okay, Rowan, you've had your audition," I said. "Now get up. You're supposed to be in bed."

She paid no attention, but slithered across the floor toward Dr. Brun, her tongue flicking in and out. "You! You tried to make me sign your black book, but I wouldn't, so now you afflict me, and—" spotting Mother Carrier huddled in the chair, "there she is! She was up in my room just now in the shape of a big red rat!"

"Rowan, stop it!" I grasped her shoulder, but she recoiled and spat at me. "You witch!" she snarled, then held out her arms piteously. "See where she's bitten me!" She palmed a needle out of her pocket and pretended to extract it from her arm. "Look! She sticks needles into me!"

She caught a glimpse of Charity's horrified face and broke up. Giggling, she threw her arms around her aunt, who bewilderedly tried to disengage herself.

"How did I do, Aunt Charity?" Rowan asked. "I know Greg's play practically by heart. I want to do Anne Putnam, but mother won't promise me the part even though she's going to be on the casting committee. You'll tell them, won't you? Tell them I really *can* act?"

Charity was still white and shaken. "Of course, darling," she said. "You terrified me. You're a great little actress." She glared at me. "You should be happy to have such a talented daughter, Mitti—you should encourage her."

207

"I do," I replied, exasperated, "but there's such a thing as nepotism."

"If you'll excuse us," Dana said, her face still slightly pale, "Dr. Brun and I will take Mrs. Carrier over to the other house."

After they had left, I shooed Rowan back to bed and then accompanied the Carriers to their car. The rain had stopped and the ground crunched with light frost.

"I'd like to bring Tyler Bishop up here sometime to explain the financial details to you," Damon said, sliding into the car.

"Don't waste your time," I told him.

He slammed the door and they drove away. The gravel scraped behind me. I whirled around, but it was only Darcy.

"Come on in," I invited her. "You gave me a start."

"I can't stay." The back porch light made her face look more weathered than ever. "Have you seen Jupiter?"

"No, I haven't. Come on in and have a brandy. You look frozen."

She drained the snifter with one gulp, but waved away a second. "Jupiter's been gone since last night. I've been looking all over for him."

"Don't worry, Darcy. That tomcat's probably out courting."

"*It* doesn't court. I've looked everywhere. I just know something's happened to him." She ran her hand through the stubble of her white hair as she leaned against the sink, a red plaid blazer flung over the familiar old faded jeans and pale blue shirt.

"I have only one kitten left," she said. "The last one— unless someone brings me another pregnant cat. I've had all the adult cats neutered."

208

"Your vet bill must be astronomical, Darcy."

"You're right, Mitti. Well, I'll be on my way. If you see Jupiter, call me—even if it's in the middle of the night."

As I was climbing into bed the phone rang. Maybe Darcy had found Jupiter—

"Hel—lo, Submit!" That same whispery voice again. "Too bad about your finger. Does it hurt? Shall we push the pin in deeper? Oh, that *did* hurt, didn't it? Would you like a pin in your navel? We can make you hurt any place we want to. Move away, Sub-mit—move away while you still have time. You witch! You pig! You sow! We hate you—"

Chapter Sixteen

The sun lay birth-bloodied upon the hills when Rowan sat down to breakfast the next morning.

"Are you sure you feel well enough for school?" I asked.

"Yeah," in a low tone. "I won't be coming home early. I'm going to the Patch—oh darn, I forgot! Iris isn't coming in today. Edna will be there, so the gang won't."

Edna Bradbury, the postmaster's wife and town gossip, could preach love and slander her neighbor in one sentence. Still, this morning I could have blessed her.

Rowan stuffed some granola into her mouth, snatched up her books and ran. As I watched the schoolbus swallow her and vanish down the hill, I ached for the parting kiss and hug she used to give me. Now I'd settle for a smile. I sat holding my coffee cup awkwardly in my left hand, the other nearly immobilized by pain. Macduff padded into the kitchen and began to chase his tail, his way of telling me he needed to go out. As I opened the door, Dana stepped in.

"How's Mother Carrier this morning?" I asked.

"Still sleeping." Her face was grim. "I do not understand your cousin's husband."

"I could have cried when he struck her. Of course, she took the brandy herself." I was trying to be fair.

"Yes, after he put the bottle so conveniently by her side. He wants to prove me incompetent to care for her." She reached in her pocket and took out her knife, slipping it out of its battered sheath. "Your finger's swollen. Let me see it."

I winced as she slit the bandage. "This should have been taken off hours ago—it's grown too tight." She pressed the nail gently, almost sending me to the floor. "I thought so. It continues to bleed under the nail and is building up pressure." She went to the stove, picked up the hot teakettle, and poured some water into a cup. Then she laid the blade of her knife across the red hot grates.

"What are you going to do?" I asked apprehensively as I saw the metal grow rosy in the blue flame.

"Don't worry. This isn't going to hurt as much as your finger does right now. Come over here and stand beside me. I want this blade to stay as hot as possible."

I obeyed hesitantly.

"Hold steady!"

I thought of the Indian's reputation for enduring pain. Biting my lower lip, I held still as the metal burned through the nail and then was withdrawn. Dark blood shot out of a tiny triangular hole, bringing unbelievable relief. I hadn't needed to be brave at all.

"This was my English grandmother's," she explained. Her hand trembled as she slipped the knife back into her pocket. "She gave it to me when she died. I almost always carry it."

As I stood over the sink, watching the dark blood ooze from the nail, I saw a shriveled, twisted thing staining the water in the cup dark brown.

"That's Indian medicine," she said, "a root I dug out of a swamp. It will help prevent infection and prepare the bed for a new nail to grow underneath. It will also deaden the pain."

"It's almost gone now."

"That's just because it feels so much better than it did a moment ago."

Dr. Brun arrived as she finished bandaging.

"You're just in time," I said. "Dana's making waffles."

"I came to see how the finger is doing."

"Then you're too late. Surgery is completed and the patient is in the recovery room." With the pain gone I was ready for anything.

"All right," I said after Dr. Brun had cleared his throat several times. "What's up? Suppose somebody starts talking."

He turned to Dana, but she remained silent.

"Then I tell you—it's about Mrs. Proctor," he said. "I've been observing her for some time now. Her deterioration has been rapid. I know it is not my business, but I'm wondering if there was a pathology report on that mole Dr. Carrier excised."

"You suspect—cancer?" I faltered, the syrup turning bitter in my mouth.

"I merely raise the question. Surely Dr. Carrier had the specimen analyzed, although," he sighed, "it is a sad fact that too many physicians neglect this. In view of the tremendous weight loss she has suffered this last year—well, Mr. Proctor is your cousin. You might ask him about it."

Syrup cascaded over Dana's waffle and plate and onto the table as she sat transfixed. I took the pitcher from her. She seemed unaware of what was going on.

"What's wrong, Dana?" Dr. Brun asked.

"The wart on her finger," she said slowly. "I never thought."

He shook his head. "I doubt that that was related. Besides, it was Dr. Carrier who excised it. You merely made it atrophy."

"But I should have warned her first, because I remember she once said something about his having removed a mole. I suppose I just assumed that a pathology was done."

"And it probably was," he soothed her.

"You're worried about melanoma, aren't you?"

"You know about that?" He turned to me, surprised.

"Clergymen's daughters learn a lot of things," I replied, and then the impact of it hit me. "Oh, dear God!"

He touched my hand. "We don't know anything of the sort. Surely Dr. Carrier took the precaution."

Dana sat stirring her coffee, her gaze drawn inward. "No, he didn't. I've been seeing it in her face all along and I didn't recognize it. I'm as guilty as he is."

"No, Dana," he admonished her, "we must not bury her yet."

"I won't be here to bury her," she said from a distance.

I didn't know what she meant, but I didn't like it, and there was no asking once she had shut the door. I shivered.

"Now, you have something to tell us?" Dr. Brun said to her.

She started, as though out of a dream. "Oh—yes." Her eyes darted to one side. "You're going to be very angry with me, Doctor. I have made much work and trouble for you. We Indians regard certain things as sacred and we do everything in our power to protect them. I had to be sure about you, Mitti. I've been watching you, analyzing you ever since you came here—"

"I know," I grinned.

"Forgive me. I have been, perhaps, rude. Last night, as I was coming down the stairs I overheard you and Dr. Carrier talking about the cave. Now I know what's in your heart and I can speak. Your aunt worried about what Charity and Damon would do with this land if they were to inherit it But if she left it to Ward, or even to them jointly, there would always be hatred between brother and sister. So when your husband was killed, she knew what she would do.

"Ward didn't need this property, but the Carriers did. They've always lived beyond their means. I'm sure Tyler Bishop and the bank virtually own them. You're going to need help, Mitti. Dr. Carrier is determined and desperate, and his wife is equally strong-willed. They'll erode you, bit by bit—like the river he hates—until they get what they want."

She paused and for a moment there was no sound in the kitchen except for the intrusive humming of the electric clock.

"Why do you apologize, my friend?" Dr. Brun asked Dana. "These problems are no fault of yours."

"I'm only coming to my confession," she said. "I haven't been fair with you. I've let you search one cave after another, while all the time I've known—if you will be patient with me, I will tell you . . ."

Within the hour the three of us were splashing our way through heaps of fallen leaves toward the cave. Above, the trees were resplendent with golds and reds and russets. But this was a fickle and fleeting beauty—one last glorious burst of fireworks and the trees would stand denuded and trembling.

Dr. Brun came prepared to climb the Matterhorn. He had changed into high laced boots, knickerbocker *Hosen*, windbreaker and heavy gloves. An *Alpenhut* decorated with a red feather and an edelweiss pin perched jauntily on top of his white hair. A camera and rucksack and a coil of rope were slung over his shoulders, a lantern and survival kit hung from his belt, and he carried pitons and a pickaxe in his arms. Every now and then I had to scrape off the leaves that stuck to his spiked boots. Dana backpacked the lunch and carried an armload of tools as well. Because of my finger they had been reluctant to let me accompany them, but a broken arm couldn't have kept me away after Dana told her story:

Her father, Maheenuk, or Two-Knives in English, had taken the amulet from my cave, but from a lower level, where he had found the remains of an unknown people. His maternal grandfather had later identified some of the artifacts as being typical of his tribe, but much older.

"Then these Indians were Nuada," I said, "not Mandan."

"We call ourselves Nuada," she replied. "The white man named us Mandan."

The missing piece in the puzzle slipped into place.

215

Subconsciously I must have known all along that this was the way it would be. Dana's father had stopped up the opening to the lower level of the cave with rocks and rubble after carefully replacing the jewelry, baskets, and pottery he'd taken out to show the old man.

In spite of his load, Dr. Brun reached the entrance to the cave first and had dumped his equipment on the ground before we arrived. He pointed to a broad wooden plank spanning the drop-off between the opening and the chambers beyond.

"I must be getting forgetful," he scolded himself. "I didn't intend to leave that plank there."

"I've been here since, and you had put it away," Dana assured him. "And I'm positive I hid it in the bushes when I left. We don't want children getting lost or hurt in there."

"Perhaps Damon and his group have been snooping around," I suggested.

"Then you must be all the more careful, Mitti," she warned.

After driving in the pitons, Dr. Brun rappelled down the sheer sides of the crevice, fastened the rope, and then guided Dana down. The far wall was undercut so that once they had gone a few feet they completely disappeared. I wasn't particularly entranced with my role of sentry. I listened wistfully to the sound of Dr. Brun's pickaxe striking against rock in the black void until the muffled echo of their voices became nearly inaudible. Then I seated myself on a rock just outside the cave mouth and got out my sketchbook and pencils. Across a deep cleft lay Bishop's Bluff, like a gigantic thunderbird sunning itself beneath the blazing blue sky. Scarlet and gold and russet filagrees were interspersed with occasional hot pinks against the dark black-green of ever-greens.

A flock of geese came honking out of the north, veered from its course to swing over my head, then circled back and resumed its southward migration. Gray fox squirrels leaped from tree to tree, pausing every once in awhile to nibble acorns and butternuts. I began blocking out a landscape, but my finger was too painful and I soon put my sketchbook aside.

Even though the sun was warm, there was a sharp chill in the wind, so, risking court martial, I abandoned my sentry post temporarily and moved into the shelter of the cave. I crossed the plank, slipped through a narrow opening, and stepped into the large chamber beyond. Jagged stalagmites rose to meet the stalactites hanging from the vaulted ceiling overhead. The beam of my flashlight bounced off the rock formations, casting shadows on the walls that resembled witches and shocks of corn reflected in a pond. A lone bat circled my head, making weird, high-pitched squeaks, then reported back to base somewhere in the hidden reaches of the cavern.

This was only the antechamber of the cave. As children, Gareth and Ward and I had penetrated much farther. The chamber beyond, I remembered, was even more vast. We had called it the "theater" because the floor at the rear was raised like a stage. Beyond that a spiral-shaped room reamed out by some primeval whirlpool led to a confluence of passages into which we had never dared venture. Someone had cleared away the pillars in the center of the first chamber to provide a broad aisle leading to the next room. Their remains lay on either side in great, disorderly heaps—works of nature that had taken aeons to form and moments to destroy.

Here and there water dripped from the ceiling as the cavern patiently set about forming new stalactites. Although there was no wind here I still felt a chill. My light routed the shadows behind the formations as I pressed forward. Something whisked by me. I stopped, holding my breath. Only the drip-drip of water and faint scuttlings in the gloom. Mice, bats, and my imagination! As I flashed my light over a rippled, varicolored limestone pillar, I became aware of a shadow that stood its ground in the murk. I moved toward the open area, turning my light this way and that, pretending I hadn't seen. As the beam fell on the column again the figure retreated behind it. I spun around and headed back toward the entrance, but it kept up with me, moving silently from pillar to pillar, pressing so close I lost my bearings and unwittingly turned toward the narrow aperture leading to the chamber beyond. In my confusion and terror I mistook it for the mouth of the cave and made a dash for it. Too late I saw my error. I whipped around in time to see someone standing behind me with arm raised. My flashlight shattered on the floor and I plunged through darkness into . . .

. . . daylight. What were those men doing back of Granny Peabody's house? And she only three days dead! One of them was hoisting something on a rope slung over a heavy tree branch. Why, they were hanging Granny's old black bitch! By law sheep killers must be hanged, but Tibby was no sheep killer. She was gagging, her tongue lolling out of her mouth, her eyes bulging white, her hind paws pawing at the air. There had been no snap to break her neck and she would swing a long time afore dying.

"What do ye?" I cried and shoved in between the men to lift up the suffering animal and prevent her from strangling.

"Leave off, woman," one of the men growled.

"But why?" Blood from a gash in her neck was trickling down my mantle. "Poor old Tibby never killed a sheep."

"Nay, worse!" The rope slackened as the man holding it gave a roar and clapped one hand to his buttocks. "She bit me! The bitch bit me, I'll swear she did!"

"How could she when I've been holding her?" I scoffed.

"Because she was Granny's familiar, given her by the Devil hisself."

"Tibby? A devil dog? Granny Peabody were no witch, only a poor, lonely old woman who pleasured in the company of a dog," I lashed out. This Roger Toothaker was a self-styled leech and Cunning Man, with neither the education of a physician nor the wit of the other. He gloried in bloodletting and applying some of the more repulsive remedies of the Cunning Man. "Belike your wenching has sent the pox to your brain!" I added.

He flushed at the insult, but his tongue rattled on. "Granny afflicted Ezekiel Conant with the boils, so Meg and I stopped up his urine in an earthen pot and baked it. Blowed up the oven, but Granny was dead the next morning—sure proof she'd set a spell on Ezekiel."

"If such a thing were possible, then you and your daughter 'ud be murderers. Have you thought about that, Roger Toothaker? Dare you accuse poor Granny o' bein' a witch when you use remedies out o' the Black Book itself? Bray Wilkins," I addressed an older man standing to one side, "surely you don't believe this nonsense. Make them let her down!" He backed away. "She's sore hurt and she was ever a good doggie. I'll warrant none o' ye thought to feed this poor beast after its mistress died."

No one stirred, but then a deep voice boomed from the outer edge of the circle. "Aye, let the animal down! Do ye explain yourselves!" A short, square-set, powerfully built man, his dark face suffused with anger, came forward. 'Twas George Burroughs, the parson of Salem Village, though not for long, I feared, if the Putnams had anything to say about it. 'Twas rumored he'd antagonized them and some other members of the church with his heretical ideas. Worse, he was known to have a sense of humor, an unseemly trait in a man o' the cloth. To me he seemed more Christian than most of his ilk. "If God's eye is on the sparrow," he was saying with pastoral dignity, "how much more is it on a faithful dog?"

Toothaker let the rope go so that the full weight of the animal descended upon me. I laid her down gently, removed the rope from her neck and began to tend to her wounds. Tibby lifted her head feebly and licked my hand. Now the men were all talking at once. Granny's spirit, they claimed, had entered the dog's body! Else how could such a weak old bitch kill George Corwin's pit bull that never lost a fight? I looked up in startled surprise. Just outside the circle lay the huge dog, its throat torn out.

"Attacked my dog without warning," Corwin whined, "my dog wot was trained for the London bear pits before I bought him and brung him here."

" 'Tis more likely you baited them into a fight," Burroughs accused him. "I've seen you do it before, George Corwin, and I trow there were wagers amongst all of ye, though that were a sin. 'Twas unseemly pride you took in your dog and many a good beast died from his fangs. Tell the truth now, man, lest your immortal soul be damned."

Corwin reddened and averted his eyes. "This hound o' hell here came runnin' across the road wi' five black imps followin' her and they all vanished into the foundation o' the house. Ripper, here, he fair went mad."

"Forsooth, you saw a chance for a fight and summoned a crowd," Burroughs said severely.

"Not a crowd, Reverend—witnesses, ye might say. So then I let Ripper go in after her—he growling all the time and his hair on end like he seed a ghost."

"You mean you sicced him on her," the pastor corrected him.

The others stirred uneasily.

" 'Tis true, isn't it?" he asked.

Samuel Braybrook hunched his shoulders defiantly. " 'Tisn't often one gets to see a dogfight."

" 'Twere no fight," Corwin continued. "The bitch ran into the hole and Ripper after her, but while he was squeezin' through she caught him by the throat. E'en then, only the old Nick himself coulda given that old bitch the strength to tear out my dog's throat."

"Or puppies!" I burst out. "Look at her tits. I'll warrant she has pups under the house and those are the imps you saw."

Burroughs was on his knees by the hole and now he brought out a squirming black pup. Four others followed. They ran to Tibby and despite her wounds began to nurse.

"Pups! Well, I'll be switched!" Samuel Braybrook began to guffaw. Soon all the rest were laughing except Corwin, who muttered a curse, slung his dead beast over his shoulder and strode away.

He'd no sooner left than a well-dressed man carrying a tiny girl no older than three, and accompanied by a thin, sour-faced woman wearing a gray mantle with a silken hood and a cap of Colbertine lace joined the group.

"Have ye been about stirring up more trouble, Reverend

Burroughs?" Mistress Ann Putnam confronted him.

"Nay, mistress," I defended him. "He spared us a deal o' pudder."

The child was staring at me with big blue eyes, a fragile thing, like a tiny china doll.

"Is this the baby Anne?" I asked. "What a bonny lass!" The child held her arms out to me and I would have taken her in mine, but her father pulled her back roughly.

"We'll have naught o' you, Goody Esty," Thomas Putnam growled, "not when your menfolk steal our rightful lands."

"Lands awarded us by the court," I replied quietly. The little girl leaned toward me again, her tiny hands reaching out for the buckle on my cloak. Her mother slapped her hands. "Have naught to do with her, Anne. 'Tis said her mother was a witch."

The child seemed to understand and began to shriek with terror.

"Let us pass," they bade me, but they weren't the Putnams, they were Damon and Charity, while the shrieking child was Rowan—and they were twisting and turning and fragmenting into nothing and I was floating up out of daylight into . . .

. . . darkness again and a realization of throbbing in my head. How long I'd been lying on the cave floor I didn't know. Gradually my mind began to sort things out. I raised my hand to my head and felt a warm, sticky liquid matting my hair. Slowly my eyes focused enough to make out the thin veil of light seeping into the chamber from the entrance. My assailant must have fled—I hoped. Painfully I began inching my way over the jagged floor. My hand closed over my broken flashlight—for a weapon if I should need it. Then something cut off the faint light from the entrance. Cautious footsteps and a swift pattering! I flattened myself to the floor and waited, my heart banging against the hard stone. But a warm tongue swiped my forehead, then yips and whines and excited barks as needle-like puppy teeth tugged at my arm. Macduff! And now strong arms were lifting me.

"Mitti! My God, what's happened to you?" Greg touched my hair. "You're bleeding!"

"Oh, Greg, thank God! I thought he'd come back and was going to kill me."

"Who was it?"

"I don't know. I just know someone attacked me. How did you and Macduff find me?"

"I dropped by your house. Darcy was outside looking for her cat."

"Hasn't she found Jupiter yet? Poor Darcy!"

"She said she'd seen you and Dr. Brun and Dana going off in this direction, looking as if you were about to make an assault on Mt. Everest. I told Macduff to make like a bloodhound. As you see, he shows great promise, although I wasn't sure if he was after a rabbit or you. Where are the others?"

I couldn't answer for shaking and laughing and crying all at the same time. His arms tightened around me and I could feel his heart beating against my cheek. It seemed so natural just to lean into him, letting my body melt into his. His lips brushed my neck, then followed hungrily up the curve of my chin until they found my mouth. My bruises and my injured finger were forgotten. Desire flamed within me, pleasure rippling up my spine and into my throat. After Owen I hadn't thought it possible ever to feel like this again, but a new love had been born in me here in the darkness—new? No, this had happened before. I ran my fingers over his face as though it were braille—I had known these lips, the long narrow nose, the deep-set eyes, slightly curved brows, the cleft in his chin and the hair waving softly over his collar . . .

His hand tugged at a hairpin, unloosing the coil at the back of my head and the whole mass came cascading down around my shoulders. *"Ah, Mary, I love thy hair—'tis silken soft."*

"Aye, Will, I love thee—all of thee."

"Will!" He pushed me away. "Why did you call me that?"

"I don't know," I murmured fuzzily. "You called me Mary."

"I did what?" He was incredulous. "That was a nasty blow you had, Mitti."

I tensed. "I'm *not* wandering in the head, if that's what you're thinking. What is it about you, Greg? When I'm with you I feel we're two other people and it terrifies me."

"You're imagining things, Mitti. Anyone would after a blow like that. We'd better call the sheriff."

I sat up. "No!"

"Why not?" My vehemence surprised him.

"Because it would—" I stopped. "I—I don't like police investigations," I said, letting myself lean against him again.

"All right," he whispered, running his lips over my nose, "but we'll have to have Damon check you out."

"Not Damon—Dr. Brun." I was getting sleepy. "Besides, I'm feeling fine now—just fine."

"Don't go to sleep on me, Mitti! You mustn't!" His voice was sharp with concern.

"Don't worry! I wouldn't miss this for the world."

"Nor I," he breathed into my neck. "Oh, Mitti, ever since you came here I've been wanting to—what's that?"

He broke off abruptly as a distant ring of metal on stone reverberated through the rock. "Where's it coming from? Another level? Is that where Dr. Brun and Dana are?"

"Y-yes," I faltered.

"Then this is—*the* cave?"

How could I answer without betraying Dana? "I don't know," I said. "We came out here today because of a—a deal Damon proposed last night. That's why I don't want him to look at my head. I don't want anyone to know about this."

Reporters are lousy lovers. "But, Mitti, this is terrific! If this *is* the cave, it's a scoop! A worldwide scoop! I'll bet the *National Geographic* will want to do a big spread on this!"

"Oh, you're jumping to conclusions, Greg," I protested. "You mustn't . . ."

"It's all right, Mitti. We can trust him."

Dana stood beside us, her lantern enveloping us in its circle of light. Immediately she was on her knees beside me. "You've been hurt! What happened?"

"It's not a deep cut," she said, examining it while I was explaining. "Must have been a glancing blow, but you're going to have a terrific headache. Did you see anyone leaving the cave, Greg?"

"No, I must've been just too late. Is it true—is this *the* cave?"

"Yes, but I beg you to keep our secret for the time being. No one must know about it—particularly Dr. Carrier."

"You ask a lot of a newspaperman," he sighed. "One

condition though when you're ready—I get first crack at the story!"

"Word of honor."

"What did you find down there?" My curiosity was an excellent analgesic.

"Bones—pottery—bits of baskets—and this." She held up a tiny blue glass bead. "The Mandans love the blue glass trade beads brought over by the early settlers. This is similar, but cruder. If it should match up with the beads the Welsh used to make on the Isle of Lundy, then we'd have a real clue. But it's going to take time to do a scientific study. A part of the roof has caved in—"

"Weren't you ever down there before?" I asked.

"No, my father wouldn't take me into the lower chambers. He said they were too sacred to be seen by one whose hair had not grayed," she explained. As she lifted her lantern she noticed the toppled formations for the first time.

"Someone's been working here!" she hissed.

"Damon?" I suggested.

"I think we should notify the sheriff—or Jim Willard," Greg said. "This would, after all, constitute trespass."

"No, you mustn't!" Dana was emphatic. "It's not just Damon's project—it's something else—I don't know what, but I feel it. I don't like intruders here," she added, swinging her lantern around and making the witches and corn shocks sway in a macabre dance. Macduff was sniffing out a scent that led him toward the inner chamber. "This is—a holy place to me," she continued. We followed her to a remote corner of the cave, where her light flickered over a mortared wall.

"My father is seated behind that," she said in a low voice. The hair on my neck stood on end. "It was his last request, so that his spirit might always watch over this cave."

She stopped as eerie howls echoed from deep within. I held tight to Greg's hand as we followed the sounds to the next chamber. Macduff was pawing and growling at something we couldn't make out in the dim light. As Dana brought her lantern forward we gasped in horror.

Blood was splashed on the walls and drying pools lay on the floor of the natural stage. Tufts of animal hair—red, white and black—were scattered here and there on the ground, and in the middle of the mess lay Jupiter's striped, tailless, mutilated body.

Chapter Seventeen

"Lo! Yonder comes the Black Man wi' his demons o' hell! There be Indians and Goody Nurse and Goody Esty and the Proctors and—Goody Corey and Goody Bishop all dancing around! Don't you see them? There, Goodman Wilkins! Your eyes be none too sharp. They're marchin' round the meetin' house yellin' to get in! Hold the door! Guard the windows! Aiyee! the Black Man's got me—he's pinching me—don't, please don't! God in Heaven help me! Draw your sword, Mr. Hutchinson! Run 'im through! Oh, there's the whole hellish bunch at the windows. Aim low, Deacon Ingersoll! Forty devils and a big black woman from Stonington! Fire! Fire! Ah, see the blood all over the ground—devils' blood! They're running away! Someone help Mercy here—she's taken bad! Abigail! What ails ye?"

"Goody Esty's choking me. She bit me, too. I'm hungry.

228

I'm going to the parsonage for supper. Picking up her cloak and walking out . . ."

"Not that way, dummy!" Rowan, who had delivered the first speech from memory, now turned on Jessica Willard in disgust. "You don't read the directions out loud!"

Rowan had won the coveted part of Anne Putnam, thanks to Charity's support. Secretly I was gratified. Not just because she was my daughter, but a strong role needs a strong actress, and it was daily more and more apparent that Rowan had inherited Owen's talent. If I could just check that artistic temperament! "That's all right, Jessica," I soothed the other girl, "you're doing fine. Rowan has had the script for weeks and this is your first crack at it. Just remember not to read the words in parentheses. Those are things you're supposed to *do*, not *say*. As for you, Rowan, you must really *see* those spectral Indians and witches outside the meeting house. Anne wasn't just putting on an act—she *believed* it. That's why she could convince her elders.

"Now Abigail Williams was just the opposite," I continued. "To her it was all a game. It was fun to be the center of attention and to have adults defer to her, but she couldn't sustain her act. When she got hungry she said to heck with it and went home."

"I don't exactly understand what was happening here, Mrs. Llewellyn," Jessica confessed. "You mean the demons and Indians were just imaginary?"

"Of course, silly!" Rowan laughed.

I frowned at her. "It's my fault, Jessica," I said. "I should have explained. In this scene the people have just poured into the meeting house from Ingersoll's ordinary—we'd call it a tavern. The girls are hallucinating

229

and screaming that Parson Burroughs and his demons are attacking Salem Village. Their elders feel they can better defend themselves from the forces of hell, which they imagine they see, by barricading themselves in the meeting house. This is one of the few funny scenes in the pageant and we'll play it for comic relief."

Cissie Osburn was still sprawled on the floor. "Don't I have any lines here?" she whined.

"Not in this scene." Her constant complaining annoyed me. "Marcy Lewis is the Putnam's servant girl and—"

"I don't want to be a servant," she pouted.

"But it's one of the best parts." I tried to be patient. "You can emote to your heart's content. Just keep convulsing—you'll be noticed, don't worry. You have lines in other scenes. All right, we'll take it from your speech again, Rowan."

A lot had happened in two weeks. Tryouts had been held for the girls' roles and some of the adult leads, and we were now rehearsing in the basement of the church on Saturday and Sunday afternoons as well as some days after school. I had become much more involved than I'd intended. From scenery designer I had progressed to co-director, actress, and casting director. In the last capacity I found myself practically alone. Except for assigning the roles of Anne Putnam and Mary Esty to Rowan and me (Greg had insisted on the latter), the casting committee had hardly functioned.

"Oh, Mitti, you've had so much more stage experience!" they insisted, and I rather enjoyed doing the casting, although I knew I'd be held accountable for any mistakes. It's not easy to build a production with amateurs; so I was guilty of type casting. It was only natural to choose Iris Faulkner for the role of Dorcas Hoar and Charity and Damon as the senior Ann Putnam and her irascible husband, Thomas. My dreams had dictated those choices, as they had Greg for William Stoughton. At first, some of them objected to their unsympathetic roles, but I reminded them that audiences remember the villains better than the heroes. Lucian also helped by consenting to play the austere Rev. Samuel Parris, in whose parsonage the trouble started, and Lucy would play his daughter Betty.

Among the adult parts, I assigned the roles of Martha and Giles Corey to Darcy and Marion Zagrodnik. Darcy was a Corey herself, and, like Martha, the dominant partner in her marriage. Nevertheless, I had begun to appreciate a quiet strength in Marion. He'd been polishing brasses in their living room the day Greg and I reluctantly brought the news about Jupiter. Keeping the truth from Darcy would have been the greater disservice, as we knew she would only continue her futile search. Marion answered the door, a tall, bony man with curly gray hair and long, veined, ring-adorned hands sticking out of billowing sleeves. He had taken the news quietly, then called Darcy. For the first time I realized that Darcy leaned on him as much as he did on her.

The part of Sarah Bibber, one of the most vindictive of the Salem accusers, had gone to Elspeth Osburn. Jim Willard, Jessica's father, was to portray another Willard—John, the constable who refused to arrest his neighbors and was therefore accused of witchcraft himself. Irv Good was a natural for Sheriff George Corwin, who not only carried out the arrests, but confiscated his prisoners' goods and left their children to beg in the streets.

Up to this point the casting committee went along with my recommendations, but they balked when I suggested that Rhoda and Darrell Jackson play Tituba, the Parrises' slave, and her husband, John Indian.

"What? Such prominent roles to outsiders?" someone objected.

"Then Lucian, Lucy, Greg, Rowan and I will all have to resign," I countered. "We're outsiders, too."

They had squirmed, not wanting to give their real reason, but Elspeth finally summed it up: "Well, not as outside as the Jacksons."

I had anticipated this by calling on the Jacksons and auditioning them privately. Rhoda read her part brilliantly and Darrell, with some coaching, would shape up. After some argument, reinforced by Greg, I won my point.

"Abigail, what ails ye?" Rowan was cueing Jessica again.

"Goody—Esty's—choking—me," Jessica read in a monotone. "See—where—she—bit—me—I'm—hungry—I'm—going—back—to—the — parsonage—for—supper." She stood there uncertainly.

"Jessica," I said as gently as possible, "even though you're not supposed to read the directions aloud, you are supposed to follow them. Let's pretend your cloak is lying on that table over there. Go and pick it up. That's the girl—now, just march off as if nothing was happening. Okay, Cissie, this is where you babble gibberish. You're all going to be doing a lot of ad libbing, girls. Only watch your language—no modern slang!"

They gathered around me as I talked. In addition to Rowan, Jessica, and Cissie, there were Linda Proctor, Lucy, Debby Cloyce, and Carol Redd. Carol's younger sister Nancy had come just to watch, but she was so cute and pert with her turned-up nose and fair hair that I promptly assigned her the role of five-year-old Dorcas Good, the youngest of the witches. Nancy was two years older, but she was small for her age. She raised her hand now.

"Yes, Nancy?" I asked.

"Did you know there's a really, truly witch here?"

The other girls shifted uneasily. "She's talking about Ruby Hobbs," Carol explained. "Kids like to go there on Halloween and throw mud at her windows and call her names."

"I bet you wouldn't dare," Cissie put in.

"I would so," Carol retorted.

"Me, too," Nancy echoed her sister.

"We could tip over her outhouse," Debby suggested.

"With her in it," Cissie added.

"Now wait a minute!" I interrupted. "I hope you don't mean that. Ruby's no witch. She's just a poor, lonely old woman."

"She's not poor," Cissie contradicted me. "They say her brother buried money in the barn and his ghost guards it."

"My dad thinks that's baloney," Jessica scoffed.

"Well, anyway, she's dirty and she's crazy," Cissie retorted. "It's scary over there. Last year Junior and I smashed pumpkins all over her porch and you know what? She came after us with a hatchet."

"I'll bet your parents didn't like your doing that," I said.

She dismissed this summarily. "They don't care. They say she's crazy, too. She never gave us treats, so she deserved it."

"Yeah," breathed Nancy, impressed by Cissie's bravery.

"Well, I'll have treats for you that night," I promised them, "so I hope you won't bother Ruby. She's too poor to buy candy."

"I don't care what Jessie's father says, my folks think she has lots of money stashed away," Debby Cloyce insisted.

"Yeah, she's an old miser," Cissie chimed in. "My mother says she must have valuable antiques. Mom's just waiting for the old bag to die so she can get some of those things on auction."

"Believe me, there's nothing of real value there," I told them. "I've been over there and—"

"You have?" in unison. "Weren't you scared?" "What's it like?" "Was it spooky?" The questions were coming too fast to be answered. Only Rowan stayed aloof, sitting cross-legged on the floor, gazing up at me with an almost hypnotic gleam in her eyes.

"Iris says Ruby can put a spell on you if you get close enough," Lucy said.

"And she can curse you, too," Rowan added deliberately, letting the words sink in. She didn't mean Ruby.

Carol rocked forward on her haunches. "Pa rents her fields," she said importantly. "One day when he was disking, she came up alongside his tractor and it konked out. Wouldn't run for half a day, but he never found anything wrong with it."

Nancy shivered and crossed her arms across her flat chest. "This year she wanted Pa to pay her more rent for her fields. When he wouldn't she said he'd be sorry. The next morning seven of our chickens were dead."

"Aw, a fox did that," Carol said scornfully.

Nancy shook her head. "Uh—uh, Pa didn't find any tracks."

"He did so."

"Did not!"

"My parents say curses can't hurt anyone," Linda observed.

"Can too!"

"Mother goes to Ruby's farm every fall to buy apples," Linda remembered, "but they weren't any good this year, they were full of worms so Mom didn't buy any."

"I'd hate to be in your mother's place," Cissie said. "Ruby's liable to make something bad happen to her."

"If Ruby should die, would my father have to preach her funeral?"

"I know one thing—if my parents have to embalm her, they'd better drive a stake through her heart," Cissie declared.

"That's *quite* enough!" I lashed out. "Do you girls realize what you've been doing? You've been acting exactly like those Salem girls did three hundred years ago. They sent twenty innocent men and women to their deaths. Are you starting in, too?"

They squirmed uneasily—all except Nancy, who was too little to catch the analogy. I would have continued the scolding, but Alison walked in.

"Okay, girls," I dropped the subject, "take it from page forty-eight. Mrs. Proctor is playing Rebecca Nurse, who was old and deaf and ill—and a very religious woman, but they hanged her anyway."

"Mrs. Proctor doesn't look that old," Jessica objected.

"Somehow that didn't come out quite right," Alison made a wry face.

"Girls," I broke in hastily, "just make up your lines as

you go along. I want you to get used to improvising. You lead off, Rowan . . ."

She immediately pitched forward on her face, shrieking, "Up there! Look up there! 'Tis Goody Nurse on that beam with a little yellow bird sucking her finger . . ."

Jessica's dubious compliment had been apt. Even in her softly cut, white jersey dress, Alison did look only a little less old and tired than Rebecca Nurse, and the lines had deepened in her fine skin. I wondered at my wisdom in assigning her the part, but she had been so anxious to do it. Where was Cissie? We needed her for this scene. I was walking toward the kitchen when genuine screams coming from the auditorium stopped me. Linda came running wildly toward me as I dashed onstage. The other girls were watching Alison in horror as great gobbets of blood gushed from her lips and down her white dress.

Chapter Eighteen

Cloyce's Market, Peacehaven's only food store, was a missing link between the old-fashioned grocery and the supermarket. Things could still be bought from bins, and the meat was cut to order. The store also served as a women's gossip exchange. Three generations of Cloyces alternated shifts. They all had high, canted foreheads, grosbeak noses, and disappearing chins; although these characteristics were watered down in Debby, the youngest member of the family. I generally left my car in Cloyce's parking lot and after rehearsal Debby and I would walk back to the store together.

The church and Cloyce's were at opposite ends of Essex Street, the main thoroughfare, along which was clustered what was left of the commercial section. I enjoyed the walk. I had spent too much time up at the Phoenix and it was fun now to renew my acquaintance with the town itself. Essex Street, named for Salem's county, was little altered. Ownership had changed in some cases, as had the nature of many of the businesses, but the newness was only cosmetic. Most of the old buildings were still there, their bricks grimed and darkened with age.

The others generally accompanied us only as far as the Patch, where the loudspeaker was a modern Pied Piper blaring rock music out into the street. Iris was usually at the door to greet the girls, her yellow eyes daring me to protest. I tried to forestall this by inviting the girls up to the Phoenix for pizza, but so far they had been unwilling to break their routine—for an obvious reason. Peacehaven was peculiarly devoid of boys their age. Junior Osburn must have been cock o' the walk while he was alive. Now only Jonah Good remained, and he was no better than a doorstop, sitting there for hours with a simpering grin until his father would come striding in, yank him roughly to his feet, and send him off on some errand. Iris, seeing the girls' need, had partitioned off half the floor space to create the semblance of a discothèque, and placed ads in the newspapers in nearby towns, thus attracting boys from there—and therein lay the chief attraction of the place.

Underneath the orange and white paint of the Clark station on the corner of the next block were the recognizable lines of the old Wadhams' filling station pagoda. The red brick edifice beyond housed the editorial office of the Peacehaven *Puritan* and Greg's apartment. The old linotypes stood abandoned in a back room, as the printing had long been contracted out to an offset press in Richland Center. I resisted the temptation to stop in, knowing the whole town would talk. There had been no repetition of the incident in the cave; Greg's visits now were pointedly concerned with the pageant. I argued with myself that it was just as well. *I* wasn't ready to commit myself either and Rowan's evident hostility toward him both troubled and annoyed me. Did she expect me to remain a widow forever?

Unlike other places, Peacehaven had kept up the old custom of having trick or treat on Halloween after dark, so we had rehearsal Saturday as usual. When Debby and I entered Cloyce's late that afternoon the store was filled with women buying what was left of Halloween candy. They descended on me instantly.

"How's Alison?" Gladys got the first question in.

It was a week since Alison had returned from the Madison hospital where she'd been put on a program of immunotherapy. Dana had mounted guard over her—to limit the visits of those who came bearing cakes and casseroles and curiosity—so I found myself in the role of unofficial press secretary.

"She's weak but improving," I said as I secured a cart for myself.

"What's that she has—melancholia?" Aunt Jenny asked.

"No—melanoma." I pushed the cart toward the baking section. Andy Cloyce had looked up from his cash register and his brother Henry was leaning over the meat counter.

"Spread to the lungs, I heard," the old woman clucked her tongue. "Can't get used to all these new-fangled diseases. In my day if a person bled from the mouth they had galloping consumption and that was it. I wish they'd stop inventing new diseases."

"It's malignant, isn't it?" That from Muriel Toothaker.

239

"I'm afraid so."

"What are her chances?"

"It's too early to tell. She could go into remission." I tried to sound encouraging.

"I must lend Alison a book I've just read," Gladys remarked. "It's about the Primal Scream—you know, the trauma we suffer at birth. Gives us all sorts of complexes and diseases, so if we can just—"

"Fiddlesticks, Glad!" Aunt Jenny interrupted. "I was the one that was hurtin' when you were born."

"Oh no, it hurt me far more, Mother. I can remember how your pelvic bones nearly busted my head when I pushed through."

"Hmph! You should have had a pain in the butt," her mother snorted. "You were a breech."

"That must have been Muriel. I distinctly remember coming headfirst." Gladys turned to me. "Alison simply must try this. It's like being born again. You see, re-experiencing your birth rids you of your physical ills and being born again rids you of your spiritual ills. You must try it sometime, Mitti."

Elspeth rescued me by coming around from the next aisle at that moment. "I hear Ward isn't speaking to Damon."

"It's worse than that," Gladys asserted. "I saw him slug him. I'd just arrived at the church to practice when Ward came tearing up the steps. They were putting Alison into the ambulance and Ward sent Damon sprawling clear down the church steps. He was yelling something about a pathology report Damon hadn't had done."

I remembered the scene all too vividly. After I had relayed Dr. Brun's warning to Ward, he'd gone to Damon who'd assured him the mole was nothing to worry about.

When Ward saw Alison on the stretcher, blood staining her mouth and white dress, he'd gone berserk.

The aftershocks had been more widespread than the initial earthquake. Bruce had rearranged his program at medical school to specialize in oncology. "I want to know more about this thing that's killing my mother," he'd said. He, at least, had a positive outlet. Linda had none. For the first time in her young life she realized that tragedies didn't just happen to other people. She retreated into a world of her own, vacillating between complete withdrawal and moments of high, unnatural hilarity. She was spending long hours at the Patch, as if she couldn't bear to go home and see her mother slip away from her.

"It just goes to show how many erroneous zones we have," Gladys was saying. "If Damon and Ward had . . ."

I nudged her. Charity was entering the store with Rosalind.

"I don't believe you've met Rosalind Bishop, Mitti," she said. She turned to Rosalind. "Mitti is hesitant about our program for developing Peacehaven. Damon tried to explain it to her, but she didn't understand. I mean to have you and Tyler and Mitti over sometime."

Rosalind gave a faint, forced smile. "Anytime, Charity," she murmured. "Mitti obviously isn't a business woman."

"Please, not now," I objected. "I have too much on my mind with Alison and the pageant."

"Of course, dear!" My cousin laid her hand on my arm. "Oh, I must tell you! I'm redecorating one of the bedrooms. Which do you think Rowan would prefer, blue or green? Or perhaps yellow?"

"Why?" I asked uneasily.

"But didn't she tell you? She's to stay at our house at

least once a week. You must share her with me, Mitti. You have two daughters and I have none." Her mouth quivered.

"Speaking of daughters," Aunt Jenny said to the banker's wife, "Muriel tells me yours is out at the witch farm."

Rosalind regarded her with eyes of tempered steel. "My daughter," she said coldly, "is with the Peace Corps."

"No, she ain't," Aunt Jenny insisted.

"Mother!" Muriel tried to stop her.

"Muriel's Harold told us," the old woman persisted. "Muriel's Harold—he *belongs* to the coven now. He said Sharon's out there with a baby."

"Do you have that crown roast ready, Henry?" Rosalind whirled so suddenly, the butcher knocked his cleaver off the chopping block, embarrassed to have been caught listening.

"Harold could have been wrong, Mother," Muriel protested.

"Wrong about a girl he's known all his life? Humph!" There was no stopping Aunt Jenny. "Harold also said he saw you and Dana out there, Mitti."

I said we'd dropped by one morning, aware Rosalind had turned her head slightly and was listening. What a sad pair they made—Charity so desperate for a child and Rosalind so desperate to disown the one she had.

"Did *you* see Sharon and her baby?" Elspeth had no mercy.

"I met a lovely girl named Maia, and she had an adorable baby boy," I equivocated as I dumped my groceries at the check-out counter. Elspeth fell into line behind me.

"It seems odd, Mitti," she said in her shrill voice, "that

242

you would let that Indian woman drag you into a den of witches."

"What seems odd to me, Elspeth," I retorted, "is that with your heritage you should make such an observation."

It was an ill-chosen remark. I knew it the moment I'd said it. I'd made no friends this afternoon.

Chapter Nineteen

Aunt Bo had made Halloween a memorable affair for the children of Peacehaven. Even though the climb up the hill was long and arduous, none would have missed our house. Dana and I continued her custom of serving doughnuts and hot cider to the goblins, monsters, and skeletons who paraded through the kitchen and living room.

Mother Carrier sat in her favorite chair holding a little blonde Indian in her lap—Cariad, who'd been dressed up by Dana. Dr. Brun, a jovial Odin in Viking costume, superintended the apple-bobbing contest. Rowan was away babysitting for the Wardwells.

Dana wore her ribbon-work Winnebago costume with headband and feather and I prevailed on Greg to don my long black monk's cape and hood and a devil's mask. Dana had been dismayed when I came down dressed as a witch. "People don't do that in Peacehaven. You won't see any of the children dressed as witches."

It was too late to change, but Greg's face confirmed Dana's words, and even the children eyed me uneasily. Cissie and Carol and Nancy lingered after the others. Nancy pulled at my false nose. "That's not yours. I like your real one. You're pretty."

I hugged her. "You're pretty, too, Nancy."

"We're gonna see a real witch tonight," she whispered.

I should have paid more attention, but at that moment Cissie began splashing water out of the apple tub at Carol.

"Nei, nei!" Dr. Brun brandished his short sword with mock ferocity. "I'll put you inside a ring of fire like Brünhilde."

Cissie had never heard of Brünhilde, but she got the idea. "Are you going to put me under a spell like you did Rowan?" she asked, intrigued.

"Nein, Mädchen," shaking his horned helmet, "there is more chance of your putting me under a spell."

Well turned, I thought, but Cissie's insinuation disturbed me.

"C'mon, Cissie," Carol tugged at her pitchfork, "let's go!"

Nancy squirmed out of my arms. "We're going on a big adventure," she trilled.

"You're not, Nancy!" Carol told her. "We're going to march you down to the bottom of the hill. Pa said he'd pick you up at nine o' clock and it's five to right now."

"How come you get to go?" Nancy pouted.

"Because I'm older."

"It's pretty late," I said doubtfully. "Your mothers will be worrying."

245

"My mother's gone to a meeting," Cissie replied, "so I can stay out as long as I want. We've had our treats—now for the tricks. Are you positive your Pa'll let you come, Carol?"

"Sure," a little uncertainly. "He doesn't care what I do 'cause I'm a girl and girls aren't worth much."

After they left, dragging a wailing Nancy with them, Dana and Dr. Brun took Mother Carrier home and I whisked Cariad off to bed. When I returned to the living room Greg had taken off my cape and had seated himself before the fire, his long legs propped up on the inglenook. I stood there, watching the firelight playing tricks with his features—deepening his eyes, giving him a harlequinesque, almost satanic expression, then, with a flicker of the flames, turning him back into the serious, gentle person I knew.

He took his feet off the stone ledge and drew me down next to him, but a sputtering sound at the window made me start.

"What's the matter? You seem fidgety tonight."

"I am," I confessed. "I've been on edge all evening—as if something bad were about to happen. So I get spooked by my own jack-o'-lanterns on the windowsill."

He laughed. "That's the way you're supposed to feel tonight. This is Samhain, the great witches' sabbat when they all go out riding on their broomsticks and the dead come back to haunt us."

I sighed. "That would be nice."

"To be haunted?"

"No, to ride a broomstick. I'd like to perch on the cusp of the moon and break off a piece of cheese."

He had withdrawn his arm and now he drew a stained, yellowed fragment of paper out of a manila envelope and held it out to me. Curiosity before romance. "What is that?" I asked.

"I was going through the Towne family genealogy last night, checking dates," he explained, "when I noticed for the first time that two pages were stuck together with something in between. I pried them apart with a paring knife and found this." He handed the fragment to me, half-reluctant to let it go, as if my touch might crumble the brittle paper. "This is a missing page from Bered Towne's diary. I think this explains the two skeletons on the tombstone."

I slanted the paper so the firelight illumined it. The script was reasonably clear, although embellished with flourishes and the archaic 's', which looked like an 'f' and took me a few seconds to get used to: "At laft"—no— "At *last* the thing which I fet"—"*set* out to do is accomplished. May God add his blessing to my deed. Ten yeres ago, during the night after my fifter"—"sister Mary was hanged for a witche, I reskewed her body from the commun pit in wich she was buried with the others and reburied it in a secrete plaice. This day did I concele her bones in the hollow I carved out of the monument for William Stoughton and I seeled them in with cement and overlaid them with that slab of marble wich is the lid. So may his spirit be trubled with the burden of her death. May she rest in peace."

Maybe the dead *did* come back at Halloween! Shivers were running up and down my arms and the back of my neck. "What a twist! How that old bachelor must be turning in his grave! And yet—" I paused, words echoing in my brain: *"Nay, William, I belong not to Satan—I belong only to God—and to thee!"*

"Perhaps some curious fate bound them together—

Stoughton and Mary Esty, I mean," I said aloud.

"I don't know what fate they would have shared," he replied stiffly, slipping the paper back into the envelope, "beyond the fact that he was her executioner."

"Maybe they'd once been lovers," I suggested.

He looked at me, incredulous. "Nothing would be more unlikely. He was gentry, she a commoner. Her life probably meant no more to him than a fly to be swatted. You're an incurable romantic, Mitti. The last thing— what the—!"

An animated ink blot bounced off the back of the sofa and onto his lap, then proceeded to lick its hind leg.

"That's Cari's new kitten," I laughed. "Darcy gave him to her. We named him Loki because he's as mischievous as the Norse Loki was."

"How do he and Macduff get along?"

"They adore each other—it's a circus around here."

Loki flexed his tiny paws and yawned, then settled down for a nap. Greg scratched him under the chin. "That purr is bigger than he is." He continued to stroke the kitten absently, but his mind was far away. "I've something else to tell you, Mitti, something you may not like . . ."

Oh, oh, he's going to marry Iris!

"Tyler Bishop came before the planning commission this week."

Was that all?

"He offered to annex Bishop's Bluff and the ravine that separates it from your property to the city, on the condition they grant him zoning for an industrial park."

"But they'd be insane to grant such a thing!" I protested. "I don't see how the location would be practical, dragging supplies up there."

"He plans to situate the industrial complex in the low area, as close to your property line as setback requirements will permit. As an added incentive, he offered to construct a water tower on top of the bluff to service the park and the city itself."

So this was to be their game! "Can we stop them?"

"You can contact the Department of Natural Resources, for one thing. They may take a dim view of a project that would overtax the already inadequate sewer system here and pollute the river. And I'll back you up with an editorial campaign."

Suddenly I was very weary. Alison, the hurly-burly of the evening, and now this—it was all too much. Tears splashed down my cheeks and his arms were around me and I was crying against his broad chest . . .

The back door slammed, springing us apart.

"I'm glad you came, Rowan," I said quickly. "I was afraid you'd meet the other girls and go off with them."

"No, they wanted me to, but I thought it was a dumb idea." Her eyes glinted in the soft light. "Do you remember my father?" she asked Greg abruptly.

He flushed. "I knew *of* him, of course."

"No one can ever take his place," Rowan said with a half sob.

"I'm sorry, Greg," I murmured as she ran from the room, "she idolized her father."

Rowan had spoiled the evening.

Rowan—Greg. The two names went round and round in my head as I tossed in my bed that night. Greg, so deeply conventional and Rowan, a barbed arrowhead in my side. When I checked her before retiring, I found her sitting cross-legged on her bed, humming softly to herself, her eyes regarding me impersonally.

"Did you know Aunt Charity is decorating a bedroom for you?"

Her fists were knotted in the covers. "It wasn't my idea," she said in a small, choked voice. "Aunt Charity's lonely. It'd be handy when I go to a party or baby-sit."

"You know I'd always come and get you if you wanted." I took her fists in my hands and gently forced them open. "I love you, Rowan. I truly love you."

She rolled away from me. "You loved Daddy, too," she whispered. "And Daddy is dead."

"You were so little—you never understood."

"It would only be once or twice a week," she mumbled, her eyes averted. "You could have Greg to yourself then."

So she was jealous of Greg—if only that was all!

"I told Aunt Charity Cari needs me. I wanted to take her with me, but she said Cari should stay here."

At least my cousin had shown *some* sense. "I think we'd better have a talk with her," I told her, twisting the tasseled cord of my robe. "Perhaps you don't know, Rowan—ever since she lost her baby girl, she's developed crushes on a succession of girls. Linda was one of them and you won't be the last. Someday she'll drop you like a hot potato."

"Oh—I don't think so," she replied dreamily, in the half light the blue of her irises almost eclipsed by her dilated pupils. "Uncle Damon wants me, too. I'm the first one he's ever wanted. Aunt Charity told me so."

Another device to drive me away? I wondered, struggling to suppress the angry words rising to my lips.

250

"Your place is here, Rowan. They'll have to understand that," I said instead.

"Iris says I'd do Aunt Charity a lot of good."

Iris! The name screamed at me. She was part of this!

"She said you and I weren't born under compatible signs and shouldn't be together too much."

"Iris isn't the only astrologer in the world, Rowan," I said, fighting to keep my voice steady. "I could take you to a dozen and we'd get a dozen different readings." I planted a shaky kiss on her forehead. "Now go to sleep, sweetheart."

Too upset to return to bed, I went down into the living room. Deciding against watching television, I scrunched down in the wingback chair and stared into the fireplace. A huge log glowed with a fiery face that winked at me, then collapsed in a shower of sparks, leaving a dark hollow where spurts of flame moved like tiny torches held by masked dancers . . .

. . . leaping about a central figure in black hood and cape, silhouetted against a low-burning fire. Faster and faster they circled, uttering weird muffled chants to the beat of a tom-tom. From the soft lilt of their West Indian dialect I knew most of them to be slaves, stolen out of their various homes in the area to perform a heathenish rite this All Hallows Eve.

I was crouching behind a clump of bushes, hoping my mare, tethered some yards away, wouldn't betray my presence. I'd stumbled across this eerie convocation while returning home from sitting up with my sister Rebecca, who'd been taken with stomach pains again. 'Twas an unseemly hour to be out, but once Rebecca had fallen asleep I insisted on riding home, for my Hannah lay a-bed with the ague. I enjoyed the clear, crisp air as my horse trotted along Meeting House road, then out across the meadows. The last of the way was marked with gulleys and hillocks and was out of sight of dwellings and the town watch. As I came over a ridge, I spied the fire and the figures swaying rhythmically around it. I dismounted and crept on alone to see what was afoot.

They were chanting in a mixture of English, West Indian, and African, of which I understood little. The tall, turbaned woman with a feather mask whose rich, deep voice dominated their litany was Tituba—no mistake—and that was her husband, the loutish John Indian, lumbering behind her. The drum slowed to a deadly beat as Tituba advanced toward the leader, carrying a bowl and a squawking chicken. He took the fowl from her, drew out a knife, and slit its breast in a manner that death would be slow. Tituba held out the bowl to catch the blood, while the worshippers responded with a chorus of sighs and grunts as the life slowly drained out of the bird. When the head hung limp, the leader tore out a handful of feathers and tossed them into the circle. There was a scramble for them, then he threw the carcass into the fire.

"Obayah Man—Obayah Man," they intoned.

"Not Obayah Man—Obayah God!" he shrilled. 'Twas not a voice I knew, but belike the goat-mask, which I could now see he was wearing, distorted it. This was no slave, this was an Englishman talking—mayhap a sailor or ship captain out of the West Indian trade.

Tituba thrust the bowl into his hands. Lifting it high, he cried, "Behold in me your Jesus-Lucifer-God!"

"Obayah God, have mercy-o!" they moaned. "Lawd, we come fo help he-o! Save us fum de duppy-o! Guard us fum de sunsum-o!"

I knew I should ride for the town watch. Heathenish rituals

252

were strictly forbidden, yet I couldn't find it in my heart to do so. These poor souls were so miserable and forlorn in their bondage. To be discovered at this would mean harsh floggings at the least.

Now the Obayah Man was walking among them, smearing their faces with chicken blood, murmuring a parody of Christian communion.

My mare neighed. At once the fire was kicked out and they dispersed, running hither and thither in the dark. I was only seconds ahead of them as I remounted and spurred my horse into flight. She vaulted a ditch, but missed her footing on the other side and I was flung over her head . . .

. . . my next recollection was being pinioned against the ground by several masked figures. The Black Man knelt, straddling me, his cloak cast aside, his face still hidden behind the hideous goatish mask. In my struggle to free myself I noticed a woman's white hand wrench my right arm back down on the ground. So all of his disciples weren't slaves!

Only a few of the assembly were still here. Most of them had fled. The Obayah Man loomed over me, his thighs white in the pale moonlight.

" 'Tis said they ha' commerce wi' the Devil at their meetings," my mother had told me. "But they get no pleasure from it, for his member be cold as ice."

I turned my head to the side. Hands forced it back into position. I cannot remember if my mother was right about the coldness—I only remember a snarl of rage and pain as I bit down hard and the Obayah Man doubled up and rolled on the ground, clutching himself and groaning. I swam in and out of consciousness as my captors struck up a death chant. The next thing I knew the Black Man was standing over me again, fully clothed now, his knife poised. Then it was snatched away from him as more masked figures leaped from the bushes and

253

drove my attackers away. By their guttural speech I knew my rescuers to be Indians. I wondered if Yawataw might be among them. They helped me to mount my horse, which one of them had caught for me, and I was on my way home once more.

'Twere no use, I knew, to report this night to the town watch. All evidence would have been removed by now, of that I was certain. Nor could I confide in Isaac. He'd think me an abandoned woman. No one would believe me. I'd only bring shame upon my family. Besides, as the cold air cleared my head, I myself began to wonder if the last part hadn't been a dream brought on by striking my head when I was thrown—or by the evil spirits everyone knew to be about on Hallowe'en. I dug my heels into the horse's flanks and . . .

. . . woke to the shrill of the telephone. I wouldn't answer! But my hand was already reaching for it.

"Mitti?" Esther Redd was crying. "Is Nancy over there?"

"No. Didn't Homer pick her up?"

Between sobs she got out her story. Homer had fallen asleep and missed his rendezvous with the girls, so they'd taken Nancy along. She'd gotten separated from them in the woods and when they couldn't find her they'd all gone home.

I'd hardly hung up when the doorbell rang. Greg had already heard that Nancy was missing. While Dana stayed with Rowan and Cari, Greg, Dr. Brun, and I thrashed through the woods, calling Nancy's name, our flashlights flushing nothing more substantial than shadows. Inevitably we came to the cave. What if she'd fallen down the crevice? Or been dragged inside? My heart thudded while Dr. Brun and Greg trained their flashlights down the drop-off: nothing, thank God!

Then a search of the upper chambers. I could hardly hold my flashlight for trembling. After an hour of futile searching we gave up. As I started away from the entrance something leaped out of the bushes and ran past me. I gave a slight scream, then realized what it had been. Frightened by a rabbit! Really, my dreams were getting the better of me!

Chapter Twenty

The hunt for Nancy continued through the next day, until by nightfall all but the law officers gave up and went home. It must have been nearly three in the morning when Macduff leaped off my bed, barking furiously at a swirling red light flashing in the windows.

Half into my robe, I answered a pounding at the back door.

"Have you found her?" My hands trembled as I tried to knot the cord at my waist, reading disaster in the sheriff's grim face. Jonah loomed in the shadows behind his father. "She—she's all right?" I quavered, trying to push it away from me, as if by doing so the truth could be reversed.

"We found her," Irv Good said harshly, "dead—in your cave."

"In my cave!" I reached for the door jamb to steady myself. "It couldn't be! Dr. Brun and I searched it thoroughly."

"You didn't go back far enough. She was in the second chamber. I've closed the cave off now, pending investigation."

I started to protest that we had been in the rear chamber, but something warned me not to.

"Have you seen Quentin Jackson?" he asked abruptly.

"No. Why?"

"He was in town today, but he's not at home now and they claim they don't know where he is. We've got evidence he's our man."

"I can't believe that!"

"Yeah? We found some of his hair clutched in her hand."

"How do you know it's his?"

His eyes narrowed. "Lady, if you'd been in police work as long as I have—oh, forget it. We've got a lot of territory to cover. If you see him or hear anything, be sure to give us a call. It's for his good, too. There's a mob forming in town."

He staggered back against the door as a great brute of a dog pushed past him and tried to force his way in. Jonah uttered a cry of sheer terror and bolted. Only a chain leash held by a deputy restrained the massive bull terrier. Saliva dripped from his mouth and a network of ugly scars stood out on his white flanks. He lunged for Macduff, his jaws working, but no sound issuing from them. Good seized the leash and jerked him back while I clung to Macduff's collar. The animal cringed at the sheriff's touch, then sprang again. The man aimed a vicious kick at the dog, which whimpered and crouched at his feet, hate red in its eyes. I felt a twinge of pity.

"Why is he mute?" I asked.

"I had his vocal cords removed. Do that with all our dogs."

"Why?" I inquired, appalled.

"They make better trackers. The quarry can't hear 'em coming."

"But how can you hear to follow?"

"Don't let 'em off the leash. Too dangerous. Might hurt somebody." He kicked the beast again as it started to rise.

"Don't—please!" Impulsively I reached out to pet the animal. The sheriff slapped my hand away.

"Don't do that, ma'am. This dog is a trained killer."

"What do you need a killer for?" Manhunts around Peacehaven?

"This is the second murder we've had in little over a year. And these are wild hills. Escaped criminals sometimes hide in them. I gotta be goin'. That nigger's out there somewhere."

Macduff bounded after the squad blinking down the hill, all legs and feathered tail. He was growing fast.

I leaned against the open door. Was this the twentieth century? A mob gathering in town, a man condemned without trial, dogs mutilated to make them better manhunters! As if in answer, an owl hooted a mournful augury nearby in the woods. Time doesn't change.

I waited until Macduff trotted back up the hill, then turned and went into the house, locking the door. The dog stiffened and growled, the puppy gone out of him.

Quentin Jackson was standing in the dark hall.

"Don't be afraid, Mrs. Llewellyn," he said, still lingering in the shadows. He held open palms to Macduff, who hesitated, then went to him, tail wagging. This was better proof of innocence than a lie detector test. No dog, not even a puppy, would have been that friendly to someone with blood on him.

"I didn't kill her," he said simply.

"H-how did you get in here?" I asked weakly.

"You forgot to lock your patio doors."

"Then you heard what the sheriff said."

He nodded. "This fellow," patting Macduff's head, "saved me. They thought their dog was after him, but he was really after me." His eyes were those of an animal at bay, begging mercy but expecting none. "Will you help me or are you like all the rest?"

Impressions flashed through my mind—the hard muscle of Irv Good's jaws, his miserable, worn little wife, the big dog cringing from those powerful scarred hands. Then I saw Quentin gently lifting Freya . . .

"You can trust me," I said simply.

"Lady," he breathed, his dark eyes still wary, "I hope you mean what you say." He shrank back into the closet as the door behind me opened and Dana walked in.

"I thought he'd be here. A county deputy questioned me, too."

"Where can we hide him? In your secret room?"

She gave a short laugh. "Not there—that's the most publicized secret in Peacehaven! I've a better idea."

"First let me check on the children," I said, as she started down the basement steps. "I want to make sure they're asleep."

Was I a little less than trusting? How long had Quentin been here? A child was dead. Why did Irv suspect him so readily? I hurried up to the bedroom level. They were both sleeping quietly.

I joined Quentin and Dana in the cellar, which was the

egg out of which the Phoenix had risen, and with its lime-washed walls it was egglike in texture, if not in shape. The original hard-packed earth had been paved. Some of the old beams remained, blackened and time-glossed; interspersed among them were the heat ducts and plumbing for the present house, so low Quentin had to stoop to get under them. Miscellaneous pieces of equipment and tools had been wedged into the rafters and forgotten, and old crocks and barrels and other junk were piled in remote corners. Lining the walls were the canned goods, preserves and pickles Dana and I had labored over in summer and fall. One tier of shelves was filled with turpentine, linseed oil, old paints, varnishes and stains—things that collect and stay forever. Dana and Quentin were already removing them.

"I've been meaning to look that stuff over and see if any of it's still good," I apologized. "Careful! You don't want to wake Rowan! Sounds travel through the registers."

"Good thing you didn't move them. This is one secret the town *doesn't* know," Dana said. "Okay, Quentin, help me."

The shelves slid aside to reveal a door where I'd thought it was just wall. Dana grasped a lever and the counterweighted door swung open slowly to reveal a dark tunnel. "This leads to my house," she explained, switching on a light in the passage. "They're not luxury accommodations, Quentin, but the room's equipped with electricity and a shower—when it rains." She smiled. "I mean—there's a vent that leads up to a grill in the lawn."

"The drain near the high bush cranberries?" I asked.

"Yes, it doubles as that. There's another drain in the floor with a catch basin underneath so the basements won't flood during a heavy rain." She shoved Quentin into the tunnel. "You'll have to stay there until we figure out what to do with you—be sure to switch off the light if you hear anyone outside."

He turned back to us as Dana started to close the door. "Will you tell my parents I'm all right? Don't use the phone—someone might listen in. Tell Mother to clean my combs and brushes and burn any hair she finds. I doubt if Good has the evidence he claims he has. He may get a search warrant and he's not above tampering with evidence if he can hang something on me."

"What does he have against you?" I asked.

"I can't tell you now, but if it works out I'll have his hide someday." He hesitated. "Was that you I saw coming away from the Faulkner house not long ago?"

I nodded, but my eyes asked more.

A shadow came into his. "I had an appointment with her, but not for what you think. I hadn't expected her to—" he stopped in embarrassment. "She's a piranha!"

"All right, all right!" Dana interrupted nervously. "We must close you in before anyone comes." We rolled the shelves back and had nearly all the goods in place when something was dislodged from the rafters and fell at my feet.

"What a strange doll!" I exclaimed curiously, picking it up. Dana dropped the candles she was about to set on the shelf. She reached for it with a trembling hand, but I held on, my hand and arm prickling from some unknown energy bombarding me. "What is it?" I whispered, both repelled and intrigued. Its long, dark hair was pulled back in a chignon like mine. The body and head were crafted of white wax and it was clothed in slacks and sweater. About its neck was a crude tinfoil facsimile of my amulet, and the thumb and middle finger of the right hand were each impaled by a pin.

"Voodoo?" I gasped.

"Not necessarily," she replied. "They had poppets like this in Salem. This is bad medicine." She snatched it away from me just as I had the furnace door open and was about to toss it into the fire chamber. "No, you mustn't! Don't you see? That's what they want you to do—destroy yourself. See? There's a long hair imbedded in the wax here. Could that be yours?"

"I—I don't know."

Dana pulled out the pins and threw them into the furnace. "These we destroy, but the poppet is you, so I will keep it safe and send its evil back to those who made it."

"Oh, really, Dana," I laughed shakily, "you don't honestly believe in such things, do you?" I tried to take it from her, but she resisted. The upstairs door opened. Rowan stared astonished as we stood there in frozen tableau, clutching the poppet, candles spilled halfway across the cellar floor.

"Wh—what are you doing?"

"We've been throwing trash away," I said quickly.

"Into the furnace? You told me never to do that."

"You're so right, Rowan," I agreed. "I was careless and Dana luckily stopped me."

She pointed to the poppet. "What's that?"

"Just a dirty old doll," Dana answered, putting it behind her. "You wouldn't want it. I'll burn it outside."

"Why are you hiding it, Dana? Why can't I . . ." Brakes squealed outside. "What's happening?"

There was no sense sparing her. "I hear Cari crying," I said after I'd told her. "You wouldn't want to leave her alone right now, would you?"

I was struggling with Macduff as I faced the sheriff again.

"Shut that damn dog up!" the lawman demanded.

"Not a chance!" I exclaimed. "If there's a criminal at large I want my dog right here. Didn't you find him?"

"No, ma'am, that nigger's somewhere around here for sure. The dogs are havin' a fit outside. I got the whole pack now."

"And a pack of people from the sound of it."

"I didn't bring them—they just came. It'll get out of hand if we don't find him."

In the evaporating night I made out Homer Redd carrying a shotgun. Most of the others were indistinguishable, but for Jim Willard who towered above the crowd as he tried to shove them back. Greg, who'd been jotting down notes, put away his notebook and went to assist him. A car jimmied itself into a vacant space and Lucian got out.

"What do you want?" I turned back to the sheriff.

"I want to search your house."

I feigned indignation. "Do you think I'd harbor a criminal?"

The pockmarks in his face deepened. "Ma'am I know nothin' except there's a murderer at large. And as for her—" he pointed at Dana, "I wouldn't trust her as far as you could throw a tomahawk."

He'd given me the edge I needed. "You've insulted my friend. You've no right here. I must ask you to leave."

The scars on his fists whitened. "Listen, lady," he snapped, "are you or are you not going to let me search this house?"

"Do you have a warrant?" I asked, bracing myself.

His jaw hardened. "So you're obstructing the law!"

"Not at all. I'm *demanding* it! *Do you have a warrant?*"

"Not yet." He tried another tack. "I was certain you'd cooperate. A little girl's been murdered. Carved up like the other one."

My grip tightened on Macduff's collar as I fought back a wave of nausea. "I assure you, the man you're looking for is not in this house," which was technically the truth. "I insist on a warrant on principle."

"I don't know if I can hold the crowd," he hedged.

"You could if you wanted to," I shot back. "Let me speak to them." Dana took Macduff. I snatched my long cape out of the closet and went outside to confront them. Their faces were becoming discernible in the dawn—hostile, menacing. Homer Redd thrust himself out in front.

"I want the man who murdered my little girl!"

"So do I, Homer," I tried to soothe him, "but do you know who he is?"

"Couldn't be no one but that Jackson feller—that was nigger hair clutched in her hand."

"A jury would have to decide that."

"Hell!" someone shouted. "No smart nigger's going to be convicted by courts today."

They closed in, their faces blurred by my panic. Greg stepped to my side. "Move back!" he ordered.

"Peacehaven once lynched an innocent man," I reminded them. "Would you want to do that again?"

"He killed my Susie!" Caleb Toothaker shouted.

Greg pushed me behind him. "You don't know that, Caleb."

Homer brandished his gun. "All we want is for the sheriff to search these buildings. That's abidin' by law and order, ain't it?"

"Not if he doesn't have a search warrant!" Greg

264

grasped the shotgun by the muzzle and with a quick flip of his wrist caught Homer by surprise and wrested the gun from him. Then, coolly, he proceeded to unload the weapon. "Now go to your homes. You can't do any good here." He handed back the empty gun.

Greg's display of sheer courage unsettled them. They shifted uneasily and some of them backed up. Not Elspeth, who edged forward, a coat thrown over her pajamas, her hair in curlers, revealing bald patches in her scalp. "Why doesn't she curse us? She can get rid of us real quick that way! Come on, folks, don't listen to this nigger-lover. She can't stop us. We can walk right over her." She pushed past Homer and the others followed her, but now Lucian confronted them.

"Brothers!" he cried, "and Sisters! Let us pray!" They bowed their heads in triggered response. "Oh, Father," he prayed, rocking back on his heels, his lids tightly closed, "help us to withhold judgment until we know that justice is being done, but—let not the culprit go free in this age when sin and crime are condoned by the highest courts. There is a higher court—Thy court, O God. Teach us where our duty lies."

What was Lucian doing? With sinking heart I saw them murmuring to each other, motioning in our direction.

"Amen! And we *know* where our duty lies." Elspeth's voice called them to action. "Let's force her!"

They pushed Lucian aside and pressed in on me. Greg spread his arms wide in an effort to hold them off.

Halt!"

The word crackled like a thunderbolt, freezing them in their tracks. Dr. Brun had suddenly appeared beside me, a ghostly figure in his long white nightshirt and light overcoat, lightning in his blue eye. Yet his voice was gentle. "Christians! Friends! None of you are law-breakers. Would you commit unlawful trespass? Mrs. Llewellyn has only demanded her rights under the law. What proof have you that she harbors a fugitive? And if you do find him, what will you do with him? Lynch him? Recreate Salem? You do not know—you cannot know—what it is like to have innocent blood on your hands." His voice broke as a look of incredible sorrow came over his face. A hush fell over the people as he talked, drawing out their anger as he would pus out of a boil. Slowly, shamefacedly, they began to disperse.

Lucian rammed his fists into his pockets. "You succeeded where I failed, Martin," he conceded wryly.

"I'll put the coffee on," I said, opening the back door.

"Sorry, Mitti," Greg said, "I have to get my story off on the wire services."

"What about you, Dr. Br—" The words froze in my mouth. The white terrier and a gaunt, one-eyed red dog were straining at their leashes, pulling the sheriff and one of his deputies toward the drain in the lawn.

"Those are fine hunters you have there," I scoffed, trembling. "There was a rabbit nest under those bushes all summer."

"Got your hunting license, Irv?" Jim Willard chimed in.

As Good unsuccessfully scoured the drain with the beam of his flashlight, the white dog suddenly lost interest in his quarry and began to pick a fight with the other animal. Cursing, he lashed out at the dogs with a booted foot and sent them cowering back to the squad cars, where they were secured separately in the caged back seats. My breathing returned to normal as the two squads zoomed off.

Before the sheriff returned from Richland Center with the warrant Dr. Brun set out for Madison with Quentin, while I delivered Quentin's instructions to his parents. When I got home I climbed up into the tower to watch for the sheriff. Something about Aunt Bo's chair made me pause. Were those hollows in the upholstery deeper than usual? As though someone was sitting there? Nonsense! Still, an invisible barrier held me back. Macduff's curly hair straightened, and with a howl he tucked his tail between his legs and bolted down the steps. Loki arched his back and spat, then overtook Macduff.

She was just as I remembered her—her pink, plump cheeks, her black, graying hair swept into a high French roll, soft tendrils escaping from her coiffure, and her mouth dimpled at each end. She shoved her acousticon toward me, cupping one hand over her ear.

"You did well today, Mitti," she said.

And then she was nothing but light waves and molecules and I was very tired. Strange what tricks the mind can play under stress . . .

But how was I to explain the acousticon lying on the desk?

Chapter Twenty-One

Peacehaven wasn't much cheered when the sheriff was unable to produce any evidence against Quentin, even though he searched the Jackson home as well as the Phoenix. But *someone* had murdered the children and in the same nightmarish way. The notion of a transient no longer held up and they were faced with the realization that whoever had done it was still among them. Doors no one had bothered to lock were locked now and the locksmith in Richland Center was thriving.

The rumor factory produced a long line of absurdities: "Their hearts were torn out and eaten." "Something sucked the blood out of them." "Dylan's coven killed them to get fat for 'flying ointment.' "

Tension mounted and undue significance was attached to incidents that in other years would have been taken in stride. The Dikes' cow broke her leg and had to be shot.

The Cloyces' pony fell dead of a heart attack. The Fosdicks' chimney caught fire. Mrs. Anson Parker sighted a UFO hovering over Bogus Bluff. And Lester Jacobs swore a phantom woman made him run his car off the road.

House, store, and car burglaries were on the increase, audio-visual equipment was stolen from the elementary school, Scotty Buckley's tavern was robbed, and someone stole Rosalind Bishop's mink cape from the coatroom of the country club.

Alison improved steadily. I dropped in on her every day, letting myself in with a key she'd given me. One afternoon, just before Christmas, I was surprised to find Lucian on his knees beside Alison, who lay on the sofa.

"No, stay, Mitti!" she called as I started to back out. "Lucian was about to leave." More an order than an observation.

He rose and stood over her. "I fear for you, Alison Proctor. I prayed this affliction would lift the scales from your eyes, but you have 'ceased not from your stubborn way,' " he paraphrased Judges. "I shall continue to pray for you," picking up his coat and hat, "but remember, 'too late' can arrive at any moment. I'm glad to see you looking so much better," he relented as he caught my angry glance. "I'll see you tonight, Mitti."

"Lucian is the bitterest medicine I have to take," Alison sighed after he'd left. "He doesn't really care about my soul—he just wants to add another fish to his string."

"Too many clergymen make soul-saving an ego trip," I agreed, perching on the cobbler's bench near the fire.

"What did he mean about tonight?" she asked slyly. "I hear he's a constant visitor at your house lately."

269

"Not really," I parried. "He and Lucy are just coming over." Rowan had been encouraging Lucian's visits, as though his presence afforded her a kind of protection from me.

For a moment all that could be heard in the darkening room was the monotonous ticking of the grandfather clock. "The shortest day of the year!" she said at last. "Hear my life ticking away?"

"Life in itself is a fatal disease," I reminded her.

"You don't really believe that, do you? You don't when you're well. I never could conceive of dying. *I* was different, *I* wouldn't grow old and die. Well, I've had to accept both inevitabilities. No," Alison waved away my half-uttered protest, "don't try to tell me it's not going to happen, that there's going to be an eleventh hour miracle. I'd hoped to see Bruce and Linda grown and established, but," her lids brimmed with tears, "I've never done anything to deserve a miracle, if they exist."

"You do seem better, Alison—even Lucian said that."

"For awhile maybe. Don't think I'm not going to fight for every day, hour and minute left me! Let's face it—I have melanoma—did you know Ward didn't want the doctors to tell me? But I insisted and I'm glad I know, even if—" she stopped and held out her hand. "You'll look out for my children, won't you, Mitti?"

"Of course," I assured her, "but don't start giving them away yet. *I* happen to believe in miracles."

"I wish I did," she spoke with fervor. "I hope Linda and Bruce won't see me—changed, particularly Linda. Bruce has his goals set, but I worry about her." Her long, wasted fingers groped along the arm of the sofa. "I can trust you not to say anything, can't I? I haven't told Ward, but she's been acting strangely. She's been hostile."

"She's probably upset by your illness," I began.

"Linda's not herself." Her voice was sharp. "She spends as little time here as possible. I think she's afraid I'll fall apart in front of her—oh, I don't know what to do!"

Was this true or had her illness made Alison prone to imaginary things? I knew nothing about the side effects of chemotherapy, but Alison seemed to be overreacting.

She rose and moved to the bookcase, where she pulled out a Bible. "You won't tell anyone! Swear it!"

"So you haven't entirely discarded your belief in God," I said after I had puzzledly complied.

"Does anyone in a foxhole? Yes, I know that's an old cliché, but that's how I feel. I want to believe, Mitti. In the hospital I tried to pray, but I was talking to blank walls. They say when people face death they get visions or revelations. I didn't."

"Perhaps you haven't been that close to death yet."

She ignored my remark. "Not that I expect any. I'm too much a doubter. If there is a God, he must despise me."

"Didn't Jesus love Thomas? My father used to reassure me, saying, 'We all doubt God at times.' My father doubt God? Impossible! 'I've asked myself,' he said, 'if I preach the Truth. We have the word of only one book and we don't even have historical proof that Jesus ever lived.' If you think you question, Alison, you should hear the debates in theological seminaries! Was there a virgin birth? Did Christ heal physical ills or only the psychosomatic? Did He raise Lazarus from the dead? Was He crucified? And did He rise from the dead? If I couldn't believe that He did, I might as well forget the Christian religion. Satan gives such logic and credibility to our doubts! That's when I thank God for Thomas, that stubborn skeptic. He couldn't accept Christ merely on faith. No, he had to touch the wounds to know they were real—and he went to India to proclaim Christ and die a martyr."

She was on the sofa again, her eyes closed. "I'm sorry," I apologized, "I didn't mean to preach."

"I was enjoying it," she protested. "I wish I'd had someone to talk to me like that. I don't like this 'ashes to ashes' business. If that's all there is, there's no point to religion, is there? Or to praying and singing hymns—or even living?"

"What you're really asking is: is there an afterlife? I believe there is—whether here or on some other plane. One lifetime isn't enough to give a person a chance to advance to the state where he is worthy to be with God."

"Lucian was right in a way," Alison said slowly. "You'd think, considering the position I'm in now, that I'd want to be born again. But I don't—not in this church, anyway. I never have. The previous minister was so modern I don't think he believed in anything. Perhaps that's why people are so drawn to Lucian. But that salvation and damnation stuff leaves me cold. He gives me the impression he considers himself the only gateway to God—almost as if he was God himself."

Lucian on the chimney rock!

"He's oddly out of place for Peacehaven," I mused. "He's type cast for a witch hunter."

She eyed me through shuttered lids. "And just what is our heritage? Do you think for one minute that we spring only from the *victims* of Salem? What do you suppose was happening in the century and a half between the witch trials and the founding of Peacehaven? The Montagues and Capulets were intermarrying, although no one here will admit that. Why, there's Putnam and Hathorne and Corwin blood running in our veins, too."

"And that's bad blood?"

"No more than any other. Which side one's on is usually an accident of birth."

I was tempted to tell her about the strange dreams I'd been having, but I refrained after a glance at her drawn face. She had closed her eyes again, her silver hair sprawled over the cushions. I rose to go.

"Don't leave yet, Mitti," she said. "I'm not asleep. Dana was here when Lucian came. I think he hates her—and fears her, too. Since I've been ill I'm more aware of things—undercurrents that I wouldn't have noticed before. Someone should warn Dana. Lucian is her deadly enemy."

I thought of Alison's warning as I listened to Lucian preach the Christmas Eve service—so unlike those I was used to. Little was done to celebrate the Nativity: one wilted poinsettia on the pulpit; no Christmas tree; no candles; no crucifix. Pagan and popish, Lucian claimed.

"On this Christmas Eve," he was saying now, "just as the Wise Men brought their gifts to the manger, won't you bring your souls to Jesus? Don't delay—tomorrow may be too late. Let me tell you about a man I once knew. His wife had given herself to Christ, but although he belonged to my church, he hadn't made his decision. He was a good man, observed all the commandments, gave to charity, loved his family, but—" He paused, savoring the congregation's rapt attention.

"He had not yet said, 'Lord, I am yours. I wish to be born again in you!' Then one night he made his deci-

273

sion—he would go to my house at once and make his commitment. Alas, my friends, the sands measuring his life had run out. On the way, a hit-and-run driver struck and killed him . . ."

Lucian dropped his hands, bringing a chill silence down on the congregation. "If only he hadn't put it off! The Lord had come and gone and this man was lost forever!" He leaned over the pulpit, drilling us with his eyes. "I see some among you who can answer, 'Yes, praise the Lord, I'm saved! I know there's a place in heaven for me; hallelujah!' But what about the rest of you? Won't someone come forward this very night?"

He was looking directly at me. I averted my eyes. There were faint stirrings in the congregation, but as yet no one moved forward.

Lucian flung out his hands. "Brothers and Sisters, Satan is among us! Two little girls have been murdered. A coven of witches lives nearby. And there are those among us who make covenant with Satan. There is a woman of alien blood who claims to heal by means of strange herbs and psychic powers. She even worships the living symbol of the Devil—a goat, a smelly, obscene male goat—"

Caper and Dana—Devil and Disciple? He'd gone too far!

"I tremble in the knowledge," he continued, "that members of our congregation have gone to this woman for her cures."

A loud "humph" greeted this. Gladys swiveled around on the organ bench to glare at her mother.

"I beg you to pray for this woman, that she may turn from her evil ways before it's too late. The Bible says, 'Thou shalt not suffer a witch to live.' " His hand gripped the pulpit. "And there is another woman for whom I ask your prayers—and for her husband, too. They're Peacehaven's own, but they are not Christians. The Lord has visited a dread disease on the woman, but still she is stiff-necked. Pray for her salvation, my friends. And now I ask you, oh you elect, on this Christmas Eve come forward to reaffirm your commitment. By your example lead those to the light who linger in darkness." Again he looked at me, but I, too, was stiff-necked. Rather than be born again in his ministry, I'd stay in the womb!

People were rising and filing past the chancel—last of all, Iris and the girls. Lucian passed his hands over one sleek head after another. Suddenly there was a shriek. One of the girls had fallen forward. My view was obstructed, but I could hear moans and a loud, coarse voice shouting obscenities. *Oh my God, it's happened to Rowan again*, I thought as I rushed forward, but I was wrong. Rowan and Cissie were supporting Lucy, her veins tracing a blue network on her transparent skin as spasms shook her frail body.

"The flames!" she screamed. "I see the flames! And the legions of Satan! Oh, they're burning me, burning me!"

Great welts and blisters had broken out on her face and arms. She contorted, then slumped back into the pew.

Chapter Twenty-Two

Greg and I stood on the bluff, gazing out over the Christmas landscape. Above us in the midnight sky, the blizzard of stars was transcendant over the bejewelled village where reds, greens, blues, and ambers in the outdoor lighting made rainbows in the snow. To somber, Puritan Salem, Peacehaven would have been a bedizened Jezebel. Windows usually dark at this hour glowed with Christmas trees and candles. Carols flowed from a loud-speaker, and far in the distance a pair of snowmobiles outlined the opposite shorelines of the river with their darting beams. It was a fragile moment, suspended in the night like a spun glass ornament dangling from the tip of a branch—perfect, yet only a tremor away from disaster. I cradled the moment in my mind, hardly daring to breathe. I didn't want to remember—I wanted only the now, but Caper's bell against the gate fractured it and brought the horror of Lucy's seizure, less than an hour before, to mind. Damon had administered a sedative while Lucian ended the service with a hasty benediction. I had expected the scheduled festivities to be canceled, but Elspeth insisted that the party she was giving the girls proceed as planned. Greg, after putting the mid-holiday issue to bed, met me at the church and brought me home. As I stepped out of his VW, the spell of the crystal night momentarily made me forget. Now, seeing Caper had brought it all back.

"I'm going to let this 'Smelly, obscene symbol of the Devil' out for a frolic," I said wryly, opening the gate. Caper catapulted through, rolled over, and, leaping high in the air, came up with a hunk of snow on his nose and began to race around the yard like a frustrated impala. "Look at him, Greg—how could Lucian say such things?"

No sooner had I said it than the little goat circled and struck Greg from the rear, pancaking him down into the snow. As I reached to give Greg a hand, my foot slipped and I fell into his arms, our lips brushing through a cloud of snow vapor.

"He may be an imp of Satan," Greg murmured, "but he maneuvers like an artist." He wiped the snow from my face. "What's wrong, Mitti? You're so quiet all of a sudden."

"Nothing . . . Let's go in. Help me decorate the tree and I will pay you in Tom and Jerries." I looked back at the little goat, standing alone and dejected in his pen. "Capricorn," I mused, "a goat could symbolize Christ as well as the Devil."

"That's a switch."

"But if Jesus really was born on December twenty-fifth—" I laid my mitten against his mouth, "Oh, I know

277

scholars dispute that, but what do *they* know? It would be logical for Christ to be a Capricorn—the scapegoat who takes away our sins."

"You really mix 'em up—astrology and Christian symbolism," he said, opening the door for me.

"It's been done before. Remember the Magi?"

"Where's Cariad?" he asked when I came into the living room with the steaming hot drinks.

"She's over at Dana's. Come down and have this while it's hot."

As I savored the frothy liquid, he sat stirring his thoughtfully. "I hope Lucy's fit won't make people reluctant to go on with the pageant," he remarked.

The pageant—always his blasted pageant! "I don't know, Greg, I have reservations about reviving the trauma of 1692. One or two performances—that would be one thing, but day after day, night after night, I wonder what effect it will have on the girls or the others."

An angry flush crept into his cheeks.

"You didn't see the whole thing tonight," I hurried on. "It was as if one of those scenes had come to life. Those were real burns. I saw fluid oozing from those blisters."

"Stigmata are a form of hysteria," he protested. "The girls in Salem Village showed similar symptoms. The wounds disappeared as quickly as they came."

"Even so, I worry about Lucy—she's such a sensitive, suggestible child."

He set down his drink and began rummaging in a box of ornaments. "If it's the pageant, then I suppose I'm guilty, too," he said, attaching a hook to a red satin ball.

278

"Perhaps we all are. How about a refill?" I asked.

"Not now, thank you. Where's the tinsel?"

"There isn't any. I don't like my ornaments to be covered up by ropes of tinsel."

"No tinsel?" he mused disappointedly. "What's Christmas without tinsel?"

"You're a terrible Puritan," I chided him. "How corrupted you are—wanting tinsel! Though honestly, Greg," I pursued my thought, "I have reservations about the pageant."

"You don't like the script?" he asked quietly.

"No, it's a great script, but it's digging up grievances that belong to the past. And it may be releasing things." I shuddered, remembering the burns crawling across Lucy's skin.

His finger lifted my chin. "You sound fresh out of Salem."

Maybe that wasn't as far out as he thought it was. My mind raced back over the months I'd been in Peacehaven: the phone calls, the poppet, my dreams, Rowan, now Lucy. "I'm beginning to understand those people," I said. "We may be more advanced in science, but we don't know any more about what lies beyond. Greed and spite were elements in the Salem tragedy, but honest fear was the catalyst. Frightened people are dangerous people, and I shudder to think what we might do given similar circumstances. That's why I'm not sure we should continue rehearsals."

"But you know theater better than any of us. If you pull out there may not be any pageant!" he protested, mounting the ladder.

279

"Would that be so bad?" I regretted saying this instantly; I was killing his dream.

"If it's Lucy you're worrying about, blame her father, not the pageant."

"Lucian does have a strange effect on people," I conceded, handing him a tiny drummer boy. "Remember how he suddenly appeared when Rowan had her seizure? And how his prayer did more to inflame than calm when the mob came after Quentin?"

"The talk is you've been seeing a lot of him."

"He comes up here with Lucy. Rowan enjoys them."

"And you?"

"It's better than lonesome evenings," I shot back.

The shaft went home. "I've been busy revising the last act," he explained. "If you desert us now, Mitti, Iris would have to take over."

That brought me around. "All right, Greg," I yielded. "Come on, let's get this tree done before New Year's Eve."

"Boy, it's hot up here!" he complained as he leaned over to put the drummer boy in place.

"Watch out! The ladder's tipping!"

He pulled back but lost his footing and slid along the teetering ladder to the floor.

"Damn!" He pushed up his shirt sleeve.

"Did you hurt yourself?"

"It's nothing. Just a sliver from the ladder."

"Well, I have a degree in splinter removal. Wait here," I returned with needle and tweezers. The sliver was lodged in his forearm near the inside of his elbow, in quite deep and broken off below the skin. As the sharp point touched him he jerked back. "I've a terror of needles."

280

"That's a common male syndrome. I'm going to have to hurt you some, but I'll be as gentle as possible."

He lay back against the arm of the sofa, his eyes closed. I slipped the needle in under the top layer of skin and exposed the tip of the splinter. After I'd lifted the end free, I latched onto it with the tweezers.

"There you are!" I held it up for him to see, but he didn't respond, just sat there rigid, staring at me wildly.

"By my faith, 'tis witchcraft!" through white lips. "Thou has put the mark o' the Devil upon me—an' I loved thee, Mary!"

The tweezers dropped from my hand. This time he had slipped through to the other side. At my touch, he sprang away from me. "Get thee gone, harlot! Get thee gone!" Then the glaze over his eyes faded. He looked around, clearly bewildered. "What happened?"

"You—you weren't yourself just now, Greg."

"I don't know what you mean," he said, fastening his cuff.

"It's always happened to me before. This is the first time—well—not quite—" I said, remembering the cave, "that it happened to you. You'd better sit down."

He didn't believe me and brushed it aside: "You know, Mitti, it's not the girls we need worry about. You're the one who's letting the pageant get to you. Naturally you'd dream about it—I know I do. And dreams never make sense. I'm flattered. I'd no idea my writing was so effective."

He took a spun glass bauble shaped like a minaret and hung it on the tree. "See how it catches the firelight!" I exclaimed, feeling an exquisite shiver as his hands suddenly framed my face.

"I prefer the firelight in your eyes," he said softly. "I

281

almost wish your dreams about Mary Esty and William Stoughton were reality. I'd write it into the pageant for you and me to act out—"

"Why act? Reality is here, Greg."

"Oh, yes!" he breathed into my hair. "I never dreamed that reality could be perfection. I'm afraid to reach for it, for fear of shattering it. Oh, Mitti, Mitti . . ." We sank down into the cushioned abyss of the sofa . . .

"Merry Christmas!"

Rowan stood over us accusingly, her eyes gleaming, her mouth drawn down into a thin arc.

"Merry Christmas to you, sweetheart! Was the party fun?"

"No, it was a drag, so Iris took me over to her house to listen to some new records. See what she gave me for Christmas?"

She thrust a pair of levis that were gaudily decorated with silver studs into my hands, and I seethed internally. *Iris—always Iris!*

"Rowan, you must always let me know where you are."

"Oh, Mother! She's an adult, and she didn't want to give me such a nice gift in front of the other girls. You know what? We went skinny dipping in her basement. The water's heated."

I fought to approach this with care—as I would someone standing at the edge of a precipice. "You know how susceptible to colds you are. We'll discuss this later. Have you heard how Lucy is?"

"Oh, she's okay. Lucian called and said her burns were gone."

"See?" Greg said triumphantly. "Sheer hysteria."

Rowan gave him a *Who asked you?* look. "Did I

interrupt something?" she asked. She knew damn well she had.

"Not at all, sweetheart," I lied. "I'll heat up the Tom and Jerries and since this is Christmas Eve you may have one."

"Okay. Be back in a minute."

She was standing by the fireplace holding a small, dark book when I returned with the drinks. "Here's a Christmas present for you," she said. "I found it up in the tower. Isn't that my grandmother's name on it?"

"That must be one of the ones I shipped to Aunt Bo when your grandmother died."

She opened a page near the beginning of the book. "Here, read this," she said, handing it to me. "Aloud."

" 'Widow Judith,' " I began, " 'was a sister of Israel Stoughton, married in England, John Denman, about 1620, and he died; she married a Smead about 1634. After the death of her husband, she came with her son, William, born in England in 1635, to be with her brother in Dorchester. His son, William Stough . . .' "

"Go on," she demanded.

" '. . . William Stoughton became Lieut. Governor, and then acting Governor of the Colony, and was for years—Chief Justice . . .' "

"I—I never read this book," I exclaimed to Greg, who had gone to the window and was standing with his back to us. "I never knew Stoughton was . . ."

Rowan slouched down onto the sofa and put her feet up on the coffee table, her hands behind her head. "You're descended from his Aunt Judith. I traced it down."

"Oh well, that's pretty distant," I pointed out.

"But you're still a Stoughton," Greg muttered, wheeling around. "No wonder you've defended Stoughton all along. And you cooked up a tale about him and Mary Esty being lovers, even tried to tell me I was once—"

"Greg, please! I didn't know what was in that book!"

"Oh, surely your mother would have talked about the ancestor who was," with sarcasm, *"His Excellency, Lieutenant Governor* of Massachusetts. Genealogy buffs thrive on titles. So you're a Stoughton! That's why you're trying to scuttle the pageant."

"Have I done something wrong?" Her eyes were sapphire innocence.

"Not at all, Rowan," he assured her. "It's time we cleared the decks. Aunt Judith—dear Aunt Judith! Oh, I can tell you about her! She and her first husband were plaintiffs in a famous lawsuit against a family of witches in Devonshire. No doubt she instructed William Stoughton in his bigotry when she lived in his home."

"And who instructed you in yours?" I flared.

"If only you'd told me at the beginning, I might have understood, but—" with a sudden movement of his arm he dislodged the minaret, which shattered at his feet. He knelt down and started to pick up the fragments. "I'm sorry, Mitti. I shouldn't have lost my temper. What does all this have to do with us?"

I turned toward the fire. "I think it has a very great deal to do with us," I said. "You think I'm a liar. I find I'm very tired, Greg. Don't bother to pick up the pieces. You've broken it and you can't put it back together again. I'm going to bed. Goodnight, Greg."

Rowan smiled in the shadows as the door closed behind him.

"And you can wipe that smirk off your face," I snapped. "If I'm descended from him, you are, too."

"No, I'm a Llewellyn, not a Stoughton. I want no part of your family, Mother."

An anguished cry sounded from the backyard. As I switched on the yardlights, I saw Dana and Greg crouching over something in Caper's pen. I ran toward them, heedless that I wore no coat and snow was crunching into my shoes. Dana turned an agonized face toward me. "I heard a sound—a scream," she quavered. "Almost human it was—then feet running and a car driving off."

She was cradling Caper's head in her arms. Someone had driven a pointed stake through his body and his blood was making dark angels in the snow.

Chapter Twenty-Three

The ancients, who began the New Year in March, showed more perception than we, for the Old Year is still in its death throes in January and February, while the New Year is locked in the earth's womb until the spring equinox. I was never more conscious of this than in my first year in Peacehaven; January and February were to me a time of loneliness and disintegration. Greg abruptly suspended publication during that time and left town—whether on vacation or business no one seemed to know. Most disturbing to me was the fact that Iris, too, had departed for parts unknown, and rumor had it they'd gone off together.

Dana was busier than ever and I worried about the drain on her. She had become drawn and distant. My offers to help were declined and I knew Dana better than to insist, but I missed our old, easy companionship.

Alison began to fail again after the New Year. She developed a chronic cough and tired easily. Although she swore she'd merely caught cold, the rest of us were skeptical, especially Ward, who'd grayed visibly.

On one of my visits I caught Dana kneeling at Alison's side, her hands uplifted over the motionless woman, from whom waves of scarlet were drawn into her own chest. Hearing my gasp, Dana whirled around and faced me with eyes black and forbidding. "You should not have come now," she mumbled.

"What are you doing?"

"I do what I must and you have no part in this."

Alison stirred slightly, but didn't wake, if sleep it was. I stumbled out, puzzled and not a little hurt. In the ensuing weeks neither she nor Dana ever mentioned the incident.

Dr. Brun was busy charting and codifying his finds. He no longer visited the cave now that snow would betray his tracks. One day he showed me an oval wicker frame with fragments of dessicated skin still clinging to it, which he had found, partly covered with rubble, in a deep recess. "This could be a frame for either a Welsh coracle or a Mandan bullboat," he explained excitedly. "They may have used boats like this to come up the river." He sighed. "This, alas, is not proof. The material and structure will have to be analyzed and dated with reasonable accuracy and that's not going to be easy."

I asked him if this time the Carbon 14 test could be used.

"You'll remember that Radiocarbon 14 works only on organic materials—things that once lived. I'm going to send skin and bone samples to the University laboratory, but they may have been contaminated by bacteria. In any case, it'll be a long time before I get an answer." Seeing my disappointment, he laid his hand on my shoulder. "Patience, my dear Mitti, is a most necessary attribute for an archaeologist—something our friends seldom develop. And now, please excuse me—I must get back to my book."

And so it went. All those I loved were drifting away from me. I was so lonely I felt a stir of pleasure when I opened the door one day to see Lucian there. Then I remembered Christmas Eve and let him stand outside with the wind and snow whipping at him until he apologized so abjectly that I relented and invited him in.

"I don't know what got into me that night," he said over a cup of steaming hot tea. "I was trying to illustrate how we are beset with a growing paganism all around us. Before I knew it I burst out about Dana's goat. To me, Caper was merely a symbol. I never dreamed anyone would take me literally."

"Start dreaming then," I said, offering him lemon. "You have tremendous influence over these people."

A flush of pleasure erased the distress in his face. "I'm delighted you think so, Mitti."

"You've polarized the whole town," I led him on. "They tell me the church nearly fell apart under your predecessor. You've made it thrive. Now your idea to revive the pageant may benefit the entire community."

"Especially if Brother Carrier's and Brother Bishop's plans are implemented," he murmured, helping himself to a doughnut.

So now I knew where *he* stood. "The people here will do anything you ask them to," I said.

He reached across the table to take my hand. "I didn't know you felt that way, Mitti."

"But it's true!" I let my fingers go limp as he squeezed them. "Your power over them is almost godlike. That's what you want, isn't it? Whose emissary are you, Lucian—God's or Satan's?"

His dark brows fused and he pulled his hand away. "What do you mean?"

"You'd have done well in Salem, Lucian. You give us a choice between a vengeful, egotistical Christ and a wicked, but heroic and fascinating Satan. That's no choice at all."

He rose, trailing powdered sugar down his black coat. "You've been listening to apostates," he said stiffly.

"My apostates don't instigate blood sacrifices," I retorted. "Sit down, Lucian—you *did* brave a storm to apologize to me."

"I told you once how beautiful you are when you're angry, Mitti," he replied. "I came to ask a favor of you. It's Lucy. She needs a woman to talk to—besides Mrs. Soames."

"What about Iris Faulkner?" an edge in my tone.

"There's always too much of a crowd around her. Lucy needs someone more like her own mother."

I was touched. "She must have died very young."

"She's still alive. She suffered a brain injury in an accident and is in a sanatorium."

"Oh, I didn't know."

"No one does here. They think I'm a widower."

Poor Gladys!

His fingers crawled up my arm. "You and I are much alike. We've lost our mates; we understand each other."

I reached up to pull his hand away, but instead his hand caught mine and refused to let go. "I hadn't thought we shared much under . . ." I broke off. His fingernail was rasping my palm. I jerked it away. "It's getting late," I said. "I must get some work done on the pageant scenery."

After he'd gone I went to the kitchen and scrubbed my hand.

I spent the rest of the afternoon in the tower, working on thumbnail sketches of pageant scenery. As I started to lay out the Gallows Hill scene, I discovered my ruler was missing. Rowan must have borrowed it. Too lazy to go downstairs to look for it, I burrowed in the drawers to see if Aunt Bo might have had one. They were crammed with papers, some typewritten, others in manuscript. Someday I must go through these—Aunt Bo, I knew, had written articles for historical publications. In the last drawer a book on Salem I'd never seen before lay on top. Several sheets of yellow copy paper had been folded and inserted into the book. I might have shoved it back into the drawer, but a note scrawled on the top of the paper caught my eye: "Mitti, read this."

My skin began to prickle as I unfolded the sheets with trembling hands. It was as if Aunt Bo was sending me a message from the grave, although, as I scanned the blotched and X'd out typing, I realized this was a rough draft of one of her articles:

Considering the widespread persecutions against witchcraft in England and Europe, the wonder is that, with the exception of a few isolated incidents, withcraft hysteria in New England was confined to the Salem area. What triggering factor in Salem was missing elsewhere? All the colonists believed in and feared witchcraft. They all suffered privations and disease, and shared a fear of Indians lurking in the forests, oppressions by the king, and the ever-present specter of early death.

"But Salem had Tituba," historians write. "Tituba started it with her voodoo tales from Barbados!" Nonsense! The colonies were full of slaves. Surely Tituba was not the only story-teller among them. No, we have to look further. I have just read with interest *Salem Possessed*, by Paul Boyer and Stephen Nissenbaum (Harvard University Press). Boyer-Nissenbaum attribute the witchcraft hysteria to al-ready existing internal factions in Salem Village society and especially the church, of which Samuel Parris was pastor. On p. 184 there is a chart of the anti-Parris network in the Salem Village con-gregation, of which faction eighteen members were accused witches and a third of those executed. On the other hand, the supporters of the witchcraft trials were overwhelmingly pro-Parris.

Still, to Messrs. Boyer and Nissenbaum, Parris was only the final straw that broke a pre-existent camel's back. They point to longstanding rivalries and jeal-ousies, land squabbles, and class struggles. The trouble with that hypothesis is that such conditions were in no way unique to Salem.

The Reverend Samuel Parris of the Salem Village church was unique, however, and I respectfully suggest that he may have been the missing ingre-dient historians have been seeking. I'm well aware that this will cause howls in history circles, but here is my argument:

Samuel Parris came to the Salem Village congregation—a backwater church known for its quarrels with its ministers—not out of choice, but because he could get no better without a theological degree. He was a Harvard dropout. When he inherited property in Barbados, he moved there and established a mercantile business between the island and the colonies. Sixteen years later, after nothing but failure, he turned to the ministry. After considerable haggling, learned as a trader no doubt, he negotiated an unusually favorable contract with the Salem Village church that included his salary, increments, bonuses, provisions, and firewood. An anti-Parris faction developed and the new minister was constantly embroiled in arguments, trying to make his parishioners live up to the contract.

Here was a man with an anti-Midas touch in all he endeavored, who was thus frustrated and bitter. Add to that the fact that there may have been a streak of insanity in his family—his son was to die a hopeless lunatic—and the conjecture that he personally took revenge on his opponents becomes entirely plausible.

Now let me digress a moment. Slavery was a fact of life in colonial Massachusetts. The colonists had brought with them an abundance of witchcraft superstitions from their homeland. It would make an interesting study, however, to assess what new dimensions had been added to their superstitions by African and West Indian beliefs. For instance, in the West Indies there are many tales of houses being pelted by stones of supernatural origin, often quite well substantiated. Nearly identical phenomena in

New England are recorded by Increase Mather in his *Lithobolia*.

Samuel Parris had lived in Barbados. Is it not probable that he observed and absorbed some of the native voodoo and obeah religion—an overlay of Indian and African beliefs with European Christianity and satanism? When Parris came to Salem Village he brought two Barbadian slaves, through whom he would have had a means of communication with other slaves in the area. In his most recent frustration, this proud, egotistical man may have turned to those other unfortunates, who often had good reason to hate their owners. What better vengeance than for the slaves to work their native magic on their masters and then make it seem that *they* were the witches?

Confessing witches in the Salem trials babbled about coven meetings in Parris' pasture. Now that could have meant any of several tracts of land which Parris acquired, either by purchase or gift prior to 1692. Historians have generally dismissed these tales of occult activities in Parris' meadow as flights of fancy by neurotic women, or downright lying. Have historians overlooked an obvious clue? Is it not possible that these "neurotic women" were telling the truth after all?

My eyes traveled to a note at the bottom of the last page written in her shaky hand—"Peacehaven has another Parris. Heaven help us!"

What wouldn't I have given to have Greg there at that moment? I doubted he'd seen this for it certainly contradicted his theory. Hers seemed the better of the two to me. It took some of the onus off William Stoughton—Greg would hate that . . . I could see a black-hooded figure conducting arcane rites by firelight. Mary Esty had never guessed who he was. Ha! I knew something she hadn't! The pageant needed rewriting. That last scribble of Aunt Bo's—strange . . .

Just then my groping hand found a ruler in the drawer. Good, I could go back to my work! Let's see—Gallows Hill—should I depict the sea in the background? It must surely have been high enough to afford a view of the salt marshes lining the shores . . . with white-crested waves shattering on the sand and gulls soaring overhead in the lowering sky, their eerie cries sounding in my ears as I ran over the expanse of sand into my old dream . . .

. . . and into his arms. His buckled hat had blown from his dark curls and lay on the ground. He folded his cape about me and we clung to each other in the wild wet wind.

"Thou munna go, my love," I pleaded. "They bring news o' smallpox in London."

"Alas, Harvard has no more degrees to offer me, sweeting. Come away with me to London, Mary."

"Would that I could," I moaned, "but wi' Mother gone, I mun care for Bered and Sarah. And thy brother'd never consent. Thou'rt not yet of age and master o' thy fortune. But bide here a year until thou art and then, God willing, I will go with thee."

"Nay, I cannot. The colony needs leaders. 'Tis my duty."

"A fine leader thou'dst make if thou shouldst sicken wi' the pox." I fingered a tiny case in my pocket which I had fashioned out of two scallop shells bound together.

"Such things are in the hands of the Almighty," he replied.

Not quite, my love! I thought.

He guided me over the dark sand to a salt encrusted rock where we would be sheltered from the wind and from sight. A ripple of flame throbbed through my body as his hand unlaced my bodice and his fingers sought my hardened nipples. Nay! I munna! I mun hold back so that, unsatisfied, he 'ud lie awake nights in London dreaming of me. With a wrench, I rolled away from him.

"What ails thee, Mary? Have I offended thee?" He reached for me to pull me back. "Before God we are man and wife."

"Nay, not yet, Will," I demurred.

"Then let us have this thing between us—let us mingle . . ."

"Our bloods," I finished his sentence as I relaced my bodice. "I'll not be thy harlot, Will. Thy wife I'll be or naught." Holding out my mother's knife, "Thy blood in my veins and mine in thine."

He pulled back his sleeve. I carved a small cross over the vein in his wrist, then did the same with mine. Our wrists bound together, our bloods mingling, we lay side by side, looking up at the gray sky and listening to the roar of the ocean that would soon lie between us. Stealthily I drew the shell case from my pocket and had it ready when at last I unbound our wrists. Before he could stop me I had daubed his wound with the smelly yellow pus I had not more than two hours gone taken from sores on my sister Sarah's hands.

"What art thou doing?" he demanded.

"Putting salve on thy wrist so 'twill mend."

"And why not on thine? Thou has left none for thyself."

"I but forgot," I lied. Nay, this was sinful. To lie would forever damn my immortal soul. "I munna trifle wi' ye, Will. 'Tis a remedy to keep thee safe from the smallpox—a thing I learned from my mother."

With a cry of horror and disgust, he plunged his arm into

the sand. "By my faith, 'tis witchcraft!" he swore. "I've heard about thy mother, but I ne'er believed it. Thou has placed the mark o' the Devil upon me! I should kill thee here and now, but I cannot, for I loved thee. May God have mercy on me for my weakness! I thank thee, O Heavenly Father, for saving me from fornicating with this woman of Babylon!"

I might have reminded him that it was I, rather than God, who'd saved him from that particular sin, but I only cried, " 'Struth, Will, I know no witchery but love!"

"Thou art the Devil's own!"

"Nay!" I knelt before him, winding my arms about his legs, but he pushed me roughly away, his face full of loathing.

"Confess, Mary, for thy soul's sake!"

"I cannot. I dare not belie myself, Will, lest I be damned."

"Nay, but thou *art* damned . . ."

A whirlwind caught him up and spun him round and round until he was sucked through a hole in space. I stumbled after, calling "Will—Will Stoughton—Greg!" He was gone, but his voice trailed behind him in the echo chamber: "Damned—damned—damned . . ."

I came to at the ringing of the telephone. "Mitti, why haven't you listened to us?" came the whisper. "We are many. Susie first—Nancy second—and then—Cariad?"

Cariad? I spiraled down the steps to the nursery. Cari lay on the floor, her head cradled on Macduff's shaggy flank and Loki nestled in the lee of her elbow. If I hadn't feared I'd frighten her, I would have snatched her up and hugged her frantically. Instead I sat down quietly on the floor beside the trio.

I must take her away from here. I'd sell the Phoenix— let Damon and the others have their way . . . but—of course! That was it! *They* must be behind the phone calls! I'd be doing the very thing they wanted. With this realization came relief. Damon and Charity weren't murderers, but they mightn't be above trying to frighten me away. If so, then this was only a cheap trick with no real threat. If I left they'd have won their point and I would have betrayed Dana and my own principles. If I were to run now, I'd keep running the rest of my life, uprooting my children time after time whenever something went wrong. And if my dreams and visions had any truth whatsoever, our karma was bound up in Peacehaven and no amount of running would save us.

Cari stirred and opened her liquid brown eyes. Her little arms reached out to me. I picked her up and held her tight while tiny fingernails explored my face, pattering over the bridge of my nose and down to my mouth.

With a peal of laughter she bounced out of my grasp and began running around the room, patting the baseboards.

"House! Cari's house!" she babbled over and over. She had made the final decision.

Chapter Twenty-Four

"Yea, though I walk through the valley of the shadow of death . . ." I found myself repeating tonight—verses I'd been taught to say when I was afraid of the dark, a fear I'd never conquered. More than ever I deplored my widowhood. Each night when I was most vulnerable must come the moment when I had to face life alone in all my weakness. Why had I quarreled with Greg? Where was he now? With Iris? I kept thinking of those moments in the cave and then Christmas Eve—the gentle strength in his long, shapely hands, the warmth of him, the shy seriousness in his brown eyes. He was a complex man, outgoing at times, withdrawn into some internal conflict at others, and I longed to work it out with him, no matter how difficult.

I felt overcome with loneliness and longing. Tears overflowed my lids—sleep seemed hopeless. I threw off the bed covers and went down to the living room, busying myself with building up the fire, then sitting, to muse, in the big chair that faced it.

I must have dozed off, for the next thing I knew, my heart was hammering as the doorbell rang. Macduff whined upstairs in Cari's room and scratched on her door.

"Lucian! What are you doing here at this hour?" I exclaimed, clutching my robe. It had been quite a while since our last encounter.

"I could see your lights from my house so I knew you must be awake," he said as he entered. "I was worried something might be wrong. Good Lord, Mitti, it's freezing in here! You're blue." As he heaped fresh wood into the grate and rekindled the fire, I huddled on the sofa with my knees drawn up. It was nice to have someone show concern, to drive the shadows away. The irritation he always roused began to ebb. Right now I didn't want argument, I wanted solicitude.

"There, that's better," he said when the flames were licking the logs. He put his arm around me, letting the warmth flow from his body into mine. I made no resistance, but let my head droop wearily against his shoulder.

"Why were you down here in the cold? Another crank call?"

Did everybody know? "Not tonight, thank heaven. I just couldn't sleep, but then I dozed off in spite of myself. I'd been thinking unhappy thoughts, I'm afraid—I just don't feel very well-liked here. It's not only the calls, it's—"

He sighed. "You've hardly conformed to Peacehaven standards, Mitti. It's not easy for them to accept an outsider, particularly when she stands in the way of progress."

"But I have to be true to my beliefs, Lucian," I said stubbornly.

He pulled me closer to him. "We'll talk about those another time," he said. "How is your work with the pageant coming? Are your girls ready for the twenty-first?"

The twenty-first of March had been chosen for the first general rehearsal and was to be a town holiday. The girls had been looking forward to working with the adults.

"I hope the weather cooperates," he went on. "I've been talking with Greg—"

"Greg?" I could feel the adrenalin pumping in my veins and I moved slightly away.

"Yes, he came back yesterday—so did Iris."

"Oh." I sat there listless as he outlined his plans for the pageant. The gallows scene, he said, should be staged up on Bishop's Bluff instead of in the park bandshell where the rest would be played. The logistics of transferring a whole audience from the park to the bluff mystified me, but Lucian felt the people could move during the intermission and that would give time for the sale of refreshments.

"There's only an old cow path to the bluff," I objected.

"That could be a problem," he conceded, "however, Tyler Bishop has promised to construct a road to the proposed water tower."

I jerked to attention. "That hasn't been voted on yet?"

"No, but Tyler says it's a cinch. Anyway, if the weather is favorable next week—"

"You don't intend to go up there at *this* time of year!"

"Why not? The weather bureau predicts a thaw.

There's that marvelous old oak for a hanging tree and then there's lumber from the old cabin that blew down. We could make a platform out of that," he continued, thinking out loud. "Of course, if it warms up too much it might be muddy—it might not be practical."

"I hope we stay in the nice warm city hall." So Greg was back—and Iris, too. It was too much a coincidence. Well, if that was the way things were, I could do nothing about it. I sat there passively as his hand stroked my arm.

He pressed his lips to my forehead. "Don't worry, we'll work it out." The gesture triggered a response in me. I needed affection so badly. I lay with my head on his shoulder, unresisting as his mouth covered mine. Then his tongue forced my lips open, his hand slipped inside my robe and found my breast beneath my nightgown. I caught his hand. "I'm sorry, Lucian, I didn't mean it that way. I shouldn't have let you . . . I said no!" He was upon me, bending me back against the sofa, tearing aside my robe.

"Are you out of your mind?" I struggled away from him, but he wrestled me down and ripped open my gown. As he fumbled with his zipper I managed to slip out from under him.

"Get out of here!" I demanded, winding my robe about me. "*You—a man of God!*"

"You need someone, Mitti, and so do I. The trouble with you, my dear Submit, is that you're still a Puritan at heart. You surprise me, daughter of a clergyman and widow of an actor. You must realize that we are all in the same profession. We give the people what they want, even if it's only illusion. I was made in God's image, as was Jesus Christ, and you're not so old-fashioned you think *he* was sexless, do you? With all the female

301

devotees he had? Mary Magdalene, Mary of Bethany—and who's to say he didn't sleep with the woman of Samaria?"

I made no attempt to conceal my disgust. "You sound like third-rate porn. Now get out!"

Instead he came at me again. His moist, cold hand caressed my neck, then tightened. I went rigid as the blood began to pound in my neck and temples. A wrong move on my part might make that hand close all the way. "You don't really want me," I half-whispered. "You only want to master me."

"And I will," he murmured, backing me toward the sofa again.

With a vicious jab I drove my knee into his groin; he doubled over.

"People should know what you are."

He gave an ugly laugh. "But you won't tell them, will you? Because they'd never believe you."

He was right, of course. "Just don't ever come near me again," I spat at him. "You—you're demonic, Lucian."

"Demonic?" he asked, confused, running his hand over his forehead as if to brush the cobwebs away. "What are you talking about, Mitti?"

The change in him was so abrupt I was caught off guard.

"Rape, Lucian—attempted, that is," I managed to stammer.

"What?" He stared in disbelief, then smiled pityingly. "Oh, my poor Mitti, I fear you've been working too hard. You must get some rest. I might have expected something like that out of Gladys, but you! I trust your hallucinations will soon pass. In the meantime, I promise not to tell anyone."

He'd done it again!

Chapter Twenty-Five

. . . "Get in there wi' ye, woman, and mind ye, dinna waste 'is Honor's time!"

Sheriff George Corwin ushered me roughly into the court chamber. Since I had sent word that I had a petition to present, I had expected the full panel of judges to be there and had even been so rash as to hope that His Excellency, Governor Sir William Phips, would be present, but only one member of the panel was there—the chief justice of the court of oyer and terminer, Lieutenant Governor William Stoughton. He was clad in a robe of deep maroon velvet, with a collar of fine lace and a narrow linen scarf knotted loosely at his throat. A black velvet skull cap crowned his flowing silver-white hair. How vast the difference between our stations! How had I once aspired to be the wife of such an aristocrat? Though surely I hadn't been in such low estate then as now, with my homespun gown grimed and torn, and my wrists and ankles fettered. Still, I had done my best to tidy my hair and Bered had brought me a fresh cap.

The justice dismissed the sheriff with a curt nod, then contemplated me with solemn, deep-set eyes.

"You are surprised to see me here alone?" he asked.

"I had thought Justice Sewall and the others would be here—and the other prisoners, Your Honor."

"They will be anon, but I wanted to talk to you alone, Mary."

My heart fluttered. So he remembered me! All during the trial he had accorded me the same treatment as the others, giving no sign of recognition. After all, he had known Mary Towne, not Mary Esty, and I mun be sore changed. Was't in his heart to render me mercy? Alas, there was no relenting in the stern countenance.

"Thank you, Your Honor," I replied, my hands clutching the document over which I had labored so diligently—not in the hope of saving my life, but the lives of those yet to come to trial. Now, in the light of this unexpected turn of events, I dared allow myself a slight glimmer of hope. Mayhap he'd see the truth in what I had written and thus the truth in me. "I have drawn up a petition—"

"Later," he waved it aside. "I want you to know I'm not insensible to the memory of—to the memory we share. 'Tis with deep sorrow that I see the plight to which your sins have brought you. My prayers for your soul have not been answered."

"By all that's holy, I am a Christian and innocent of this crime!" I burst out.

"Mary, Mary," he groaned; and for the first time I was aware of the struggle going on within him, "do not lie to me. I have the mark of your infamy upon me!" He drew back the sleeve of his robe to display a faint white scar.

"Have ye not been free of smallpox all your life?"

"I hope I was spared through the grace of God, not through the work of the Devil," he remarked with asperity.

"Nay, Wi . . . Your Honor, 'tis not the mark o' Satan. 'Tis a thing o' nature and comes from God, though I know not how it works."

His mouth drooped. "The apple which Eve gave to Adam was a thing of nature, but it was evil. But let us to the point. I plead with you to confess your sins and be received back into the fold. I like not to sign your death warrant, Mary."

"I cannot confess to a lie! Better you condemn me to hang than God condemn my immortal soul," I cried.

He dropped his head in his hands, then looked up at me again, his face drawn taut. "Thou art beautiful yet, Mary." He'd fallen into the old form of address. "I had not thought to find thee so after all these years. And thine eyes are innocent as a newborn lamb's. Oh, God," he groaned, ramming his fist down on the table, "how artfully the Fiend disguises his own." He rang a small silver bell. "I have done what I could. Bring in the prisoners, sheriff," he said as Corwin stuck his head through the door.

As the accused filed in, Justice Samuel Sewall and the rest of the court entered by another door and took their places on either side of Stoughton. Dorcas stood just a bit in front of the other prisoners, her head high and defiance in her eyes.

"You have a statement you wish to make to the court, Goody Hoar?" the chief justice asked.

"Aye, Your Honour," curtseying. "I wish to turn from my sinful ways. I 'ave ne'er signed the Devil's book, but I confess I 'ave oft danced with the coven in the minister's meadow, as

305

she," pointing at me, "can well testify, for she were there, too, dancin' wi' the Black Man and a-suckin' his pizzle."

"She lies!" I gasped. I was seeing a white hand wrestling my arm to the ground.

Stoughton brought down his gavel. "Be silent, woman!"

The irons cut into my wrists as Corwin jerked me back.

"Can you pay for the food the state has furnished you in prison?" Sewall asked her.

"Aye, that I can. I pray for a little time to lead a life o' good deeds and penance," she replied with cloying humility.

Stoughton brought down his gavel again. "Then let this woman be released when she has paid the proper indemnities."

I was shaking with outrage. How could he believe her lies and turn his back on my innocencye? Had our love been for nought?

"And now, Goody Esty," he addressed me coldly, "you have a petition you wish read to the court?"

"One moment!" The Reverend Samuel Parris had risen in the courtroom. "Do we grant a hearing to a convicted witch?"

The chief justice threw him a saturnine glance. "Why yes, Mr. Parris, we must not deny any one of these miserable creatures a last chance for repentance."

"Thank you, Your Honour," I whispered, barely able to control my voice. I lifted the paper with difficulty, weighted down as my arms were by the shackles, and began to read:

"The humbl petition of Mary Eastick unto his Excellencyes, Sr Wm Phipps and to the honourd Judge and Bench now Stting in Ju—Judicature," my tongue stumbled over the word, "in Salem and the Reverend ministers humbly sheweth:

"That whereas your poor and humble Petitioner being condemned to die Doe humbly begg of you to take it in your Judicious and pious considerations that your Poor and humble petitioner, knowing my own Innocencye, Blised be the Lord for it, and," looking at Dorcas, "seeing plainly the wiles and subtility of my accusers, by myselfe cannot but Judg charitably of others that are going ye same way of myselfe if the Lord stepps not mightily in. I was confined a whole month upon the same account that I am condemned now for and then cleared by the afflicted persons as some of Your Honours know and in two dayes time I was cryed out upon by them and have been confined and now am condemned to die. The Lord above knows my Innocencye then and likewise does now, as att the great day will be known to men and Angells—I Petition to Your Honours not for my own life, for I know I must die and my appointed time is sett," gazing straight at Stoughton, "but the Lord he knowes it is that if it be possible no more Innocent blood may be shed which undoubtidly cannot be Avoyded in the way and course you go in. I question not but Your Honours doe to the uttmost of your Power in the discovery and Selecting of witchcraft and witches and would not be gulty of Innocent blood for the world but by my oun Innocencye I know you are in the wrong way. The Lord in his infinite mercye direct you in this great work if it be his blessed will that no more Innocent blood be shed. I would humbly begg of you that Your Honours would be pleased to examine theis Aflicted Persons strictly and keep them apart some time and likewise to try some of these confessing wiches," with a glance toward Dorcas, "I being confident there is severall of them has belyed themselves and others, as will appeare, if not in this world, I am sure in the world to come, whither I am now agoing and I Question not but youle see an alteration of theis things. They say myselfe and others having made a League with the Divel, we cannot confesse. I know, and the Lord knows, as will shortly appeare, they belye me and so I Question not but they Doe others. The Lord above, who is the Searcher of all hearts, knowes that as I shall answer it at the Tribunall seat that I know not the least thinge of witchcraft, therefore I cannot, I dare not belye my own soule. I beg you Honours not to deny this my humble petition from a poor dying innocent person and I Question not but the Lord will give a blessing to yor endevers."

Before I finished, the afflicted girls had come in and now . . .

Rowan ran to me and threw white powder in my eyes. Gregory Towne rose from the judge's bench. "Petition denied!" he roared. He held out his arm to Dorcas—no, Iris—and they waltzed out of the room as he shouted "Petition denied . . . Petition denied . . ."

It was past noon when I awoke, the weight of the irons still on my wrists. Dana had taken Cariad to her house so I could catch up on the sleep I'd lost after Lucian's visit the night before. I dressed and went over to pick her up. When the ancient brass knocker failed to bring an answer, I shoved the door open and walked in.

The wooden floors reverberated under my feet as I went from room to room. Unwashed luncheon dishes in the sink loomed ominously—Dana was meticulous about such things. I opened the door to the cellar, but it was completely dark. After finding the bedrooms on the second floor empty, I remembered the secret room that could be reached only by a hidden stair leading out of the back parlor. I retraced my steps and opened the cupboard door in the chimney, which was supposed to be a storage place for wood, but, as in Hawthorne's house, had a false back, beyond which were rickety, hand-hewn steps leading to the upper room. Something caught at my hair.

I darted back, then laughed—shakily—as I lifted a gray kitten down from the mantel. "Phantom, you imp!" I scolded and set him down near the battered ball of yarn that was his plaything.

At the top of the stairs, I knocked at the heavy door, reluctant to simply walk in. Dana had never invited me up here so I had no desire to violate her privacy, but when there was no answer, I turned the knob and entered. The only light in the room came from one small, diamond-paned window, and at first I thought the chamber was empty, but then with a start I saw Dana kneeling at a low altar that was draped in fine, dun-colored buckskin, beaded and fringed. A fur pouch, handsomely trimmed with quillwork, lay on the top, at either end of which was a low-burning candle. Above, on the wall, hung a natural crucifix of a gnarled branch that had grown over another to form a cross with the twisted torso of a crucified man. Next to that was a large turtle shell decorated with designs done in red clay—a Mandan totem, I remembered.

Dana took no notice of my entrance, but continued to move her lips soundlessly over a small clay figure in her hand—Alison staring up at me in miniature! Strands of gray hair sprouting from the top of the head were fashioned into a figure eight at the back of the neck. Draped loosely about the body was a flowing silk caftan of Moorish design in shades of blue, red, and gold on a white background, made from a swatch of the material used in a real caftan Dana had sewn for Alison. I groped for the wall to steady myself, in that moment of shock my mind reverting to the stereotype of witch, which connoted only evil. Was Dana a witch draining Alison's life away? Was she behind the phone calls? Had she made the wax image of me? It was there, too, on a shelf, wrapped in plastic. And where was Cariad?

Still, Dana seemed not to be praying to the doll, but for it, or for the woman it represented. She raised her eyes to the rough crucifix, pulled back her blouse from her shoulder and uttered a hoarse cry that made me reel to my knees. Red flames leaping from Alison's image entered Dana's body with such a jolt that she fell backward. An ugly red mark spread its tentacles across her bare shoulder just above the left breast, growing darker until it was almost black. Just as quickly it was gone. Dana lay still a moment, then sat up slowly, seeing me for the first time.

"I—I didn't mean to intrude," I stammered. "I was looking for Cariad and couldn't find anybody."

"It is no matter," she said brusquely, buttoning her blouse. Then, anxiously, "You won't tell, will you? If people here were to know I could not finish what I have started to do."

"Just what is that?" I wasn't sure I wanted her to finish either. "And where is my baby?"

I had to steel myself against the hurt in her eyes as she answered simply, "Dr. Brun took her and Mother Carrier for a drive. They should be back soon. As for this—" she picked up the miniature Alison, "I cannot talk about it even to you. I only beg you to trust me—not to betray me."

I was confused and appalled to find her practicing anything so primitive as image magic. She saw my hesitation. "It is not as you think," she assured me. "The poppet has no power. It only helps me to visualize as I meditate."

"Why have you kept the one of me?"

"Because whoever made it wanted it destroyed and wanted to destroy you."

I shook my head. "How can an intelligent woman like you believe that the destruction of a doll could affect me?"

"The doll is nothing," she answered. "It is only a lump of wax. It is their belief in it—their hate—that I fear. But I have another reason for keeping it—as evidence in case we find out who's making the calls." She still read doubt in my face. "As you can see, the workmanship in the two dolls is very different."

It was a good point. Dana's workmanship was superior.

"But—about Alison—" I began, still unconvinced.

She gripped my arm. "Already Alison is healing. But no one must know of this. Will you keep my secret?"

I nodded numbly as the front door banged, announcing the return of Dr. Brun and the others.

"Will you stay?" she asked.

I told her I must meet Rowan when she returned from school.

Cari was fast asleep when I took her from Dr. Brun's arms. As I walked home I wondered if Dr. Brun had ever been up in Dana's chapel and if so, what he thought of it. But I couldn't ask him. I had given my word.

The phone was ringing as I entered the back hall. My first instinct was to ignore it, but what if Rowan was calling? Balancing Cari on the kitchen counter, I answered.

"When are you going to listen to us, Mitti? What if the same thing should happen to your daughter that happened to Susie and Nancy? Move away, Mitti—if you love your daughter, move away . . ."

There was a stealthy click, then the dial tone, then a recording saying, "If you'd like to make a call, please hang up and try again . . ." and still I stood there, mesmerized, my right arm clutching Cari, until the phone began hurling insults at me. I might have remained there longer but for a scratching at the back door. A small white rectangle had been shoved underneath. I picked it up and turned it over. My cry of horror awakened Cari, who began to wail. It was a snapshot of Rowan—someone had bloodied her with a felt tip pen. I ran to the window just in time to see Jonah Good lumbering into the woods.

Chapter Twenty-Six

Rearing up from the borderline between lawn and woods was a venerable oak which at some time in its history had taken a bolt of lightning that had split a portion of the trunk vertically, like a greenstick fracture. Yet it had continued to live, though its foliage was now so sparse its top stood out stark and bald against the other trees. Still, leaves sprouted each spring from lower branches and no one had the heart to suggest that this veteran, which must have presided over Indian councils, be cut down. Now, in the final week before the general rehearsal, a sudden thaw had set in and strong southwest winds twisted the arthritic giant unmercifully until his complaints were loud and agonized and I wondered if euthanasia might not be the kindest course.

And while he grumbled, thousands of freshets were bursting from the hillsides, emptying into temporary lakes in the hollows until they overflowed and sent hundreds of miniature cataracts down the slopes, which in turn became torrents boiling into the rapidly rising river. The sandbars were completely submerged and Mother Carrier's old house, as expected, succumbed. Before the end of the week the river was spilling over into other portions of the city. Ward's lumberyard was inundated and in spite of extensive sandbagging many basements were flooded, including the one at the Community church. Nevertheless, most people were pleased with the warming trend. They seemed little concerned that their town was being washed away.

But I remained chill and taut. I should report that last call and that snapshot to Jim Willard, but could I trust him not to relay my complaint to the sheriff? At the bottom of the photo had been the words, "Tell the police and you're *all* dead!"

I was losing control—life was moving around me with prismatic distortion. Whom could I trust? Even Dr. Brun and Dana seemed alien to me. Rowan had become even more distanced—we groped through the week like shadow-boxers. With the general rehearsal almost upon us, how could I think? How could I plan a course of action? Afterward, I rationalized, perhaps my mind would clear and I could tackle my problem.

I saw Greg only briefly at a pageant committee meeting at the church the night before the rehearsal. All during the evening, I felt his eyes on me, but when I faced him he turned away. Iris snuggled next to him, and since I arrived late I didn't know if they had come together or separately. After the meeting she took him by the arm and drew him toward me.

"You look as if you'd survived the Wisconsin winter,"

314

she said. "As for me, I prefer Jamaica. Don't you, Greg?"

His answer told me nothing. "My mother loved Jamaica," he replied. "Excuse me, ladies, I have some rewriting to do."

She followed me as I went out to my car. "Nothing like giving us the deep freeze," she remarked, clearly annoyed.

"What? Oh yes, Greg," I made a pretense of indifference. "Any flooding at your place?" Wishful thinking.

She smiled. "No, the house is too high. The basement is filled so I can't swim, but it's fascinating to watch Peacehaven being shredded, bit by bit. I saw Mother Carrier's roof go downriver." She opened the door of her Porsche, parked behind my car. "How about coming over for a drink?"

A drink with her was the last thing I needed. "No, thank you, Iris. I must get home."

As I pulled away from the curb, I could see in my rearview mirror that she was still standing next to her car. I hadn't proceeded very far when I noticed a light in the police headquarters at the city hall, directly across the street from the newspaper office. On impulse I swerved my car into the parking lot. I desperately needed someone to talk to—I couldn't wait any longer. If Gareth could trust Jim . . .

He motioned me to a seat while he completed a call, then leaned back in his chair, his hands behind his head, his long legs sticking through the kneehole of his desk. As I began to talk his old swivel chair creaked forward and he leaned across the desk, concern deepening in his forehead. I felt thankful for this kind-hearted man, who listened quietly, giving me his full attention. Suddenly I knew I was doing the right thing and I began to pour out my story. I hadn't gotten very far when he stopped me.

"I'm sorry, Mitti. Working hours are over. Would you mind giving me a lift home?"

"Sorry to have been so abrupt," he apologized in my car. "Walls have ears."

"You think your office might be bugged?"

"I found a tap on my phone last week and another in the register behind my desk in October. Don't take me home yet," he said as we neared his house. "I want to hear the rest of your story."

I headed my car in the direction of the bluff road and took up my narrative again—the attack in the cave, the phone calls, Damon's grandiose plans, and the horrid snapshot. I tried to cover everything, yet all the time I couldn't shake the feeling that I was leaving out something—something important, but what was it?

As I talked, I began to be aware of car lights behind us, making every turn we did. We were following a narrow, winding road in and around the bluffs, their rugged Indian faces showing eerily in the beam of our headlights. Those other lights were still following us around the curves, appearing and disappearing with the undulations of the road. Some farmer returning home after a visit to Buckley's, I told myself, but now Jim's hand was groping under the dashboard, then under the front seat. Swearing softly, he brought out a tiny rectangular object that had been fastened by a magnet to the metal under the seat and tossed it out the window.

My hands trembled on the wheel. "Was that what I think it was?"

"Yes, and I'm a damn fool for not checking. That was an FM monitoring unit. By tuning into a vacant FM wavelength, whoever's following us in the vehicle back there heard everything we said. Someone got to your car while you were in my office. Did anyone see you go in?"

"I suppose Iris did."

"That figures," he said grimly.

"But that's not a Porsche behind us."

"She would have had time to alert someone else. There's a crossroad hidden behind a curve about a quarter of a mile down. Take it to the left and douse your lights. Maybe we'll be lucky."

Whoever was following hesitated, then continued on. By this time Jim was out of the car and around to my side. "Move over," he ordered. "I'll drive."

We doubled back, then drove off onto byroads unknown to me, crossing our own path several times until we'd apparently lost our tail.

"Why would anyone want to bug us?" I asked.

"Because you and I constitute threats to certain individuals' plans here in town. It's only lately that I've been aware of it and have been able to piece some of it together. It started after Iris came. They made no move while your aunt was still alive because they were confident she'd leave her property to Charity and they could do what they wanted with it. Damon and Charity are being used, but they don't know it. A number of Peacehaven's most prominent citizens are involved. Tyler Bishop is nominally at the head, although from information I've received, Iris is the liaison with the outside interests through an ex-lover. She knows what she's doing, but I'm convinced that in their greed, Tyler and his associates have never inquired too closely into the background of this 'syndicate.' Anyone who blocks them must be eliminated one way or another and that includes you, Mitti—and Dana."

"You mean this—" my stomach felt queasy, "this 'syndicate' has underworld connections?"

"Not just connections. It *is* underworld."

"Do you have any proof?"

"Let's backtrack a little. Remember the night you hid Quentin in that old tunnel between your houses?" I gasped audibly. "I'm probably the only one in town who knows about that tunnel. I wired it for electricity when Dad still had the hardware store."

"And you didn't betray us when those dogs were sniffing around the drain!" I exclaimed warmly.

"Quentin's working for an investigative committee appointed by the governor. According to information they have, some underworld figures are planning to establish a resort and condominium development here as a cover for a variety of illegal activities, including drugs and the dogfighting racket."

"I'm confused. I saw Quentin going to Iris' house one day. I know she was expecting him because—" I described my visit to the Faulkner home.

Jim chuckled. "He told me about that. He'd made a date to interrogate her—about the dogs and about Mark's death. But she met him as though he'd made an assignation—either to try to compromise him or she thought he really was on the make. She probably sicced Irv on to Quentin when Nancy was killed."

I was struck by the irony. "So Quentin is our law and order man, while the pillars of Peacehaven are on the side of the bad guys! Come to think of it, Quentin once mentioned something about dogfights to me—"

"He's death on dogfighters—thinks his dog was stolen by one, probably to be used as bait for the fighting dogs. They also use cats and kittens, you know—dangle them

318

in mesh bags in front of the dogs, then snatch them away while still alive and let the dogs finish them off the next day."

"Jupiter!" I gasped, gripping the dashboard.

"What?"

"Darcy's cat. We found his body in the cave. And she's lost other cats since." Without betraying Dana's and Dr. Brun's errand, I told him about our excursion.

"They must have had a trial run," he conjectured. "Quentin thought they would. I'll bet Irv Good went in there to destroy evidence and you surprised him, so he attacked you. Why didn't *we* think of *your cave*? It's a perfect place for a dogfight operation, because even if Irv mutes his dogs, the others wouldn't be muted, and a cave would contain the noise so that—"

"Irv!" My head was reeling. "You mean he's . . ."

"He's a trainer. His dogs are professional fighters."

"He said he uses them for police work."

"That's his story. He cuts his dogs' vocal cords so they won't draw attention. Besides, mute fighting dogs present a terrifying spectacle. Good dogs sell for several grand apiece. Quentin and I couldn't locate his training quarters. We figured they must be on his own farm, but there's absolutely nothing there."

"I still can't get over Quentin's being a government investigator," 1 said. "That would surprise a lot of people."

"I think it surprised him, but at least he may have the satisfaction of bagging a sheriff." He grinned, slowing as we passed a "winding road" warning.

"How about Jonah?" I blurted out my question before I even had it well formulated in my mind.

"Jonah?" He looked puzzled. "Oh, you mean the dogs?

Well, in most things, Jonah's his father's robot—obeys him blindly and mindlessly, but he's afraid of dogs—*all* dogs."

"Yes, I know," I remembered how terrified the boy had been of the big white dog. "I didn't mean that. What I meant was—why was Irv Good so anxious to blame Nancy's murder on Quentin? Do you suppose he was trying to protect his own son?"

"That'd be a better motive than what I suspect was his true one. No, as a matter of fact, my wife and I played pinochle with the Goods that night, and Jonah sat and watched us all evening."

Well, rule that one out, I thought—then, as though a flashbulb had popped in my brain, it came to me—what I'd been trying to remember!

"The cave wouldn't be suitable for boarding dogs as it is now, would it?" Privately I knew Dr. Brun would have seen anything like that going on.

"No, there's no road leading to it," Jim agreed. "Which still leaves the question—where *does* he keep them?"

"Ruby Hobbs told Dana and me last summer that Irv's been renting her barn."

Jim slapped his knee. "That's it, Mitti! It all fits together! I wouldn't be surprised if Irv leased it before Ruby's brother died. A few days before that, Old Man Hobbs had an argument with Lester Jacobs down at the feed store. Lester was slightly plastered that day—as usual—and he began to josh old Hobbs about what a firetrap of a barn he had. Hobbs got mad and told him that the barn was more valuable than anyone knew. I think that's how the rumor about Hobbs burying money in the barn got around. Saay," he drawled, "we're less than a mile from there now—I'd like to check something. Are you game?"

I wasn't sure my car was as we bounced, lights out, over the choppy, axle-grinding tractor path leading to the barnyard. "Safer than taking the main drive," he explained, easing through one last chuckhole before stopping behind a windbreak of spruces. We sprinted across to the barn on the side away from the house. An owl hooted an alert, but the groans of the old windmill helped cover our approach.

The door to the cowbarn was boarded up, but as Jim leaned against it to listen, one of the boards slipped out of place and would have fallen if he hadn't caught it and forced in a loose nail. Jim caught my arm. There it was! Sniffing, then a scratching on the other side. But now my ears picked up another sound—the hum of an engine coming along the main farm drive. We reached the shelter of the spruces just as the lights of a truck turned a bend and flooded the barnyard. Irv Good got out, carrying something squirming in a bag, and went up the ramp to the granary floor. Jim pulled me down on the half-frozen ground.

"I don't think he saw us," he whispered.

As I lay there, my heart pounding against the ground, the sheriff opened the padlock and pushed aside the big door. A dog sprang for him. He cursed it and kicked it to one side as he entered. We could hear his boots echoing on the steps from the loft to the floor below. An unearthly screech sounded faintly through the thick fieldstone walls, then silence. After a long while he returned, still carrying the now limp sack; climbed into the truck; and drove away.

"He must have one dog on guard duty and the rest in cages," Jim remarked as we picked our way back over the tractor lane.

"What was that terrible sound?" I asked, shivering.

"Probably a cat, but it doesn't make sense. He wasn't in there long enough to be training his dogs. If my theory is right, I imagine old Irv was pretty shaken when he found the children's bodies. I think the poor kids wandered in there—there're all kinds of stories about buried money and stuff—and were attacked by the guard dog. Irv found them, but since he couldn't afford to have them connected with his operation, he carved those symbols on them, then moved the bodies."

I was too shocked to get a word in before Jim smashed his fist on the steering wheel. "No wonder Quentin's the fall guy! I'll bet all our meetings have been bugged. I'll drive over to Madison tonight to see him. We're going to have to act fast. Quentin can get a detachment of state police and a warrant to search the barn tomorrow night during rehearsal. Will Irv be there?"

"Yes, he plays Sheriff George Corwin, who confiscated the witches' property and left their children to beg in the streets. Typecasting," I added with a shaky laugh. It was easy to picture Irv Good turning orphans into the street . . . and then I was seeing him standing over a dying white dog, while a black one struggled at the end of a rope. "*Attacked my dog without warning,*" he was saying, "*my dog wot was trained in the London bear pits . . .*"

Jim switched on the lights when we reached the county road, bringing me back to the present. I leaned against the seat, thinking about tomorrow. The Peacehaven council had declared a holiday as a kick-off to engender enthusiasm and publicity. The rehearsal was to be held in the oversized council chamber at city hall that doubled as an auditorium.

Alison would be there. She was in another remission and was determined to continue in the part of Rebecca Nurse. Her improvement was little short of a miracle. But in contrast to this new burst of energy on Alison's part, Dana seemed to be losing her old vitality. I remembered Dana kneeling before her altar, holding out the poppet of Alison, with the ugly mark spreading above her left breast . . .

"Wake up, Mitti," Jim said, turning off the ignition. "You looked so relaxed just now I hated to disturb you, but I'd better head home pretty quick. My wife will be wondering what happened to me, and I have to get to Madison before morning."

"I wasn't sleeping," I told him. "I could have dropped you off at your house."

"Not a chance. I always escort ladies to their door," he said gallantly. "With my long legs, I'll be home in less than five minutes." An apprehensive note came into his voice. "Strange thing, I just saw Irv's truck on the way down from your house. He must have beaten us here; wonder what he wanted."

The answer lay on my doorstep in a bloodied sack—a mangled heap of gray fur that had once been Phantom. So that was what had screamed in the barn! Irv must have thought he'd gotten my cat, but Loki had been locked in the house. Whoever'd spied on Jim and me must have relayed the information to Irv and this was his way of telling me to clear out. As I swayed dizzily against

323

the wall of the house there was a loud crack. Aged fibers had given away, and with a woodsy shriek, the ancient oak came crashing down like a movie clapstick, setting the cameras in motion for action for which there would be no retakes.

Chapter Twenty-Seven

"Mary Esty, how can you afflict these children so and not repent?" The judge peered down at me, his face severe below the wig that fringed his black skullcap.

"She chokes me—oh, she chokes me kuz I wunna sign in the Black Book!" Mercy Lewis rolled at my feet. Her own groping fingers had produced the red blotches on her neck. The other girls mimicked her, chanting a scurrilous litany, until Anne Putnam suddenly sprang up and pointed to the beams overhead. "There! There's her spectral shape a-sittin' there—with a fat green snake windin' round her wrist! See how it sucks her thumb—ooh, now it's changed into a little yellow bird! Mary Esty, come down from there and stop afflicting me!"

"Come down, come down!" her companions chorused.

Their elders stared in fascination, fancying they saw my shape and a snake and a bird among the empty trusses.

" 'Tis some strange delusion has struck the child," I faltered. "I know nought o't."

Anne fell to the ground, shrieking that nails and pins were being driven into her, and indeed, I watched wounds erupt from her fair skin. My heart skipped a beat, then raced wildly as the others began to develop similar symptoms. It couldn't be so and yet 'twas. Anne was not the sly minx Mercy Lewis was, and I believed her tortures genuine.

The judge's eyes bored into me, raking my soul. "How can you say you know nothing when you see these tormented?"

"Would you have me accuse myself?"

"Yes, if you be guilty. How far have you complied with Satan whereby he takes this advantage against you?"

"Sir, I never complied but prayed against him all my days. What would you have me do?" I pleaded, searching his face for some remnant of the affection he once bore me; but there was none.

"Confess, if you be guilty!" he thundered.

A flux of love, hurt, and fear welled in my throat and I was forced to clear it. At once the girls began to clear their throats. My hands went to my mouth. Theirs did likewise. What could I do against such conspiracy?

An ancient crone tottered towards the bench—Margaret Redington, my neighbor, whom I had cured of the King's Evil and to whom I had brought fresh meat when she had none.

"Come February," she began in a quavery voice, "I was at Goodman Esty's and talking with his wife about an infirmity I had and presently after I fell into a most solemn condition and sometime later I was exceeding ill and that night Goody Esty appeared to me and proffered

326

me a piece of fresh meat and I told her 'twas not fit for the dogs and I would have none of it and then she vanished away."

My heart quailed. How could the woman lie so? She had snatched at the meat—good meat—and wolfed it before her sister returned home so she wouldn't have to share it. Ironically, I'd always suspected *her* of being a witch.

Now Samuel Smith took the stand, uncommon sober, but reeking of stale urine and vomit. "I was one night at the house of Isaac Estick of Topsfield," he said, nervously drawing his hand over hair slick with bear grease, "and I was as far as I know too rude in discourse, and the above Estick's wife said to me that I might rue it hereafter. And as I was going home that night about a quarter of a mile from the said Estick's house by a stone wall, I received a little blow on my shoulder with I know not what and the stone wall rattled very much which affrighted me. My horse also was affrighted very much, but I cannot give the reason of it."

That old tale again, born in his cups.

"Mary Esty, what have you to say to this?" the judge asked.

Oh, Will, Will, how can you believe such lies? "I will say it—I am clear of this sin," I declared aloud.

He gaveled down the noise. "Of what sin?" he demanded.

"Of witchcraft."

Stroking his chin, as though unsure of himself, he turned to the witnesses. "Are you certain this is the woman?"

The girls promptly began to bark and bleat and mew. Some crawled around on all fours. Mercy Lewis crept forward and rolled at my feet. I clenched my hands to suppress a desire to slap her. She reared on her haunches and clenched her hands. Instinctively I unclenched mine, whereupon she relaxed hers.

Judge Stoughton had not failed to notice.

"Look, now your hands are open, hers are open."

"Indeed, so it is with children who play 'Simon Says,' " I retorted, which caused Mary Warren and Betty Hubbard to hold their breaths until their faces purpled, and Anne Putnam cried out, "Oh, Goody Esty, Goody Esty, you are the woman!"

The strain of the day had taken its toll and I lowered my head to drive away the faintness that threatened to engulf me. So, too, did the heads of the young girls droop, then slowly twist nearly halfway round. The elder Ann Putnam pushed them aside and ran toward me. "Put up her head!" she cried. "For while her head is down the necks of these be broken!"

As the sheriff jerked my head upright the girls straightened theirs.

" 'Tis she," the elder Ann continued, "who with her sister Rebecca, murdered my babies while they were yet in the cradle—forsooth, some yet in the womb. And eke my sister's babes, so that she died of grief. Night after night these butchered innocents come to me in their winding sheets and beg me to avenge them."

Stoughton's eyes bored into me. "And thou sayst this is not witchcraft, Mary?" He'd used my first name and the old form of speech! Yet he gave no other sign of recognition.

" 'Tis an evil spirit," I conceded, trying not to flinch as a frenzied Sarah Bibber dug her sharp nails into my scalp, "but whether it be witchcraft, I do not know." That there was something diabolic afoot I did not doubt.

"She wanted us to sign the Devil's Book," they chorused. "She flew in my window at night and sat on my bed with the book," Abigail Williams cried out. Betty Parris, the minister's daughter, prowled on all fours, yowling like a cat in heat.

"Let the accused touch the afflicted so she may draw her devils back into herself," the judge ordered.

One by one the girls were brought to me and Sheriff Corwin forced me to lay my hands on them. As I touched the soft flesh, each "victim" ceased her struggles and let herself be led away quietly. It took three men to bring Betty Parris to me, spitting and scratching, a great ball swelling in her throat. Stoughton went livid. "Woman, withdraw *all* thy devils!" he roared. "Wouldst thou slay this child before our eyes?"

"I know nought o' devils," I protested. "I have no power to stop this. I fear for the child as do you."

Betty pushed her ash blonde hair away from her eyes. "Nay, 'tis not Goody Esty afflicts me. 'Tis the demons I see in *all* o' *ye!* Oh, ye are sore possessed . . ."

"Cut! Cut!" Lucian hurried forward, script in hand. "Lucy, those weren't your lines. Where'd you get them?"

Lucy stood trembling, her lips white and her eyes downcast behind the thick lenses. "I don't know," she murmured. "I'll try to do it right the next time."

"Well, we've been going at it pretty hard," he relented. "Take five, everyone. Good work, girls."

They drifted off toward the refreshment tables, loaded

with confections from nearly every oven in Peacehaven.

"You've trained the girls well, Mitti," Lucian said. "And you adults are coming along, too, even though you still have to use your scripts, except for Mitti and Greg." He turned to Elspeth. "Your characterization of Sarah Bibber is excellent, but don't be so realistic. We don't want Mitti torn to pieces before the pageant. And, Charity, you've got to project more for Mistress Ann Putnam. One thing puzzles me, though," he continued, turning to Greg. "Why did you switch to the second person singular when you addressed Mary at the last? I thought you said according to your research the 'you' form was fairly universal by 1692 instead of the 'thou.' Did you change the script?"

"I wasn't aware I was doing it," Greg replied.

Homer Redd came up, stuffing his mouth with blitz torte. "You were too sober as Samuel Smith, Homer," Lucian told him. "Don't you think he might have taken a belt or so to fortify himself? Like you do when you go to the dentist." The farmer reddened. "Oh, and you, Irv, pick up your cues faster—lay Mitti's hands on the girls immediately. You ought to know how a sheriff acts. As for you, Aunt Jenny, you're playing Goody Redington too young. She was at least seventy." Sheer flattery! He knew damn well Aunt Jenny was over eighty.

The rehearsal had been going on since noon. Lucian had urged us to wear costumes, even at rehearsal, to help us get into our roles. I'd had a hard time to keep from staring at Greg. He was attired exactly as Stoughton had been in my dream, with maroon robe, black skull cap, and linen and lace neckpiece. "You've done a superb job, Mitti," he said. "I—I want to apologize for the way I acted at Christmas. You're not scuttling the pageant—

you're making it with your portrayal of Mary Esty."

"You were uncommonly convincing yourself, Greg," I countered, keeping my tone cool, though my heart pounded and I hid my shaking hands in the folds of my long dark-green gown. "Where did you get your costume? It looks so—authentic."

"I had it copied from Stoughton's portrait in the Harvard archives, where I've been working the last two months."

"I thought you were in Jamaica."

"Jamaica?" He was puzzled. "I haven't been there since I was a little boy. No, to tell you the truth, you'd made me question some of my theories and I went back for additional research."

I turned my head to hide my relief. "I have something for you. I found an article on Salem that Aunt Bo started and apparently never finished. It gives a new light on the whole subject. Read it. You might want to make some changes in the pageant."

He put the copies I'd made into his pocket, but the old wariness came into his eyes. I added quickly, "You've done a clever job of weaving in the actual trial testimony. When I speak my lines I feel little shivers to think I'm saying the same words Mary Esty did three centuries ago. And you play a hanging judge with a vengeance."

"I want to show Stoughton as he was—bigoted, cruel and self-righteous."

"He didn't think that of himself. You have to believe his lines in order to make the audience believe you."

"You really can't accept your ancestor for what he was, can you?" The spurt of anger passed. "I'm sorry, I shouldn't have said that. What do you think was Stoughton's motive?"

331

"Fear, Greg, stark fear."

Iris wedged herself between us, interlacing her fingers with his. "Greg, darling, can we go over our scene together? I want to be sure I have my part right."

"Oh, you'll do fine, Iris," he assured her. "I was just about to offer Mitti some refreshment. Would you join us?"

"Why don't you two go ahead?" I suggested. "I'm not hungry, and one witch at a time is enough for you, Greg."

Iris tugged at his arm. Reluctantly—I hoped—he followed her to the table.

I walked over to Darcy and Marion, who were going over their lines in the corner. "Can't you rest even for a minute?" I asked them.

"Oh, I could," Darcy drawled, "but Marion's nervous about the scene where he gets pressed to death."

"What's so hard about that?" I asked. "All you have to do is moan and cry out, 'More rocks! More rocks!' "

"But some of the guys might get carried away," he worried.

No wonder, after the harassment he'd suffered at the hands of the town bullies! "I'll speak to Lucian. We ought to have rocks made of foam rubber or papier maché. Relax! The way we're going today, we won't get to the last act."

Darcy grabbed my arm. "Well, glory be! There's Alison!"

Ward and Bruce were helping Alison with her coat. She'd insisted she felt well enough to be at the rehearsal. "I hope I'm not late," she said now. "Ward made me rest all morning." Her eyes sparkled and it was hard to believe her appearance of health was only a reprieve, not a pardon.

"We put your big scene off until later," I reassured her.

Lucian climbed onto the stage and blew his whistle. "Since we're running a little late," he announced, "we won't try the third act today. I'd planned to move us all up to Bishop's Bluff for the gallows scene, since the ground's frozen again, but there's not going to be time. Lucy, take it again from the second scene where you accuse Tituba of having bewitched you. You direct, Mitti—I have to do Parris. Damon," he called to the doctor, who was talking to Tyler Bishop, "you're in this, so get on up here."

"Good thing Lucian has some sense," Ward growled in my ear. "I'd never have let Alison go up on that bluff tonight."

Lucy dragged her feet up the steps to the stage and lay down across the three chairs that were a makeshift bed. She was ominously white, but Lucian seemed not to notice. She began to moan and gnaw at the blanket which had been thrown over her, then suddenly stopped. "Please, Daddy," she whimpered, "I don't want to do this part again today. Can we do something else?"

"Nonsense, the scene needs work," Lucian objected.

Lucy put aside her glasses and resumed her position.

"Betty, child," Lucian gave his line, "what ails thee?"

Her convulsions increased until those gathered around her had to hold her down on the bed.

"Tell us, Betty, in the name of Almighty God!" he commanded.

"Don't say that name!" she shrieked, her hands over her ears. "I can't bear it!" She fell back in a swoon and Andy Cloyce, as Dr. Griggs, took hold of her wrist.

"Her pulse is weak and rapid," he said, "dangerous for a child of her delicate nature. Bleeding would be of no

333

avail. This is not a natural disorder. The evil hand is upon her.''

"Hmmph!'' Damon, who played the irascible Thomas Putnam, sniffed. "Just as my wife said—an evil spirit walks among us. Tell us, Miss Betty, who has done this thing?''

This was Lucy's cue to sit up, point to Rhoda Jackson crouching at the foot of the bed and cry out, "Tituba—oh, Tituba!'' Instead, she wailed, "Iris—oh, Iris!''

Iris, who was clinging to Greg's arm, went rigid as curious eyes turned to her, but she quickly regained her composure. "The child's right, Lucian. She isn't well. She needs rest.''

Her father glared at her. "I don't know what's gotten into you, Lucy. Apologize at once!''

She slid down from the platform and dragged toward Iris, her head drooping. A shiver went through her as the woman took her hand. "I'm sorry, Iris,'' she murmured.

"Okay, okay, everyone,'' Lucian barked, "we'll try the last act.''

As we were taking our positions, the outside door banged and Dana came hobbling into the auditorium, wisps of hair straying about her face. "Cariad's gone! Gone!''

Sheriff Good took command at once. "All officers and reserves are immediately ordered to duty!'' He turned to Dana. "All right, what happened? And none o' your Indian lies!'' he added menacingly.

Dana leaned wearily against the refreshment table. "Cari wanted to go out, so I bundled her up and put her out in her play yard to romp with her dog while I fixed supper. Then I heard the dog yowling and went to see what was the matter. Cariad was gone and the dog was trying to jump out." She handed the sheriff a torn piece of brown corduroy. "I found this on the ground. Outside the fence there were huge footprints in the frost."

"Maybe her dog would track her," Jim Willard suggested.

She shook her head. "Just as I was getting into my car to come down here, I saw him clear the fence and dash off into the woods. I tried to call him back, but he was gone."

Someone spoke up. "This is a sabbat night for the coven—when they make sacrifices."

"Jim!" Good barked at Willard, "take a posse over to the witch farm and round 'em up!"

"I'll need a warrant," Jim objected.

The sheriff's face flushed. "You fool around gettin' a warrant when they got a child in their hands?"

"You don't know that."

Homer Redd shook his fist in Jim's face. "You goddam halfass cop! No wonder kids get murdered around here!" He sprang up on the stage. "Who'll follow me? We'll round 'em up!"

"Okay, I'm deputizing you, Homer," Irv told him. "You, too, Scotty. Jim, get on the radio and call in the regular deputies, and then you and Caleb go get those two-way radios out of your office."

A vision of Jonah Good darting into the woods came into my mind. Had he been the one all along? But Jim had accounted for him on Halloween. Still, he might have had time after the Willards had gone home that night. "Jim!" I grabbed his sleeve as he passed below the stage. "The Hobbs farm!" Then in a whisper, "Is Quentin coming?"

"I'm giving orders," Irv barked. "*I'll* check the Hobbs

farm. No, you don't, doc," he directed at Damon who had said something in a low voice, "I want you to stay right where we can find you."

While Irv had his head turned Jim gave me a thumbs-up sign. So Quentin would be there. But would Jonah take her to the farm?

The eerie notes of an Indian chant sounded above the hubbub. Dana had slumped to the floor and was swaying back and forth, chanting a prayer to *Maoona*.

"What's she doing?" Edna asked in a loud whisper. "Do you suppose she's talking in tongues?"

"Praying to her heathen gods, most likely," Gladys sniffed.

"That's Winnebago," I said. "*Maoona* is their name for the Creator and *Hayninklra* was his fair-skinned son who taught them wisdom and how to make medicine."

"I'm sure that's not one of Jehovah's tongues," Gladys retorted. "Lucian tells me my tongue sounds like Hebrew—God's own language."

"You wouldn't know Hebrew from Winnebago," Aunt Jenny snapped. "You don't even know what you're sayin', I bet."

"Only God knows that," Gladys said sanctimoniously.

"Or the Devil," the old woman shot back.

"Really, Mother!"

Dana dropped her head on her breast in an attitude of dejection. "I can't see!" she moaned. "My powers are spent. I cannot see her."

The world around me was breaking up into bits and pieces, like garbled film clips. Mothers were rounding up their younger children, afraid they, too, might disappear. The Redd baby was crying.

"Please!" I cried. "Somebody find my child!"

Alison's arm encircled my waist. "They'll find her,

336

Mitti, I know they will," she tried to comfort me. "Don't you worry—good heavens, what's she doing?"

Rowan was prancing around the stage, riding an invisible horse. "Giddy-ap, old Robin-Dobbin, Giddy-ap!" in a coarse, heavy voice that changed to a loud whinny, as though horse and rider were one. "Up wi' ye, ye spavined nag! Horse 'n hattock!" She leaped onto one of the chairs in Lucy's makeshift bed. The other girls crowded in close as everyone turned to watch. Rowan went through the motions of dismounting and slapping the horse on the rump to send him away, then turned slowly around to us, glassy-eyed and flushed.

A shiver ran through the crowd as her eyes riveted on something in the back of the room. I followed her gaze to yellow-green eyes. Iris made a slight movement of her hand. Rowan fell forward, her tongue protruding until she gagged. One after the other the girls joined in. Cissie Osburn was bleating like a goat; Linda beat her head upon the floor. Dorcas Redd stood aloof at first, but when Debby and Jessica pulled her down, she, too, was caught up in the frenzy. All the tricks I'd taught them were being played in deadly earnest now.

Iris nodded her head slightly. Instantly Rowan threw herself at Dana's feet. "Remove your spell!" my daughter pleaded. "Let us be!" She reached up and caught at Dana's outstretched hands, followed by the other girls, one by one, ceasing their cries the moment they touched her.

"Woman, what have you to say?" Lucian demanded.

"I love Cariad," Dana protested. "I would protect her with my life."

"Listen, everyone, please!" Alison pleaded. "Dana wouldn't . . ."

"Stay out of this!" Damon snapped at her.

"Don't you tell me what to do!" she lashed out. "Dana's cured me, which is more than you did! She laid her hands upon me and drew the poison from my body. I'm healed. Ward doesn't believe that yet, but he will."

As Ward tried to draw Alison away, Cissie Osburn bounded forward. "Oh, Goody Nurse, 'tis you who've been sitting on my bed at night!" She dug her hands into the chignon at the nape of Alison's neck. Ward pushed Cissie away, lifted Alison and strode out.

"God help us!" Lucian cried. "The evil is upon us. Satan's emissaries lurk among us, and we must discover them."

"Iris knows!" Cissie cried out. "The Devil showed her his Black Book. She said so."

Lucian turned to her. "Is that true, Iris?"

She bowed her head, the lovely penitent to all eyes but mine. "The Devil knew I was weak," she confessed in a soft voice. "He asked me to sign his book and showed me the names of those who had already done so. I was tempted, but I stalled. Each time he returned, the list had grown, and I knew I couldn't hold out much longer. That is when I went to you for help, Lucian. You brought me to Christ, and Satan came no more." She sighed. "But perhaps I did wrong to shield those whose names were in the book."

"God bless you, Sister," Lucian soothed her. "He would want you to unmask those who covenant with Satan."

We were balanced on two spheres of time—the seventeenth century and the twentieth. How could these people revert to the error of Salem when their own ancestors had died of it? These weren't the people I'd known—even their speech was unnatural.

338

"The names!" Lucian prodded.

"Must I?" Iris seemed near fainting.

"For the sake of the innocent," he urged.

She swayed dizzily. "Dana," she murmured. "She was the first."

"I knew it! I knew it!" Homer bawled. "Her and her fancy potions. Now the doc says Esther can't have any more kids, so I won't ever have a son, and I know Dana had a hand in that somehow."

"Hush, Homer!" his wife tried to quiet him.

"Shut up, woman! Or are you in league with her?"

"And there was old Mrs. Pudeator."

Aunt Jenny! Impossible! I could see their astonishment. Gladys paled. "I begged you not to take that Indian woman's medicines, Mother."

"Goodness knows what was in them," Muriel put in.

"You're cowards, both of you," the old woman wailed. "Only afraid for your own skins. Wish I'd aborted the both o' you." Her face puckered and tears began running down her cheeks, as she thumped with her cane toward the door.

"Stop that woman! Arrest her!" Good shouted to Jim, who had returned with the radios.

"On what charge?" Jim asked simply.

"He won't help, Irv," Iris cried. "He's one, too."

A shudder ran through the crowd. Gentle Jim Willard! Jessica confronted her father. "Is that why you wouldn't let me go to the Patch this week, Daddy? Were you afraid Iris would tell on you?"

Jim's face went gray. Irv Good ripped the deputy badge from his coat, then motioned to another deputy to guard him and Aunt Jenny, who had already been taken into custody by her son-in-law.

"And Darcy is another." Iris had warmed to her mission. "She sacrifices her cats to her gods. That's why she has so few left."

"You goddam, lying bitch!" Darcy raged.

"You heard her curse me," Iris said meekly.

"Anyone else?" Lucian asked.

"I didn't see all the names. And one is too embarrassing for me to mention."

"God will defend you," Lucian assured her gently.

"He tried to rape me."

"Who was he?" Elspeth echoed a universal curiosity.

Iris bit her lip. "Quentin Jackson," she whispered. The sheriff's eyes lit.

"Anyone else?" Lucian asked.

"No—yes, I almost forgot! He pretends to be holy, but he conjures up demons in caves—Dr. Martin Brun!"

She waited for the sensation her last announcement had made to die down. "And there was yet another—she who caused her cousin to drown . . ."

"I knew it all the time! She killed my Junior!" Elspeth Osburn came menacingly toward me. "And maybe she killed her baby," she screeched. "After all, she can have plenty more by screwing the Devil."

"Elspeth!" Melvin remonstrated. "My wife hasn't been herself," he apologized, trying to draw her away.

They closed in on me, their excitement mounting. I put my arm around Dana, as much for support as to help her. *They're not going to find Cariad,* I despaired. *They're going to stay here and hunt witches!* I plucked at Greg's sleeve. "You're a newspaperman, Greg—you can't believe these wild accusations. They've gone crazy. They don't even care about my baby!"

340

He didn't answer—merely stood with his hands gripping the lectern, tortured eyes staring off into space.

"Greg?" I asked uncertainly. Then, "Will?"

He saw me for the first time. "You are right for once, Mary Esty. We must be certain justice is done." The room hushed as his gavel crashed down on the stand.

"Let the Indian woman be examined in private for the devil's mark," he declared.

"Why in private?" Iris asked contemptuously.

Her question triggered a response in Rowan, who sprang at Dana and ripped the blouse from her shoulders. A shock wave ran through the hall. Just above Dana's left breast was a black mole.

"The devil's tit!" Elspeth shrieked. Immediately the girls screamed that Dana was tormenting them again, and one by one they touched her. Cissie raked her nails across the mole, leaving angry red welts on either side. Drops of blood slowly gathered on Dana's breast. So this was the price of Alison's cure!

"She's the woman who made me wreck my car!" Lester Jacobs exclaimed. "And I saw her fly right off into the trees!"

"Yeah, and she stopped my tractor dead!" Homer declared.

Lucian was kneeling center stage. His hands were clasped, his eyes on the ceiling, his lips moving in prayer.

"He's a saint!" someone whispered.

"The Lord has spoken to me," he cried out suddenly. "While the search goes on, the rest of us must seek Him in a high place to pray for the safety of the child and for those lost souls. We'll light a bonfire on Bishop's Bluff to be a beacon for the searchers. There we will wait until the child is found. We will take the accused with us and pray for their deliverance from Satan."

At least he got them going, I thought thankfully, as the hall cleared. The small children and the elderly were whisked home. I grabbed my cape from its hook and wrapped it high around my chin, hoping to join the hunt, but Damon caught my arm.

"You, too, Submit," he said.

I looked back. Greg still stood by the lectern, staring at the gavel in his hand. Slowly he laid it down and went for his coat. Then, as if in afterthought, he returned to the lectern, picked up the gavel, and stuffed it in his coat pocket. As Damon steered me through the door with the others, Greg—or was it Will?—followed us out into the night.

Chapter Twenty-Eight

Shadowed eye sockets in the firelight made masks of the faces of those gathered on Bishop's Bluff. Only the hardiest, angriest, and most curious had reached the top, some having given up on the rugged cowpath and gone home to their television sets. Firewood ripped from the dilapidated shack was now a blazing beacon for miles around, for night had clamped its lid down over the landscape. Our numbers had thinned, but one by one those hunting for Cariad were arriving, either to report or to give up and stay. Lanterns and flashlights flickered like fireflies here and there among the hills. In the distance a sleepless coyote howled his woes to a jagged sickle of moon and a screech owl somewhere in the night warned of impending disaster.

The drop in temperature had turned the mud-furrowed slopes into a frozen corduroy that twisted ankles and tripped up our feet. Dana stumbled along near the head of the column. Jim Willard, the Jacksons, and the Zagrodniks, under Caleb's hawklike eye, took turns making chairs with their hands to carry Aunt Jenny up the steep incline. About halfway up I saw Dana falter and almost go down. Someone had thrust a gallon jug of liquid—liquor, I supposed—into her hands and the weight of it had thrown her off balance. I scrambled forward and took the bottle away from her just as she slipped to her knees again. She was breathing hard and her lameness was more pronounced. Tyler Bishop caught up with us. "What's going on here?"

"She lost her balance."

"Come here, Mel," he called to the undertaker. "Take this gasoline on up ahead so they can start the bonfire." Again Dana staggered and I slipped my arm into hers to support her. She shivered and tried to pull away. "I don't deserve your help," she panted, but she leaned on me heavily, seeming to draw strength from me, for her steps quickened, her weight on my arm decreased and she regained the breath to speak.

"The stars do not decree our fate," she said. "We sow our fate in the stars and when they come round again we must reap according to what we have sown. Once I betrayed a friend—not deliberately—but I helped cause her death and I was unable to save her—or," her voice fell, "too cowardly. She and her mother had been good to me and my people, had saved some of us from the spotted disease, but other white people had been bad. We wanted to frighten the white man so he would go away from Naumkeag, so we danced with the slaves at their sabbats. They drank of our magic and we of theirs until we brewed a strong poison for our enemies. The Obayah

344

Man instructed us. We drove their cattle into the sea, weakened their axles so their wheels fell off, threw stones at their houses, and planted toads and snakes and strange animals in their beds and in the meeting house, while the slaves hid poppets where they would be found and spread evil rumors about those whom the Obayah Man chose. I did not think my poison could hurt my friend because she didn't belong to the Obayah Man's church and owned no slave, but it did. Vengeance is not justice; it is a stone thrown into the waters and makes no distinction between innocent and guilty. You will need to remember that tonight, Mitti."

My mind slipped gears between past and present. She knew nothing of my dreams, yet this might have been Yawataw walking beside me. Her fingers tightened on my wrist.

"The world is full of demons," she continued, "material and immaterial, but for every demon there are a thousand good spirits—angels you call them—if we only make use of them. One of these is Forgiveness, who is only a little less strong than Love."

"But we must have discipline and punishment," I argued.

"To forgive doesn't require us to condone," she said. "As for discipline and punishment—they are the responsibility of the law and society. I speak of the individual spirit—our responsibility is to seek after angels, not demons. They're all about us and it is up to us to choose. Because I chose wrongly, my friend, her sister and others died. I have paid my debt to the sister, but I have other debts to pay tonight."

Was she out of her head or was I dreaming this, too? The wind sang around us and the air was filled with voices. When we reached the top of the bluff Dana was separated from me and herded to one side where the accused were assembled under a large oak on the smoke-laden side of the fire. She mounted a small, wobbly platform, her face muffled in the hood of her cloak. Caleb leaned on his shotgun beside her, the blue veins in his nose glistening in the firelight. At his order, his charges seated themselves on the ground. Darcy and Marion huddled together in silence. Aunt Jenny lay with her head in Rhoda Jackson's lap, shivering under the blanket someone had thrown over her, while Jim Willard and Darrell Jackson sat to one side.

They were the goats. I was kept among the sheep on the leeward side of the fire, possibly because they hadn't made up their minds about me in spite of Iris' denunciation. It was my child who was missing and they were torn between pity and vengeance.

Though I was close to the fire, its warmth failed to drive the chill from my heart. How could I remain here in this madness when my child was lost somewhere out there? But Damon kept a firm grip on me and I was as much a prisoner as those on the other side of the fire.

Rowan, too, had tried to join the hunt, but had been ordered back, for which I was grateful. Now she remained silent, among the gibbering girls, her head downcast. Iris stood next to her, eyes riveted on the fire, her mouth curved in a slight smile. Esther had left her baby with Mrs. Soames and now was trying to calm Mrs. Willard. Greg was nowhere to be seen. Was his one of those lights out there in the dark?

Lucian stood with his back so close to the flames he seemed almost to have risen out of them. He held his bible in his hands, its pages bristling with white reference cards. After a moment of silent prayer, he opened to one of the selections.

"Brothers and Sisters," his voice rose above the wind and the crackling wood, "we have come to a difficult moment in the history of this community. We who have loathed witch-hunters are forced to face the reality that traffickers with Satan do exist and must be ferreted out and either made to turn from their sinful ways or be cast out. Even so did Lucifer attack Salem. There his weapons were superstition and fear. Do not think because we gather to cast Satan out of our society that we have become witchhunters as they did three centuries ago. The Evil One uses strategems to confuse our thinking. Where our ancestors were too strict, we have been too liberal. We define evil as a mental disease. Satan would crow with delight if we were to liken the sufferings of these girls to the vicious behavior of those maids in Salem. The Puritans *believed* in Satan and feared him. We, all too often, neither believe in him nor fear him; thus are all the more vulnerable to his delusions. Now witches can brazenly parade their blasphemy before us and all we do is say, 'How quaint!' "

A prolonged nervous titter formed a descant over mutterings around the fire. Someone started to clap, then stopped.

"Strange things," Lucian continued when they had quieted, "have been going on in Peacehaven, from trivial incidents to murder. You have tolerated the presence of pagans and atheists. Saint John wrote of a similar situation in Revelation: 'I know thy works, and charity, and service, and faith, and thy patience . . . Notwith-

347

standing I have a few things against thee, because thou sufferest that woman Jezebel,' " turning his head slowly toward Dana, " 'which calleth herself a prophetess, to teach and to seduce my servants to commit fornication, and to eat things sacrificed unto idols.'

"Now you are asking, 'Lucian, when have we commited fornication with her?—eaten things sacrificed unto idols?' I say to hold commerce with her is mental fornication and to drink of her potions is to eat meat sacrificed unto idols." He pointed to Aunt Jenny. "Who knows what poisons she's been given?"

"What of the poison you feed these people, Lucian Leroi?" Aunt Jenny cried out from the other side of the fire.

The crowd began to murmur angrily. "Be tolerant toward our elderly sister," Lucian stilled them. "She may have done this in all innocence at first. I perceive that this one," he held out his hand to Gladys, "repents having fetched those 'medicines' for her mother. Is that not so, my child?"

Gladys' opulent bosom began to heave. "I did it because they eased her pains, but I wasn't the only one. Muriel was guilty, too."

Her sister shot her an angry look.

"Both of you acted out of compassion," he said gently. "Tell me, did you ever see the Indian woman making strange signs over her potions or uttering magical words?"

"Oh no, never—that is, not until the rehearsal tonight," Muriel exclaimed.

"We-ell," Gladys groped to please, "there *was* a faraway look in her eyes at times."

348

"What about the love potion *you* asked for, Glad?" Muriel had her revenge.

"Ah, Gladys, even you?" Lucian asked sadly.

Now the tears came. "I—I was desperate. I found Dana tending her goat—she asked *him* if he thought I should have it."

Sickened, I remembered Dana's whimsical way with Caper.

"And did he—this goat—answer?"

"He seemed angry. He hit her with his head and she fell down and worshiped him." Oh, Caper and his antics! If only Greg were here, he could tell how Caper knocked him down.

"Worshiped him?" The minister reeled with horror.

"She talked to him in a strange tongue . . ."

Scolded him in Winnebago, no doubt.

"And did she give you the potion?"

"No, she said what I desired was not to be—that y . . ."

Lucian stopped her mouth with his fingers. "That is enough, my child. Your secrets are your own. Praise the Lord; He protected you.

"So," he continued, "we have heard testimony that this woman dispensed magic potions and bowed down to a goatish god. Hear now what the Lord saith, 'Whosoever lieth with a beast shall surely be put to death. He that sacrificeth unto any god, save unto the Lord only, he shall be utterly destroyed . . . There shall not be found among you anyone that maketh his son or daughter to pass through the fire . . .' "

"That's Submit!" Elspeth screamed. *"She put my son through the fire!* There's your witch! Why isn't *she* with the accused?"

349

Her question foundered as Homer Redd and Lester Jacobs, carrying shotguns, came up the path. "We went to the witch farm," Homer reported, "but they must have had their sabbat somewhere else. We didn't find them anywhere."

"Probably taken off somewhere with the baby," Lester added.

Charity came over to me. "I—I hope they find Cari, Mitti. I know I haven't been very friendly . . . hate me if you wish . . . but don't be too hard on Damon, please. He's obsessed with the idea of restoring Peacehaven. He cares about nothing else—not even me. He says I'm weak and neurotic. I don't think he ever really loved me. He thought he was marrying a fortune. I wish I didn't love him, but I do. I shouldn't go on like this—maybe I really am neurotic—I just wanted you to know I'm sorry."

But my anguish had turned to unrelenting rage. "Oh, yes, you're sorry! You had no qualms about trying to steal Rowan from me or trying to drive me and my children from our home! I suppose you were in on those phone calls, too!"

She lowered her eyes. "I didn't make any. I didn't like the idea, but Damon and the others insisted on them. Iris was most often your caller."

She was a miserable spectacle crouching there, the tears running down her cheeks, but her very passivity infuriated me. Why didn't she scream at me, recount my shortcomings—anything to give me license to let loose my full wrath?

"Charity!" I sneered. "What mockery your name!" I taunted, hoping to provoke a retort, but she remained mute, fueling the rage that boiled within me, building up

350

a power that forced my lips open. "May God str—" the valve closed on my anger and choked the words back as Lucian took up his sermon again.

" 'There shall not be found among you anyone that maketh his son or daughter to pass through the fire or useth divination . . . or an enchanter or a witch . . . or a wizard or a necromancer. For all that do these things are an abomination unto the Lord.'

" 'Neither shalt thou lie with any beast to defile thyself therewith, neither shall any woman stand before a beast to lie down thereto.' Did not this woman here lie down before her beast?"

"That she did!" Gladys affirmed.

"I don't believe it!" Esther's courage flared momentarily.

"Are you her disciple, woman?" Lucian thundered.

"I? Oh, no!" Her courage had flickered out. The girls had gone into spasms again—all but Rowan. "Stop it, Carol!" Esther shrieked, grabbing her daughter's arm. At once the girl desisted and so did the others as, one by one, they touched the distraught woman.

"Do you confess your guilt?" Lucian demanded.

She fell to her knees, her hands covering her face. "I do," she whispered, sobbing. So this is what Mary Esty meant by confessing witches who belied themselves to save their lives!

"Praise the Lord!" the minister rejoiced. "We've snatched a soul from the brink of hell!"

More steps on the path. One of Good's men reported, "No sign of the baby. Irv's gone for his dogs, and Scotty and the Cloyces are bringing Dr. Brun and Mother Carrier."

"*My* mother?" Damon exclaimed. "Why her? This is too much strain for her."

"Didn't Lucian say *anyone* who's trafficked with the Devil?" Tyler Bishop shouted.

"But she's *my* mother," the doctor said through gritted teeth.

"What difference does that make?" Bishop persisted. He would have said more, but the Cloyce brothers and Dr. Brun arrived, carrying Damon's mother, who moaned as they laid her down next to Aunt Jenny. Dr. Brun knelt by her side and listened to her heart, felt her swollen ankles and turned to Damon.

"Do you have any digitalis for IV injection, doctor?"

"I have digoxin." Damon took a hypodermic syringe and an ampule of the medication from his bag; Dr. Brun administered the shot.

"I want to move her out of the smoke," Damon continued. "She's having difficulty breathing." Ignoring protests, the two doctors carried her over to the "sheep" side of the fire.

"She was fine before we left the house," Dr. Brun said. "I had just returned and knew nothing about the kidnaping until these fellows burst in with their guns and dragged us up here."

Mother Carrier was regaining consciousness and her chest rales had subsided. Elspeth confronted Dr. Brun. "So you'd just returned—from your coven, no doubt. What did you do with the baby?"

Again she was thwarted, this time by the arrival of Scotty Buckley, loaded with boxes and the wicker boat frame. "We found these in the wizard's room," he told them, depositing Dr. Brun's precious specimens in a jumble on the ground.

352

Rosalind Bishop picked up the frame. "What's this?"

"That," said Iris, "is part of a witch's cradle, a device for meditation. The witch suspends himself in it. This one is broken."

"She's lying. I've seen that before," I spoke up. "It's a boat frame. Dr. Brun found it . . ."

A warning flash in Dr. Brun's eye stopped me from betraying the secret of the cave! Then the warning turned to agony as Lucian took the frame from Rosalind and tossed it into the fire.

Elspeth ripped open another box. "There's nothing in here but old bones!"

"Into the flames with those, too!" Lucian ordered.

One by one, all of Dr. Brun's painstakingly collected specimens went into the fire. I turned my head, unable to bear the hurt in his eyes.

"You knew these were sorcerers' devices, Submit," Lucian rebuked me.

He turned to another marker in his bible. "You have all seen the mark of the beast—or Devil—upon this Indian woman," he reminded the crowd. "John says in Revelation: 'And the beast was taken, and with him the false prophet that wrought miracles before him, with which he deceived them that had received the mark of the beast . . . these were . . . cast alive into a lake of fire burning with brimstone!' "

Something burst out of the bushes. People gasped and cringed, but it was Greg, his wig askew and the hem of his robe torn. He held up a tiny pink dress, ripped and bloodied. I felt myself sink to the ground. Damon lifted me and forced me to stand.

"This was lying near the cave," Greg panted.

Lucian took the garment from Greg's hand and raised it

353

over his head in the firelight. When I saw the blood-stains, I sagged again. Damon pushed my head down between my knees until I was conscious once more and with consciousness came reason. Cariad hadn't been wearing that dress today! She'd had on blue overalls—and Dana would have put a snowsuit on her. That dress had been missing from the outside line since the day Jonah had slipped the snapshot under my door.

"Has anyone investigated the cave?" Lucian asked.

"A couple of deputies had just finished when I got there," Greg replied. "They found nothing."

"How come they didn't see this?" Homer asked incredulously.

"I don't know."

But I thought I did. *Someone had dropped it where Greg would find it!* But did Jonah have cunning like that?

I tried to tell them, tried to scream out that someone had planted this, but it was impossible to be heard over the frenzy that seized them—not only the girls this time, but the older women and some of the men—as well. They linked their arms and began to sway, like the witch shadows in the cave, intoning mesmerically in the night as Iris led them in their chant.

Higher and higher rose their keening, their bodies contorted, their eyes rolling, as the Black Man of my dream read from his Black Book. "The hand of Satan is upon them," Lucian shouted to Greg, who appeared to nod in agreement. "Who are those that afflict them?"

A blast from Caleb's shotgun brought the chant to an abrupt end. "What's wrong, Caleb?" Lucian asked the hardware dealer, who was waving his gun and cursing.

354

"Jim Willard's disappeared. Sneaked out when I wasn't looking."

"That's a hell of a note," Homer growled. "If you couldn't keep an eye on 'em, why didn't you ask for help?"

"You were supposed to assist without being asked," Caleb snapped back. "Did you think you'd gone off duty?"

"I suppose no one knows *when* he escaped," Tyler put in.

Caleb pointed his gun at the prisoners. "I bet they know."

They sat there impassive; then Darcy chuckled. "You didn't think we'd tell, did you? Besides, we've been enjoying your show."

"Silence, woman!" Lucian thundered. "Who among you afflicted these girls and these women?"

There was no answer but the hissing of the dwindling flames. Andy Cloyce threw more wood on the fire to rebuild it. Hank had the gasoline jug ready to soak the boards, but the rotten wood caught by itself, so he put the almost full bottle out in the dark beyond the range of the fire.

Now, out of the lull, came a slithering sound. My blood turned cold as I saw the girls squirming across the ground toward the accused.

"Touch us! Heal us! Take back your devils!" they pleaded, pawing the prisoners, one after the other, but this time it did them no good. And on they came, circling the fire on their bellies until they faced me, their tongues lolling from their mouths, their long hair sweeping the ground. At a signal from Iris, Rowan sprang up and

355

confronted me. "Why don't you tell them the truth, Mother? Tell them what *you* are. You're one of them, aren't you? You *wanted* Cari dead, didn't you? Am I next?" She whirled onto the others. "She killed my father! She cursed him and he died. She killed him; *she* killed him! Make her tell you what she did with Cari— *make her tell you!*"

My hand flew to my throat at the horror of it. Hopelessly I saw their hands do likewise. Elspeth rushed at me, froth on her lips. "Didn't I say so? She killed my boy! He left my house that morning, so handsome, so full of life." Her eyes were mad in the firelight. "Make her confess!" She pointed to the two doors that had been taken down from the shack to use in the pressing scene. "Crush the truth out of her! Press her!"

During her tirade some of the men had been fastening a rope to an overhanging branch of the oak tree and passing the noose around Dana's neck . . .

Now they advanced on me, carrying the doors. Dr. Brun sprang in front of me, but Caleb clipped him on the head with the gun stock and he went down heavily. I was thrown to the ground and dragged toward the prisoners. I struggled to free myself, screaming to Greg to help me, but the man standing tall above me, still in his judicial robe, his gavel raised, was not Gregory Towne. Then the heavy door hid his face from me entirely.

It came, the first rock crashing down on the wood—not much more than a pebble—then a boulder, striking just above my ribs and sending pain racketing through my body—another—and another—then a shower of them, driving splinters into me. I thought of the woman Christ saved from stoning—oh, Jesus, help me! My lungs flattened with the weight—blood burst from a thousand places . . .

"Stop it! Stop it!" Greg's voice, and someone clawing at the rocks and trying to drag them away.

"She may have had enough." Lucian's voice. "Rip away that loose board by her head and give her a chance to recant."

"She's innocent!" Greg screamed, struggling futilely to break away from someone restraining him. "I swear she's innocent. Kill me! I tell you this is murder!"

"Not if it is ordained by God!" Lucian retorted. He leaned down and wiped my face with Cari's dress. "Do you confess, my child? God can still forgive you."

I retched and turned my head away, seeing a figure in a goatish mask . . .

He leaned down further and whispered in my ear, "Don't you know me yet? Why must you always obstruct me?"

I peered into his face—the many faces he'd worn throughout the ages. Memories came rushing into my disordered brain, phantasms which receded before I could sort them out . . . the man who would be God, sinking lower each time around . . . Phaeton in his chariot . . . Icarus on melting wings . . . Simon Magus plummeting from his tower . . . Samuel Parris playing God to the slaves and with his parishioners' lives . . . Lucian on the chimney rock . . .

Now he was on his knees beside me. "I can save you," he repeated. "Only submit to me!" Then, in a voice audible to the rest, "Confess, Submit, if you would save yourself."

"We are waiting—Submit," Lucian persisted.

Submit—submit—submit! Through the pain glazing my eyes I could see their faces ringing me with hate. Their eyes were black slits in the firelight, but here and there I could pick them out . . . Tituba standing in Elspeth's place . . . Master Thomas Putnam—Damon . . . Dorcas . . .

"Don't you know us, Submit?"

"Yes, your name is Legion," I moaned, "and you have entered into swine."

They clapped their hands and danced around. "You didn't guess! You lost your chance. We are *all* Satan, didn't you know?"

They screeched their loathing as the vision faded. Lucian rose and silenced them. Holding his hands high, he cried, *"Thou shalt not suffer a witch to live!"*

As if triggered by his words, the gasoline jug, trailing a lighted wick, came hurtling out of the dark, splashing the small group around Dana with a million droplets. Flames followed in their wake. I was protected by the door, but the others' clothes were ablaze, screams splitting the night. I saw Marion, his hair and beard alight, push Darcy onto free ground, rolling her over and over until the flames were extinguished. But by now he was a torch. Rhoda managed to get out of the fire, and Dr. Brun caught Darrell's hand, pulling him to Rhoda's side. They lay there beating their blazing garments. Then Dr. Brun dragged Aunt Jenny out of the flames and tried vainly to breathe life into her. Greg plunged into the fire, had to retreat to cast off his smoldering robe, then into the inferno again in an attempt to reach Dana, only to be driven back, then try again.

Before the fire was fully upon her, Dana's voice was

heard above the shrieks and groans of the dying. "*Maoona* forgive them! As a sign, let the river be turned back from Peacehaven . . ."

A spasm of coughing racked her. Lifting up her bound hands, she cried: "*Hay-nink-lra!*"

That was all. The flimsy platform had mercifully burned out from under her and the rope spared her the torture of the flames.

At the moment her body stiffened with the jerk of the rope, the ground rocked beneath us. A deathly quiet descended on the people of Peacehaven, who clung to each other in horror. Not even in Salem had witches been *burned!* Then, in the silence, I heard the thin wail of a child. Quentin burst into the circle with Cariad in his arms!

The door was lifted from me and Greg's arms were around me, supporting me, for I knew I was hurt, yet I was divorced from the pain in this moment of joy and tragedy. Rowan had taken Cari from Quentin and was regarding me with a strange, unreadable expression. Cariad reached out her arms to me, but I hadn't the strength to lift her. I could only touch her cheeks and her lips and her sturdy little body, assuring myself that she, at least, was unharmed.

They were quiet as Quentin told his story. Jonah, on his father's orders, had taken Cari. Since he couldn't drive, he'd had to carry the child over the back of the bluff and across Ruby's fields on his way to the witch farm, where he'd been told to wait. Irv then intended to stage a dramatic rescue, as he hadn't meant to kill the child—only frighten me into leaving Peacehaven and incriminate the coven at the same time. Macduff caught up with Jonah and Cari on the Hobbs farm. The terrified boy fled across the barnyard toward the woodshed. But when he saw he couldn't outstrip the dog, he'd dropped Cari near the barn. It was sometime after that that the great white fighting dog had managed to break through the loose boards and had attacked. While Jonah cowered in the woodshed, Macduff, young as he was, took on the terrier, dodging this way and that to divert him from the child. He was no match for the beast, but he was younger and faster, and by maneuvering kept the bull terrier at bay just long enough. The slashing teeth were at Macduff's throat when a state trooper's bullet dropped the maddened animal. Just then Irv Good had burst upon them, and when he saw Quentin and the troopers and the blood from the dogs, he'd panicked.

"You'll never catch me!" he'd screamed, dashing into the barn and up the stairs, slamming down the trapdoor. They'd heard him cursing and banging open the cage doors, trying to recruit a defense squad. But he had lost control of his animals. Here was the man who had beaten and brutalized them. One sprang for his throat and then the whole pack was on him. Before the troopers could reach him, Irv Good lay dying, but he'd gasped out a confession in his last moments. With that and what they had seen and what Jonah had been able to tell them, they'd pretty well pieced together the whole puzzle by the time Jim Willard came stumbling into the barnyard, winded and barely able to tell them what was going on up on the bluff. "Get up there with the child," he'd begged Quentin, who was tending Macduff's injuries. "If you don't, something terrible will happen."

"What about my Carol?" Homer wanted to know.

"And my Susie?" Muriel cried.

"We figure they wandered into the barn looking for the money old Hobbs was supposed to have hidden in there and were killed by the guard dog. Irv didn't dare have them traced to his barn, so he'd planted the bodies elsewhere."

They were still mute with shock after Quentin had finished. Then it came, the instinctive reaction of a people ashamed, each blaming the others. The sickening stench of burned flesh was nothing compared to the stench in our souls.

Linda broke open the abscess. "It was Iris! She told me my mother would die if I didn't do what she said," she sobbed.

"Like making phone calls." Debbie.

"Mother and I made the little car and the poppet of Mitti—with hair Rowan got for us." Cissie sounded rather proud.

"We'll all burn in hell," Carol wailed.

"No, we won't," Cissie assured her. "Lucian said we were doing God's work by driving out the unfaithful. The grown-ups were in on it, too."

"Iris is guilty," an older voice cried.

"And Lucian, too!"

"And Elspeth!" Muriel.

"Tyler Bishop!" Damon.

"Damon and Charity!" Tyler Bishop.

"Caleb!" Homer.

"Homer!" Caleb.

As they turned viciously on each other, my eyes were blinded by the fury and hatred in me. I trembled with a terrible power and I knew that if I just uttered the words I could damn them all. But Dana had forgiven them. "Forgiveness is only a little less strong than Love," she had said. Love was beyond me at that moment, but forgiveness was just barely within reach, something I, as Mary Esty, had not quite achieved on this side of the wall.

Charity stood before me, holding her arms out in supplication. "Can you ever forgive us, Mitti?"

Pushing Greg's blistered hands gently away, I stood alone. This I had to do for myself.

"I—I forgive you," I whispered to them—and to Owen.

Then the blackness rushed in on me, but following me into the dark were Rowan's eyes, moist and shining with love.

Epilogue

Peacehaven's day of penance has ended and Bishop's Bluff stands brooding over its ugly memories. The dignitaries and reporters and sightseers have all left. 'Twill surprise me if today's ritual of penance will be repeated for twenty years as was the one in Massachusetts colony nigh three centuries ago. These people seem not as strict in such observances. Yet I cannot think they will ever be able to look on the scarred and sullied crest of that bluff without paying a silent penance.

Now, on this warm May Eve, as sunset pales into twilight, Submit—Mitti—that other part of me—lies dreaming on the soft new grass in her sanctuary in the wood. And since she is here, I must be here, too, for she and I are one, though at times we separate as far as the silver cord can stretch. But Mary Eastick is only one part of me, for I have lived before, again and again, and I'll not know the sum of myself until I have played out all my lives.

Mitti is but a se'ennight home from the hospital, for she suffered internal injuries that terrible night and lay in a coma for days, during which she slipped through the invisible wall into our world and she and I were one with our memories and our loved ones.

Greg left town without seeing her after he knew she was out of danger, and returned only today—which saddened Mitti, who as yet doesn't understand that he had to come to terms with himself before he could face her again.

Mitti's forgiveness was more than Lucian could bear. To forgive is godly, to be forgiven, mortal. His body was found the next morning at the bottom of Tomahawk Rock. No one knows where Iris is. She closed the Patch and shut herself up in the old house. When Jim Willard, the new sheriff, went to see her, he found the house vacant. Some think she drowned. Perhaps her lover claimed her and she swims with him now in that shadowy world beneath the waters.

Dr. Brun still lives in Dana's house and Mrs. Soames is his housekeeper. He's Peacehaven's new minister, at least until the people are mended. He has given up the search for Prince Madog's descendants, for the tremor that shook the earth when Dana died crushed the thin floor of the upper cave, causing it to collapse inward onto the lower level. To Dr. Brun and Mitti it was a sign that Peacehaven—and the world—are not ready for the truth.

Folk came from afar to attend today's service—a few, mayhap, to hear the famous Dr. Brun preach, the rest, sensation seekers. But what began as adventure was transformed into a sobering occasion and all joined in experiencing a collective guilt. And the governor came to announce a new project for harnessing the river and reclaiming lost lands . . . *"As a sign, let the river be turned back from Peacehaven . . ."*

All the townspeople were there today—all who were able, that is. Mother Carrier, who now lives with Charity and Damon and her great-grandson, was, naturally, too feeble to come. The girls clustered together as usual, but they were no longer a nucleus for destruction. Lucy, who's being adopted by Dr. Brun, stood fearfully to one side, her face pale and pinched behind those enormous spectacles, until Rowan put her arm around her and drew her gently into the group.

Conspicuously absent were Rosalind and Tyler Bishop. When the real estate bubble burst, the Bishops tried to flee with stolen funds, but Caleb Toothaker, who knew his half-brother too well, intercepted them as they were leaving the bank, and, as deputy sheriff, arrested them. They, in turn, accused him of having gone to the till himself.

Endless questions arise. For some the answers will come in time, for others never. Who threw the gasoline bomb? Only the guilty one knows and must live with that knowledge—if he can. Yet even that crime must be shared to some extent by each and everyone in Peacehaven.

"We walked in clouds and could not see our way. And we have most cause to be humbled for error . . . which cannot be retrieved." Thus, with the words of the Reverend John Hale, written nearly three centuries ago, did Dr. Brun begin his homily today. After a brief, eloquent address, he motioned to Rowan. She came forward hesitantly, then faced the crowd, biting her lip, her chin slightly tilted.

"I desire," she said in a clear, tremulous voice, "to be

humbled before God for the accusing of several persons of a grievous crime, whereby their lives were taken away from them, whom now I have just grounds and good reason to believe they were innocent persons; and that it was a great delusion of Satan that deceived me in that sad time, whereby I justly fear I have been instrumental with others, though ignorantly and unwittingly, to bring upon myself and this land the guilt of innocent blood . . ."

So far 'twas Anne Putnam's confession of guilt that Rowan was quoting, but suddenly she burst out with words of her own: "I blamed my mother for Junior's death—but most of all for my father's."

She stopped to wipe away the tears coursing down her cheeks. "Mother never told me the truth about my father because she didn't want me to think badly of him. And I probably would have, but now I know he fell into error because he was afraid of failure and of not being able to provide for mother and Cariad and me. Dr. Brun says God has surely forgiven him because he didn't know what he was doing, therefore so must I. I only hope God can forgive me for what I have done. I can't bring back those for whose deaths I must share the blame, but I can spend the rest of my life trying to prove to my mother how much I love her." The last whispered words were all but lost as she rushed into Mitti's arms.

All the while Will—nay, Greg now—stood there, knotting and unknotting his fists. "I can't let this child take all the blame," he spoke out. "I helped sow the seeds of this thing with my blind prejudice and my obsessive promotion of the pageant."

Still the implacable judge, poor Will! Someday perhaps he will learn to forgive himself. Yet better the man

366

who takes others' sins as well as his own unto himself than he who tries to sluff his sins off on others. For in the tragedies of Salem and Peacehaven look not for one villain—look to us all.

As for Mitti, she has learned what I could not in this life—to forgive. Perhaps, before she and I are one again on this side, she will have learned to love all humanity—but if not, the stars will come round again.

So Mitti still dreams in her sanctuary. I can feel the strength flowing into her from the wellspring of nature, for this is Beltane, when all things burst forth in renewed splendor and the dead, dry deeds of the past are cast aside. The last fingers of pink in the western sky have grayed and a soft breeze is filtering through the leaves to brush Mitti's face. And I must hurry to rejoin her, because he—her love and mine—has made peace with himself at last, and at this moment has just entered the woods.